Acclaim for

Other Gods

Book I of *The Averillan Chronicles*

"Women prevail in Barbara Reichmuth Geisler's first novel, *Other Gods: The Averillan Chronicles*, set in the aftermath of the Norman invasion of England in the mid-12th century. Dame Averilla struggles to protect her Benedictine abbey when an important book is stolen, another nun goes missing, and an alleged witch suddenly returns."

— *Publishers Weekly*

"An unfamiliar time and place are brought to life, the scene and characters so perfectly imagined that one is immediately drawn into the lives and concerns of the abbey nuns. Readers will learn a great deal about the time and place, while being entertained by an enthralling story."

— *The Living Church*

"A fascinating blend of mystery, history, anthropology, and arcane and religious studies. Highly recommended!"

— *Ellen Pass Brandt, San Rafael, Calif.*

"It's good on every level: the excitement of the detective story, the information about the old customs and the use of herbs, and the emphasis on redemption and committing oneself to God. Dame Averilla should go to an infirmarers' convention and meet Brother Cadfael."

— *Sue Adamson, Greenbrae*

"It grabbed me from the very first page. If this were a film, the little man from the *Chronicle* would be out of his seat applauding! Put me at the top of the waiting list if you write a sequel."

— *Eleanor Stacy, Walnut Creek*

"I was enthralled. F   ···tions of nature and the English woods ring so true."

an, *Gillingham Dorset*

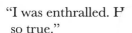

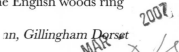

Graven Images

Acknowledgements

I WOULD LIKE TO EXPRESS my heartfelt thanks and gratitude to the following, who kindly read and interpreted the various incarnations of this novel and have been helpful in more ways than I can enumerate.

Mary Ann Shaffer, Carolyn Cavalier, Nancy Tornga, Rita Ching, Elizabeth Geisler, Melissa Trafton, Alexis Ford, Lauren John, Bill Geisler, Leslie Ross, Christine Simon, Grace Morris, Elen Brandt, Barbara Joy, Leslie Lee, Mary Aleander, Julia Fromholz, John Cooperpoole, Jayne Davis, France Bark, Stephanie Rosencrans, and Michael Brechner.

Graven Images

The Averillan Chronicles

Book II

A NOVEL BY

BARBARA REICHMUTH GEISLER

LOST
COAST
PRESS

35674045232585

GRAVEN IMAGES
THE AVERILLAN CHRONICLES, BOOK II
Copyright © 2004 by Barbara Reichmuth Geisler

Lost Coast Press
155 Cypress Street
Fort Bragg, California 95437
(707) 964-9520
Fax: 707-964-7531
http:\\www.cypresshouse.com

Book and cover design: Michael Brechner/Cypress House

ISBN 1-882897-84-6
Library of Congress Control Number: 2004104090

Book production by Cypress House

Manufactured in the USA
2 4 6 8 9 7 5 3 1

*For Melissa and
Elizabeth
Love
As far as God
can reach*

St. Matthew

Thou shalt not make unto thee any graven image, nor any likeness of any thing that is in heaven above, or that is in the earth beneath, or that is in the water under the earth: thou shalt not bow down thyself to them, nor serve them ...

Exodus 20:4 – 5, King James Version

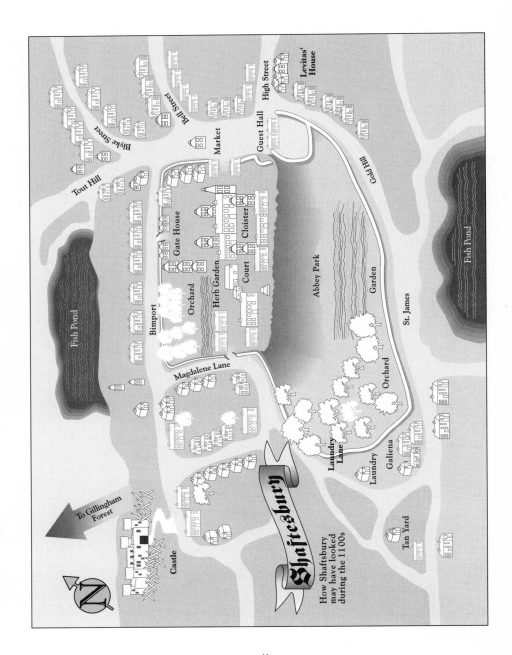

Shaftesbury

How Shaftsbury
may have looked
during the 1100s

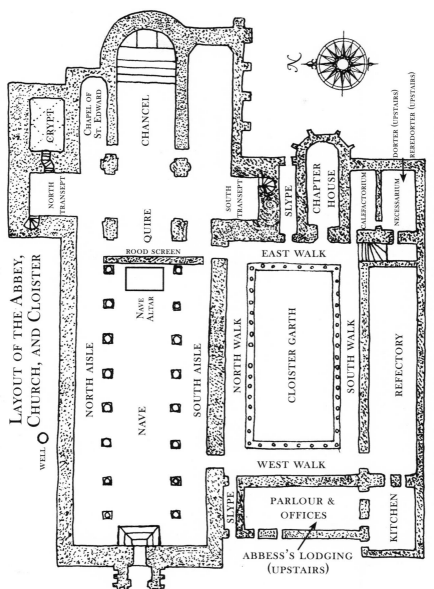

LAYOUT OF THE ABBEY,
CHURCH, AND CLOISTER

WELL

CRYPT

CHAPEL OF ST. EDWARD

CHANCEL

NORTH TRANSEPT

QUIRE

ROOD SCREEN

NAVE ALTAR

NORTH AISLE

NAVE

SOUTH AISLE

SOUTH TRANSEPT

SLYPE

CHAPTER HOUSE

CALEFACTORIUM

DORTER (UPSTAIRS)

REREDORTER (UPSTAIRS)

NECESSARIUM

EAST WALK

NORTH WALK

CLOISTER GARTH

SOUTH WALK

REFECTORY

WEST WALK

SLYPE

PARLOUR & OFFICES

KITCHEN

ABBESS'S LODGING
(UPSTAIRS)

Floor plan based on and with permission from the Shaftesbury Abbey Museum and Gardens

xiii

OPUS DEI OR THE WORK OF GOD

(Daily Rota of the seven offices of psalms,
plus times of recreation, meals, and activities)

Matins — 1 a.m.

Lauds — 1:30 a.m.
Prime — 6 a.m. or daybreak*, directly
precedes mixtum (breakfast)

Terce — 9 a.m.
Chapter Mass — 9:30 a.m.,† precedes
chapter in the chapter house (20 min.)

Sext — Noon

Followed by dinner and midday rest;

Afterward, labor, study and recreation

Nones — 3 p.m.

Vespers — Sunset

Supper

Evening Collation (short reading)

Compline - 8 p.m. (Not necessarily in the choir of the church)

To bed

Doors locked

Absolute silence until prime

---

*Times varied with the season and hours of daylight.
† On Sundays and festivals, instead of Chapter Mass, High Mass is
celebrated at 11 a.m. following chapter.

In the Town

Bayard — *the reeve's older son, brother to Jared and Sister Cadilla*

Robert Bradshaw — *bailiff, husband of Mavis,*
    father of Mary and Clement

Master Chapman — *abbey steward*

Damasa — *daughter of Master Chapman*

Hannah — *deceased daughter to Levitas and Rebekkah*

Hugo — *renowned carver and artisan*

Jared — *reeve's younger son, works as a shepherd*

Margary de Huseldure — *courtly widow. Donor of money*
    for reredos

John — *master mason*

Master Samuel Levitas — *sometimes called Levi, town moneyer*
    and goldsmith

Lovick, Borack's-son — *a cotter or peasant ranking just above a slave*

Mavis — *wife of Bailiff Bradshaw, mother of Mary and Clement*

Mary — *daughter to Robert and Mavis Bradshaw, goose-girl*

Ralf — *orphaned boy, apprentice to Master Hugo*

Rebekkah — *deceased wife of Levitas, mother of Hannah*

Reeve — *father of Bayard, Jared, and Sister Cadilla*

Savette — *Lovick's daughter, sister to Todd and Simon*

Simon — *Lovick's older son, brother to Todd and Savette*

Todd — *Lovick's younger son, brother to Simon and Savette*

Tom — *second to Bailiff Bradshaw*

Only those who play a major part in the book are listed.
All butMaster Hugo are fictitious.

In the Abbey:

Abbess — Emma
Former abbess — *Cecily FitzHamon*

Choir Nuns

Dame Aethwulfa — *retired and in the infirmary*
Dame Agnes — *former cellarer — in the home farm*
Dame Alburga — *mistress of ceremonies*
Dame Alice — *assistant to sub prioress*
Dame Anne — *in charge of the home farm*
Dame Averilla — *sacrist*
Dame Celine — *portress*
Dame Edith — *illuminator*
Dame Helewise — *assistant to Sister Cadilla in the infirmary*
Dame Joan — *assistant t-o Dame Anne on the home farm*
Dame Maura — *mistress of church work*
Dame Osburga — *prioress; previously assistant sacrist*
Dame Perpetua — *cellarer*
Dame Petronella — *novice mistress*

Claustral or Lay Sisters

(Not required to sing in choir or to read)

Novices

Sister Cantile
Sister Mavern
Sister Theodosia

Sister Cadilla — *infirmaress; daughter of the reeve*
Sister Clayetta — *in charge of the abbess' rooms*
Sister Fayga — *in charge of the laundry*

MALE OFFICERS

Warren and Abward — *night porters*
Father Boniface — *nun's priest*
Father William — *parish priest*
Father Merowald — *deceased priest*

At the time, there were perhaps eighty nuns at Shaftesbury. Only those who play a major part are mentioned. All except Emma are fictitious.

CHAPTER ONE

SHAFTESBURY, JANUARY 1140

MONDAY LATE AFTERNOON, BEFORE VESPERS

Jared peered down the track leading away from the abbey ponds and absently adjusted the filthy wool binding that kept the cold from his hands. He was a tall young man with the hardened shoulders of an outdoor laborer. His full lips and long dark lashes gave him a sullen, even truculent, look.

Under a ceiling of mist, where the washing stream dribbled away from the abbey laundry, *right where the goose girl had said she would be,* a figure was indeed bending and turning, snatching washing from the bushes and rumpling it into her basket. Jared shook his head in exasperation. *Midwinter, and almost Vespers,* he thought, *but Savette won't leave her washing until a warmer day! Only one in the whole village who is so dainty.*

"She's been there this while," the goose girl persisted, using her long stick to prod a reluctant gander.

Jared had known he'd have to tell Savette. *I can't keep it from her any longer,* he thought as he watched. But he'd hoped — fervently hoped — she'd hear by way of gossip from an old wife at the wellhead, and then he'd be spared the telling.

1

He scratched an eyebrow, pulled up his belt, and started toward the slight form, feeling Mary's eyes on his back. As he drew nearer, he could see, even with the height of the drying bushes between them, that it was indeed Savette. No one else for miles around had the same slight frame and slender waist. But she seemed subdued. When her left foot squelched into the mud, she barely noticed, and only belatedly did she pull off her clog and hold it into the dribble of moving water. When no more linen lay stiff on the bushes, she hoisted the reed basket onto her outthrust hip.

Jared pushed aside the drying bushes, and his foot cracked on a piece of rutted ice. Savette started and looked up. Inwardly, Jared groaned. The weeks he had been avoiding her seemed parched, like a thirst. "Unquenchable," Father Merowald would have called it. Now, like a hare seeing a fox, Savette's body stilled, her eyes widening in uncertainty. One strand of pale hair blew across her eyes. She raised a hand to push it back. Before he could stop himself, Jared had grabbed her to him, not even noticing the dull creak as her wash basket hit the ground, aware only of the crush of her breasts, the warmth of her familiar wood-smoke woman scent, and the silk of her hair.

There was a tear. Gently, he thumbed it away, opening his hand to circle her lips. She kissed his palm. When his hand nudged the wadmal scarf from her shoulders and slid down to cup her breast, she didn't resist. The shudder that ran through her body jolted through him and he pushed himself more urgently against the small swelling below her womb, combing his fingers into the mass of her hair and pulling her head back, while he nibbled on the fullness of her lower lip.

A raven cried somewhere above them. Jared wiped the moisture from his mouth and pulled away. "Not here," he said, his voice hoarse. "They … someone … "

Jared pulled her through the bushes, pushing aside denuded twigs as he led her into a small dell completely surrounded by the dense wall of waist-high alder and hazel. The dell was sheltered, the short yellowed grass free from ice and springy from the frost beneath.

He shrugged out of his sheepskin and laid it on the ground. Kneeling on top of it, he took her hand and pulled her to him, caressing her down and onto the fleece. Pushing up her rough gown, he caressed the skin above her hose with the grease-smooth hands of a shepherd. When she shivered, he bent his head and kissed the insides of her thighs, flicking his tongue.

When they were done, and lay facing one another, her head on his arm, she spoke. "Jared?"

"Umm," he tried to make his voice lazy, somnolent with satisfaction, but knew his arm was tense. She raised her head and kissed the almost-feminine smoothness of it. Before he was able to respond, she rolled on top of him, put her elbows on his chest, and giggled. "Because of your slight of me these past weeks, 'twill be your penance to lie now against the cold of the ground." Her blond plaits, tangled from their lovemaking, had loosened and fell in two wings as she leaned over him; brushing the tail of one against his lips, she asked, "Love me?"

He rested his arm across his eyes. The pause lengthened.

Her hand slithered down his body and she grinned coyly. "Shall I make you say it?"

"Nay." He pushed away her hand. Seeing her stricken look, he temporized. "Oh, I love you, well know you that, but it won't ... we can't ... "

Wary, the peculiar answer cautioning her, she whispered, "Jared?

He gave her a long look, trying to tell her, not wanting to say it.

"Jared," her voice rose. "I have your troth."

"Troth?" He tried to keep his voice level. "Savette, you know it can't be."

3

She tried to pull his arm away from his eyes so she could read the meaning in them. "But, Jared," her voice rose, "it was a plight troth."

"You must give me back the ring."

She slid off him, "No," and pushing down her skirt, she hugged her knees to her chest. "No. It was a gift. From you to me."

Jared tried to grab her hand from her knees. "Savette." It was a voice of frustration. "I can give you nothing. Nothing but starvation and misery. It was a dream. A dream we both dreamed. You …" He lifted his hand as if to caress her face, but she drew back. He rubbed his head just below his widow's peak, as if in pain. "I know what I have to do, but during the harvest, I forgot. When I was with you, nothing else mattered."

She bit her lip and hid her face against her knees. "No." The cloth of her gonelle muffled her voice. "Jared, it was a plight troth. It cannot be dissolved, not without …" she broke off, shaking her head. "I will go to the bailiff."

"Don't you see?" he tried again. "Here, I can never be more than I am. I intended, before you—always—to go into the Church. To get away. I know words, and I can write. But now, with Father Merowald gone …" He clenched his empty fist and rubbed his brow, the supplication naked in his eyes. "Without Father Merowald, I have no one to tell me what monastery to go to, no one to send me there. I don't know where to go …."

There was silence.

"What I have, though—the only thing I still have—is words; the words and the writing. I can read and write. And that, is … something." Despite her blank silence, his voice had swerved out of despair.

"The Church?" Savette raised her head. "You would enter the Church? No. No! Jared …"

There was no sound but the muted dribble of the brook. Her voice was low then, from deep in her throat, but clear. "Jared, I am with child."

4

He stared at the rounded back, disbelieving, his mouth open.

"I have known," she continued, her voice drab, "this while. I thought to wait to tell you. But you have been so slight with me ... I thought perhaps ... "

"Child?" He finally found his voice.

"Aye. Your child, Jared. And mine. We must wed. To avoid the tax. The church is not possible for you ... with a child."

"My child? It cannot be."

She raised her head and finally allowed herself to plead. "I — you — didn't seem to ... want ... "

His raven hair, long in front but shaved in the back in the fashion of the Normans of the conquest, had slipped over one eye. He pushed it away to glare at her. "I will pay." The words came out gritted, intending to hurt.

Savette looked as if she had been slapped. "No. You plighted me your troth, Jared." Then, as if all it needed was to be said, "And no monastery will have you with a plight troth left behind."

"It was not real, the plight troth." In his panic, he meant to hurt, aimed to hurt. "Not in front of the church, was it? No bargain with your father or brothers, was there? Just between us two. Your word against mine now."

Savette struggled to rise. He felt her movement and grabbed her arm. Much stronger and quicker, his great height levering his advantage, he tumbled her over and held her down, his hands clamping her wrists to the ground.

Like a cornered cat, she struggled and fought, biting at his hands; then, finally exhausted, she lay still. "I still have the ring," she hissed. And I shall keep it. It is my proof."

He brought her hands together over her head and held them with his left hand. With his right, he reached for the ring, fumbling between her breasts where she wore it, his mouth a rictus of determination. He pulled from her gonelle the silk ribbon tied around her neck, a ribbon he had given her as a fairing at

5

Michaelmas. He slid his knife from its sheath.

Her eyes widened in horror. "Jared, no!"

The knife sliced easily through the silk.

"I will not live like a servant at every man's bidding," he growled, shoving the ring into his scrip. "No more." He released her hands and rose to one knee. With a bitter smile, he continued, "Truth be known, I go not into the Church. I shall indeed wed. Master Chapman has offered me Damasa."

A furrow broke across Savette's brow, and she lay still until bitter comprehension narrowed her eyes. The hot anger that welled into her cheeks erased the hurt that had numbed her. "Aye," she spat. "I see it now. Saw it. At the grape harvest. I did not understand it then. I thought you had some kindness for her. But no, it was not that at all ..." She looked at him with disgust, a venomous hurt scourging away the ache. "You may have the ring," she said, the words hoarse and low in her throat, her face contorted. "But when you stand before the church door with Damasa, I shall indeed tell of this broken troth. She rose to her elbow. "When they ask if anyone knows anything against the marriage, I shall tell. It shall not be the shame of my babe." Her hands now loosed, she wiggled backwards from beside his knee. "Nor shall it be my shame. It is yours, and your name shall bear it. Damasa can have you, if she so wills." Savette scrambled to her feet, bending so she could growl into his face. "But even Damasa has her limits. I know her as you do not. And I know Abbess Emma."

Fear clawed Jared's bowels as he absently wiped the spittle from his face. *The abbess. I hadn't thought about the abbess. She won't easily allow a marriage when a troth has been plighted to another. No more than she would allow Master Chapman to buy my freedom to train as a clerc to him. Who wants a lying clerc? No one. Certainly not this abbess.*

His anger mastering him, he reached for her. She had turned and was stumbling through the bushes toward the stream, but had only reached the path when he grabbed her and started to shake her. Savette's head whipped back and forth and her eyes curled back.

"No. Not to me," he yelled. This you shall not do." And then, "Try to trap me with a child? Ye're no more with child than I!"

"Nooo. Nooo. I am with child, Jared. I carry our child."

"Speak you of love. What do you know of love, if you would do this to me?" He shoved her viciously away. Sneering, he finished, "What kind of love do you have that you try to trap a man like this? In a life of slavery?"

She stumbled. The back of her foot caught on a root. She wobbled, her arms milling back and forth. Jared watched as she overbalanced into the stream. *Serves her right*, he thought, anger foaming red behind his eyes. He patted at his scrip for the feel of the ring, and a sense of freedom washed over him. *Now I have a ring for Damasa. I won't even have to plead with the Jew again to lend me enough.*

Jared looked up to where a few trees clung to the cliff below the abbey. The ledges and flanks were clothed in mist. No one could have seen them. After carefully rearranging his tunic and braes, Jared shot a parting glance in Savette's direction. She had fallen half in and half out of the stream, one leg cocked at a peculiar angle, still caught in the root that had made her stumble. She had not yet pulled herself out of the water. It perplexed him as he took a few steps backward up the path. *She is so still. Why doesn't she get up, wipe the blood from her face, and glare at me; try to get my pity, force me to relent?* A flicker of worry plucked at his anger, but just as he was about to yield, he thought he saw a small movement. *She is just trying to get me to return; to feel sorry for her. Well, it won't work. Not now and not later. Master Chapman will surely think of a way to silence her.*

7

Chapter Two

Shaftesbury, January 1140

After Vespers

I

When Vespers had ended in the great church of the Abbey of the Virgin Mary and Edward King and Martyr at Shaftesbury, one of the black-robed figures detached herself from the line of solemnly pacing nuns. She was a tall woman, with the supple grace of a young birch, her eyes the peridot green of moving leaves. This was Emma, and it was she who ruled the convent. When Abbess Cecily had died, Emma had been a compromise candidate for abbess, as she was of mixed parentage, half-Norman and half-English. But the nuns had chosen her for another reason altogether. Emma was not in the least interested in being abbess. During the election, Dame Petronella had whispered to the novices — who could only watch and were not allowed to vote — "It is better to choose one who does not want to be abbess than to choose one who does." Had they been asked, however, her nuns would have put it differently. They would have declared that it was her wisdom, strength, and peace, her inner sanctity and her watery mysticism, that had given them their faith in her.

The worst part of it is that an abbess has to decide, Emma thought now as she hurried down the north walk and past the cloister garth, where a recent ice storm had reduced the grass to shards and the plants to skeletons. She continued on through the slype and started across the inner court. *Who am I to make judgments for the whole community? It is not my gift. It never was.* The antiphon that preceded the Magnificat sung during Sunday's Vespers still rang in her ears: "When the wine failed, Jesus bade the water pots be filled with water; which water was turned to wine, alleluia."

Jesus can turn water into wine; would that I could turn snowflakes into gold. Such debts, and I have to decide what to do; whom to pay. The previous year had been tumultuous, but the problems Emma had faced had been more in the realm of the nurturing of souls, and she had been confident in her role, buttressed by God. *But now, I alone must assess what is to be done.* Emma pursed her lips and paused, allowing her eyes to rest on the ebb of the downs flowing black against a meager sunset. *January,* she sighed deeply, and tried to force herself to weigh her problems against the reality of eternity. The diffused pinks of the drifting clouds folded inward as she watched, until all that remained were alternating bands of brilliant rouge and troubled gray. The worry in her melted somewhat. *We may be locked away, but at least You give us Your sunsets.* When a faint sound of laughter drifted up from Saint James, she relaxed even further, seeing the scene in her mind; two men — *two ordinary men* — breathing plumes of vapor and feeding the abbey oxen. *Feeding. At least there was still food enough.*

Emma crunched down the iced gravel path leading to the infirmary, ducked under the water dripping from the eaves, and pushed open the door. She passed the dim arcades where the rows of beds were filled with the results of the prolonged cold: coughs and chilblains and running noses. The rains of November had not only been early, but had also been unusually cold, icing the ruts and denuding the trees. In addition, because it was built on a hilltop, Shaftesbury bore the brunt of the weather.

At the beginning of Advent, the first of December and the start of the church year, the prioress, old Dame Aethwulfa, crippled by severe rheumatism, had retired to the warmth of the infirmary. Aethwulfa's retirement came at an opportune time, for with Advent came the distribution of offices, when each member of the community was assigned her duties for the coming year. The Benedictine rule required that all members be able to assume any of the myriad tasks that occupied the nuns when they were not in the church. Dame Osburga, a quiet woman who managed to complete her tasks with little fuss, was chosen as the new prioress, and in time, her solid administrative mind would balance the more spiritual gifts of Abbess Emma. For the present, however, Osburga was too perplexed by her new responsibilities to be able to offer Emma the counsel she needed. Thus Emma had taken to visiting Dame Aethwulfa every day after Vespers and supper, ostensibly to tell the old prioress of the day's events, but really to lean on the old lady's wisdom. Today, Emma would skip supper. She was restless, eager to have the advice of the prioress, and to confide in her this bouquet of worries she could share with no other soul.

Her eyes lowered, Emma now seated herself on the stool beside Aethwulfa's bed, pressing her skirts into neat folds and tucking her hands into her wide black sleeves. Dame Aethwulfa's bed was in the crossing of the transept of the infirmary, close to the central hearth, where her old bones and gnarled hands could be warmed by the bustling winter fires. The abbess sat for a moment, pretending, *not entirely pretending,* to savor the unaccustomed warmth.

The prioress was the first to speak, her apple-doll face wrinkling into lines of concern. "Something is bothering you, I think, and has been for some time now."

Emma sighed, finally looking up. "We have enormous debts."

"Debts, my lady?" Aethwulfa's look of confusion was quickly supplanted by that expression that comes to the aged when the fear of forgetting comes upon them.

"No, you didn't know. I myself didn't know until recently."

"Debts? To Master Levitas? I—"

"You didn't know because Abbess Cecily went around you; had Joan borrow from Master Levitas. Poor Joan was vulnerable to anything Cecily said or did from the very first day Cecily arrived in the abbey, all cloaked and booted and beautiful, so Joan did as Cecily bid her."

"Cecily did not have enough money to finish the rebuilding of the oratory?" the prioress' voice trembled. "But I thought the Duchess of Gloucester had given Cecily a huge gift. Or that the King..."

"We all did. But Cecily ran out of money and feared the community would deny funds from the general coffers. It was Dame Joan, in her role as bursar, who did the borrowing. Cecily told Joan—believed it herself—that more pilgrims would be drawn to abbey if it were bigger and grander. With an increased number of pilgrims would come increased gifts, which could repay Master Levitas."

"And so..."

"When Cecily died, Joan tried to make ends meet. Instead of confessing to the community, she went right on borrowing, trying to hide what Cecily had done."

"So you worry about how to repay what we owe?"

"Aye." Emma took a deep breath. "But there is more. Master Chapman—why that man was ever appointed steward I cannot understand—knew of Joan's dealings. Instead of informing me, he kept the knowledge to himself."

"But why would he so?" The wise old eyes became more intent.

"Because Joan knew — had been told by Peter the metalworker — that Master Chapman was in the habit of taking a bit here and a bit there from the rents and tithes. It became a pact of silence between them. Fear of each other meant that neither would tell on the other."

"And you have known this?"

"Aye. Emma nodded. "The knowledge came to me right after Christmastide, from Margaret de Huseldure. She had given the money for a silver reredos in her husband's memory. Master Hugo, a sculptor at Bury Saint Edmund's, had been commissioned to create it. Margaret came to me wondering why nothing had been done. She's a strong woman, is Margaret. She suspected that our lack of action boded ill and decided to tell me of it. At any rate, the sculptor, Master Hugo should soon arrive — "

"And we have not the money to pay him."

"I suppose I must dismiss Master Chapman .... I like not the feeling that he values us so little. I like not the feeling that Joan was in a kind of bondage to him."

They wrestled with the problem in silence, only the ticking of the fire disturbing the quiet. Dame Aethwulfa offered, "The reeve is an honest man."

The abbess rubbed two fingers across her mouth before speaking, as if to hold the words at bay. "Aye, the reeve is an honest and good man, but for all his trustworthiness, he can neither read nor write."

"His son, Jared, can both read and write."

"You suggest we elevate Jared to the rank of steward?"

"Nay, my lady. I am not as confused as that. If I remember aright, Jared is not only headstrong, but self-centered. Both are attributes that will be smoothed by the pumice of age. He is goodhearted, I think. I suggest you elevate his father, the reeve, to the rank of steward, and allow his son to do his reading and writing, in the role of secretary. It is not unheard of. Let the reeve righten the evil Master Chapman has wrought, and at the same time straighten the kinks of youth that beset his son. In time, I think, Jared could be taught to value the ways of honor."

"And then I must tell the chapter of the debts. I do need to tell them, don't I? Such a huge amount. We'd have to sell all the grain in the tithe barn just to replace the silver Margaret de Huseldure gave for the reredos." Emma shook her head.

The silence was interrupted by an incessant coughing and the soft steps of Sister Cadilla as she went to the patient.

"Is there something more?"

"Dame Averilla is not at peace."

"Aye?"

"When Joan was here in the infirmary with Averilla, I hoped their intimacy would ease the way for the forgiveness that must enter Averilla's heart. It did not. Now Averilla is sacrist, and she seems to hug her anger to herself. I used to think of Averilla as my faithful lion, ready to protect the abbey from any threat, but now . . ."

Dame Aethwulfa marked the grim look in the abbess' eyes. "Give the problem to God, my dear. If God has something He wants you to do, He will tell you."

"I will try. He has been elusive of late." The abbess' voice was hollow.

For a moment, Dame Aethwulfa couldn't find words to counter the desperation she sensed in her superior's voice. Trying, she said, "At least you don't have to tell them of the perfidy of the steward. That is yours alone to solve and does not require the cumbersome witness of discussion." Realizing that the solemn silence that greeted her words meant there was no consolation in them, the prioress faltered, "Rest, my lady, in God's peace. I will pray for you."

Chapter Three

Shaftesbury
Monday, late afternoon after Vespers

I

At first, Savette was aware only of the rainbows, luminous spots, pure and rounded, overlapping and starlit. Water? *Did it rain? Again? After the snow? No. Water on my eyelashes. But if it's not rain …*

When next she knew, she knew only pain. Behind her eyes a throbbing seared her temple. *Hurts.* The pain scorched and then hardened, like a snake expanding and contracting its coils. Very close, someone whimpered plaintively, like a new kitten. *Me? Hurt.*

Nearby, but not as close as the moaning, there was a wet sound. *A pot left to boil? No. Water. The brook. I was washing.*

Fighting a numbing fatigue, she raised her hand to the pain. *Head. Hurts.* She then examined her hand. Red filled the gap where the rainbow had been. *Blood on my hand?*

From somewhere else, but because she could hear it, *it must be nearby,* a whistle creased the sound of water. *A familiar whistle.* Two shorts and one long. *Not a bird. The goose girl. Little Mary leading the geese. To the ponds? Away from them?* The familiar

14

image of the child pushed away the sight of the blood on her hand. She let the hand drop, and saw in her mind's eye the ungainly geese, following the girl, swinging wide their feet and hissing their irritation at being moved from the scanty fodder near the ponds; pausing now and again to pull at an ice-scarred blade of knotgrass.

Mary could help me.

"Mary!" Savette called, but her voice was hoarse and low, and sounded against the water like nothing more than another disgruntled crow.

2

ON THE OTHER SIDE OF THE HILL FROM WHERE SAVETTE LAY, a man, a boy, a donkey, and a dog passed through a small copse and paused. The four had traveled for a good distance along the Portway from Salisbury, perhaps ten miles, safely above any dangers that might be hidden in the valleys and woods below. For the last several miles, however, the lay of the land had forced them to descend from the heights and pass through a series of small woods and fields. It had made the man, the artist known as Master Hugo, nervous, this forced inability to see ahead or around. The winter's dusk was close at hand, the four of them were obviously unprotected, and the threat of masterless men or outlaws was very sear in his recent memory. But now, with their goal in sight, Master Hugo paused. Atop the hill ahead of them, like a Norse longboat riding a wave, stood an immense building above a swell of rime-covered huts.

This man was a long-awaited sculptor, commissioned by the abbey nuns to carve for them a reredos to hang behind one of their altars. He had hard inquisitive eyes and huge hands. Master Hugo was well known among the clergy who hired such men to decorate the great abbeys and churches they built for themselves and for the greater glory of God. He had seen many such buildings

15

in his travels, and he nodded now, both pleased and somewhat surprised by the size of this abbey. He had not expected it.

Master Hugo's only human companion was a half-starved boy who followed rather too closely, leading a bemused-looking donkey and a huge dog. The boy's name was Ralf, and, as Hugo stopped, Ralf skidded on a patch of leftover ice and bumped into his master. As the big man whirled around, Ralf cowered and whispered by way of distraction, "Master? Yon? Be that Shaftesbury?"

Through clenched teeth Master Hugo answered, his voice exasperated, "Aye, Ralf, that be Shaftesbury." Not for the first time he regretted encumbering himself with this boy. When he had first met Ralf, however, the boy, or rather his dog, had seemed a godsend …

IT HAD BEEN WINTER AND HUGO and his donkey, Bithric, had been traveling a circuitous route from Bury St. Edmunds toward Shaftesbury. Master Hugo had been, for the last few minutes, trying to entice the recalcitrant donkey close enough to nab the lead rope. So far, every time the man moved, the donkey shifted his weight and minced a few steps farther away. The sun slipped toward the hills that hugged the horizon. Slowly, and for no apparent reason, Bithric stepped forward and allowed himself and his rope to be caught, wisps of yellowing grasses drooping from his munching jaws. Hugo grabbed the rope and, looping it around his wrist, scrabbled through the wicker panniers hanging lopsidedly from a wooden bow-like structure on either side of the donkey. "Thank God," he whispered aloud, fondling the leather bundles one by one. Repacking them, hands shaking, he reiterated, "Thank God."

Shattering the silence and startling Hugo, a rook lifted from a nearby apple tree, jeered, and twisted into flight. As he looked toward the drunken old tree, nude for the winter, Hugo saw, unnervingly close and eerily motionless, a boy who had so melded into the tree's shadow that Hugo had not even seen him.

They stared at one another. The boy's hair was rank with filth, and he had the extended belly of starvation. Hugo had seen relics in Norman churches with more flesh on them than this boy had skeining his shins.

"What is it, boy?" Assuming another trap, Hugo's voice was hostile. He dropped the donkey's lead and reached for the heavy hammer slotted into his belt.

The boy pointed. Hugo turned and saw the charred remains of a ravaged hamlet just visible behind the tree. *A trap?* Hugo asked himself. *Or was he what he seemed, the detritus of the war. Just flotsam in the way of a petty earl or thane or outlaw who, unhampered by the king's might, had burned his village. Mayhap the same one who had attacked and killed...*

Still uncertain, unwilling to turn his back on the boy for fear of who else might be hidden somewhere near, he asked, "The vill? Yours?"

The boy nodded.

"But you live?"

The boy looked blank. Hugo's bushy eyebrows drew together. *Perhaps it is a trap, and the boy doesn't know what to say.*

"I," the single word was vomited, the voice under it hoarse and unused. Again, the boy spoke. "I." Then, "I was in the forest." His mouth moistened as he used his tongue. "I was beating acorns from the trees for the pigs. I heard the screams."

"Didn't they come into the forest after you when they'd burned the village?"

"Aye, they did." The boy paused. "There is a cave."

The boy did not move as he spoke. He was poised, though, watching.

He's as scared of me as I am of him, Hugo thought, and began

17

to relax. "How many days has it been?"

"Many. Beyond reckoning."

"You ate the pigs?"

"The pigs were taken when they came to find ... any who were hidden. There are ... others ... in the forest who make better use of a pit than I."

Hugo turned back to the panniers, carefully retied the straps, and then fiddled with the girth, stretching it under the donkey's belly. *So, it's not an outlaw ruse. Just another lost bit,* he thought, ignoring the boy, satisfied that he posed no threat. *Probably wants to come with me.* Hugo turned and started to lead the donkey through the frost-scarred grasses and back up the hill whence he had come. Regaining the track, he limped along, trying to remember the way he was to go, his whole body crying out against the beating it had taken earlier. *Of no more use would he be to me than ...* After a quarter mile Hugo stopped, ostensibly to scan the distance, and, despising himself, looked back. The boy was straggling behind him. "'Sblood," Hugo muttered aloud.

He waited as the boy sidled closer, panting, his face white. He looked up, eyes beseeching. "I could work for ye," he said. "For food. With winter there is no more food to find."

Hugo's voice was firm. "Have little eno' for myself. Naught else. G'wan. Back to where'er ... " and he pivoted, yanking the donkey, shoulders hunched, unwilling to contemplate the completion of the thought.

After that, Hugo jolted along as quickly as his bruised body would permit, avoiding the icy ruts and muddy potholes, and even more avidly avoiding looking behind him. Finally, he saw faint traces of smoke curling into the mist. As he neared what he expected to be another village, Hugo saw that it was not only a village, but bigger than the remains of the scrawny one near which he had found the boy. This village was surrounded by a sturdy earthwork mound topped with pikes, and there was a square tower, though only of wood, which rose to give the defenders a view of the surrounding countryside.

"No." The boy's shout came from behind him like a whip.

Clenching his jaw, ready to curse the brat away, Hugo turned. The boy's eyes were enormous, his pallor heightened.

"No?" Hugo shrugged. "Why not? Can't stay out here o'ernight." Then, curious despite himself, he asked, "The baron, er, thane of this burgh? 'Twas he as came to your village?" *Might be true,* Hugo thought under his words. *What's to say that those in the village won't attack me once I am within their gate? Who's to say that it wasn't men from this very village who earlier attacked us?* Hugo stroked the beech-wood handle of the hammer ready at his hip.

Ralf nodded. "Aye. Was as ye say."

Hugo looked appraisingly at the boy, and then took a long look at their surroundings. Nothing moved against the beginning streaks of sunset. "Won't make Winchester this night, that be certain," he grumbled. "So ... " and without another word Hugo yanked the donkey's lead and headed for the clutch of thatched hayricks, squatting like huge onions on the field to the north, their thatch thick to keep the wet from the grain. The boy followed. At the last haystack, the one farthest up the hill and with the best view, Hugo turned and, the lead knotted around his arm, again untied a strap that closed the donkey's panniers. He fumbled past the leather-wrapped tools and pulled out a sturdy peg, which he pounded into the ground, not too near the haystack. Placing a hobble around the donkey's hooves, he turned to find the boy next to the panniers.

"Take 'em off?" the boy asked, pointing to the baskets.

"Aye. Then take handfuls of grass and rub 'im. He can be left. He'll do as he pleases."

"Should I not take him to the stream?" The boy's hands were shaking as he fumbled with the knots.

"No." Hugo's voice was sharp, then softer. "We were just at the

19

stream, not long before you ... appeared. I was with others. We were attacked."

"I saw them go." When Ralf had tugged down the withy baskets, Hugo busied himself with drawing from them the various sacks and parcels, among which was a wadmal bag that he proffered to the boy. *Might as well give him a bit to eat for the warning he gave me. I would've entered that vill and they would surely have recognized me.* As he held out the bag, Hugo asked, "Hep ye a name?"

"Aye. Ralf."

The boy looked longer at the bag uncertain. Hugo juggled it.

"Here ye go, Ralf. Take it."

Ralf opened the bag and looked up without comprehension.

"Eat. It's food. Raisins, er, dried grapes, quite precious, actually. And almonds."

Ralf put a tentative hand into the bag and drew out one small wrinkled raisin, not plump, but dried from storing and gritty with seeds. Tentatively, he put it into his mouth and tasted. The sweet taste surprised him and he smiled. Without looking again at the man, the boy reached into the bag again and again, grabbing out handfuls of mixed raisins and nuts and stuffing them into his mouth.

Hugo pointed to the bag, "Go easy, or the gut'll throw it right back. I know." Hugo again busied himself with the baskets, and then turned back to the boy with a leathern flask of wine. "It is raw, but I warrant that it will make no difference to you."

Ralf looked at Hugo wordlessly and then took a long draught. Hugo thought he could distinguish every muscle in the boy's gullet as he gulped.

"You don't want to take too much of that, either."

Hugo took a bite of a cold pasty and chewed slowly, savoring the mouthful. After a moment he removed another pasty and nudged it toward Ralf. Eyes on Hugo's face, Ralf slowly reached for it, as if at any moment his fingers would be cut off. Then he ate, stuffing the food into his mouth with both hands. When he was finished, he pulled the back of his wrist across his mouth.

"I understand, lad," Hugo said, "that you have had naught to eat for many a day. But 'tis better to take it slow-like." He withdrew some dried meat and pushed the larger slab toward the boy. "This'll slow ye down." Ralf turned over the thin, dry shingle. "Go ahead. Eat. 'Twill do ye no harm." After a brief and unsuccessful tussle with the stringy mass, Ralf compromised by sucking on it.

While they were eating, Bithric had sidled closer and closer until his quivering underbelly was brushing Hugo's hair. Hugo frowned and struggled upright, using the animal for a lever. He looked around. A small wind rustled the last few leaves left atop the hay. The donkey stamped a hind hoof. Ralf remained where he was, pulling at his meat, unconcerned. *Too unconcerned.* Hugo locked his jaw. Bithric, ears forward, backed toward the uphill side of the stack, dragging his hobble rope along with him, trying to put Hugo between himself and . . . *and what?* Hugo cocked his head. *Is something there? Is this boy, seemingly so innocent, really one of a party of masterless men?*

"Who goes there?"

No answer.

There? Dammit, there is *someone. Stupid to take on this brat. Unknown. What an idiot I am!*

The boy half-lifted his head, shot a quick glance toward Hugo, and took another suck on the beef. An owl gave a halfhearted croak. Hugo slid the hammer from of its loop. Ralf looked at him once again, and then put two fingers to his lips, emitting a piercing whistle. Bithric jumped backward, straining against the peg.

Below them, closer than Hugo would have thought possible, a gray-black shadow slunk out from under the gloom below the nearest stack.

A wolf?

21

Ralf didn't move.

Hugo had seen wolves in Paris during the famine. *No, not quite a wolf... the head is too square, and the body is tall, tall and thin with longer legs than the wolves I saw slinking across the frozen Seine.*

Without looking around, relaxed, the boy again put two fingers to his lips and again he whistled.

The burr-laden animal came and sat beside Ralf, its slab of tongue lolling. Hugo gazed, rapt. The half-curled wiry hair blended into the dusk, shadow into shadow. The dog, *it must be a dog,* Hugo thought, *is calm and fearless. At least 'tis not a pack of thieving scum.*

"A wolfhound?" Hugo asked.

Ralf nodded.

"Yours?"

"Now. Left fer dead, he was. An arrow miscast. I stayed with him. He was warm."

"So that's how you survived."

"Aye."

That's how I will now survive this journey. The boy needs me. I need protection. A wolfhound can kill and will bark a warning. Then, when I get to Shaftesbury, I can figure out what to do with them. Now, though, the boy can help with the donkey. Before the thought was finished, Hugo heard his tongue say, "I might be able to use a boy, now that I think on it. I would feed you."

"Yea, master." The boy's voice was thick with phlegm. "And I—I have a bit of knowledge with animals, though not with, um, ponies. But..."

"Donkeys." Hugo hastened to correct. "Bithric, here, is a donkey." *First my life is spared.* Hugo thought beneath his words, *but I am left defenseless and without protection. Then just as suddenly, a guard is provided,* he reminded himself, *and a servent.* Aloud he said. "Takes much the same care as ... pigs, I suppose. For the rest,

22

I can teach you what I know."

Ralf raised his head, eyes defiant. "The dog too must come. He—he can help. He can catch things. Pigeons, squirrels, hedgehogs. I have stayed alive on hedgehogs."

"Better than dried beef, eh?" Hugo found himself relaxing into a smile and grudgingly admiring the grit that had enabled the boy to stay alive. *And a boy with a dog does not belong to a party of masterless men. At least this one doesn't.*

Ralf looked up to see if Hugo was joking, but he didn't allow himself a smile. Earnestly, he added, "And—and he will protect us."

"I imagine so. If he is to travel with us, however, ye needs make peace come between him and yon donkey. Bithric has some suspicions. Hep the wolfhound a name?"

"Aye. Tindal."

"Tindal?"

"I made it up." Ralf's voice was muffled by the piece of half-chewed beef. "Had to call him some'ut."

Hugo smiled. "Well, Tindal."

Pushing his ears forward at the sound of his name, the dog looked Hugo in the eyes.

"We may as well be friends," Hugo held out a hand.

The dog's yellow eyes probed those of the man. After a bit, Tindal rose from his haunches, and, putting his ears back and down in a dog smile, crossed the space with a grave dignity that forbade the familiarity of a caress. Again the two held each other's eyes. Finally, the dog put his head lightly against the man's hand, sniffed, and returned to Ralf.

"What if I had not liked him? Or he me?" asked Hugo raising an eyebrow.

"I would not 'ave come." Ralf's voice held no sense of embarrassment, just a strong certainty. His dignity matched the dog's.

Impressed, and further relieved, Hugo busied himself with the bags. "I have nothing for your friend."

23

"He catches his own."

"Well then, now might be the time to introduce him to Bithric. I say again, lad, the two must get along. I can go nowhere without Bithric. If ye are to be useful to me," he slipped the sack back into the leather bag, "ye must deal with both, and no jealousy from either."

As Ralf stood, brushing a thawed leaf from the back of his tunic, Tindal rose from his crouch. Ralf whispered something. Hugo thought it might be English, but was not sure. The dog, however, understood and stayed where he was. Ralf inched his way up the hill toward Bithric, alone and quivering against the shadowed night. Hugo heard another sound from Ralf; this time it was a snuffling and whickering so much like a donkey's that Hugo thought for a moment the sound had come from Bithric. He watched, mesmerized. Bithric stayed where he was, ears forward, nervous feet stamping, eyes switching from boy to dog. Slowly, the donkey backed away. Ralf waited. Presently, he yanked from his scrip a withered and shrunken apple. *Must have pulled it from the tree where we met.* "You'll like this," Hugo heard him say. "Let's try." Still whickering softly and muttering, Ralf crept closer. When he was within five paces, he stretched his hand flat. Slowly, daintily, Bithric sidled up to the boy, eyes hawking to the dog that had remained motionless and half-crouched at the side of the fire. As the donkey stretched his neck for the dried fruit, Ralf whistled for the dog.

"Then happened that which I never thought I'd see," Hugo would later tell the abbess. "That dog is almost as high as the donkey, and yet, there was something the lad did between them, some sign — the dog came up just so far and then sat, looking at the donkey, as if for permission, ears forward, sort of beseeching, and earnest. The lad, you see, was silent, just willing them. Knew I not better, I would have thought witchery, or some language far beyond the hearing of men. And then the dog simply came up

24

to the boy, slow-like, and nuzzled into his other hand, the one by the boy's side. The donkey watched, not nervous anymore, I wot, but trusting of the boy. They are good friends, now, Bithric and Tindal, and there is a lightness between them."

"Bring him down, lad," was all that Hugo had said at the time, and Ralf had taken the noseband and led the donkey back to the fire, the dog pacing on the other side of the boy and a bit forward.

NOW, AS THEY STOOD LOOKING toward Shaftesbury, Hugo finally answered Ralf's question. "Aye, Ralf, it be Shaftesbury." He narrowed his eyes in concentration. "Strange place to site it, though. So far from the water. Not a river or stream, not even a brook nearby."

The last rays of the sun shone fitfully through green-tinged clouds. *So, now we're here, I must figure how to use this boy.* Hugo brought his lower lip over his upper and started slowly forward. *I'm getting old. Tired. Not a good time to take on another responsibility.* The trip with Ralf had been grueling. During their stay in Salisbury, while Hugo priced silver and gold and heard tales of the ravages of the civil war, the days had turned blustery and cold. When they had finally started to cross the fourteen miles of carpet ground that made up the great plain from Salisbury, they had hardly been able to see for the mists and rain. They had slogged on across, following insensible routes around and through the mud and potholes, often reduced to following the lead of the wolfhound. Too often they had had to stop to pull Bithric, useless except to carry Hugo's tools, out of a mud hole. More than once they had been forced to ask brusque shepherds, their sheep close-huddled, heavy-shouldered rams stamping, which way to turn. Here, though, in the abbey demesne, below

25

the hill of Shaftesbury, the mists had lifted. The fields had been ploughed in the fall, and the furrows made black stripes against the white ridges of the earlier snowfall.

Hugo walked a few more feet before he again stopped, remembering that he and Ralf had been talking. "Aye, lad, that be Shaftesbury," he returned to the former thought. "But know you what that is?" and he pointed to the huge edifice atop the mound.

"Er, Shaftesbury?" The boy dragged his attention from the dog, which was eyeing a shepherd and his sheep traveling toward them.

"Aye, but do you see?"

Ralf gazed again at the bulky rampart, awed by the size of the building. It dwarfed the grainy-colored huts like a hen with her chickens. "A castle?"

"No. That's the thing. Not a castle, not a castle at all. A church. And more. Those buildings—that fortress—is the abode of women."

"Women?"

"Aye. 'Tis a nunnery, boy. Those stones house women. Dainty and well-bred women, at that! The Abbey of the Virgin Mary and Edward, King and Martyr."

They stood a moment longer, looking at the hill, black bushes against the white of the snow, and above that the teeth of the palisade that circled the summit.

The flock of blank-eyed sheep were now almost on them. "Good shepherd, this," Hugo commented, interrupting Ralf's reverie. "Takes his flock east with the night. That keeps the sun from their eyes."

As the sheep roiled hip-deep around them, they watched the shepherd's dog belly-slink behind some of the more recalcitrant ewes. Touching his cap as he ambled by, the shepherd grunted, "Abbey has a guest hall. Gate closes a bit after dark." As if to underline his words, a bell tolled gently above them in the town.

26

Ralf stopped, struck by the purity of the bronze tone.

"Vespers," Hugo said. They pray, nuns and monks do, seven times a day. Or, at least, that's what the monks at Saint Edmund's did. To and from the church all day long, seven times at least. Know your numbers, boy?"

Ralf shook his head, a scowl hardening his jaw. "Naw, I wot one and two. For the many? That be for 'em as works with other things." Beneath the grime, a flush claimed his ears. "A stick does me fine."

"If you are to work with me," Hugo said firmly, "you need to know. I ask for 'seven points,' you need to bring me seven. You can start with your fingers."

Hugo looked again at the town, absently rubbing his beard. *So, if they still want to hire me, who is it exactly will come here to see my work? To a convent of women? Who will ever see what my hands create? When I designed the doors for Saint Edmund's — better doors by far than those at Santa Sabina in Rome — people stopped to stare as they traveled through Bury, and the name 'Master Hugo' was repeated. The pilgrims who came to ask favors of Saint Edmund's left amazed by my doors. But who will come here, to Shaftesbury? No one but soldiers and shepherds can even find the place!*

"Come on," he finally said to the boy, who was now kicking at sheep pellets. "Best be in afore nightfall."

Chapter Four

Shaftesbury

Monday, late afternoon after Vespers

I

The image of the geese that fleetingly occupied Savette was overwhelmed by a sense of the numbing cold creeping in and around the pain in her head. *I am in the water. He left me here.* A tear started. This new pain shredded something soft deep within her. *Oh, God, no. Please, no. Jared!* This pain was nothing like the other. Black pain. *Jared with Damasa?* Her brow furrowed. *Damasa? How could he?* It wasn't possible. *He loves me. Did love me.* This man was someone she didn't know. *I would like to die. To just stay here and die.* She didn't feel the cold anymore. *I can just lie here with the sound of the water and …* Her eyes closed. Then flew open. *The babe. The babe would die with m … Do I care now? When but a week ago I would 'ave rid me of it?*

Savette forced herself to roll onto her shoulder. Rocks, *not pebbles, rocks,* stabbed through the wet clothing and into her flesh. She lifted her left arm and scrabbled for the root. *If I had 'na tripped on the root.* Grasping the slimy roundness —*Let it be*

28

strong — Savette pulled her body up the shallow bank and managed to lift her head to look around. There was nowhere else to go, nothing else to grab. The big rock the women used for washing was too far away. "I don't ... can't ... " The tension seeped out of her arms and she rolled onto her stomach, the meager spurt of energy squandered.

Her nose dropped into the water and she inhaled. Sputtering, gasping, and coughing, she roused. *How long ... ?* She didn't know. *Some time.* Instinctively, achingly, the rocks scraping them, she drew her legs up under her. As her shoulders rose from the blanket of water, the air seemed colder. Her eye was seeing the red again. *Not on my hand. In the water. The sunset? Red water from the last of the sunset? No. Swirls like blood. Of course it is. From my head. Oh, God.*

2

IN HIS COTTAGE ON THE HIGH STREET, several paces from the Shaftesbury marketplace, Lovick, Borack's-son, bent over the dregs of a fire. Rime still rimmed the window ledges, and because it was cold he had reluctantly pulled the shutters to their casings. He was waiting, more worried than he liked to admit, for his daughter to return home. She made the bleak years of age bearable. He smiled faintly, remembering her birth. Indeed, she had been a beautiful babe. Even to him, never sentimental about such things, she had been ... perfect. His wife had named her Savette. He had been appalled, thinking it a Norman name. It wasn't. Had been her godmother's name, and "she was Saxon, with great blue eyes." A man's wife, after a painful birthing, cannot be denied, so Savette was named. "She is a beauty, Lovick. 'Twill be easy to get a good marriage with a name like Savette. Means safety."

So, now he sat, waiting. Age and toil had tarnished the young man he had been, outlining his sinews, giving his sparse beard a mangy cast, scarring rivulets down his cheeks. *So, where is she?* Carefully, he placed a root and a handful of bark slivers on the embers and studied them, his eyes blank. *Not like Savette to linger past the Vespers bell — dinner not yet started, the hearth cold.*

The two-room cot in which he stood was of wattle — woven twigs and branches plastered over with daub — and was dark. Any light that tried to enter had to angle through the one narrow window or rise from the fire on the tiled hearth in the middle of the room.

Lovick glanced with distaste at the lumps of cabbage and onion at the bottom of the iron pot. *Lads'll be back, though, soon eno'. Might 'ave seen 'er.*

As if called, the door blustered open, and two young, full-bodied men stumbled into the house, the wind beating in after them, flinging smoke and ash from the hearth into the room and sending a lick of flame around the root. Simon, the older of the two, built like an ox, with bright eyes and a short beard, cupped his hands and blew into them.

"'Tis that cold out there. Snow again afore long. What's with the paltry fire? Savette? Where's my girl?"

Lovick stirred at the now melting mess in the pot. "Naught about."

"Naught about?" Simon looked blank, intent in shrugging off the filthy sheepskin cloak, then looked at Lovick, brows furrowed. "Where, then?"

"With Jared, like as not," said Todd, the words slurred around the heel of the morning's loaf. Todd was leaner than Simon, and darker, with the hooded eyes of a hawk.

Simon whirled. "Eno' o' tha'. She's a good lass. Keeps our dad."

"I said naught about that." Todd pushed his brother's hand from his chest. "Safe from danger she be with Jared. Friend though 'e be o' mine, too sure of 'is own self, lately, with all the maids. Not just Savette. 'At's the sum of it."

"Savette's not been here this while," Lovick interrupted. "'Tisn't like her. Some'ut ... " His voice was querulous. "Simon," he said, "there's a good lad. Go along the Bimport. 'Tis just Vespers and the light'll soon be gone. Ask at the tavern on the High Street. Mayhap someone'll 'ave seen 'er. Todd? Down to the ponds with ye. She was intent on the washing."

"Threshing barn?" Todd suggested, his Adam's apple bobbing with the last swallow of bread.

"Nay. Wash's not back."

Simon hauled his sheepskin from the peg on which he had just flung it. "Be certain ye ask of all, have they seen ... "

"Aye, aye." Todd was out the door to look for Savette, even before Lovick had finished his instructions. "Stacking wood for the abbess all day, and now this," he muttered just loud enough so that Simon, behind him, could hear his words. "She can't e'en manage to do the washing withou' trouble."

Simon glowered at his younger brother's back, but ignored the taunt.

Gold Hill, the steep track that led to the bottom of the hill, was deserted, though a ray of light knifed under the goldsmith's door and through his shutters. *That one can afford to light cressets,* Todd thought, *even afore full dark. Probably has wax tapers.*

From opposite the goldsmith's, Todd paused to look down on the splatter of huts that nestled against the lower slopes of the hill. The tiny parish of St. James. As best he could see within the fingers of mist, nothing moved. *Could she have run away to Salisbury with Jared? Nay,* he thought, shaking his head. *Wouldn't leave Lovick, would she? Even if she did, what could Jared do for the year and a day he'd need to become a freeman?*

At the bottom of the hill, any light that managed to peep through the shutters of the cottages was muzzy in the winter damp. A desultory wind rummaged through the few soggy leaves scattered among the icy ruts, but it had not the bite that it carried on top of the hill. Todd looked uncertainly down the path beside the

31

stream. The bushes on which the village women dried their laundry were pockets of deeper shadow. He took a few wobbly steps along the path, feeling for the familiar rocks. As children they'd played here, floating pieces of bark with leaves for sails while their mother beat the washing with wooden paddles. The path seemed to have changed since then. *Where does Savette wash the clothes? Where Moder did? Near that rock that juts out into the stream?* After a few more feet, he felt the path turn further into the bank, leaving the stream. *Where is that damn rock? Did I pass it? Did I pass her? In the bushes? In the water? Wouldn't she call out? Mayhap leave 'er basket?*

He tried to listen for some sound of her, but the ticking of the wind and the moist whispering of the stream covered all sound. *Hopeless.* As he moved forward, his foot turned on a mossy rock and slipped off into the mud.

"'Sblood! Todd scrambled upright and, shaking his wet foot, yelled downstream, "Savette. 'Ey, Savette."

Nothing.

Todd bit his lip. *Scaring myself and I can't see a thing. 'Tis a waste of time.* Back on the track, he tried to see through the mist down to the abbey's laundry house, *but it'll be shuttered against the night. She wouldn't have gone there, anyway.*

"Savette." His voice sounded hoarse even to his ears, hoarse and scared.

"Savette." Louder.

No one in St. James opened a door or looked out.

Chapter Five

Monday, early night after Vespers

I

Sister Cadilla hurried up the hill, clammy threads of fog clinging to her habit. A strong woman, she was, with a square face, high forehead, and the ice-blue eyes of her Saxon forebears. She hated to be out in the fogs of winter—fugs, really, of smoke and mists and ghostly forms that brought the nuns to the infirmary with colds and coughs. So many were now there that she'd had little time recently to check on the herbs drying in the officina, the little hut at the back of the herbarium. It'd been more than a week, she suspected. She'd take a moment now. It was on her way, and it was warm.

As she scraped open the door to the officina, Cadilla could hear, muffled by the heavy fog, the muted "ba-a-a" of the sheep, and the shepherd's horn as he led them to their pens. She shut the door. The herbarium cat rose from his place by the fire, arched his back, and gave her a murmur of greeting. As she bent to steep her hands in the warm fur, hoping to stop their shaking, she gave a little sniff. *Was that a hint of mold? That hollow, wet smell?* The loudest smells in the officina—rosemary, lavender, and thyme — crashed against her senses, but beneath them lay an undertone, a wet resonance, that was slightly off. *Yes, a mold was starting.*

On top of the now-ashy coals, Cadilla upended a bavin of brush stored ready next to the hearth, gave it a twist to allow the air to circulate, and softly blew until a small flame darted up the bundle of dried grasses and twigs. When the runnels of fire were stronger, she added three pieces of kindling and turned to the drying trays. The window above them was shuttered, its upper half covered in thin sheets of waxed parchment, which kept out some of the moisture and allowed in enough light for her to work — *but on a winter afternoon, I still need a fire to be able to see.*

Cadilla peered at the most recently stacked of the drying trays, lifting them one after another, sifting along the warp that kept the layers apart. Absently, she felt the leaves, plucking one here, another there, to be discarded. She nodded to herself. *The coals in the curfew alone can't keep the officina warm enough. The air is too moist.* She'd ask the chapter for more wood. From now until late spring, she'd have to keep a fire going, banked but burning, day and night.

As she fingered a tray of drying parsley, Cadilla's mind veered onto the changes brought about by the distribution of offices of the New Year. *Why,* she grumbled to herself, *did the abbess remove Dame Averilla from the infirmary now, when I need her? Only nun as ever really knew me — only one as ever tried.* Cadilla's fingers slid into a patch of slime — *always parsley isn't it? Leaves be too close together. But if Dame Averilla 'adn 'a been taken from the infirmary, the abbess wouldna 'ave given the place to me, so ...*

Beyond all thought or reasonable expectation, Cadilla, daughter of the reeve, English to her fingertips, and a lay sister or domicilla — one who had no dowry — had been appointed infirmaress of the abbey. Shaftesbury was one of the few abbeys where such a breach in tradition would be tolerated. Because it was one of the oldest and richest abbeys in the kingdom—certainly one of the largest, and a royal foundation as well—the nuns of Shaftesbury did very much as they pleased. Somehow, they managed to avoid the petty alliances and resulting squabbles between Norman and English nuns that beset other foundations, and sometimes, albeit rarely, the chapter did allow a lay sister to hold a position of responsibility.

Under Abbess Cecily, she acknowledged, *I would never 'a been appointed infirmaress, but Abbess Emma, probably 'cause 'er moder was English, now she saw the good in me. Lucky, too, that Shaftesbury be rich, else I would 'av had to 'av a dowry.* A great wave of emotion overwhelmed her. The weight and enormity of her good fortune broke through her anxiety and fear. Tears, one after another, trickled down her cheeks. She stood unmoving. Then, as if a momentous decision had been made, Cadilla reached under her wimple and pulled out a leather cord from which hung a triangular stone.

The little stone had been a gift from her brother, who had found it near the barrows. He had drilled a hole in it for a cord, and the little stone had nestled between her breasts ever since. The "elf bolt" had become a talisman. Many people had them—they brought luck. Cadilla touched it when she felt threatened or thwarted or in need of help.

She held it up now, to the light, looking at it as if seeing it for the first time, remembering how Dame Averilla had flinched when first she saw it, with disgust. *As if 'twas a salamander or a noxious toad or such like.* When Averilla had asked about it, *only the once, I'll grant 'er that—ye'd 'a thought she was seeing an adder. Didn't cast it out, though. 'Twas as well she didn't. That would 'a set me to, it would.*

All thought of the parsley gone, Cadilla gazed fondly at the elf bolt, and with some awe. *Almost the shape of an arrowhead, 'tis*, she thought, examining the rounded, fingernail slices along the edges. *I 'ave 'ad it for so long. Hard to give up, it'll be. I must, though. Told St. Edward I would. Told him that I wouldn't rub it or watch how it turned any more, if he'd just let me stay in the infirmary.* She sighed and then brightened as a thought hit her. *That's how Saint Edward did it, I warrant. 'Twas easy enough for him. Made Emma take the post of abbess. Then 'e made Dame Averilla disobey the abbess, so the abbess 'ad to punish 'er by taking 'er from the infirmary.* Cadilla felt a momentary pang of conscience at having caused Averilla sorrow. *By the rood, 'twas Saint Edward's choice as how to do it. I just asked him as he would let me stay. I did not ask to be infirmaress.*

Cadilla turned the elf bolt between thumb and forefinger. *But how do I rid myself of it? If I throw it away, I will remember and hallow the spot. Others do that. Why, old Ingrid never passes the miller's corn crib without crossing herself, and even Damasa turned around three times under the spring moon, wanting a husband. If I threw it away, I'd allays know where it was, waiting to be used, if I needed to ask something of it. I might even go dig it up. I allays could. So how do I rid myself of it?*

The thought appeared so suddenly that it seemed to come from God: *Give the elf bolt to St. Edward.*

A niche, she knew, had been carved into the bottom of the little statue of Saint Edward that stood at the entrance to the infirmary chapel. She could push the elf bolt into the niche until it was wedged so tightly that it couldn't be moved. *That'd be the way to do it.*

Cadilla had been praying to the statue of Saint Edward for as long as she could remember. It wasn't that she didn't like God—after all, hadn't she appealed to God last year in the forest when she was praying for Averilla? But this little Saint Edward was approachable.

No one knew where the statue had come from. Some said he

36

had been carved from the tusks of the fantastical heavy beasts that dwelt on great sheets of ice far to the north. Long ago, when the bones of King Edward were transferred to Shaftesbury, the statue was placed near the font, but in the lee of the doorway. It had been difficult to see in the brooding darkness of the sturdy and nearly windowless Anglo-Saxon church. Everyone assumed that the statue had come with the bones of the saint, and it had given the pilgrims another special place to pray.

To Cadilla, as a child, the figurine had been an irresistible attraction. At the close of the day, after she had driven the geese back to their owners, she would creep into the church and stand listening to the swirling of the nuns' voices as they sang Vespers. Her mind, though, would be fixed on the myth and beauty of the boy king. Saint Edward was everything Cadilla most admired: aristocratic, serene, and ascetic. The statue had a becoming manliness, the tapered fingers hooked into a wide belt slung carelessly across thin hips. Loops hanging from the belt ought to have held both dagger and sword, but they were empty — no swords, not even a tiny one, in a church. The sightless eyes beheld some distant vision, and the image seemed far above the world's petty distractions, even the perfidy of his stepmother. It was to Saint Edward that Cadilla had taken her childish woes, asking his help in all matters of distress, her father's solemn quietude, her mother's despair. Indeed, for most of those who managed to find it, the carven ivory figure held more than a little charm. The features had a kind of delicacy and wit to them that the stories about Edward affirmed. So different was Edward's life from that which Cadilla knew or ever thought to have, so different was he from any man who might have looked with favor on her big boned, un-feminine tall body, or the bright blue eyes in the moon-shaped face. So different were his long-fingered hands from Cadilla's, both large and work-callused. What had started as a childish fantasy soon turned to adulation.

At the beginning of the reconstruction of the abbey, undertaken by the former abbess, Cecily FitzHamon, the ivory image was removed from the narthex and placed for safekeeping atop a cornice at the entrance to the infirmary chapel. Cadilla, a humble lay sister assigned to work in the infirmary, saw this as a sign that she should take her requests to Edward and no longer rely on the elf bolt when she wanted something.

So, now, as the newly appointed infirmaress, Cadilla took her deepest fears, her most intimate worries, to Edward, and spent what little time she had on her knees before him. Edward, she was sure, heard and helped her.

Cadilla had asked Edward to help her be admitted to this very abbey, and despite her common upbringing, the fact that she was English, and that she had no dowry, Cadilla had been accepted. As a lay sister, it was true, but accepted anyway, the dowry waived because of her recognized skill with herbs. And look at where she was now. Infirmaress. Unheard of that such a position be given to a lay sister. All because of her prayers to Edward. *Or the nightly rubbing of the elf bolt,* something inside her whispered. She would put the elf bolt in the hollow at the bottom of the statue of King Edward. There it would be safe.

It was cold as Cadilla stepped from the officina. The air seemed textured, almost as if it were firming up in preparation for ice. She was glad to lift the latch of the infirmary door and step down onto the swept and washed tiles. That had been one of Dame Averilla's more peculiar notions: she had been convinced that rushes were dirty, and their presence on the floor promoted disease. The infirmary certainly smelled better without them. As Cadilla traversed the length of the room, her eyes, with the rote of long experience, took in every detail, a mussed coverlet here, a prolonged snoring or a restless tossing there.

Cadilla's mind returned to the uses to which she had put the elf bolt. Last year, she had been afraid that Dame Edith would be raised over her in the infirmary. At the full moon she had dipped the elf bolt in cows' milk... So, at the change of duties at the New Year, Abbess Emma had placed Edith in the cloister to be the abbey illuminator, while Cadilla, to the surprise of many, was given charge of the infirmary. Since she didn't really have anything against Dame Edith, Cadilla hadn't put a spell on her. After all, Edith had made the effort to teach her the sticky and sliding words of Norman French, and now the drawled patter of the Norman nuns had become easier for her to understand. *Now they can't whisper behind my back.* She sniffed the air for any unusual scent of pus or putrifaction. *Verily—aye, that would be Edith's word, 'verily.'* Cadilla hadn't made much of an effort to learn French before her advancement, so consumed had she been with making her own mark; on not being looked down upon, on being respected. *But now I need to understand what ails them. To be fair, the old nuns were always courteous. The English nuns. English like King Edward and King Ethelred. No, even more than courteous, they were kind. 'Verily,' I was prickly. Holding all the nuns off, afraid to open myself, always keeping up my shield. Just like Goliath. Not only big and clumsy, and they so dainty, but armoring myself against sneers about Fader. Holding up my shield against taunts and giggles behind hands.*

As she now walked the length of the infirmary, Cadilla didn't need to stop to attend anyone. Most of her patients were asleep, or at least their eyes were closed. That in itself was sign enough for her that what she intended was right. It meant that Edward agreed that it would be better if no one were privy to her actions, and more important, he agreed to accept the elf bolt.

Instead of turning into the chapel at the transept, Cadilla made her way into the work area where the braziers and pre-pared tisanes and small pots of ointments were kept in readiness. Again she pulled up the cord from beneath her tunic and slipped it over her head. Taking the sharpest knife from a slotted board,

39

she sliced through the cord and pulled it out of the hole in the jagged piece of stone.

At the statue of Saint Edward, she paused and bowed, put out both hands, lifted the ivory statue, and with slow, ceremonious steps, holding it before her, laid the little figurine on the altar, bowed low, and then knelt. *Not quite right to upend the statue and insert the elf bolt. Some'ut obscene, is it?*

"Saint Edward," she said softly. "You have been my help, my savior. Hear my plea. Accept this gift. Keep it safe. I know it is wrong to believe in the power of such things, and so I give it to you, knowing that with you it will no longer tempt me."

With nothing more to say, and fearing the arrival of someone else, Cadilla pushed the little arrowhead into the niche in the statue. She then took one of the cressets that always were lighted at the sides of the chapel, and lighted one of the altar candles. Patiently, she dripped wax over the niche until the opening was completely sealed.

Chapter Six

Monday evening after Vespers

I

By the time Master Hugo and Ralf reached the gate at the top of the incline, the other latecomers had melded into the throng that was jostling to get inside the barricade before night. Pack mules kicked at donkeys, peddlers shoved at beggars, and all were pushed by the hungry townsfolk with faggots of wood on their backs or bags of chips slung from yokes, their worn tunics streaked burnt red and sullen umber against the off-white of the well-used snow. None, Hugo noticed, lacked footwear, albeit rags in many cases, and most had hoods to cover their heads, or shabby wicker peasant hats.

As they waited to pass into the town, Hugo examined the surrounding palisade — a barricade of sharpened stakes wound with brambles. He had already noted with some interest the series of ice-studded ponds surrounding the base of the hill. For a town this size, the place was effectively and efficiently fortified. *Man'd think twice afore trying to get at this convent. But then again, who'd want to get in?*

When it was their turn to pass the gatekeeper, Hugo had barely opened the first basket on the donkey's back before the man

41

motioned them past. "Naw, no fee, Master. The lady abbess be expecting ye. 'Tis her gate, after all, and she be paying. Glad to see ye, she'll be." Hugo felt mild surprise. Is *it so obvious who I am and how I make a living?*

On the other side of the gate, the High Street echoed the turmoil of evening. People shouted, pigs squealed, and children pointed sharp voices at one another as they streaked between adult legs. Nearby, a gander squawked and pecked at a goose hidden beneath the huge wheels of an ox cart. Rebuffed, he lifted his bulky wings and hissed a string of dreary blats at his unwilling mate.

Ralf's eyes widened as they passed a forge where piles of alder charcoal were stacked between scythes dulled in the harvest. The blacksmith, haloed by the still-bright coals, held a bent coulter in long tongs against the anvil, while the ploughman, tunic hiked above cloth-banded legs, leaned against a post and picked his teeth with a thorn, obviously enjoying the warmth of the fire.

"It needs to be reset," Hugo replied resignedly to yet another of Ralf's interminable questions, "the coulter does. Otherwise, comes next plowing, the plow'll leave a rest between the ridges, and thistles will spring up. The winter gives 'em time to repair such like."

The houses of the town seemed ordinary to Hugo, even some-what prosperous — wattle plastered with daub, but sturdy and well thatched. Some were two-storied, with stone bases and exterior steps leading up to the second floor. At a sign and a lantern, he stopped. "Glad o' this, I be." After flinging the donkey's rope around a post, he started to push his way through the crowded doorway.

A thick-necked young man wearing a soiled sheepskin stepped directly into Hugo's path. Looking Hugo up and down, he curled his lip and said, "God prosper you."

Surprised, Hugo responded, "And you as well," and waited for the man to move. When the young man stayed put, Hugo placed his equally massive arm against the man's chest and said, "If we might get some ale?" The man spat and kept his place, forcing Hugo and Ralf against other bodies as they stumbled into the alehouse.

The room was large, the length of a barn, with heavy beams holding up the thatch. The rich, steamy smell of brewing ale hung heavy in the smoke. A group of men near the measly fire talked in growled whispers, while others sat, heads together, around the trestle tables lining the walls.

Wordlessly, Hugo held out their horns to the tapster.

"Ye're lucky this night," the tapster said, eyeing them. "We've just broached a cask of the August ale. 'Tis Mistress Meredith's. We 'ave many as can put a clever hand to brewing, but her ale ... " His words were the common hospitality expected by travelers, but his eyes observed Hugo carefully — his clothes, his gait, the lie of his hair.

Hugo pointed his chin back toward the crowd at the door. "'Tis not a saint's day, I think?"

"Always a reason for ale." The tapster didn't smile. "One o' the maids from the town 'as gone missing. The lad to the front of the door be brother to her. Name o' Simon. Questioning strangers."

Hugo glanced back at the door, nodded, put down a small coin with King Stephen's head on it, and pointed to the platter of brown-crusted pasties stacked on a shelf. Giving one to Ralf, Hugo shouldered a path to the end of the table farthest from both door and fire.

2

STRUGGLING BACK UP GOLD HILL, Todd forced himself to try to think logically. *The abbey. Of course. The nuns had often needed Savette for one reason or another. She had helped there before.*

43.

At the top of the hill, puffing from the climb, he knocked at the porter's lodge in one of the twin towers of the gatehouse. A stout shutter, small and square, in the small gate used by those on foot, slid slowly back and a lined face peered out at him as he stood under the flickering waves of a fire basket. It was Dame Celine.

"Dame?"

"Aye. And may God keep you safe this night, too, son of Lovick. In what way may we be of service?"

"Er, may God keep you, Dame Celine. Have you seen my sister Savette? She has gone missing. Came she here on some errand?"

"No, lad. Why, 'tis after Vespers. All are gone by then." She looked doubtfully at the whiteness of his face. "But I shall ask." Forgetting to close the shutter, she hobbled toward the inner court and disappeared.

When the apple-doll face reappeared at the slot, it was gray with worry, the small eyes larger in their anxiety. "No, lad. I am that sorry, but she has not been here this day. Dame Averilla, the infirmaress as was" — Todd started to back away, fearing a rambling monologue, — "said that Savette came by a bit ago, but has not seen her since."

Todd hesitated. "Here? Today?"

"Nay, lad. A day or so ago, 'twas. Perhaps longer. She did not say. But not this day. Of that I am sure."

"A day ago? But she mentioned no such errand."

"Our prayers will be with you. And with her," Dame Celine said as she started to slide the shutter. "I myself shall go now to pray."

A lot of good that'll do.

Todd reached his father's cottage at a half-run, real fear beginning inside him. He found Lovick, despite the freezing air, seated on the bench outside, his hands between his legs, his breath steaming in the torch light. A crowd of men had already gathered, swarming like gnats around a center, stamping their feet in the dirty bits

44

of snow and blowing on their hands.

Tom, the bailiff's second, was also just ariving.

Not seeing Tom, Lovick looked up hopefully at Todd and asked, "At the stream?"

"Nay." Todd shook his head. "I asked at the abbey as well. They 'ave not seen her. Mayhap ... " he let the sentence trail off.

"Torches," Tom broke in. "With the mist thickening, we'll need torches. Try to retrace her steps. Two parties. Cedric, ye take one." Tom turned to Todd. "Not by the stream, ye say?"

"Nay. I followed the path some ways, not far, ye wist, for the mist. Then I fell. I could see naught for the bushes. Seemed no point to look further."

"Well, take torches with ye now and seek again along the banks of the stream. See if she fell in, or tripped. Not likely, but who knows? Be cautious. Can't do much at night, and we risk fouling the tracks, if tracks there be. If we find her not tonight, at first light we'll look again. But tonight mayhap we can still hear her, if she be in need of help. There warn't no cause fer her to wander? After nuts or roots?"

"Nay," Lovick said firmly, certain. "Those she collected in the fall and stored. And there was our dinner to get on. Allays did what she should and when. Wanted everything just so." He looked down. "That was the way she was. A good maid."

"Simon?" Tom asked.

"He went to the alehouse to ask if any had seen or heard tell of her. To talk to strangers ... "

Robert Bradshaw, the bailiff, the man charged with keeping the peace in the town and protecting the abbey, had arrived somewhat after Tom. Robert had stayed on the fringes of the crowd, unnoticed, picking at his teeth with his knife, and watching. It was Tom's business, this, the finding of lost things. Tom was the best tracker for miles around, and he had taken charge as Robert had ordered him to.

45

But Robert knew men. So now, as Tom organized the searchers, Robert absently put his knife in its sheath and watched from the shadows, trying to catch something false. *Jared,* he thought, scratching above his mustache as he often did when in thought. His eye rested on a youth with heavy black brows and a hint of a mustache above a full upper lip. The lad hovered on the far side of the crowd. *Wasn't it Jared who was oft with Savette at harvest time?*

Sensing the bailiff's eyes on him, Jared spoke up, his voice overloud. "The carver has arrived."

At Jared's voice, Todd whirled and, puffing like an adder, lunged at him. He grabbed the neck of Jared's tunic and pulled him forward until their noses almost touched. "What did you do wi' 'er. Where 'ave you taken 'er?"

"Hey! Wha?" Jared slammed his fist upward against the hand on his tunic, but Todd was already butting his head into Jared's chest and at the same time pummeling his back. Jared hammered his free fist against Todd's ear again and again until they both went down, locked together, scrabbling in the dust. Other hands hauled them apart, and Jared, coughing, wiped his mouth with the back of his hand and glared at Todd. "She 'as na mare to do wi' me. You remember that."

3

HUGO, AT THE REAR OF THE ALEHOUSE, was enjoying his pasty. Ralf, having wolfed his down, perfunctorily wiped his lips and twisted toward the sounds of a scuffle that sounded like it was building into a brawl.

"Just Gloucester's men, I—" Hugo said around a mouthful of pasty. Ralf was no longer listening to Hugo. Dropping his horn, Ralf bolted from the bench and, like an eel through marsh weed, slid in and out among the hips and knees of the crowd around the door, all the while howling like a berserker, "No, nooo."

Aware of their position as strangers, Hugo rose and proceeded more courteously to the front. The yells and growls coming from the yard had ominously increased since Ralf had shoved his way through, and had then been replaced by a menacing silence. Reaching the door, Hugo's height allowed him to see over the crowd. In the misted lantern light, a bug caught in amber, lay the man who'd barred them from the alehouse — Simon, the tapster'd named him — and over him, his menace barely tethered, crouched Tindal, teeth inches from Simon's bulging neck, his black, belly-lifted snarl audible across the silence.

A boy — 'sblood, it's Ralf — approached from the torch light, his words, "Tindal! Down!" overriding the dog's droning growl. The dog hesitated. His eyes wavered. Then he lowered himself onto his haunches, not sitting, still coiled, but presenting a pre-tense at obedience.

Appalled — "I was already trying to justify myself to you," Hugo would later tell the abbess — Hugo shouldered himself forward, put one hand on the scruff of Ralf's neck and at the same time pulled from his belt his heavy hammer. Teeth bared, Hugo scythed the intervening space with the hammer, clearing the arc around them.

Hugo's back, however, was undefended; he felt the sharp sting of a knife at his throat. "Drop the hammer." From the side, another man snaked an arm around the boy and twisted the scrawny arm behind Ralf's back in a hammerlock of such force that Hugo was sure the arm would break.

"Defend," The command was uttered with such assurance that Hugo was amazed that it was the same boy. The dog slid back into a crouch, teeth inches from Simon's throat.

An impasse.

From the corner of his eye, Hugo saw the light glance off sharpened steel.

"You kill that dog," Hugo bellowed despite the knife at his own throat, "and by the rood, ye'll answer to the abbess."

Before anyone could move, from further up the street came the sound of the watch: "Way, make way."

A maid from the inn scuttled forward and then retreated, held at bay by one look from the dog.

"Simon, what the devil ... ?" The crowd cleared a space for the bailiff.

Simon's eyes teared. He said nothing.

"I saw it all, Bailiff." The voice was that of an older woman, the only woman, save the serving maid, in the crowd. Though her smile revealed several gaps, her kerchief was of a clean white. "Simon 'as been asken after Savette. Was just trying to make sure this donkey," and she pointed at Bithric — neglected, irritated, ears back — "carries only what he ought. Savette missing and all ... "

"Call off the dog." The bailiff's voice held no fear.

"Not quite yet."

The holds around Hugo and Ralf had tightened. The bailiff fixed Hugo with a cold glare. "Well, man, declare yourself."

Hugo glared back, undaunted by the knife at his throat, "I am Master Hugo, carver, late of the Abbey of Saint Edmunds at Bury, here to see the lady abbess, at her bidding, to create a reredos for her altar." Aware of the impact of his words, eyes cold and ominous, Hugo said evenly, "Is this, Master Bailiff, your usual way of welcome? A strange representative of Christ this lady abbess must be."

"'Tis not her way, nor ours either. But a maid, as was told you, has gone missing," and the Bailiff calmly raised a hand in command. Hugo felt cool air on his neck as the knife was removed. "You are a stranger," the bailiff continued, "Simon was right to question. Now," it was a command, "the dog."

Ralf glanced up at Hugo and, after the pause of a moment, said evenly, "Tindal. Back."

48

This time — "I imagine he was a trained war dog," Hugo would later continue to the abbess — the dog backed two paces and sat, eyes still fixed on Simon.

Cautiously, Simon wiped his arm across his mouth and licked at the bloody tooth marks on his arm. Placing his other arm beneath him, he levered himself from the ground and muttered to the bailiff, "Aye. So it was. Wanted to see what 'is bags 'ad." Here, Simon glowered over at Hugo. "Who knows who or what this man might 'ave been. Never seen afore this night. Could be … anyone."

Chapter Seven

Monday Evening After Compline

It was just after Compline by the time Master Hugo and the bailiff arrived at yet another gate, this the main gate of the abbey gatehouse. Robert pounded on the thick boards, and the gatekeeper, Abward, made a show of coming down the stairs from the upper rooms and creaking back a slot set in one of the boards. "It be after Compline," he growled peering through the grille and holding back a yawn. Belatedly recognizing the bailiff in the torch light, he straightened, "Is aught amiss?"

Robert explained.

"Ye be knowing as well as I," Abward said, "that all in the abbey must be locked after Compline. Abbess be abed by now."

Robert glanced through toward the inner court and thought he saw a light in the upper window above the bursar's office. "Compline is just now finished. Mayhap Abbess Emma is not yet abed. Ask Sister Clayetta."

Abward was dubious. "Iffen she wanted—"

"Now," Robert commanded. "Tell Sister Clayetta 'tis Master Hugo."

Abbess Emma had not retired to the barren inner room in which she slept when important guests needed to be entertained or some other matter kept her up past Compline. She was seated in the outer of the two rooms that comprised her lodgings, a room used as both office and dining room. Her face was drawn from fatigue, for she was still trying to puzzle out from which accounts Master Chapman had taken the money.

At her hesitant "Deo gratis," Master Hugo followed the bailiff and Sister Clayetta into the room. Candlelight flickered and fluttered against the paneling and the closed shutters. The remains of a sparse meal, some crusty bread and a wooden bowl, lay on one of two tables. The abbess sat at the other, a stack of rolled parchment beside her, one roll lying open on her table.

The abbess looked up in surprise and no little consternation as the two men were bundled into the room by a grumbling Sister Clayetta. "Well you wist, Master Bailiff, that Compline—" but whatever else she intended to say was interrupted by the Bailiff.

"My lady, I bring you Master Hugo."

She raised her eyebrows and then stood, coming around the table.

Master Hugo looked to the abbess like an irritated and very dirty rooster. Wide across the chest from his work, Hugo was further puffed up with the dregs of his anger. His gray-brown hair and beard went in all directions despite an obvious and none-too-successful attempt to smooth them. Both gorget and tunic were travel-stained and dirty, and the sour, yeasty smell of old ale preceded him.

Giving the abbess time to collect herself, Robert added, "You need to know as well, my lady, that the maid Savette has gone missing.

Emma's eyes immediately fastened on those of the bailiff and she whispered, "Lovick's daughter?"

"Aye. Simon, Savette's older brother, was at the tavern, asking any strangers …

Robert related the events while the abbess looked from one

man to the other, her face little betraying her thoughts.

"I bid you well come, Master," she said when Robert had finished the story. "Despite your previous reception, I must assure you that we are glad to have you with us. Your fame precedes you."

"My lady," Hugo said, bowing his head, and noticing for the first time the bloodied scratch that ran along his hand. He hid it behind his back. "My journeying was somewhat precarious," he said, "even before the events of this day had run their course." He didn't elaborate, but scrabbled to lift the leather flap of his scrip. Drawing out a large tome bound in boards and covered in plain leather, he added, "I bring with me as well a book sent you by Abbot Anselm of Saint Edmunds. He said you had written requesting to borrow our copy of Boethius in order that your scribes might copy it."

The abbess took the book, opened the cover, and looked at the first page. She raised her eyes and smiled. "Dame Edith, our illuminator, as well as our scribes, will be glad of this. She has long hoped to see it. You come unaccompanied?" She raised a skeptical eyebrow. Few traveled unaccompanied.

"I started with a party of merchants. We were attacked on the road. I alone survived, and from then on I went very slowly, taking great care about where the next steps led." His eyes gazed into the distance of his mind.

Hugo hadn't seen them coming, but then, none of them had. The first whiff he had had of them, like a dog smelling a bear, had been the flicker of his horse's ears, twitching to an unfamiliar nicker.

With the civil war tightening muscular coils around England, solitary travel had become absolutely foolhardy. Thus, in Bury

St. Edmund's, Hugo had managed to join a caravan of merchants following the market fairs. These weren't big fairs — not like those of St. Denis and Bruges on the continent — but smaller gatherings held around convenient saints' days in the summer: St. John's in June, Our Lady in August, Michaelmas in September, and Candlemas in February. Hugo could just as well have joined with a band of pilgrims, but merchants were armed and ready to defend themselves. Pilgrims tended to be defenseless, easy prey for marauders, innocently carrying their alms and oblations to present at the shrine of a favored saint, and blissfully unaware that anyone knew they did so. In any case, pilgrims didn't travel when the roads were mucky.

The caravan Hugo joined had more than fifty men, all seasoned, armed, and ready to defend their wares. In loaded wicker panniers, their mules and donkeys carried silks from Spain and Constantinople, furs from Kiev, steel from Damascus and Toledo, paper from China, and the heavy felted wool of Flanders.

That day they had been following a track that meandered along a hill crest covered in scrub and gorse and barbered by the wind. Even though the day was cold, they needed to water the stock and had just started down a convenient gully toward a stream. They were nearing the denuded willows and aspen hugging a redness in their twigs that presaged spring not so far off when Hugo's horse flicked his ears.

Hugo was in his usual spot in the caravan — toward the back and to the left — in order to keep his donkey from the fierce kicks of the horses. There was an alarmed whicker further up the line. Hugo stopped and listened, and then he too felt, rather than heard, the thunderous vibration of many hooves and the gritty scraping of unsheathed swords. The brigands came down on the caravan like a wall of water, bent forward over their horses' necks, teeth clenched, and swords drawn.

The well-timed whinny was enough to save Hugo. As soon as he heard it and recognized the meaning of the accompanying thunder, he slipped his feet from the stirrups, knotted his heavy body into as much of a ball as he could, and rolled down the remaining slope and into the mush at the water's edge. Cushioned by the flexible reeds and white-headed cattails, his body settled into the muck with little more than a quiver of twigs.

The merchants Hugo was riding with were all killed. Ruthlessly and with practiced efficiency, they were run through before they had time to unsheathe their weapons. Hugo watched from his wet refuge as one after another died. Merchants, even armed merchants, were no match for outlaws.

Hugo stayed where he was. The bodies splayed above him soon drenched his senses in the sickly iron smell of blood. One of the murdered men rolled into the reeds alongside Hugo. He hesitated to push off the man's outflung arm. He watched, disgusted, as a fly settled on the dead man's still-open eye and kneaded its legs on the last glimmer of sight. This man had just yesterday bought Hugo a tankard of ale. He quietly retched.

The merchants' animals and Hugo's horse were quickly rounded up, tied together, and led away, necks stretched, eyes wild. Along with the horses went the two-wheeled carts and Hugo's small, long-eared donkey, his dainty hooves leaving small runes atop the deep indentations made by the horses.

Hugo stayed hidden until the sun was well down the western sky, and then managed to unfold frozen knees and ankles from the reeds. At the top of the gully, nothing along the wayside moved. Not even the wind.

"Won't do," he muttered to himself, eager to hear the normalcy of a voice, even his own, "to continue along this track. Needs keep to the woods. Go slow. Aware." *And when night falls, what then?* "Climb a tree?" he muttered aloud in answer to his thought, talking to himself. *Talking to myself, am I? That can't be a good sign.* "More scared than I thought."

54

Hugo had gone only the length of a hide when he heard the snapping of a twig. He flattened himself against a tree and waited. The sound was not repeated. And then there came the solitary click of a dainty hoof against a pebble. Slowly, and with practiced caution, Hugo peered around the tree. "God is good," he whispered before he could stop himself, for there, as vulnerable and trusting as a young maid, was the donkey, the wicker panniers on his back intact, though crooked.

How Bithric escaped, Hugo never knew. "We'll have to get from here to Winchester alone," he said to the donkey. "'Twon't be easy now, without the horse. *Without the others to guard us.* "You see that, don't you? No hee-haws now, or games." *If you value my life.* The donkey had minced backwards.

"I AM NOT ENTIRELY UNACCOMPANIED, HOWEVER. I have one companion. An apprentice."

"Is he with you?"

"Aye."

"Mayhap I might meet him."

"My apprentice?" Hugo gaped.

"It is well for me to know every soul who sets foot within the abbey courts. Especially every man."

"He is a boy."

"And boys."

"As you will, my lady."

Hugo started to the door. Suspecting that he might yell for the boy, before he could open it, Emma said, "Go you softly, Master. It is after Compline. The time of our Great Silence."

"The boy, mind you," Emma would tell Dame Aethwulfa, "is not far from starvation, by the look of him. His ragged tunic barely covered the knobs of elbows and shoulders. I can't help

55

but wonder ... But his eyes are clear."

Ralf entered, but stood at the door, blinking at the light, and momentarily overwhelmed by such trappings and luxury as he had never before seen.

"This is Ralf." Hugo's voice was gruff.

"Ah."

The abbess and Ralf looked at one another, with surprise on her part and immediate adulation on his. "I have a dog," Ralf blurted, before she could say anything.

"My lady, the dog can be kept without," Hugo interrupted, clearly embarrassed.

"But, Master ... " Ralf swiveled his head to the man standing beside him. "You said ... "

"The boy gave me a look of such pleading and betrayal that I decided God was warning me to walk softly with him," Emma mused later to the old prioress.

"We, the enclosed," she said to Ralf's sullen look, "are allowed no pets. It distracts us, and detracts from our concentration on God. But," she added "there are cats in the abbey, for mice, and a dog or so in the stables, for rats. "I would meet this dog of yours before I decide on his accommodation."

Ralf scrambled to the door, yanked it open, and whistled. Before he had finished, Sister Clayetta had sidled into the room, keeping her back to the door and her eyes on the dog "who seemed to have mounted the outside staircase on his own, and from what I could tell was seated outside my lodgings, holding Clayetta hostage."

Tindal paced into the room and sat next to Ralf. Sister Clayetta scuttled out.

"Has he a name."

"Tindal."

"The dog crossed to me," Emma would continue to Aethwulfa, "as if to one of long acquaintance, as if what he could sense or smell told him everything he needed to know. He put his head

56

under my hand and pressed his forehead into my habit and sat down beside me, looking at the other two as if he, not they, had been requested into my presence."

"A wolfhound?" she asked. "Is it true what they say, that such dogs can look into your eyes and see the good or evil there?"

"I think so," Ralf mumbled and added "my lady," casting a sidelong look at Hugo to see that he was saying it right. Hugo's teeth tightened.

"He — he saved me at the tavern just now," Ralf blurted as the abbess patted the square head at her hip.

"Is that true?" the abbess looked to Hugo. As briefly as possible he explained those parts of the encounter with Simon, mostly concerning the dog, which the bailiff, for the sake of brevity, had omitted. The abbess' eyes narrowed."

"In that case, this Tindal will be a valuable addition to the abbey while you bide with us. However," she looked straight at Ralf, "he must remain by your side at all times. We have pilgrims and other timid souls to whom he might seem fearsome. For now, I bid you sweet sleep."

"My lady," Hugo said, his words detaining her as she was turning from them, "might it be possible for me to see the altar where I am to work?"

"Now?" she asked.

"I would my mind have as much time as possible to visualize the commission. A reredos of beaten silver is a daunting task."

She gave him a long appraising look and nodded. "To see the chapel and altar will not be difficult. There are always two watchers praying at the shrine. Sister Clayetta has a key to the oratory. She and the bailiff will lead you there."

CHAPTER EIGHT

MONDAY LATE NIGHT;

AFTER COMPLINE, BEFORE MATINS

I

Standing behind Sister Clayetta beneath the flickering light of the fire basket in the north porch of the oratory, Ralf rubbed his arms for warmth and buried his face in Tindal's thick fur. Clayetta peered first at one key, then another. The wind had risen while they were with the abbess; the snow was now all around them, and cold, much colder than it had been earlier below in the fields.

The bailiff had bid them good night at the gate separating the inner and outer courts.

"Snow," the nun now muttered pleasantly as she inserted an "E"-shaped key into the belly of the hanging lock. She stepped aside to allow Hugo to slot back the bar that fastened the door, which, grating open, revealed a cave of still darkness. To their left, straws of light pricked the gloom. The smell of old incense and burnt wick was not unpleasant, nor was the cool must of new stone that overlay it. The great building seemed less imposing, cocooned as they were within the coverlet of the dark.

On their way across the inner court, Hugo had snatched up a smooth piece of slate left by the masons. As they moved up the north aisle behind Sister Clayetta, Hugo produced a piece of charcoal from a pouch dangling from his belt. Head cocked to the side, he jotted squiggles and lines on the slate.

The candlelit portion of the church toward which they progressed proved to be a small chapel, the fine beeswax candles, always burning for Saint Edward, haloed by a cold-induced vapor. There was much more of the building off to the right, but that was now hidden in darkness. Here, in the chapel, two silent figures, black-veiled and still, knelt before the altar, on which stood a box. It was covered in leather, with smooth, bright blue medallions of enamel, gold leaves intertwined between them. The box was shaped like a little house on legs, seemingly held together with pins. Below its lid was a scene with simple figures, their heads in relief.

Hugo, oblivious to everything else, meandered through the chapel, scribbling continuously on the slate and mumbling quietly to himself, as if in conversation. "No. 'Twouldn't seem right. Well, yes, that would work, but . . . " There was a space of quiet. Then, "No, no it won't."

After the first bemused glances, the three nuns — Sister Clayetta had taken her place beside the other two — took little notice of either Hugo or Ralf or the silent gray-black dog that followed them.

Ralf propped himself against the back wall of the chapel and nestled beside the dog. From this sideways angle the altar was quite simple. The stone at its center front, Ralf noticed, was quite worn. Hugo answered Ralf's questions as they left the church. "The pressure of the priests leaning against it. And the stone is chipped," Hugo continued. "Not quarried from round about here, I warrant." He then scribbled on his piece of stone and motioned to Ralf to follow him.

Becoming aware of their leaving, Sister Clayetta bundled herself after them and escorted them to their lodgings in the outer court above one of the stables.

2

DESPITE THE LATENESS OF THE HOUR, Dame Averilla the new abbey sacarist was in the sacristy under the rood loft while Hugo was examining the North Chapel. Averilla was tall, with a ready, gap-toothed smile, eyes the color of a stormy morning, and the long-legged gait of a blue heron. She was engaged in polishing one of the huge silver-gilt candlesticks that usually stood beside the nave altar. These, and all the rest of the silver, gold, gilt, and brass that glittered in the abbey, the sacrist and any assistant assigned to her had to keep polished and shining. With Candlemas day not far off—the beginning of February—it was important that all the candelabra, especially these two enormous works of art, be gleaming in readiness. Candlemas was a particularly important feast for the abbey, for it hallowed the purification of Our Lady, one of Shaftesbury's patron saints. In her mind's eye, Dame Averilla could see the solemn mass that would be celebrated that day. She saw the nuns as they filed to the high altar, their candles held high in anticipation of light, while all the villagers watched and prayed for the snow that would ensure an abundant harvest. Averilla made a mental note to search in the forest for snowdrops, the "Fair Maids" of February, to adorn the high altar.

This polishing of the abbey silver was one small part of Dame Averilla's new duties. When the abbess had removed her from her former position as infirmaress, Averilla had been numb, off kilter, even unable to sleep. She had always relished the out-of-doors duties delegated to the infirmaress, the back-bending work in the herbarium, and the ministry to the aged and frail in the infirmary and in the village. She had felt fulfilled and worthwhile as she stooped over pallets to offer healing herbs, or to caress a gnarled hand. She had stood in awe of the strange life-giving trembling that overwhelmed her as, kneeling with a priest beside a sickbed, a miracle would sneak into the convulsed limbs, or they would share with the dying something of the shining, all-encompassing moment of death.

The abbess had removed Averilla from the infirmary deliberately, as if cauterizing a fester. *Indeed, it had been a fester, mayhap even a carbuncle*, Averilla now thought remembering those past trespasses. Averilla had not only disobeyed several precise orders given her by the abbess, but had started to believe that her gift of healing stemmed from inside her and not from the hand of God.

The worst part of her punishment was being asked to forgive Dame Joan for her betrayal of Dame Agnes. Before the abbess had relieved Averilla of her duties in the infirmary, she had insisted that Averilla herself must be the one to minister to Joan, and to help her recover from her self-inflicted wounds.

Dame Agnes, the woman Dame Joan had so grievously harmed, was also in the infirmary. Averilla had wanted to be the one to comfort Agnes. That, however, wasn't the lesson Averilla needed to learn; the abbess, the obedientaries, even God Himself, it seemed, wanted Averilla to minister not to Agnes, but to Joan.

She had done so, though at first Averilla seemed able to manage only the most fragile of kindnesses. Finding that the others in the infirmary — Sister Cadilla or the then Sister Helewise — refused to help when Joan whimpered, Averilla had been forced to tend her. The others would raise their heads, look in Joan's direction, and then resume their tasks. Averilla would sigh loudly, spend longer than necessary washing her hands, dry them as if wringing a towel, and finally, unable to put it off, she would attend to Joan.

Apparently, the intimacy was no easier for Joan, who refused to meet Averilla's eyes when asking for whatever it was she needed—to be turned on her pallet, to have ointment rubbed on the leg. *That was the hardest part, of course, the touching*. The broken leg had knit together. The wound—after the brief fester of the holy pus, the smell of which had been excruciating—had healed, but Averilla had had to rub oil of arnica onto the leg and spend time massaging it each day. The abbess' plan had neither helped Averilla forgive Joan, nor had it allowed Joan to forget the evil she had done.

When Averilla had confessed this hardness of heart to Father Merowald, he suggested that she try praying for Joan, but Averilla had been unable to. *I didn't want to.* "Nor did you want to use your healing power, that strange gift that rests in your hands," the abbess had said, hard-eyed. "You withheld God's gift from her." Even so, Joan had healed, and left the infirmary, and Averilla had gone to take up her new duties in the sacristy. As best they could the two avoided each other.

But, before Averilla could assume her duties as the abbey sacrist, she had had to endure the punishment called for in the Rule of St. Benedict. She had been required to lie face down on the cold tiles of the oratory floor, spread as if on the cross, each part of her body in direct contact with the cold. *Is hell fire? No, hell is cold, the cruel dearth that separates the dead from the quick.* Two days she had stayed on the floor, counting each excruciating moment, aware of the numbness that slowly overtook her until—she had been pleading with the Lord to help her—she realized that she had never before thrown her whole being on His mercy. *Why did it take pain to make me ask?* she now wondered. *I, a professed nun, ought to have recognized my lack of reliance on Him.* The bounty of God's response had been a revelation. Averilla had melded into a trance of such beauty that even now the memory of it suffused her with the sweetness of its unaccustomed peace.

Physically, Averilla had taken on her new duties as sacrist, but she sulked, and wouldn't meet the calm eyes of the abbess. Her prayers were dry and she felt claustrophobic in the church. At the end of each day, during recreation, she would hurry to the edge of the park and gaze across the ocean of the downs, gulping in great mouthfuls of air and letting the wind blow in her face.

She neither forgave nor prayed for Joan.

But it doesn't really matter so much anymore. I rarely see her, she told herself now as she finished the slow, careful polishing.

3

As Hugo and Ralf were departing into the night, and Averilla was lighting the candles and adjusting the lectern, the nuns were gathering behind the door to the night stairs for the office of Matins. In a monastic community, the church is never quiet for long. "Seven times will I praise thee, oh my God," say the psalms, and so Benedictines throughout all the ages have taken it upon themselves to do so, even in the cold, silent stretches of the night while others sleep. A single delicate chime sounded from Mary Minor, the littlest of the abbey bells, and Dame Alburga, clear-throated, intoned, "Oh Lord, open Thou my lips."

As the porter swung wide the door leading into the church, the nuns repeated, their voices scratchy, unused, heavy with the night:

"And my mouth shall show forth Thy praise."

Then, in unison, they chanted Psalm Three:

"Lord, how are they increased that trouble me! Many are they that rise up against me."

The women glided into the church like so many otters through dark water, ducking beneath the stone rood screen and emerging into the choir, where they were greeted by flickering candles beside the choir stalls. Just two candles, and yet, seen in such darkness, the very essence of brilliant light. Night after night each woman swam from the darkness into the light, an ever-present reminder of the gift of the Son.

One by one they mounted the two steps onto the wooden dais which shielded their feet from the cold stone floor. The choir was a room within a room, a wooden windbreak against the cold, drafty cavern that was the church. Carved of oak, the stalls provided each woman a niche with armrests, backs, and little canopies to keep out the worst of the winter. Each nun had her own stall, given to her at her solemn profession and hers unto death. In a community where absolutely nothing was owned by the individual, the stall was a place of safety and familiarity, where the self could feel her separateness from the overwhelming oneness of the group.

As she mounted the stairs, Dame Edith, newly selected abbey illuminator, found her gaze again held by the little carving on the handhold of the stall at the foot of the dais. Each nun was wont to rest her hand on the bald head of "Eadric," the little carved gnome that gave them balance. His head polished by time, he had become a sort of talisman, despite his leer and the fingers in his ears.

Does such a carving offend God? Edith wondered as she intoned the responses to the psalm. *Bernard of Clairvaux would say that it distracts the supplicant from God. Do we here at Shaftesbury believe we have to touch Eadric to be safe or lucky or in tune? Do we really believe in gnomes?*

Reaching her place, Edith leaned gratefully against the curved seat, which braced the nuns as they stood. She was tired, and felt that her mind, despite the night's brisk cold, was like the roe deer she had been drawing during the fore-Nones: skittish, bounding here and there, unable to settle on anything.

What was I thinking about just now?

Edith repeated with the others the correct responses.

I'm not listening, she thought. *I haven't heard a word that has issued from my own lips.* The vision of the deer surrounded by tendrils and vines usurped her focus while the Gospel was read. *Where in this Gospel is my word or phrase to meditate upon? I know not even what Gospel she reads from. John? No, no, it is Mark.* It was time to sing again, and for a moment of rebellion Edith thought, *Mayhap I will not. Mayhap I will go back to the infirmary and lie abed for nights and days.*

In the Abbey of the Virgin Mary and Edward King and Martyr, the office of Matins was followed by that of Lauds. It was not stipulated in Benedict's rule that the two be sung one directly after the other, but it was possible for the abbess to make such a decision; in this case the decision not to wake the community twice. Between the two offices there was time, an allotted pause when most of the community walked with their thoughts around the darkened cloister. It was a time for seeing stars and calming any inner turmoil brought upon by the anxieties of the dream world. It was rare, not forbidden, but rare, that they spoke, so it shocked the abbess to find Dame Edith beside her as she paced.

"Mother?" The voice was a whisper, but distress peeked through.

"Dame Edith?"

"Mother, is it wrong to spend our resources glorifying God?" Her lower lip trembled. "For if it is, I should — would be better employed in serving the sick, would I not?" The tears that were forever threatening to spill trickled one by one down her cheeks.

Emma's eyes softened. "Never is it wrong to glorify God. Never. David was a man after God's own heart because he praised him, but God is ever pleased by balance. He allowed David to praise him in song, but didn't allow him to build the temple. Remember, too, how Jesus spoke to Martha and Mary. He said not that Martha's household duties were wrong, but that there was a time for worship at His feet, too. You, Dame Edith, spent many years

65

serving the sick. It is time to renew yourself in creation."

"But Abbot Bernard of Clairvaux speaks against such decorations."

"Aye, he does. Remember Sister Cantile's words a week ago in chapter?"

Edith shook her head, but of course the abbess couldn't see the motion. She spoke anyway into the silence. "Sister Cantile spoke true. She said the pillars in the cloister walk, which have monsters and wicked faces carved onto them, wouldn't leave her mind and kept her from concentrating on God. I think that those faces are wrong, but copying anything in nature or on the earth cannot be unpleasing to God, for all was created by God and mirrors a part of him"

Chapter Nine

Tuesday

Very early morning before Prime

I

After Matins and Lauds, it rained until the bell for Prime had rung, rained with a tenacious ferocity, the drops splatting on the abbey stones and then rushing in freezing brown rivulets down Gold Hill.

Before first light, as dawn smudged the east and drizzled through the shutters, Lovick clambered out of a fitful sleep and turned eagerly to the bench where Savette slept. The skins were smooth; she had not been there. Hearing men from the garrison and some villagers already gathering outside the door, he shuffled out to sit numbly on the same bench he had sat on the night before, unaware of the freezing wet of the plank. Those around him moved like ants in a disturbed hill. Tom was already ordering the men in various directions for the hue and cry. *Useless*, Lovick thought. *One way or another, she's gone.*

A small hand, flat and dimpled, crawled onto his gnarled old one, and a little girl raised blue eyes to him. It was the bailiff's daughter, Mary, not more than five, with the white-blonde hair of her father's family. "I saw her," she lisped through her tiny milk teeth.

He ignored her.

"I saw her." Mary stamped her foot and, leaning toward him, yelled into his ear as if he were deaf. "I saw her."

He responded slowly, as if from a dream. "Saw her? Where? Where, lass?" He grabbed her shoulders and she winced.

"By the stream." She had his attention now and was determined to draw the story out. "'Twas not yet Vespers. I was with the geese and ... "

"By the stream?"

"Aye. The stream from the ponds." It seemed to Lovick as if the street had suddenly become silent; certainly the half-formed groups in front of him were still. "It was time to start back." Mary continued. "Savette was taking linen from the bushes. The sun had most gone and it was horrible drear." With the deviousness of a spoiled child, Mary saved the best for last. "Jared was seeking her. Asket me had I seen her. I told him where she was. He will know." Satisfied, Mary looked up demurely from beneath her lashes.

"But Jared was here last night." The old man's voice, even to his ears, sounded high and querulous.

"Down by the stream?" Tom took Mary by the shoulders and turned her toward him, digging his fingers into her. "You saw them together? And have told no one afore this?"

"Oow. Leave go," she shrieked, and squirmed against him. "I'll tell my fader."

Tom gritted his teeth and turned to his men, changing his orders. "Best start there. Last place she was seen. We'll retrace her steps — be thorough — in the bushes, on the banks. She might have washed up against the bend."

Washed up? Lovick thought. *But that'd mean ...*

DAWN WAS STABBING HOLES THROUGH the few stable shutters when Ralf, beside Hugo, started to twitch and mumble, his smooth brow furrowed. "Nooo. Eeiiirggh!" Ralf's half-volume voice sounded like a mewling kitten, full of terrified anguish. Hugo awoke, pushed himself up onto his elbow, and leaned over the thrashing boy. Tindal, on the other side of Ralf, lifted his lip in just the beginning of a snarl. Fearing to wake Ralf, and wanting to avoid being bitten, Hugo started to croon, his voice just slightly above the whisper of the wind, "Sanctus, Sanctus, Sanctus, Dominus deus Sabaoth. Pleni sunt celi et terra ... "

"Wha–" As Ralf opened his eyes in bewilderment, Tindal slurped his great tongue across the boy's face. "What, why ... " Finally, "Where?" Knuckling his eyes. "Is it still night?"

"Aye, lad. You were dreaming."

"They were coming for her. "

"Her? "

"My moder. They, they, " he rubbed his eyes as if to remove the image. "They ... "

"Killed her? " Hugo prodded.

"Aye. But first ... " Great sobs racked his body. Tears streamed down his cheeks. The edges of his mouth trembled into a grimace. "Took her. Pushed up her tunic. She screamed. I ... " Ralf's chin convulsed into ripples of pain, "couldn't do anything." His mouth twitched. "Stayed hidden in the thatch. She screamed and screamed and screamed. In my dream, I heard her voice and I could do naught. Naught ... I — I — I stay safe while ... " He looked up at Hugo.

"Oh, lad. " Hugo kept his eyes firmly fixed on the shutter.

"Then ... " Ralf was confused, not wanting to see into the distance of his mind. "Her screams stopped ... finally. And I, I hid. The last — the last took his knife and — and slit her." Ralf's movement was so sudden that it took Hugo by surprise. Pushing himself up to his knees, the boy stumbled over the dog, and, wobbling to the far side of the loft, vomited his nothingness into the straw. Wiping his chin with a shaking hand, he blundered back onto the makeshift bed, cradling his head in Tindal's fur and clutching great tufts of it between his fingers.

It seemed just a moment before Ralf slid back into an exhausted sleep, his hand limp in the dog's hair.

Becoming aware of the rustling movement of men outside the abbey walls, Hugo lay for a moment, listening to the bustle and hawking as those on the High Street gathered, for something. *What? A hunt? Yes, a hunt. The maid. Still not found,* he guessed, plucking a few pieces of straw from his hair as he stretched. Ralf was still deaf to it, prone, lying with one hand near his mouth, his cheeks flushed, the hard, pinched look of starvation softened by sleep. *Sleep'll do him good.* Tindal opened an eye and watched Hugo crawl over to the hole in the floor that led from the loft down to the stables. The steps were steep, hewn from a single log. He smiled, remembering how the dog had climbed to the loft the night before, long legs at impossible crouching angles, claws biting into the wood as every tendon strained.

At the bottom of the steps, the stable door opened onto the outer court. Grooms seemed to be dealing with a great number of horses. Gloucester's knights, by the look of the trappings. Sun motes glinted against the flank of a bay gelding, and Hugo paused, entranced by the beauty of the line. The huge hooves were cloaked in shining hair. *Horses. Fascinating. Could I carve a horse or horses on the reredos? What story could it be? Christ at the well with the Samaritan woman? No, not Christ. This was to be a shrine to St. Edward. Whoever he was, he must have had horses.* Hugo looked around for a privy. Not seeing one, he started to fumble in his braes.

"Not here, master." croaked a passing ostler. "Privy's yon," and pointed to a hut.

The enclosed were very particular about cleanliness, Hugo knew. *Been too long in the forest, I have.* He found the privy and when he had finished started for the well to pull water for Bithric.

The well house was chilly with the morning. The wellhead was a great stone basin, as round as it was high. Moisture clung to the stone, and a lush growth of moss flourished in the crevices between the rocks. Hugo trailed his hand around the upper surface, fingering the carvings, seeing with his hands. *Ancient,* he thought. The leaf scrolls and carved ropes winding the surface were cracked with time. *Even so, it is majestic.* He lowered the leather bucket and let the liquid silver swirl over its rim and creep slowly up. Only then did he allow himself a long drink from one of the hanging ladles.

Hugo watered Bithric, then went and roused a sluggish Ralf. They entered the guest hall, where everyone but the nuns and high-ranking guests ate. The crowd comprised travelers, soldiers, pilgrims, and those about business in the town. One of the nuns — guest mistress, Hugo guessed — made them welcome in a reserved manner and handed each of them a large hunk of maslin bread and a wedge of cheese. Another woman, a lay sister, filled wooden tumblers with watered ale.

3

FARTHER DOWN THE SLOPE OF GOLD HILL, in a room behind his shop, the goldsmith, Master Levitas, rolled over on his fleece. Since first light he had lain abed listening to the mournful sound of the hue and cry. *Poor soul,* he thought, and prayed for whoever it was. *Bad times, these are, and not just for Jews — for everyone.*

As if in pain, he stretched his legs from under the fleece and elbowed himself into a sitting position. A spate of coughing gripped him then, and like a dog shaking a rabbit, savaged his frail body. But the cough itself was impotent, a wet gurgling below his throat.

71

This morning, often now, he hadn't enough breath for anything more vigorous than a halfhearted bark. He sat, head between white knees, just trying to breathe. Aloud, alone, and into the empty room, he croaked the words, the familiar words, words he had spoken every morning on waking since he could first lisp out cogent sound, as had his father before him. "Hear, O Israel, the Lord our God, the Lord is one. Blessed be His kingdom forever and ever." As he spoke, his voice planed into a sonorous cadence, a hesitation that emphasized and drew out the vowels, a particular signature of voice. The words were the same, and he said them, but the fire behind them had been extinguished.

Master Levitas tried, rather unsuccessfully, to neaten his beard, an untidy gray with streaks of black. With a great effort of will against the numbing fatigue, he stood up, his ankles thin and long-veined, the cold seeping into his feet. Shuffling barefoot across the room, he unlatched and opened the wooden shutters and let his eyes stray across the great sweep of downs that roiled away to the south, looking for the searchers. Closer by, a finger of sun fidgeted on the massive wall that buttressed the abbey park, but the sky over the downs was still weak, weak and flat and white. He could see no sign of the hue and cry. There was sure to be more rain, perhaps by tonight. Certainly tomorrow.

The house in which Levitas stood was one of those that clung precariously to the side of Gold Hill, and for which he paid the lady abbess an exorbitant sum in rent. All the other goldsmiths and moneylenders, Jews to a one, had left Shaftesbury more than a year ago. An atavistic fear had clutched at them, and one by one they had gone. "We don't do well in wars," one had muttered. "Or in the country. We need the king's might."

English Jews had relied on the king's protection since William the Conqueror had brought them from France. Henry had protected them by a special charter. But now there was no king. Instead, the English were skirmishing across the land in a civil war in which the heir, the Empress Matilda, daughter of Henry I and widow of the Holy Roman Emperor, battled her cousin, Stephen of Blois, for her throne. The countryside had been repeatedly pillaged and looted by prowling anarchy. When the other Jews had left Shaftesbury to be closer to London and the king, Master Levitas hadn't gone with them. "Too old," he had told them. "Rebekkah is gone," they had told each other. *Shaftesbury is familiar*, he told himself, and *the nuns need me.*

It was true, the nuns did need him, but the townsfolk were another matter altogether. They envied him his wealth, suspected his ways, and hated his religion. *This winter they seem to have more hostility than they were wont to have. Why? The cold, the bad harvest, the civil war?* A frisson of awareness slithered up his spine. *This lack of Rebekkah, it sucks me dry.*

The opaque whiteness of the mist had now reached the hill, dimming even the close outlines, but Levitas was no longer looking. His mind's eye reached backward in time, and he beheld not his wife, Rebekkah, part of his soul, but their joy, their daughter Hannah.

FROM THE VERY FIRST THE CHILD HAD GIVEN THEM — him, Rebekkah, everyone — pleasure. She had enchanted those who beheld her, and had delighted in following her father, helping at his bench, even going to the abbey, where her musical laughter had been subtly subdued by the windows and the silence and the music. While he had spoken with the assistant sacrist — Dame Osburga it had been then — Hannah would wander off, trailing her hand across a carving or a pillar, her eyes glazed in thought. Once he had found her squatting on the tiles and tracing the patterns that hung in the glass-colored air and slated across the floor and up the pillars.

The nuns had loved her, cherished her. "She will become one of us," Dame Osburga had teased as they had watched the child, who couldn't have been more than six, her head back, craning to see the light dancing though the glass. It had been, Levitas now remembered, during an office — Sext, he thought. But it was the day before a feast day, and Dame Osburga had needed the repaired paten because it matched the festal silver. Otherwise, Master Levitas would never have interrupted the nuns during an office. But that day he had been summoned. Dame Osburga had not minded missing Sext: "My need for the proper vessels..." she had fluttered her hands meaningfully. But the pure-voiced chant echoing through the vault had produced in Hannah a state close to rapture. She had started to twirl in the aisle, her skirts out and around her, lost in a bubble of cascading light and sound. Master Levitas had hurriedly left, but not before Dame Osburga had said, rubbing sand into his soul, "You see, her heart has responded to Christ."

He hadn't allowed his anger — disgust? affront? — to show, but from then on, he and Rebekkah had been careful to shield the growing girl from further contact with the nuns.

"It is as well," he had said to Hannah's hurt and bewildered eyes, placing one small block in the beginning shield-wall between them. "It is time that you learned of your mother's arts, not mine."

Rebekkah, a cherisher of family and hearth, had thrown her entire being into the tender weaving of the feminine arts around her one fledgling. But Hannah had felt deprived of freedom and choice and of the otherness of her father's world. The solemn silence that quickly succeeded Hannah's angry response to her female bondage of task after menial task had created a breastplate that was increasingly impervious to Rebekkah's devotion. Even Hannah's hair had refused to settle into the plaits that fashion and Rebekkah had tried to demand, wicking out around the ribbons and curling riotously over her brow. Throughout Hannah's babyhood, it was true, Rebekkah had allowed the cloud of curls to frame the merry, round face and the star-sapphire eyes that peeped out of thought. As maidenhood overtook the child, Rebekkah could no longer allow such a loss of control. "We must not seem different," Rebekkah had maintained, a ribbon drooping out of her mouth as she struggled to tame the curls.

Hannah was thirteen — only thirteen — when it happened, Levitas now remembered, the pain a fiery spout within him. He tried to refuse the memory of that leaden time, forcing his mind back toward the six-year-old child skipping along beside her mother, her basket precariously swinging in her hand. But even then there had been tension. One day, as the two of them were mounting to the market, Hannah had swung the basket in a circle around itself and it had dropped nothing. Rebekkah's lips had become thin and rigid as she gave an irritated shake to the child's arm.

"They may accept us now," Rebekkah had later told Levitas, "because King Henry needs the Jews and protects us. But what will happen in the future? What if the next king withdraws this shelter? We are only tolerated because of the king's might. With that gone they will use any excuse to persecute us. Someone will remember that everything stayed in her basket when she held it upside down, and she will be called a witch."

Rebekkah was right, of course. Times were changing. Probably the famine of 1135 had started it; kine dying in the field where they stood; children's arms like brittle twigs. It had been awful, gruesome beyond belief. Master Levitas had filled the outstretched hands, all of them, lending and lending and lending ever more of his silver. Afterward, they hadn't thanked him for his generosity. Instead, they had hated him for their need.

He shook his head now as he remembered and dragged his thoughts back. *I won't think of that now. It makes me sad. No, it's Hannah I want to remember — happy and light.* But his mind recused him. Thoughts of Hannah could never more drag anything but grief into his heart, always the same painful memory.

75

She had been twelve, *no, it was thirteen; thirteen with the beginning bloom of maidenhood.* She had sprung up to woman's height in the previous year. That day, *that horrible day,* had been the first time she wore her new maiden's gonelle over the pleated shift. The gonelle had been of a spring green, with bands of embroidery on hem and sleeves, and had fallen to below the knee to show off the pleats of the shift. Hannah had been so proud of that shift of pleats; had stitched it herself and had wound the fabric around a broomstick as fashion demanded, undaunted by pricked fingers, undeterred by Rebekkah's cautions against vanity.

Before they left for the market that day, the two of them had quarreled. A simple disobedience? A fear of the future? Levitas never really knew. The quarrel had been irrevocably emphasized and besmirched by the events that followed it.

As the two women prepared to leave the house that morning, silence shouting between them, Hannah had turned obediently to her father and given him a reverence as she had been taught. But it was stiff, lacking her usual grace, and she had refused to meet his eye. He had reached out his hand, expecting to take her chin in his fingertips to see if he could ease the trouble, but Rebekkah's voice had lashed between them. "Leave us, Hannah. I would address your father. Alone."

The sullen glance Hannah had shot her mother was meant to be seen.

"Samuel, I despair," Rebekkah started a well-worn litany. "She grows into one I know not."

There had been a thump from above as Hannah had intentionally flopped herself onto the floor of the loft, effectively disrupting her mother's words, words Hannah was intended to hear, he now supposed. *Else wouldn't Rebekkah have made some sign? Taken him out to talk? Started the bellows?* But she had done none of those things.

"She will be a woman soon," he had tried to mollify his wife.

"This happens, I think, in maids, this sullen changefulness."

"She used to be biddable."

He reached his hand again, this time finding the chin he sought, and forced Rebekkah to look at him, to let her mind soar in his spirit.

"It happens," he had continued earnestly. "I saw my sisters do the same. It can be even worse between a father and his son. They come to blows. Mothers and daughters? All quarrel and frown, signifying only that she soon will be that which God has created her to be. She will not be the image of her mother, as she probably secretly yearns to be" — here Rebekkah gave a pleased moue of dismissal — "but she will come close. She must think she arrives at adulthood by her own choices. For that to be, she must have the opportunity to not choose your ways. She must detach. Wife, unfortunately mayhap, the love that binds you to your one fledgling is so very strong that the knife needed to cut it must be the sharper. You will have her again, my love, when she has passed this time."

The two of them, the daughter two angry paces ahead of her mother, had trudged up to the market for the last time.

It had happened with so little warning, as if the hand of God was already poised to strike. At least that was the way he always saw it. He had heard enough from Rebekkah's babbled terror and others' tales to imprint the scene forever on his heart.

Rebekkah had been about one errand or another, nothing that was of importance. That too had haunted her. "I was looking at a basket of ribbons, Samuel," she had wailed, "only a basket of ribbons." In those first hours, he had tried to pat the torment from her, soothe her, but it hadn't worked — not then, not later.

Rebekkah hadn't noticed the sound at first. There was always a drumming of hooves, from here or there; hard to distinguish over the creaking of the wheels of an oxcart, the bleating of sheep unwilling to move, or the shouts of a cattle drover. But that time, with an unworldly premonition, her ear had tuned to the speed of the sound and the sheer thunder of it. By then it was too late.

The Shaftesbury marketplace was crowded at the best of times, squeezed as it was on the slanted flatness at the top of Gold Hill, crammed between the abbey walls on one side and the tumble of alleys and houses on the other, all trying to cling to the available land atop the hill. There would have been no way to see their coming for the jumble of stalls and banners and the height of the hill, all of which would have blocked any view, so there had been no time to jump out of their way. They swept from the High Street and into the market like clouds before a streaming winter wind, all menace and height and a dreadful pounding of hooves. There were four of them — although some said five — and they had whipped their horses, the heavy steeds of knighthood, through the market, thrashing through the stalls and the people with less concern than if they had been standing grain. Rebekkah spoke for too long about the squeals of a pig; how they had filled her ears and gone on and on. She remembered as well the soft body of the woman next to her as she fell, her heavy breasts flattening against Rebekkah's thigh, the flesh oozing down Rebekkah's body like a great fall of mud. Rebekkah had been dazed by the fullness of the moment; the sheer volume of sensory impression made by the pig and the woman had invaded and occupied her memory. Then — others said — she had started to call out, the mother-bleat for a lost lamb, neither thought nor foreknowledge, but fear paramount in her cry. There was no answering whimper. The poultry stall where Hannah had been fondling the chicks was now a beaver dam of jagged spars. Here and there, people scrambled to their feet, or numbly picked up their wares. One man was trying to pen apples that rolled toward the slant of the hill, their bright red lost in a miasma of dust. Hannah wasn't anywhere. Rebekkah's bleat became a shriek of terror as she stumbled through the chaos, lifting a banner here, pulling up a misplaced stanchion there, screeching and crying and hysterical. When Rebekkah found her, Hannah had been neat and tidy and still breathing, just a small issue of blood oozing from the mass of springy curls. She had been hit in the head, they thought. By one of the hooves? A sword? No one seemed to know. "I seen that stallion rear up as they be taught for battle. Up over her head," old Enid kept repeating. But few believed the old crone at the best of times. There was just the one bruise and a beginning blueness on her temple.

They had brought Hannah home, several townsmen carrying her — not a Jew among them.

Levitas had resisted asking the nuns for help. Other Jews then lived in the town. They were eager with counsel. They knew of these things. A physician, one of their own, was called from Winchester. Taught in Jerusalem, he had been, and learned at Salamanca from the Moors. After a week of bleeding and hot irons and stinking poultices, the man had shaken his head in despair and then retreated back to Winchester, sure that it must have been some fault of the maid or her father, a punishment from God.

Rebekkah had pleaded, distraught, for Dame Averilla to come from the abbey. "They might be able to help," she had cried, and had then added, further piercing her husband's bruised heart, soldering his will against allowing the nuns, "They too know God." When finally she had prevailed, it had been by tweaking his pride. "Samuel, Samuel," she had then pleaded, "Let not this happen. Our only babe! It cannot hurt to ask them! How can we have done nothing?"

"Much ashamed," he said now to the morning mist.

And so, finally, he had dragged himself up to plead at the gate, but even then his pride had forbidden him to pound on it. Dame Averilla, the infirmaress then, a woman he knew from her forays into the town, had caught up with him as he had stumbled back down the hill.

"Master Levitas," she had said, shifting her heavy scrip to her other shoulder. "We heard, and we have been praying."

He had refused to meet her eyes. "Are your prayers so much more efficacious than are ours?" he flailed at her, his voice gruff.

She had flinched and said, her voice newly soft, "I truly believe not. Only that we have added ours to yours. Your dear Hannah has brought joy to all who have seen her."

Dame Averilla had tried her arts, had stayed up night after night. Nothing seemed to work. White, listless, enervated, Hannah slipped into sleep and died.

Rebekkah had literally torn her breast, her wails vomited from her heart. For days she had been inconsolable. Levitas had tried to comfort her. "My beloved, you have been a good mother, a fine caretaker of this gift from God. You have not spurned His gift, but have cherished it and made Him glad."

She had shaken her head. A tear had run across her still smooth cheek to her chin.

Their neighbors had been solicitous — to a point.

He had gone to the minyan expecting solace. But since the burial had occurred, and the Song of the Dead had been sung, they expected him, and even more, Rebekkah, to go on, as if nothing had happened. But that was impossible; everything had happened, and the gulf between them and him had become a cavern, and there was no bridge across.

After a number of weeks, several of the men had come to Levitas. "Samuel," they said sagely. "It is your right, your job, to succor this wife."

As if I had not been trying. "She is inconsolable," he had said.

It hadn't soothed them. They had seemed to think, "If tenderness will not do it, you must insist. The whole community ..." Leaving the sentence unfinished, they had glanced meaningfully toward the abbey, as if one of the nuns, or the abbess herself, might come down and complain about Rebekkah's moans.

"All you are concerned about," Levitas had growled, "is the appearance. The nuns understand." And he had slammed the door on his "friends."

Rebekkah had heard them, deep in her mind. Levitas knew this because she had nodded dully when he had spoken to her. Her eyes seemed to register his words, glinting for a moment in recognition and then dulling into themselves.

After that, Rebekkah had grieved differently; she had become painfully silent, toiling for a cleanliness and spotlessness in the house, muting her words, staying in bed — not their marriage bed, but the pallet that had been Hannah's. "It has her smell." She had alternated between frenzied cleaning and the deepest melancholy.

Then, too, he had wanted vengeance on the riders. Everyone knew who they were. Levitas had wanted them tried. He knew that if he went alone to the bailiff he would have no standing. He had pleaded with them. "If we go together ... the strength of numbers ... the king's justiciar will come through these parts and we have the king's protection." But it had been useless. They had been afraid, and had called it common sense. Patiently, they had explained, "Indeed, the king does favor us, but not when pitted against his barons. He is embroiled in a war. If it came to trial, Samuel, think you that the friends and fathers of these youths would find against them? We will not help you in this." One of them had tried to ease the lash of their words: "It would have been different during the reign of Henry, much different then. But now we would merely raise their ire."

If not in this, he had reasoned to himself, *what use to me are they?* He shunned them. Kept to himself.

After more months, Rebekkah refused to rise from her bed. She had tried once. One of her friends had visited, and Rebek-

81

kah stumbled out to greet her, her hair in tangles down her back, drifts lying across her breast, her white shift of nighttime torn in places and soiled at the hem. The woman had turned pale, had given one horrified look at the vision of grief. "I am sorry to have disturbed you," she had whispered, and stumbled out the door, entirely forgetting to offer Rebekkah the cake she had brought.

Rebekkah had smiled then at Levitas as she leaned against the doorpost to the bedroom. It had been a smile of irony and understanding, a glint of mockery in her eye. "You see, Samuel," she had said, "I embarrass you before them all. Your precious community. The chosen people. If this is the way your God shows how He loves you, what does He do with those He hates?" And she had stumbled back into the room, refused to eat, and within the month had died.

God, it seemed, had abandoned him.

"My God, my God, lift me high above my pain and my distress."

Psalm 69 was little help, and when, with the increasing anarchy of the civil war, the Jewish community sought refuge in London, he had not gone with them.

Despising himself for being unable to lead his thoughts away, Levitas now returned to the hearth, where a bit of last night's fire huddled under the small clay pot called a curfew. He threw twists of rush onto the embers and sifted through the pile of wood for a twig the right size. A heel of hard-crusted bread and a sliver of cheese remained from the previous night's meal, and there would be cold pottage in the pot.

He sighed. Yesterday, before she left, his maid had made the sign of the cross over herself. She despised him. Called him "Levi" — not even "Master Levi," certainly not "Master Levitas" — and took his money. Since the other Jews had gone, few called him Master Levitas. A few of the nuns did; most of the townsfolk called him Levi; not even his name left to him — he a Jew, for whom name was of utmost importance.

He sneered in disgust. *It never gets better, does it?* When he had last been in Salisbury, the word had followed him like an eerie echo, slithering among the dregs of the populace — *Bloodsucker* — as if any Jew would even consider drinking blood. Didn't these Christians read enough of the Bible to know that consuming blood was not only forbidden, but an abomination?

4

AFTER BREAKING THEIR FAST IN THE GUEST HALL, Ralf sloshed behind Master Hugo along the path that wound through the burial ground between the hall and the great conventual church. When he would gladly have stopped to watch two men pounding a piece of hardwood into a notch in a piece of stone, Hugo shook his head and said, "They wet that wood so it swells and splits the stone, but now's not the time to watch." Walking almost backwards in order to keep his eyes on the masons, Ralf followed Hugo around to the west front, where two slim towers, half-finished, loomed above a newly carved tympanum of the Last Judgment.

"Get the best impression of a church from the processional entrance." Hugo said. "Always the best way to understand a church. What you saw last night will be fair changed by the light." As Hugo pushed open the iron-banded door, Ralf gasped and stopped, transfixed by an overwhelming wave of sight and sound.

The vestibule they had entered was open to the nave. One pure, silver voice swirled up and around the nave, clear and hollow and polished. Before its echoes had had a chance to ebb, like the surge of the tide, other voices, chaste and sweet and ethereal, entwined themselves with the first, undulating around it and caressing it. Hugo knew that nothing in Ralf's life had prepared him for such incorporeal peace and clarity. The silver tones tinkled, floated, slid down the sides of the huge bulk of the church like a great fall of light. Hugo found himself hoping that the wave of sound would pierce to the very depths of Ralf's soul and cauterize the pain hunkering there.

"That be the nuns at their worship," Hugo whispered, unnecessarily. "'Prime,' this office is called." There was a pause, and Ralf looked at his master in perplexity and disappointment, for the song had been too short. "They'll be at it again, soon. One will read from the Bible for a bit now." After a moment, Hugo continued. "I have not heard women before. Monks, I have heard. Their voices be different, more like boulders falling in a winter's torrent. Nuns' voices be to monks' like a flower is to a newly forged sword."

As the two of them crept into the nave, Ralf was overawed by the immensity of the interior space. Columns, like the guardians of God, round, full, and strong, marched down the incredible length of space, storming eternity. But the magnificence of the stone was nothing in comparison to the light: shimmers of virginal light danced, floated, and glowed upon the floor between the stone columns, and splashed onto the walls that rose above them like sides of a cavern, up and up and up. Ralf raised his eyes, bewildered. Jewels, it seemed, had been stuck somehow into the window bays, blue sapphires and rubies and saffron-colored stones, like the crystals he had once found in a stream, or the jewels he had seen on the brooch that Byron De Chafney wore. The red, blues, and yellows were as pure as the singing voices, the light brighter than he had ever imagined. Coming in from a world clothed in the grays and duns of wadmal and wool, a world cocooned in the muted sage of stone and slate and the dried browns of the dirty snow, he had stepped into this place where a moving rainbow of light cascaded from heaven, transmuting gloom into glory.

Ralf tagged behind Hugo, holding onto the man's work tunic

84

in order to keep his eyes aloft, craning his neck this way and that, stretching his eyes into the fire and tracery as light and color and story danced over him. The color, like the sound that swirled again through the nave, washed from him the last lingering motes of despair and darkness, and he was aware of nothing but a pounding joy at this liquid fall of light and sound.

Even Hugo was impressed, though stained glass was not a new concept to him. He peered into the space before him, critically calculating the stone angles and curves, the incredible upthrust. After a while, sensing Ralf's awe, Hugo stopped analyzing and allowed himself simply to appreciate the fact that the clouds had parted enough to allow in the morning light. *It is like a folktale in full color. Better than painted walls. Very like mosaics, but better — vitalized, enlivened. Light changes everything, absolutely everything. Even stone cannot remain the same under its scrutiny. If light can change color and make it a thing of such ethereal beauty, then the light shining though a man ... if ... if ... a man were glass, and let everything he did be changed by God ... ?*

5

THE NUNS SINGING PRIME BEHIND THE ROOD SCREEN knew by the pausing sounds of the steps who it was that had joined them in the church. In the way of all small communities, after Matins and by Lauds of the previous night, the entire community had been informed not only that Savette had gone missing and that "their" sculptor had arrived, but that he and his apprentice and "a dog" had been in a tavern brawl. The story had been passed through the abbey from the youngest serving maid to the prioress. They had all heard. And it was exciting. Not just the fight between the dog and Simon, but the very presence of a man among them. The possibility of his presence in the choir had been discussed in chapter earlier in the year. They had decided against allowing him into this very private part of the church.

"And with good reason," Dame Osburga, recently appointed prioress, had been firm.

Margaret de Huseldure had intended a reredos for the high altar that stood in the choir, their choir, separated from the more public spaces by the high wooden choir stalls and the rood screen, a wall of stone that bisected the nave into two distinct spaces.

"Mother," Dame Osburga had opened the discussion, "we have had men in the outer and inner courts: soldiers, barons, masons in plenty. Even kings," she added, remembering that King Canute had died there. "Glaziers, pilgrims, and priests are always in the church, have had access to the cloister. The bailiff is here often. Haven't we had our prayer life in the church disrupted enough during these weary years of building? Since the oratory was reconsecrated, none but priests have been allowed in the choir or the cloister. These places are ours, where we, as sisters, can just be. We know one another. When we creep into the sanctity of the choir to be alone with God, to feel his presence, we are free, then, to weep and tell Him of our needs, even in the wee hours of the night. It is there that we can allow ourselves to fall into his embrace. It would be neither easy nor kind to open the choir again to a man, one foreign to our thoughts and ways, a stranger always there, tapping with his tools, puttering around. There would be temptation." Osburga had lowered her eyes, a blush rising under the pure white of her clean wimple and staining her cheek with a mottled blotchiness.

"Dame Osburga," Abbess Emma had agreed, "It is as you say. Small joy to me would be any gift if by it you were divorced from the companionship of God." She paused. "I think it wise that the sculptor, this Master Hugo, be requested to create not a reredos for the high altar, as Margaret intends. Such would place him within our privacy. It is vital," she smiled, "that no gift, however important the giver, cause disruption to our spiritual lives. Thus, it is my will that what is to be carved shall be a reredos for the altar at the shrine of Saint Edward."

The hum of astonished voices had bubbled into whispers and threatened to break into talking. The abbess held up a hand. "We must not behave like old women hoarding to ourselves all our jewels. It would be gracious, I think, to allow this new beauty to the pilgrims. It is important that they have sparks to light their contemplation. They, who cannot have the solace of the written word, have need of the consolation of images to spark their souls. The beauty of it will not be lost to us, either; we shall have a chance to gaze on it of a night whenever we watch at the shrine."

CHAPTER TEN

TUESDAY

MID-MORNING, DURING TERCE

I

As Hugo and Ralf moved farther up the nave and into the transept, Hugo suddenly halted and gazed up into the lantern tower. Like a rock thrown by a child, a bird traced a circuitous path across the light. Hugo frowned. Lantern towers were dangerous. Hadn't that in Winchester collapsed into the transept, obliterating the tomb of the late King William Rufus? The king was said to be evil, but even so, it was uncanny, the falling in of that tower over the King's tomb.

"Master, wha ... "

"Later," Hugo whispered, nodding to the pilgrims at prayer before the chapel altar, and, pressing on the boy's shoulder, they both knelt. From this position on his knees, Hugo was intent on examining the reliquary. *Twice as long as it is high. Pleasing size, though.* "Probably of wood underneath. They often are," Hugo whispered to Ralf, who had no idea what his master was speaking of. The box was covered in leather and embossed with a filigree of twining studs. "Brass," he added. Ralf looked confused. "No, surely not." *Must be copper for the studs.* The lid was fastened by a stout hasp and firmly locked. Hugo's eyes were riveted to the numerous medallions decorating the leather lid. Each bordered medallion was a separate lunette, circular or oval, six on each side, enameled in hues of blue, turquoise, and green; designs that twisted into the likeness of beasts and birds, fantastic forms, pecking and coiling or with wings outspread, rife with symbolism. "Enamel work, that be. On copper and then gilded. Champleve." The twisting style was a favorite of Hugo's. It reached something Celt within him. Hadn't he used it himself in the illuminations for the Great Bible at St. Edmunds, twining each image to conform to its limited space? "The outlines are called 'cloisons,'" he continued, "and made of copper, though they be gilded; similar, ye wist, to the lead that holds the stained glass in the windows." Ralf looked up.

Why, Hugo wondered, *am I answering his questions before he has even asked?*

In perplexity at himself, Hugo stood to observe the hanging behind the altar. "The needlework behind the altar," he would later tell Ralf over the evening meal, "is well done indeed. 'English Work,' it's called. Recognized all over the empire it is. The one behind the altar was probably done by the nuns here. Fine linen, bleached and then embroidered. When we next look at it, notice that it too has a kind of cloison." Hugo took a sip of watered ale, and, remembering where he was, stifled a belch and went on. "That's gold, lad, twined around silk. It's called 'gold-work.' Probably find a building called a 'brode hall' here in the abbey among all the other buildings in the outer court. It'll be a workroom for the nuns to sew. Like as not 'twill have a north light."

The scene portrayed on the hanging was a complete story with two figures, a man and a woman, a king and queen. Though the man was smaller than the woman, his crown was larger.

In one scene they seemed to be talking, while in the other she was stabbing him. *Probably the story of the death of this Saint Edward,* Hugo thought.

Effective. I wonder if the nuns will want more about this saint for the reredos. "Ralf," Hugo now said, "go out the north door and to your left. The thatched buildings that lean against the church there, that be the mason's yard. Find me a piece of slate, flat like, biggest ye can carry, and bring it here." He moved to one of the transept piers and sat, his mind in the turmoil of creation, images flocking to him like birds on a cornfield.

As soon as Ralf lugged the slate into the chapel and placed it on Hugo's knees, Hugo drew his charcoal from behind his ear and started to draw, slashing out three distinct panels, as if the image would desert him if he slackened his speed. Ralf stood and watched, fascinated, his eye following the sharp charcoal, his face mobile as it mirrored his opinion of each stroke.

2

AFTER THE SEARCHERS HAD HURRIED OFF TO THE STREAM, Tom went in search of Jared.

The crone who opened the reeve's heavy door was stooped with age. Her two lower teeth smacked against her upper lip in a repetitive motion. She wore no wimple, and gray strands of hair lay stiff against the white-pink flesh of her scalp.

"Jared." Tom was abrupt. The woman turned her back on Tom and limped across the room to nudge at the heap of skins sprawled against the back wall. Jared's head appeared, his eyes bleary and unfocused.

"Bailiffsmanwantsye." The woman's vowels were unintelligible to Tom, as she spoke without teeth, but seemingly she communicated sense to Jared. He glanced warily toward the door. Outside, behind Tom's back, the searchers' voices echoed like a

demented plainchant: "Saaaaveeeette." Drawn out. "Veeeeette"
Wailed. "Saaaaveeeette" Hallooed. As if the very winds were
calling for her.

"Mary, the bailiff's daughter," Tom sneered as Jared stumbled
across to him, "says she saw you with Savette."

Jared nodded his head and ran his hand through his hair.

"Aye," Jared said. Then, belatedly, a look of fear mounting
his eyes. "She's not back?"

Tom shook his head.

As the meaning of the hue and cry cleansed the fog in his
brain, Jared blanched. "Then ... "

Tom waited.

"Aye — we spoke, down by the pond." Jared gestured over his
shoulder with a thumb.

Tom still waited.

"We, well, she — she — we had ... " he shrugged his shoulders
and smiled, just a man among men, "this summer."

"Aye," Tom said dryly, "at the harvest. And yester e'en?"

"I had — had to tell her about — about ... I am plight troth ... with
the steward's daughter. She — Savette ye wist — was angry.
Last night I thought she'd run off somewhere and 'ud soon be
back."

"Ye spoke not of this yester e'en."

Jared ran his hand through his hair. "I thought she'd be
soon home. And with Todd there, ready to tear out my throat?
Think I be daft?"

"I think ye be daft to not be with them searching for her."

3

FINISHING UP IN THE SACRISTY, Dame Averilla was surprised by a
slight tapping on the wooden latchet. Looking up, she found herself
face to face with Master Hugo. Despite the fame that preceded

him, the carver seemed to Averilla thoroughly unprepossessing. He was older than she had expected, with grizzled, somewhat thinning hair and a dun-colored beard picked out with gray. His eyes, though, were clear and hazel, the color of Chilmark stone, and held a surety — *or was it arrogance* — in their depth.

"May you speak?" he asked.

She nodded.

He gestured vaguely around the church. "I know a bit about the hours of prayer. I would know where you would have me work? There seems not a place in the mason's yard. I would be in their way. Would it be possible to work in the chapel? There would be tapping, from my hammers. Any sawing I can do outside."

"We are much used to the noise of creation," she responded with a rueful moue. "This new oratory has been too many years in the fashioning. We have learned to make do with the cloister and the choir for our solitude. No one but our community may enter either place. I am certain you will be aware of our needs. And," as an afterthought, "of course, your 'tapping' must stop during the offices."

He nodded, and then asked, "Have you time to accompany me to the reliquary chapel? I would that we agree on the placement of my tools."

He followed her across the north aisle and into the chapel. He had propped his slate against the back wall, but obviously it would require a stand if he intended to carve inside.

"It would be better for you to be inside for the carving?" Averilla asked skeptically.

"If possible. This winter light hits different surfaces differently." He smiled deprecatingly. "And the church is warmer. My hands need to be agile."

Dame Averilla frowned. She was not watching him as he spoke, but had her eye on a covey of pilgrims in deep prayer

92

before the altar. A few were audibly muttering to the reliquary. "You wish to be as close to the altar as possible?"

"Aye."

"Then we need, I think, to move the reliquary for the time you are with us. No pilgrim or any who would put themselves close to Saint Edward should have their prayers interrupted." She glanced toward the choir. "I will ask the abbess.

"You would transfer the reliquary to the nave altar for my convenience?" Hugo was amazed.

Averilla arched her brow. "You, Master Hugo, are of concern, of course. But our main concern is for the spiritual needs of the pilgrims."

His surprise was obvious. "Even so, I thank you. It will make it much easier for me."

Averilla made a perfunctory bow and started to turn toward the choir.

"Dame?" Hugo pointed to the slate for her inspection. "I have made some preliminary scribbles. I would show you them."

"I need speak to the abbess before..." Averilla began, but, despite herself, took the two steps to where his slate leaned against the wall and looked at it. "Ah," she sighed and looked into his eyes. "How do you create an image so real with so few lines?" She glanced from the slate to the altar and back again, her eye measuring the space. "'Tis a bold concept indeed, Master Hugo. You well deserve your reputation."

4

BEFORE MASS, BUT AFTER PRIME, the abbess mounted to her lodgings. The hue and cry of the early morning, and the cluttered whispering of the women in the cloister, had drained her. Even the soft ba-a-a-ing of the sheep rising from the downs seemed mournful.

The loss of the girl, Savette, the abbess thought, *and I can't even remember what she looked like. She is one of my sheep, and I didn't even know her name."*

"Once inside my parlour, however," the abbess would later tell Aethwulfa, "I completely forgot her. Can you imagine it, so obsessed was I by the debts, that my mind could leave a young woman hurt, desolate, perhaps dead? We owe Master Levitas so very much money!"

The abbess paused and regained a portion of composure. "I heard no knock, but before Sister Clayetta could stop him, Father Boniface appeared. The audacity of entering unannounced! "Then he stumbled over the sill, and I felt sorry for him, so pompous and yet so tangled in his robes had he become. I prayed to see him as God does. As one of God's creatures."

"And did you?"

"Before I could get that far, he kissed my ring."

"Not something you enjoy overmuch."

"Then he sat."

"Without invitation?"

"Indeed."

"He said, 'My bishop, Henry of Winchester, has decided, on my advice and that of well-traveled others, to follow the example of Rome. Bishop Henry requires that the candles for the Mass be placed atop the altar instead of to the side, where they tend to hinder the priest. It is a superior position symbolically, of course, representing the fire and presence of the Holy Spirit. Thus the candles beside the altar here at Shaftesbury must be removed.' Can you imagine? Removing the huge candelabra Abbess Cecily commissioned as copies of those in Gloucester? 'Have the masons . . .' here he wafted his hand, as if speaking of inconsequential men, men without names, with no real being, only function, ' . . . remove the candelabra from the paving stones.

94

As soon as possible. It will, of course, make it easier for me to celebrate the Masses."

"And you said?" Dame Aethwulfa smiled in anticipation.

"I am a baron of the realm. My oath of fealty is to the king, not to his brother, even if he is the papal legate. In church matters, my obedience is to the bishop of Salisbury, not that of Winchester. You, Sir Priest, while in this abbey, are here under my sufferance and direction. Your duties are confined to celebrations of the Mass, and, in times of stress and by invitation only, as confessor to those souls who entrust themselves to you. You may leave us.'

"I will need to confess this trespass, I suppose." She paused in thinking about it. "But not, perhaps, today."

"When Father Boniface finally left," Emma continued her monologue to the old prioress, "I went to the oratory. The man is like a bedbug, he so itches my purpose. I was in no fit state to attend Mass. I needed solitude. The oratory was amazingly quiet. Dame Averilla was speaking with the carver, but they were in the reliquary chapel, and their voices were low pitched."

The agony of her responsibilities had carved rivulets in what had been, before her election as abbess, an unusually serene face.

"Why did they choose me?" she burst out in frustration, startling the prioress. "I am not good at this. I don't like entertaining knights and nobles, I ... " Aethwulfa brought her hand from beneath the coverlet and patted that of the abbess. After a moment, as they both stared at the too-prominent veins in the old lady's hand and the blotches of purple-brown where the thin skin had taken a bruise and bled beneath, the abbess took a deep breath and continued. "I went and sat in one of the 'nobodies.'"

She didn't need to explain to Dame Aethwulfa about the stalls at the bottom of the choir, which were reserved for postulants and novices who had yet to be assigned stalls of their own. "To sit in the abbatial chair just then would only have reminded me of everything that was burdening me."

Aethwulfa nodded, understanding the leaden weight of power.

"I wanted to be comforted. The scraping and thumping of Master Hugo's assistant was more comforting than disruptive. Their voices—Averilla and the carver—were like the sound of one's parents talking before sleep comes."

"Oh, Dame, I seem to be fighting everything and everyone." Recognizing her lack of control, the abbess forcibly stilled herself. "Do you know what Bishop Roger said on the day of my consecration?" He said, 'It is not a matter of imposing upon them your will. My dear, the secret is in *not* using your power.' But I don't want this power."

"You must listen."

"But I am so tired, so focused on this problem that I can't even pray. I tried to let go, but all I could do was repeat, 'Now I lay me down to sleep' over and over."

"Could you finally pray?"

The abbess sighed deeply, "Yes. Finally."

Aethwulfa noted the subtle release of lines on her superior's face. *Mayhap*, the old woman thought, *she slips into prayer as I do, seeing behind my eyes the flashes of red and drifting motes of yellow.*

"I had a vision," the abbess muttered.

The prioress stiffened herself into quietude. It was rare that Emma allowed anyone so far in.

"I found myself alone with Christ, walking to Calvary. The road was pitted and dotted with lumps of gravel, and the dust was thick on my ankles. It was hot, so very hot. A Roman on his horse blocked my path. He was between Christ and me. I—I panicked. Then I heard a voice. His voice. Surely He should

96

have been engulfed in His own pain, but even from His pain He forced Himself to speak."

"And what did He say, my dear?"

The abbess looked down, embarrassed. "He said, 'I am with you.' It was so beautiful. His eyes. And then, just as I had found solace, it was broken. Dame Alburga had decided, just at that moment, to practice the novices in the choir. A new trope. I hadn't heard them enter, but suddenly ... "

Alburga's words right then, Aethwulfa decided, must have been like a thunderclap in Emma's mind, so deeply engrossed would she have been in prayer. Aethwulfa had seen it happen before. The person praying would tremble and then stand bleary-eyed like a babe awakened from deep sleep.

"The oratory should be a place of quiet," Emma fretted. "Not just during the office, but at all times."

Aethwulfa allowed herself to raise an eyebrow. "Yes," and then slightly hesitant, "Indeed, Saint Benedict so ordered."

"The novices were so sincere and sweet. They are so eager to give their best to God. In this new trope, Michael and the angels are fighting the devil. The novices' voices are like the softness of the winds of May. A chill ran up my spine as I listened and understood what Alburga was attempting; the mature singers standing for the fierce strength of Michael defending God against the devil, who, of course, is not allowed a tone, but speaks, his voice quavering."

"Did you stop them?"

"No."

"Well, then."

Then, finally, when they had all left, I saw Dame Averilla coming toward me."

"And you averted your eyes?" Averted eyes were the monastic response to allow privacy.

"Of course, but she spoke anyway. And it was important. She

thought we ought to move the reliquary so that Master Hugo might not disturb the pilgrims when he works. It seemed a — a kind of lesson. My prayers had been interrupted, over and over again, in order that I understand that the prayers of others must not be. Mayhap I would have balked at moving the reliquary had I not been so prickled by the constant intrusions."

"So, what did you do?"

"Asked her to find Father Boniface. It was too early for him to be vesting for Mass. He would probably be in his lodgings. And to form the procession."

"It seems a rather hurried decision."

"Aye. But then, when I approached the chapel to receive the procession, I understood her concern. Master Hugo was standing, looking around, not noisy, you understand, but there. Ralf — did I tell you he has an assistant — was busy with a sort of table, and that was disturbing. And the dog, Tindal, was thumping his tail.

"I have not seen it, but from what you have said, the dog alone might be enough to alarm the pilgrims."

"Master Hugo had his assistant move the boards to make way for the procession."

Aethwulfa enjoyed envisioning it: the whoosh as the great doors were opened, the quiet rustle of feet against stone as the sweeping wool carried across the silence. Then, the voice of Dame Alburga intoning the antiphon, the notes rising loud under the lantern tower, echoing, repeating, responding, as the procession passed down the south aisle. They probably crossed the west front and started to return up the north aisle.

"Father Boniface, though, looked more pinched than even he is wont to look." The abbess broke into her thoughts. "I suppose he liked not my usurpation of the rite."

"No. I don't imagine he did." The prioress allowed a twinkle to flash as she saw the procession in her mind's eye. She saw

98

the abbess bowing to the priest and to the four obedientaries, who then detached themselves from the procession. All five women accompanied the priest as he removed the reliquary from the altar. Overcoming their awe, several pilgrims probably jostled each other as they tried to get as close as possible to the sacred relics. A few reached out to touch the priest's robe ....

HUGO, STILL IN THE NAVE, followed the pilgrims. *It is uncanny,* he thought, *how these monastics can flick into a liturgy at the turn of an eye. Why, they hadn't had a thought of this before the sacrist talked to me.*

The nave of the church, the great rectangular portion, still partly unfinished, was perhaps the longest that Hugo had ever seen. It, too, was divided into parts, one for the lay sisters, and the rest for the laity of the town, who were to remain behind a wooden grille with a small gate or latchet to it. It appeared that the nuns intended to allow the laity into the claustral part of the nave for the sake of those on pilgrimage, as the dividing gate remained ajar. The pilgrims flowed through it and up to the nave altar, where, with much ceremony, the priest placed the reliquary.

As the rite went forward, with much incense and chanting — the priest too could drag ponderous words from nowhere — Hugo's gaze was attracted by the great rood screen behind the nave altar. Massive and built entirely of stone, it dwarfed the people standing in front of it and around the altar. Niches, both open into the choir behind and closed, housing saints, seated and standing, were bordered with elaborate vine-like traceries that softened and lightened the immense wall. As his eye traveled over the complicated design, Hugo noticed a pair of huge candlesticks standing beside and immediately behind the altar. Each was more than five feet high, intricately cast and then gilded. Bronze, probably, he decided. The casting would have been complex for something both weighty and delicate. *It's quite brilliant,* he thought, *the way the movement of the metal echoes the flames that rise from the beeswax.*

Chapter Eleven

Tuesday

Mid-morning, after Terce

I

The search party easily found Savette before the bells for Chapter Mass had begun tolling.

Lovick knew they had found her by the ominous quiet, as if a knife had sliced through the hue and cry. He waited, leaden, for Robert's knock.

"Aye." Saying nothing else, Lovick rose. Robert led him down Gold Hill. He stumbled, his gait tottering, his eyes glazed and listless.

The whole town seemed to have crowded onto the slender path, the dingle, woolen cloaks smelling like wet dog. All Lovick would later remember of that moment was the silent parting of them, the lapping sound of the water overlaying the silence, and most of all, the way their eyes were averted.

Savette looked to Lovick in death more beautiful than she had ever been in her short life, more beautiful, but different. *Someone else. Not my Savette. Not my daughter.* He lurched to his knees. He heard a hoarse bellow from very near, and threw himself down on her, felt tears, and knew he wept, wept in a great, blinding, unknowing grief heaved up from the pod of his being. He remembered nothing after that. The others stood silent, watching as he gently cupped her cheek with his hand and moved a stray tendril from her brow. At length, some departed in reverence for his sorrow. Simon and Todd stood together behind him, lips mashed into grimaces as they tried not to cry. Finally, Simon put his hand on the sharp bones of his father's shoulder. The old man managed to rise, and Simon led him, stumbling, home. Father William, the parish priest, hands dangling, walked behind them.

2

TODD WAS LEFT WITH THE OTHERS. His numbness became colored behind his eyes, purple amid spatters of red. The body that lay before him was not his sister. The hair was mussed and lay in stringy slender mats. The clothes were sodden. What there must have been of blood had been washed away. Someone had shut her eyes.

Guilt splashed orange across his consciousness. She had been a trial to him, no doubt about that. He had even told himself that he hated her. As a child, he had hated her way of bursting in on his games, hated the way she had teased him with pinches and taunts, hated when she had goaded him into punches. Always it was his ears that had been boxed. He remembered how at twelve she had tagged after him. His friends had mocked it.

The sound of a voice pried open the numbness of Todd's trance. *Jared!* He raised his eyes.

"How?" Jared asked, stumbling down the path behind Tom, his voice surprisingly high, looking around the blank faces, as they parted for him. "I saw her, here, yester e'en afore Vespers."

102

"Aye. So we hear tell." John the Mason's eyes were flat, and his voice grim.

Todd's lips lifted around his teeth. He balled his fists, turned, and lunged. Hands shot out, twisted Todd's arm into a hammerlock, and yanked back his head by a hank of hair. From beneath his brows he glared at Jared.

Tom was trying to hold Jared, but Jared was seemingly unaware of him; unaware of those watching; unaware of anything but the blue-white body. Tears streaming down his face, Jared shrugged off Tom's hand, knelt beside the body, and with his forefinger touched her lips. His voice, when he finally spoke, hoarse on the silence, was strained. "Think ye she tripped on a root," he looked around, "and hit her head?" Drowned most like. Then crawled . . . "

"What do ye care?" Todd's lips curled, and to his shame the last words squeaked. "Ye — ye got rid of her as soon as ye had her maidenhead."

Jared clenched his teeth and looked steadily at the man who had been his friend. "Ye wist naught."

The first man to move was John the Mason, who, grim jawed and ignoring Jared, bent to the girl's body. Gently, carefully, he slid his fingers under Savette's head and left shoulder. Shaking their heads, others moved to help.

Jared, too, wormed his hands toward the body, but before he could touch her, Todd tore from the restraining hands, leaned across the body, placed the heel of his hand on Jared's chest, and thrust him back. "Don't even think of touching her," he growled. "Go to the other wenches ye be so sicker with. Might not be so sweet on ye when ye tell them they needs be ready to prepare a body. But never shall ye again lay so much as a finger on Savette's hair. Never," and Todd spat.

The corpse bearers wound their way along the stream and then headed up the longer, easier track to the top of the hill.

When they had disappeared from sight, Jared reached up and wiped away the glob of phlegm from his cheek. Avoiding all eye contact, he started toward Gold Hill, and, one by one, his friends slouched after him. "They always travel in a pack, that group," Tom would later tell the bailiff. "And I don't trust 'em. Not a one. That's the thing of it."

By the time they had reached Gold Hill, Jared's followers had formed a clot around him. They were unusually silent and all too aware of the crunching of their feet on the bits of iced gravel. Finally, one of them punched Jared on the shoulder, an empathetic thump; the best he could do, not knowing the words or even the emotion behind them.

Another muttered, looking around, "More snow, afore long."

Silence.

They had already climbed halfway up Gold Hill and were across from the goldsmith's when another braved. "Aye, we'll be freezing, and there'll be the Jew with a huge great fire, and beeswax candles, and a fatted calf." The shutters were opened and there was movement within. "But will 'e give us just a bit of 'is hoard to warm our cots? Makes us grovel for it, 'e will. Always makes us grovel."

The closer they climbed, the more their minds coalesced. "About to go out, don' ye think?"

Jared was only half listening.

"Take a maid or a child."

"An' eat 'em."

"Aye, that they do. And suck their blood."

Opposite the house, Jared stopped. The others looked to him for direction. "Steal babes?" he asked, his brow furrowing.

"Aye. Un found just the other day. In the forest."

"Let's give 'im a taste of 'is own."

Faster than thought they were gone, slipping into one of the cramped alleys that meandered between the houses.

104

THE FLACCID FLESH HANGING FROM THE SCAFFOLD of Master Levitas' bones was stringy, like one of the carcasses at the tannery. He was scrubbing himself with a coarse bit of burrel, stingy with his small amount of warmed water.

By the time he had finished his bath he was blue and his skin prickled with the cold. Like the good Jew he was, he was always fastidious, but today he was to deliver a repaired chalice to Dame Averilla. There was a sense of rightness in his dealings with Averilla. She saw him; he existed to her. Levitas shrugged into a clean linen chainse. Over the soft fabric he slid a woolen tunic, followed by his mantle. He chose his best. Rebekkah had embellished it with embroidery at the hem, had decorated it with pearls and gold thread. Briskly, he pulled at the mantle and fastened it at his waist with an ornate belt from which hung his money pouch and his larger scrip. He put the calfskin pouch containing the chalice into the scrip, flung it over his shoulder, and covered it with his cloak. Opening the door, he peered first up the hill and then down.

Even though he had looked, Master Levitas wouldn't have seen Jared and his friends, for they weren't there. As soon as he was out on the hill and away from the relative safety of his shop, they oozed like cats from the cracks between the houses, first one, then more. Later, when he thought about it, he would decide that they had been waiting for him. Because he was focused on the climb and the icy stones, all he saw were two dirty hard-leather shoes directly in his path. He tried to sidestep; the feet followed him. He jerked his head in surprise. The youth was familiar. *Jared? Yes, Jared. Bought something. What? A ring? Then wanted to borrow more, just the other day. Why borrow again? For an eating knife? Yes. That was it.* The recognition took Master Levitas but a second. Here in the street, Jared seemed enormous. Not only was he uphill of the goldsmith, but even in the most equal of circumstances, Master Levitas would be considered only of average height, whereas Jared was taller than any man in the burgh save the bailiff, John the Mason, and the smith.

Levitas watched Jared's callused hands clench and unclench above tattered hose, the huge shoulders splayed back, widened in hostility, like a cat in anger. Master Levitas politely veered to the right. Jared moved with him, softly, menacingly, on the balls of his feet. There was a hiss from behind. The old man glanced over his shoulder. Three more had grouped behind him, their eyes slitted. They squeezed him toward the wall. With a sinking feeling, Levitas knew that no one would come to his rescue. Then Jared pushed him. The goldsmith stumbled back. From behind him a foot snaked out and sliced across the back of his legs. The old man's knees released, buckling under him, and he fell backward heavily on his tail bone, gashing his left wrist and forearm on the metal latch that held the door to the drains. Pain lumbered through his pelvis, hovered around his wrists, and lanced fire up his arm. He looked up at Jared in understanding, then lowered his eyes in submission. "Never," his father had once told him, "when you meet a bully — and you will meet bullies — never confront him, or them. It gives them the excuse they need. And above all, lower your gaze." Levitas did so now, as he crouched and didn't try to rise.

Infuriated by his submission, Jared grabbed under the Jew's lowered chin and caught hold of the fibula, the brooch that fastened the cloak at his neck. "We know all about you, old man," he said. "You can't get away with it." Jared curled his lip. "Learn to look over your shoulder. And bolt your door. The bailiff and the cage are far too good for your kind, bloodsucker." Before the old man could react, Jared was pulling him up by the brooch, pressing his hand against the goldsmith's windpipe and

106

lifting him off his feet. The brooch resisted only momentarily; the shaft slowly bent and then popped from its housing. The sharp end gashed a long stroke from beneath Levitas' jaw and up across his cheek. He coughed and then gagged.

"Christ killer." Jared sneered, but desultorily, for he was looking in awed greed at his newly acquired brooch. He grinned.

The tallest of the other young men narrowed his eyes as he looked at Jared, at the blue black hair, the long lashes, the sky-blue eyes. "Warrant Damasa'll be pleased by that little bit."

Hoping to be ignored by them, hoping they had gotten what they wanted, Master Levitas remained doubled over, trying to regain his breath, spittle dripping from his mouth.

Jared had stilled at Damasa's name, but after a moment and with renewed viciousness, he refocused on the Jew, slamming his staff into the old man's groin and hissing, "Murderer. Women and children not safe from the likes of you."

Black thunder engulfed Master Levitas and he fell. Even then they didn't leave him alone, but aimed calculated kicks at his face until the old man's sinuses gave in a flow of blood and mucus. From the ground, even with the agony usurping his body, he sensed the four of them slip back between the closely stacked houses, taking with them the purse that had dangled invitingly from his belt.

Surprising himself, despite the pain, the lack of breath, and the bewildering problem of how to arise, Master Levitas found he was focused on the repaired chalice. *They left me the chalice. Please, God, let me not have fallen on it.*

4

EMMA FIXED HER EYES ON THE PLAIN WOODEN CRUCIFIX. *I feel, Lord, as if I am slipping off a cliff; holding on, yet still slipping. Where are You? Always I have felt Your presence beside me. I had only to open myself to You, and tears would pinch my heart, a swallowing of myself in You. But where are You now? I cannot find you.*

There was a rap on the door.

"Deo gratis," the customary words. Emma's heart sank. She didn't want to see anyone. *But an abbess must, mustn't she, stop herself even from trying to speak to God.*

Sister Clayetta held the door. "Master Chapman, my lady," as the steward strode into the room.

Of medium height, Master Chapman's body carried the signs of good living, but his face, Emma thought, was sharp like that of a fox. His hair curled to his shoulders and his brown beard was pointed. His long tunic was of heavy Flanders wool, dyed in a pale blue and trimmed with fur. Emma had to force herself to meet the steward's eyes. *Since I heard of his deceit, he looks different to me, crafty. Coward that I am, I have ignored what I know and allowed him to continue.*

Master Chapman coughed to get her attention, and then without the least formality, said, "A missive, my lady, from the king." Still standing, he drew a rolled parchment from the folds of his sleeve. From where she sat she could see the great wax seal, the multiple ribbons dangling.

From the king? She frowned. *The seal is broken!*

He unrolled and started to read.

Why have I not before seen his condescension? I can read as well as he.

Stopping himself after the salutation, Master Chapman looked up. "It concerns the lands given us by Richard de Sto-claro near Wareham, my lady . . . ."

But that is what he has always done, isn't it? Made us feel that things are just too complicated for nuns to understand.

Oblivious of her inattention, Master Chapman continued, " . . . lands given, if I remember aright, during the reign of—let

108

me see — not Alfred, Ethelred mayhap … "

Why was he, and not I, presented with this letter?

" … are being reclaimed by the crown."

She held out her hand for the document, eyes narrowing. "Which crown?"

Her voice was sharp and she noticed his head jerk slightly.

So engrossed have I been in my piety that this — this fungus has spread. Although the community elected me for my serenity, I cannot just abrogate all responsibility.

Master Chapman's eyes narrowed as he handed over the rolled parchment and tried to calculate what the abbess was thinking, what had changed in her attitude. "Stephen of Blois, Lady, is the king. Though he may have usurped it, the crown sits on his head, not on his cousin's, and he is desperately in need of money to fight her. He is again claiming that de Stoclaro's lands were always a part of the crown's moiety. Probably, it is the fish that he needs, or perhaps the tactical advantage, so near the sea as those lands are. He is sending to us to relinquish to him the tithes and taxes we have collected over the last years."

"I thought this matter had been decided when I stood before him right after he had stolen the crown." Emma's voice was even. She glanced at the letter, noting the salutation: 'To Emma,' it read, 'Abbess of the Abbey of the Virgin Mary and Edward King and Martyr at Shaftesbury, Greetings.'

"This is addressed to me."

He flushed. Just slightly. "I — it has always been the custom to have me intercept any — "

She held up her hand to forestall further explanation. "Any and all missives directed to the Abbess of Shaftesbury shall be delivered directly to me, and the seals shall be broken by my own hand." Again she held him with her eyes. "Surely the herald went not first to you, but entered the abbey forecourt?"

"As I said, Lady, the custom was ... "

"You intercepted him?"

Master Chapman's eyes held no look of repentance, but one of irritation and dislike.

"I shall draft King Stephen a letter refusing to relinquish that which is rightfully ours."

Master Chapman smoothly interrupted. "May I suggest, my lady, that you go to Winchester yourself?"

And what mischief would you get into in my absence? Aloud, she said, with a real note of indignation, "You would have me, a woman and a nun, travel amidst armies marching hither and yon across the land? Heard you not of the firing of Nottingham, or the betrayal that transpired at Lincoln during Christmastide? At any rate," her voice took on a dry note of fatigue, "precarious as this issue may be for us, 'tis not the time for traveling. Not until April do pilgrims venture forth, when the roads are again solid after the wet. No, Master Chapman, I do not intend to venture out into a quagmire. Let Stephen find a way to wrest from us those tithes. He can ill afford to spend the men to force us."

Master Chapman bowed and would have taken that as a dismissal, turning his bulky form toward the door when she stopped him with her voice. "It is meet that you should come to me just now. I have been much perplexed by these accounts. The rolls indicate that we have not garnered as much from even the home farms as we were wont to do. Can you think of any reason for that discrepancy?"

If the man flushed with guilty memory, she did not see it. Smoothly, with his usual garnishes, he frowned as if in concentration and said, "If you remember, my lady, there was a drought this year past and the harvest was late."

She held up a hand to stop the inevitable flow of words. "Not so much as to make the difference that I find between the accounts of the recent years compared with past years with like weather."

"Surely, my lady, the sub-prioress and I have handled these matters successfully for many years." He recognized his mistake and retreated, "Although it is true that Dame Joan ... " He didn't finish the sentence, choosing to lay the entire blame on Joan.

Emma gave him a sweet smile, although above it, her eyes were steel. "I may be mistaken, but I think the discrepancies are of a different kind than the confusion Joan created to shield Cecily. I will continue to study it. Myself." He was now on notice. She would see what he would do about it.

CHAPTER TWELVE

TUESDAY, MID-MORNING

I

elt good, Jared thought as he reached the top of Gold Hill, rolling his shoulders as if to put his muscles back into place, *to give the Jew a taste of the pain he gives others.* He sent a final derisive glance at the man still slumped in the road, retching. *Must be true what they say, about killing babes. So secret 'e is about that back room and the loft. And we all know he keeps no swine.*

Jared was alone. The others had vanished into the squalid alleys slotted between the houses. Even the market was deserted for the wind and the cold *and the grief.* Jared rubbed his arms. Within him, panic rose hot, no longer concealed beneath rage. *"Murderer," they'll call me. Already think I done it. Didn't mean to, though.*

At least Fader wasn't there when they found 'er. The reeve had left early for Tisbury. *Or to check a sheepfold.* Jared couldn't remember. *That look would come into his eyes. Sorrow and further disappointment. What if I meet him now. coming back from the tithe barn?*

Jared's eye strayed toward the forest. *Could run away. To*

the outlaws and masterless men. The image of a skeleton, dry sinews taut, dangling from the hanging oak came unbidden to his mind. *Outlaws're no better fed than the rest of us. Nor rich. What use 'ud I be, anyrood, to them?*

His feet, without conscious purpose, were taking him across the market and down Tout Hill. His mind veered back to his father. *I just won't be here. Won't be anywhere around when he gets back to Shaftesbury. For certes, when he stops by the tavern, I'll be asleep. Or something.*

The path he chose skirted one of the abbey fishponds. There were splashes of white on the surface as riffles beat across it. Periodically, a veil of spray would skitter and slide, running before the force of the wind.

Shaftesbury. Always so windy. Moder hated the wind. He allowed his mind to wallow in the comforting memory of her. The feel of her hair. *Shiny.* Her hair had been shiny. On summer mornings, at waking, the slats of light from the shutters had shimmered against it. On a winter's evening, the glow of the fire had danced on the strands as she brushed it.

Let me burrow into it. Sometimes. Or nuzzle her neck and lie against her breasts.

Savette's breasts. He stooped to pick up a pebble and tossed it toward the ponds.

Wouldn't let me near, her Moder wouldn't, when the wind crept around the mound.

With the thought of the wind, the comforting memory of his mother rayed into splintered shards.

"Prowled." She'd said "prowled" and her eyes had become haunted.

As if the hounds of hell were tearing at her shift.

She had paced and flitted from one thing to another, had snapped at him and at Cadilla, finding fault, angry.

Always pecking away at the marrow of us when the winds

blew. Or mayhap it was the sickness of that last babe. Puling mass, with its coughing cries, and that sour, wet smell. Mayhap that was what had hunted through her mind, whipping her thoughts just like that spray before the wind.

But Jared had been fiercely and totally hers; she could do no wrong. And she?

She loved me.

Loved him with a fever that had become almost frantic after the last babe had died.

Imperceptibly, she had taken her grief and despair and bound them all into a bleakness of soul that she focused on their Norman oppressors. Her misery for the lost babe not assuaged, she had sorrowed too for the loss of the ancient familial socage, for the loss of their status; in all, she grieved for what was no longer theirs to give to him and his brother. Her woe focused on Jared, for Bayard had married an only child who had lands of her own. Only Jared was bereft of his rights. Her despair would in turn anger the reeve, the red rage of grief skimming his eyes. Unable to give her what she wanted, unable to suspend the rising tide of her tirade, he would threaten her with the stocks of a scold.

In the end, when Jared was seven, lines of work and fatigue and the gnawing misery of loss had etched themselves under her eyes.

"If only . . . " she would start, the words spoken to Jared but with a half-veiled glance at his father, "'twould be yours. Knowest thou that? Orchard Farm. Yours. By rights, as it was my father's and his father's before him. To the times long gone." The reeve would growl, "Enough!" into the fire, or slam his fist against the table.

Timidly, she would then grab at Jared, pressing him to her. He had hated the harsh digging of her nails into his skin, hated the irrational look in her eyes, the madness of her grief.

"It is as will be, woman," his father would shout. "There be naught I can do. Naught! Hearest thou?" he would yell. "Why tormentest thou me? 'Twas the Conqueror himself who took it, and that long ago, when your fader was but a child. Ye well heard him tell it. There was naught then, there be naught now, that the likes of us can do against the king's honor. They tried rebellion. What did it bring but a castle where houses had stood? There is naught to be changed of it. Naught."

Then there were the long silences as he stared into the fire. Sometimes he would continue, as if there had been nothing between, "Besides, this abbess be a fair mistress. Wife, it could be worse. Much worse."

His mother's anguish and his father's grim resignation had eaten away at the young soul growing within Jared; had grated, too, on his young body as he toiled after the plow or brought in the sheep droppings, doing all he could to help the family.

And so, Jared now thought, striding between the ice-sodden grasses that bent at the edge of the forest, *she dribbled herself away.* And then there were no more words. Gone. Gone from the house. Buried with her. His father had taken to eating his meals in the grim silence of the morning or evening light, saving his words as if they were precious, storing them up to be used sparingly and with regret.

"Not even our language," he had said once, goaded on by something in the fire, "is left to us. Not even the beauty of our language." Finally, it seemed to Jared, that his father spoke not at all.

In those years after his mother's death, after Cadilla had gone in desperation into the abbey, his father had worked even harder than before, had toiled against age. "Work be hallow*ed*," he had once said, putting the emphasis on the end of the word. "Mayhap they be our overlords, but I still have my foot on the land. No one, no one can take away from me what I've done.

115

It be done. And past. And of my making. Canna' be changed. Even if I get nothing from it. 'Twas I as did it, and the land be better for it."

Inevitably, because of his unceasing toil, Jared's father had been elected reeve. After that, he was the one elected again and again, shouldering the job when no one else would take it, the hated job of reeve, a go-between, a mouthpiece for the steward to the forced English labor, a scapegoat for both factions. If the Normans did not blame him for the paucity of the harvest, the village blamed him for the hard work. He took the responsibility for all of it. "Half mad 'e be," Jared had heard one of the old men mutter, "but 'tis easier on us than 'twere before.' 'E takes it all unto hisself."

Rifts that threatened to grow into chasms were smoothed over by a chosen few of his father's hoarded words. He would listen to a man for hours. He was able to understand under the spoken words more than just a report about the spoilage of hay in the yardland or the farrowing of a sow before her time, and he would smooth the grief by sharing it. He would always take the time to sit with a man in the alehouse of an evening, to buy him a horn of the widow's ale, to listen to the words of anguish that flowed from parched lips, listen to the beating of a man's heart against the bars of a fate that had walled him within drab days of toil and despair. He would take the time to patch and mend the inevitable split between two men when their strips were unevenly divided and the fall plowing offered nothing but thistles among the rows. It was his job to prod the lax and comfort the ill, to wring out of them the hard-won fruit of the land. And he had a heart big enough for such a burden. He was able to see the merit in making sure the ponds were well slaked with lime. He saw the worth of the new water-driven mills, useless in Shaftesbury, there being no streams; even so he had understood the value of the concept

116

and had used it on other of the abbey's fishponds. So, when the new idea of allowing the wind to drive mills had come from Normandy, he had been elated and had gone so far as to install one to grind the town's grain. Most people hated that mill. The superstitious still made the sign of the cross as they passed. They wanted to grind their grain in the time-hallowed way, by hand; didn't want to have to pay for that which they could do on their own. But the reeve had seen farther than they had. Such an improvement gave the abbey more wealth. Then, in the future, he assured them, when the burgh need a release from the abbey, a favor, an easing of their burdens, he would only need to remind the steward of the mill.

And yet, and yet, Jared thought as he squatted down to study the long-short-long-short pattern of the weasel track in a patch of protected snow, *Fader will ne'er — no matter how hard he tries, no matter what friendship he wins among warring parties, no matter how much greater the harvest — Fader will ne'er be more than he be. Normans trample 'is fields in a hunt, hooves flinging seeds to the birds. 'E be no more to them than a serf, filthy and stinking. Just a tool. Less to them than their horses.*

Jared looked around at the series of branching paths. A denuded log lay broken on his left; on his right a small brook stair-stepped between iced banks. He stared at them, seeing in his mind's eye the market square of the previous day. A squire, probably one of Gloucester's men, had ridden arrogantly through the market, his horse on a tight rein, hooves dancing insolently, its hindquarters knocking the stalls, spilling wares this way and that. When Jared had yelled, the squire had glanced toward him, sneered, and spurred his mount. *Didn't even bother to respond,* Jared thought. *I was less than nothing to him. It's the horses, make the difference between us.* Horses had been why William the Bastard had won at the Battle of Hastings. Horses were what ate up the good land, literally ate it up. Horses were what put the Normans up, out of reach of English swords. Cowards. Wouldn't get down and fight. Stayed up on their horses and looked down. *On me. On us all.* He fingered the handle at his side, imagining it was the sword he had seen at Peter the metalworker's. It had been a broadsword of Damascene steel, the hilt and knuckle-bow inlaid in gold. *If only I had a sword. Not just an eating knife. But mayhap now I'll be able to afford a sword.*

And pay my debt to the Jew. Jared saw the face of Master Levitas in his mind as, he, Jared had again humbled himself, had again asked, had again been polite.

"May I borrow a pittance, *your suckerness?* Just fer the knife, not even a sword *yer bloodiness. Course he hadn't called him names, not then.* He whipped at a tangle of ivy with his sling. The memory reddened his mind. *Damned Jew hadn't believed he could repay the loan. Probably couldn't have then.* Master Levi had just said, had the nerve to remind him, *him Jared Reeve's son,* in that whiny voice he had, "You already owe, you know, for the ring." Had then asked, "Can ye afford aught more, lad?" *Questioning his honor. The arrogance.*

Couldn't crush me, though. Some may think I be as rotten as the corpse of a badger burst wide. Not old Father Merowald. The old priest always saw something in me.

Father Merowald had always taken the more promising village lads to teach. Some paid, but not all. Jared could still remember the Bible stories the old man had told. David. Over and over. "Remember, Jared," he had said, "David triumphed. Over them all."

Then, when the old man had wanted him to learn to parse a phrase, Jared had been surprised by the fierce joy it had given him, the power of knowledge. The old man had watched him as he nagged at the meaning of a word or at the deeper meanings below the meaning. Jared had been proud to see the old cleric smile. Smile or no, though, Father Merowald had not missed Jared's impatience with the slowness of the others. "Lad," the priest had cautioned, "they are far younger than you are. More important than the knowledge of words is patience. You will never get what you want without it."

Father Merowald had held the key to Jared's future. "The only sure way for an Englishman to rise," he had told Jared, is through the Church." And Jared had an aptitude for learning. Vowel sounds came easily to him, tripped off his tongue. His long fingers had deftly held the sharpened goose quill. He had written in the several scripts required of a clerc with equal ease. The old priest had taught him language, and then had, slowly at first, started to prepare him for a life in the church; had started, imperceptibly, to pave the way by telling him bible stories, and allowing Jared to assist at the mass and to light the candles. They were little things, but important.

Then, Father Merowald had died. *A month ago now. While it was still raining. Before winter had frozen us.*

"Gone to the worms," Jared now muttered. "No one to send me to a monastery." He shook his head and pulled the toggles of his sheepskin jerkin tighter, then stopped to rewrap his hands with the strips of linen.

"Didn't even know where to look for a monastery," he mumbled into the silent forest. *Out there past Gillingham somewhere is the Abbey of Tewkesbury. No longer where it used to be in Cranborne Chase. Just like that Father Merowald died and there was no one to show me. No one who could ask the abbess for me; no one to tell me how to ask for admittance*

Visions of Savette soughed into his mind as he chose a path at random and started down it. The soft, rounded curve of her cheek, the long, smooth bend of her neck, and he gasped as a fiery longing seared through his groin. The reality of her and the honey of their pleasure had made him forget his aim in life,

119

the desire of his soul, the honing of his mind. She had satisfied his gnawing need for place and power; had deadened the disappointment and confusion that came when he watched his father at the backbreaking, unrewarding work. With the soft green scent of hay in his nostrils, with the warmth of sweat on his loins, he had plunged into the heady, all-consuming taste of a woman. From deep inside the embers of that dubious fire, heedless of all contagion, he had indeed plighted to Savette his troth. *Me! A plight troth!*

"Now, though, all be changed," he again spoke aloud to the denuded trees. "Literally everything."

2

DAME ALBURGA WAS INTONING THE SECOND ANTIPHON before Psalm 118 when the nuns heard the sound of many feet shuffling up the nave aisle, feet gritty and heavy on the tiles with an ominous weariness to their gait. Alburga's voice didn't falter, and her sleeves continued to waft beneath her flapping hand as she intoned the words:

"Thy light is come, O Jerusalem, and the glory of the Lord is risen upon thee; the Gentiles shall walk in thy light."

Antiphons, short prefaces to the psalms were inserted into the office so all members of the choir would start on the same note, but hearing the feet several of the nuns glanced briefly away from the Psalter, with its enormous square, black notes, and a few voices wavered.

The feet tramped closer. Alburga didn't falter, but many of the choir, achingly curious to know what was happening, faded into silence.

The feet stopped.

Silence.

Then: "Dame Averilla."

Silence.

Again: "Dame Averilla!"

The nuns glanced at one another.

"Dame Averilla!"

No one had ever before had the temerity to bellow to one of the nuns during an office.

"Unheard of."

"Disrespectful."

"The portress was once requested to fetch the abbess."

But to interrupt the Divine Office?

"Intolerable."

The words of Psalm 118, trailed into a mewing whisper as one after another of the choir looked over at Dame Averilla with varying degrees of exasperation and irritation.

"Interrupting an office in order to display Dame Averilla's gift for healing!" Since the time John the Mason's fall had ended not in death but in life, Averilla had thought she was blessed with a gift. They, all the rest of the community, had endured interruptions occasioned by requests from all and sundry for her attention. Novices had been sent running here and there to fetch Averilla at odd hours. Once, the service vessels had been left unclean because Averilla had been busy with a broken leg. She continued to try to heal despite strict instructions from the abbess that she confine herself to the sacristy and leave the healing ministry to Sister Cadilla and Dame Helewise. And now this blatant interruption.

It was insufferable!

Alburga continued to sing. "Nothing," she always taught the novices, "may be allowed to come between us and our praise of God." So she sang, and the hefty purity of her deep-throated solo wove through the dim reaches of the nave like a drift of autumnal smoke.

121

Dame Averilla took a half step toward the rood screen and then stopped. "It was unthinkable, really," Dame Petronella would later remember, "that those men should so interrupt the office." "But at least," Dame Marguerite would gently remind her superior, "we hadn't as yet got to the Mass. Think ye that the abbess would have allowed any interruption then?"

The bellow came again, from more voices this time, and it was clear that whoever was outside was not to be deterred. Giving in, the abbess nodded to Averilla, who slipped out of her stall and down the two shallow steps, rubbing her hand absently on the little carved dwarf image, Eadric, which served as handhold on the last stair. The office limped on around her, despite the fact that the minds of those singing were obviously distracted. More than one note wobbled away from the correct tone.

The hue and cry has stopped, Averilla thought as she tiptoed across the floor of the choir. *They've found Savette. It must be Savette.* She exited through a small latchet and hurried to the north aisle where eight men stood around a body.

A needle of hope lanced her thoughts: *Lord, let her still live.*

As she approached, John the Mason spoke. "Dame, we ... "

Before he could finish, Averilla had kilted her skirts to kneel beside the still form. *Too still.* The cold wetness of the body, the parchment face and waxy skin were telltale. *There is no hope here.* Averilla placed her finger beneath the girl's jaw where life always registered its presence with a gentle, warm thumping. Then she rose. Finding no place for her hands, feeling them shake despite her willed control, Averilla whispered, "She lives no more."

John moved forward. "We would have ye do your magic with the girl, as ye did fer me last year when I fell. With Father Merowald, ye wist ... "

She reached out a hand to stop him before he could go any

122

further and shook her head. "John, misunderstand not. The maid is long dead."

"But you ... last year ... I ... "

"John, you lived. I — I cannot bring back to life one long dead. This maid ... would that I could," she finished lamely.

"But our Lord ... "

Averilla stepped back as if he had slapped her.

3

LEAVING THE UNPREMEDITATED rite in which the community had moved the reliquary, Father Boniface strode across the outer court in irritation. *Liturgies should be planned, not just cobbled together on the spur of the moment. Prayers must be thought out.* The abbess might be the ruler of the abbey, but he was in charge of the liturgy. *The audacity. Usurping my rights!* Father Boniface reached the gatehouse and started up the stairs.

Her effrontery about the candles — Not only to him, but to the pope. How dare she? The temerity to disagree. He was not just a man, but a priest? It was not merely a matter of candles!

The tempo of his tread across the planks increased: back and forth, back and forth. *Monastics were too involved in the trappings. No time for God. Have a name for that in Rome. 'Sacristy rat.' Don't really want to be close to Christ. Just want the trappings, the beauty. All this fuss over the carver.* The sound of the bell for Chapter Mass startled him, and he felt a pang of guilt that he had not been praying, preparing himself for it; guilt that only served to increase his ire toward the abbess. *Use the money they're paying the carver to feed the poor. Not add more 'graven images' to the oratory.*

Trying to marshal his thoughts, he straightened his cassock and flung on the green-black cloak that had served him since long before his sojourn in Rome. Hurrying down the well-worn treads, he checked his fingernails and ducked to avoid the adz-scarred lintel. He swept by the gatekeeper, without acknowledgment. *Hard enough,* he thought as he stepped into the daylight, *to try to keep the nuns straight, all in black as they are, much less try to keep in mind the name of every English flunky attached to the abbey.* He slowed, so as not to be seen hurrying across the outer court. *After all, the Mass can't start without me. Give them time to reflect. Spend so much time singing. Shouldn't be surprised — have no time for prayer. Too busy practicing tropes and designing liturgies. Worse even than monks. Why was I placed in a house of women? Didn't ever much care about women. Well, cousin Eleanor. But that was different. We were just children.* He smiled to himself as he deftly avoided an ostler trying to calm a skittish horse, remembering his young cousin, remembering how she'd slipped into the trees. "To listen to the birds," she had said. *Wanted to get away,* he remembered, as he passed through the gate from the outer to the inner court. *To get away from the carping gossip of the women in the solar with their pricking needles.*

At sixteen — *was I ever that young?* — his head had been full of the songs of the trouveres.

Deciding to take a short cut to the sacristy, he pushed his way into the mason's yard, and headed for the small side door that opened into the north transept. With winter upon them, a set of planks and canvases had been erected over the entire yard to give the masons shelter from the north wind.

Father Boniface veered neither right nor left, but headed straight for the north door. *It's been boarded up. Shouldn't have boarded it up. I always use this door. They know that.* Three men were heading toward him, hefting between them a huge log. The two on the far end, facing forward, saw him, but the lead man was walking backwards. "Ware!" one shouted. It was too late. The leader looked over his shoulder, saw Boniface, and tried to veer out of the way, but the weight of the log was against him, and he stumbled and fell on one knee. "By the cross, Father, what do you think ye're doing in here?"

Boniface turned and glared. "In the future, I suggest you watch where you are going." His voice was stern. The workman's return look, however, was more disgusted than chastised as he struggled to keep the log from falling from his shoulder and onto his bent knee. Others rushed toward him to lift it from his shoulder.

"Sorry, Father," one of the others muttered, sounding more irritated than regretful.

Two others, passing a look amongst them, scrambled to remove the planks and the canvas from the unused door. With a nod, Boniface swept into the transept, ostentatiously brushing the sleeves of his cassock and leaning down to shake the dust from his hem. As he crossed the transept toward the sacristy, he saw the nuns just processioning through the abbess' door on the other side of the transept. Something about one of them brought back his train of thought.

Eleanor. He had been content to watch her and occasionally strum the lyre, musing on the way the sun danced through the ribbons on her newly bundled hair. He had thought, had felt, had known, that she cared for him, too. *Of course she did. We had secret places and went riding together, played hide-and-go-seek on our horses in the spring.* His mind's eye saw the spring green of the grass, the tiny daisies, the yellow of the dandelions and the ever-present bluebells under the trees. He saw the two giggling children as they tried to hide the full-flanked bulk of their palfreys behind clumps of trees. *We tried to elude the others, everyone.* She had giggled at that, and leaned forward over her horse's neck, sharing the secret with him in her eyes. Telling him ...

Then, one summer's day, it had ended. They stopped beside

125

a secluded pond — they had found it earlier in the year and considered it their own — to revel in the sun and tear into the soft crunch of the new bread they had filched from the pantry. The strawberries had been ripe just then, the little wild ones that stained their teeth. And of course there had been a round of cheese. When they had finished eating, without even a nod to maidenly daintiness and discretion, she had shrugged out of her gonelle and splashed eel-like into the blue-black depths of the pond. He had seen her then, new-eyed, had seen the side of her, smooth like a fish, skin glowing over the radiations of her ribs, and the plumpness of a breast, with its pink rose of a nipple just starting. With that dive, everything had changed. An invitation had been issued, he had been sure of it, and he had felt the eruption of a new and fiery longing. Hard pressed, he had shed his clothes, proud to show her the new fullness of his own body, eager to respond to the invitation. She had swum away from him, coaxing, teasing. When he tried to catch her, had swum up breathless with the exertion, she dunked his head beneath the cold. Sputtering to the surface, he found her gone, flashing away in a rainbow of turbulent water. She had risen then from the reeds at the edge of the pond, making no attempt to conceal the length of her body as she traversed the shallows, hadn't hidden behind a bush to slide the dry gonelle over the wetness of her; had flaunted her lithe femaleness at him. So, when he in turn had blundered through the marshes, she had barely glanced at him as she languidly tried to untangle the mess the water and the weeds had made of her plaits. She was so close. He had placed one hand firmly on her small breast, encircling her waist with his arm, drawing her to him.

As Boniface now drew open the sacristy door, a gust of wind slammed it with the same swift violence of her reaction. She had slapped him. He thought they had stood there looking at one another, her eyes blazing, her fire further inflaming him. He had wanted her, all of her. But her words — "How dare you?" — wilted his ardor and confused him.

"How dare you?" she had spat again.

"But you — I thought," he had stammered limply. "You undressed in front of me."

Her brow had furrowed in incomprehension. "You are my cousin. Not a man. A cousin."

He had known then, had understood with an enormous sense of shame, that she had never even thought of him, except to tease him. With certainty he realized that she had been teasing him. It had been on purpose, all of it. And it had amused her. He had flushed. And she had known that he knew. She reached a hand over to his arm, but he threw it off. "You are my cousin," she kept repeating as if that made any difference. "I am betrothed. You know that." His height, his slightness, she hadn't known he was alive. *Not as a man.*

Both sacristy and vestry were hidden under the rood loft, and separated from the choir by the bulk of the stone rood screen. Dismissing the memories of Eleanor as best he could, Father Boniface entered the vestry with its panels of polished wood, the floor covered by a carpet brought by somebody's brother from the Holy Land. It was a place of beauty, and Father Boniface deliberately made the sign of the cross and tried to focus on each action as he vested, trying, albeit futilely, to imbue his mind and actions with God. The chasuble was laid over a table, the stole making the "chi rho" on top of it, his amice and alb beside them. There was a prie dieu for his use along the wall. But it was hard today. His knees were tight in the bending. It was only with the strongest of efforts that he was able to kneel.

"Father," he prayed as he tried to give himself to God. Without warning, a vision of the morning flashed across his mind's eye. The masons. And the procession before that. And then having to speak to that Dame Averilla. *I wish she weren't the one I had to deal with as sacristan.* For a start, she was taller than he was. No prayer came. Father Boniface rose, shrugged into the long white alb, flipped the amice over his head, and tied the strings under his chin. *The abbess. Refusing to listen to the orders of the pope.*

When his head emerged from the amice and he had straightened it into a high collar around his neck, he lifted his stole and kissed the cross on the center back. Instead of putting it around his neck, he looked at it, an eternity swirling through his mind.

You must not go in to Mass like this.

It was a tiny voice within him and he didn't want to listen. But it was insistent. Grudgingly, with an enormous effort of will, he forced himself back down and onto his knees. *Oh, God, help me, listen to me. This scorpion within me. How I harbor it. I am not fit for this task, not fit to be one of your priests.*

There was movement outside in choir. *They are expecting. Not me. A priest. Oh, God, only say the word, and I shall be healed.* Heaving a great sigh, he rose, again carefully kissing the cross, and hung the stole around his neck. *I will never be healed.*

4

ALL THAT MORNING, EVEN BEFORE THE DEAD maid was brought into their midst, the abbess had seemed strangely distant to the rest of the nuns. The young woman's death was serious, but Savette was unknown to most of them. They prayed dutifully for her unshriven soul during Mass, but their minds were focused with real alarm on the change in the behavior of their abbess.

"She was distracted all through Matins and Lauds, as well as Prime," Petronella whispered to Alburga as they filed into the chapter house.

"And short with me as we were practicing the trope," Alburga responded, still smarting from the earlier rebuke. "So, 'tisn't Savette's death that disturbs her peace. Mayhap 'tis Dame Averilla's trying to heal the dead girl."

"And," she hesitated, "did ye notice, she paused before taking the host, just for a bit before receiving?"

"Father Boniface?"

"Mayhap. He is always so punctilious."

"Fastidious."

"Could it be that the abbess does not accept his priesthood?"

Shocked silence.

"Probably another matter?'

"She can't suspect her own sanctity?"

"Then why did she not feel worthy to receive?"

So it was with a certain restlessness that they gathered in the chapter house.

The abbess' sermon that morning was dry. "I was bored, actually. I must need sleep," Dame Alburga said later, smarting not just about the trope, but about the unpremeditated liturgy "about which I was not consulted."

The chapter house benches were arranged along the wall so that all could both see and be seen. Before asking them to consider the "Affairs of the House," the abbess looked around the serried faces, familiar faces, as known to her as the lines that crossed her own palm, *and dear.* Her heart ached. *It's I who bring this weight into their midst.* She saw herself dragging the debt like a large bag with ropes attached to her shoulders, the way she'd seen the masons pulling a huge rock into the oratory that very morning.

I am taking too long. There were little movements as the community wondered why she didn't speak. Emma licked her lips and opened her mouth. "As most of you know by now, last night, after Compline, Master Hugo arrived, accompanied by an apprentice … " She saw several glances as the women began to comprehend the strangeness of such a man being accompanied by only one other. " … and a dog." A rustle ran around the seated knees. "I have allowed the dog to stay." Smiles flitted across some faces; others hid their eyes to avoid censuring the decision of their superior.

"Of course, it *is* her prerogative," Dame Alice would later remark, her words measured as she tried to incorporate this seeming deviation from the rule.

"Indeed," Dame Anne would concur, "Benedict says nothing about guests in the abbey having pets. *We* can't have pets." Dame Anne loved all creatures indiscriminately, large and small, "even spiders," one of the novices had once shrieked.

When the abbess opened her mouth to speak of the debts, she found she couldn't do it. She tried to speak about the inability to pay for the reredos. The words would not come. With renewed energy she said, "It has been brought to my notice that there is a change being wrought within the church that involves us all.

She paused, "Apparently, it is the custom in the papal chapel to place candles not behind or beside the altar, but upon it. Father Boniface tells me that it is the "will" of the Bishop of Winchester, who, as we know, is the papal legate, that all places of worship in England follow this new custom."

There were murmurs of surprise and angst. "I, too," her voice rose over the rustle of dismay, "dislike any change, particularly when I understand not the reason. I bring the matter to you now, for it might be that we would be well advised to institute this practice in our own chapel of Saint Edward."

A hissing slid across the room, "I hate change," Petronella whispered, "of any kind, but for him to tell us how to arrange the church!"

The abbess' voice rose as she held up a hand against the murmurs. "We would thus be adhering to that which will soon be, if not required, at least expected of us. At our own altar, the high altar, where our hearts reside, we needn't change our placement of the candles. No one sees that altar but our community alone."

All were surprised when Dame Agnes stood. "I mislike following the changes of the leaders of the Church as they winkle their way between spirit and thought. 'Tis not for me to say whether moving the candles is right or wrong, but I would counsel that we weigh this carefully before making a change in the fabric of our life."

Dame Felda rose. "Mayhap. But since the Holy Father orders it?"

From another, "Is it the right of Rome to so dictate?"

"The candles," Dame Petronella was ponderous, "symbolize candles held in the catacombs by the faithful."

"The Light of Christ."

"The fire of the Holy Spirit." Four were standing now. Usually, they would pass a thought like a child's toy, understanding fully from a few selected words what was meant—a synchronism of thought. But sometimes, as now, seemingly out of nowhere, the differing views would rankle into a boil.

I feel so alone, Emma thought. *Even after so many years. I hate this stepping out from the crowd, of losing the comfort of the communal mind, of being no longer just one of the swarm. I could just tell them what to do, and have done with their uncertainty. Did Christ ever feel this vacillation? No,* she answered herself—*or, mayhap, yes.*

The abbess cleared her throat. Those who had risen in dispute seated themselves. "What I have just told you, my dear daughters in Christ, is more in the nature of information than a matter for discussion. The candles on the shrine are to be moved. Those next to the high altar and those beside the nave altar are too large to move. They shall remain."

The abbess could avoid the subject of debt no longer.

"I wish," she said, "to speak now of the proposed reredos. The altar reredos that was commissioned by Margaret de Husel-dure was to have been of silver. That is no longer possible. But Master Hugo is here, and I must tell him something about what we expect him to create. We have spent much — too much — in these last years on the new oratory. The money that Margaret gave for the reredos has been used elsewise. There are other debts as well."

There was silence, deep, profound, and appalled. Emma chose to let it lie. For most of the community, raised in wealth as they had been, many of them coming from royal lineage, the idea of debt was foreign. They had no place in their sequestered minds to place such a concept.

Finally, Dame Helewise stood. Practical and forthright, she always felt like a breath of fresh air, and Emma looked at her in relief. "Are the debts large, Mother?"

"They are huge." Now that the boil had been lanced, Emma found that the words flowed freely, and she felt an incredible sense of relief to share that which she alone had borne so long. "Apparently, Abbess Cecily anticipated monies from her sister, the Duchess of Gloucester, which had been promised at the death of their father, Robert FitzHamon." *This all sounds so reasonable,* Emma thought. *Of course it is the truth I am telling them. Just not all of it. At least most of them know some of Joan's part in it. Perhaps it is my business to know such things but not share them.* "However," she continued, "because of the civil war, because the Duke of Gloucester must defend his sister the empress with men and arms, the monies promised Cecily were withheld. The monies due us from the crown are also being withheld. The king needs all he can find to pay for his part in the war."

Dame Helewise was still standing.

"Dame?"

"Then you are telling us, Mother, that although she no longer had the money for it, Abbess Cecily continued to build? That she funded the building by borrowing?"

"Yes, that is what I am saying."

"That we have no money to buy the silver for the reredos?"

Beneath her sleeves, Emma started to pick at her nails. *Why, Lord, did you thrust this on me? I am not the one they need for this.* "We will need" she continued over her interior prayer, "all our resources for the poor, every grain in all the tithe barns. The cold season started unusually early and promises to be long. Because of the drought, the harvest was sparse. We may not let people starve because we have spent the Lord's grain."

The abbess paused. "Remember, our Lord gives two kinds of bread to feed on: that for the body and that for the soul; we must try to serve both at our table." All the nuns looked troubled; some looked shocked. Dame Edith seemed on the verge of tears. "We must feed the poor, honor our commitment to Margaret de Huseldure, and begin to repay our debts, and none of these may be at the expense of any other."

They thought about it.

The silence lengthened.

Dame Helewise was still standing. Again the abbess nodded. "Ivory?"

The abbess thought about it. "I know not. I will have to ask."

Still Dame Helewise had not resumed her place.

"Dame?"

"These debts of which you spoke. To whom do we owe these monies? From whom have we borrowed?" The young woman waited for the concept to sink in to all their minds. "And how do we intend to repay?"

"We borrowed from Master Levitas. We used the abbey plate as collateral. He will give us time to repay. If we cannot, then — then we must give him the silver or gold from our treasury. For now …"

Dame Anne, in charge of the home farm, had been standing as well, waiting patiently to be noticed. The abbess sighed. Dame Anne was good at what she did, but given a chance to speak, *She always seems to start with Adam and Eve.*

Hearing the abbess sigh, Dame Anne blushed, only too aware of her loquacity. "Lady, two years past, an ancient oak at the home farm was felled in the great storm. The carver can have that wood if he will. It is in the mason's yard. Has been there, drying. Master Mason wanted it for the dove house, I believe. It was cut in half and into lengths before it was hauled up to the abbey on a slide, but mayhap it might serve the purpose." Dame Anne sat down.

The abbess, ashamed of her rudeness, softened her voice. "Thank you, Dame Anne, for your foresight and for all your care of us. Master Hugo shall be so informed."

"Then we are agreed?"

"Agreed on what, Mother?" Only Dame Alburga could have had the courage to ask that question.

The abbess breathed deeply and sorted her thoughts. *What indeed?* she wondered. "I felt," she would tell Dame Aethwulfa, like a father might when forbidding his daughter a longed-for fairing. Aloud she said, "I will propose to Master Hugo that he carve the figures and scenes for the reredos out of wood or ivory. Mayhap wood can later be silvered. I know not how it is done. But already Master Hugo has a design in his mind, and has asked that we look at it and give him our thoughts. Mayhap Dame Agnes, Dame Edith, Dame Maura, and Dame Joan might come later this morning, somewhat before Sext — I will have a bell rung when Master Hugo is ready — to look at the design he has traced out on his plaster."

Dame Joan reddened with pleasure at being included among those considered "talented," and Dame Edith paled, not with the idea of being thought talented, but with that of meeting an artist for whom she felt such admiration.

"I would that we come to a speedy consensus. I hate to detain Master Hugo for a carving in–in wood when he had expected a much more profitable commission."

As the abbess spoke the last sentence, the words came very slowly, and a surprising sequence of expressions passed over her face: wonder, then surprise, and finally, consternation, as if the thought had just now been inserted into her consciousness by the discussion of wood that directly preceded it. She said, "There is another matter that must be addressed." Again she paused, testing the idea with her mind. Steeling herself, hating to chastise one of her beloved daughters publicly, she thought, *I may not be able to make Averilla understand the depth of her hubris in this matter of healing, but perhaps I can help her to be at peace with Joan.*

She now said, "There are various strenuous tasks, necessary for the functioning of the house, which it would not be in the spirit of Benedict to hire others to do, such as the threshing or the cutting of wood for the warming room. We at Shaftesbury have made it our custom to leave these jobs to the young backs and strong arms of the novices. There comes with such work, as we all remember, a feeling of empathy, a bonding among those assigned these tasks. To help reestablish the sisterly affection and forgiveness so recently disturbed between them, I have decided that Dame Averilla and Dame Joan be required to saw into lengths that which is left from the oak when Master Hugo has taken what he needs."

Startled to hear their names, both Averilla and Joan immediately cast down their eyes. A fiery blush mounted on Dame Averilla's cheeks. Dame Joan paled.

5

Master Levitas lay stunned. He crawled across Gold Hill and, using the side of his house, stood up. After a while he found himself beside the brode hall. He knew the building—it was where the nuns embroidered liturgical vestments in silk and secular pieces on linen. The English nuns' skill was renowned all over the continent; so famous was their embroidery that it was called "English Work." But Levitas had never before had occasion to enter the brode hall. Hearing a step behind him, sudden terror overcame the hesitance he felt. Glancing fearfully over his shoulder, he pushed open the door, trembling so badly that he leaned against its frame to keep from falling. With his strangely darkening sight, he beheld a blur of color and light. Sound echoed in his ears like the tumbling waves of church bells from far off. Inexplicable dark spots swirled around the room, as if a fire had been put out, and charred bits of leaf and twig were lifting on the wind.

Soft hands grabbed him under his elbows and half-led, half-pushed him onto a stool. Docilely, he allowed his head to be pressed down between his knees. It felt comfortable. He breathed deeply of a soft, clean scent. *What is that? Fabric? Yes, fabric. Haven't smelt freshly fulled fabric since—since Rebekkah died. Comfortable. Does fabric absorb the smell of a woman?*

A movement caught the corner of his eye. He raised his head. The black specks had stopped whirling. He looked around, awed that a place of such beauty could be so near and yet so unknown even to him, who so often came to see the nuns. *Perhaps it isn't here. Perhaps I have died. Perhaps the youth so injured me. No. This is a building.* He looked up. The whole northern wall was incut with an unusual number of small windows. *North-facing.* All of the windows were covered in glazed parchment, allowing numerous shafts of light into the room. *More light than ... Light to work in.*

It was the light that chased the fog from the goldsmith's brain. His artist's eye recognized the curious arrangement of the windows, acknowledged the usefulness while his being still trembled with the physical and mental pain of the assault. Finally, his eyes came to rest on the grave gaze of a nun he had never before seen. He gawked at her in surprise and then mused on this aberration as if he had all the time in the world; as if he were not interrupting whatever it was she had been doing; as if he were not fleeing for his very life. *That I do not know her is not strange in itself. Most of the nuns are sequestered.*

This nun, whoever she was, stood serene, the planes of her face unmarred by wrinkles, the skin pulled taut by youth. Only the great gray eyes expressed the depth of her compassion. Levitas lowered his eyes and bowed his head. "Most ashamed. Should not presume to enter here, but—"

"You are in pain," The warmth in the woman's voice managed to splinter his confusion. "I thought you might faint. I can give you a drink." She looked around vaguely, as if a flagon might unaccountably appear with the strength of her willing. Then, wryly conceding her own incompetence, she fluttered her hands and, turning, said, "I shall send for warmed wine."

"No. No, don't. Please. Please" he urged. "Sit back down. At—at your loom. I have interrupted you." To his dismay, he started to cough, and weakly waved his hand in a sitting motion. Probably afraid that denying his request would worsen his discomfort, the young nun sat. His cough was wet and hacking, and accomplished nothing but to redden two spots on his cadaverous gray cheeks. When he again had breath, he croaked, "Continue please with what you were doing ... I just need a—a moment."

Could it be that she doesn't know me; doesn't know that I am a Jew. Treats me with respect. Ironic. Youths were so savagely aware of my religion.

Needing to breathe, and wanting more than anything to be no

trouble to anyone, with the last of his strength he croaked, "Please, continue. Tell me what you are doing. It will let me rest."

Doubting, she moved further onto the cushioned bench and glanced worriedly over her shoulder, saying coaxingly, "You cannot see from over there. Not well." She patted the bench. "Truly," she arched an eyebrow, "if you come here I can be sure that you will not again faint."

Pulling a deep breath through his teeth so as not to resume the repugnant coughing, he crabbed over to her, put his hand on what he had taken to be a loom, and slumped onto the cushioned bench.

On closer inspection the apparatus proved to be an oblong frame of wood, onto which linen had been attached with long running stitches of a coarse thread. Three feet in length and probably two in width, the frame was supported by a sturdy pole underneath. The whole thing was similar in arrangement to a reader's lectern, or to one of the desks he had seen scribes use. The frame was situated in such a way that the light fell on the work. The embroiderer's back — for such seemed her occupation — was to the windows. He shifted on the bench, fascinated despite his fatigue, terror, and despair.

She spoke, "See, I am making a story, with my needle and wool on a linen ground." She looked at him to see if there was comprehension in his eyes. To her he still seemed dazed, but his interest reassured her and she continued, though still somewhat dubiously. "I — I see the world in my mind. I am not in it, but separated from it. I know not why. It is a great sorrow to me. I cannot feel. Not close. Nor can I draw. Not with the ability of Dame Edith. So she draws what I see for me. I tell her and she places here, with lines of ink on the linen, my visions. Then I fill in her pictures with floss. You see. Here are the men during the battle."

Levitas focused, and the figures she addressed were indeed lifelike. "They seem so sad." He looked more closely. "All of them.

138

Dame, is there no happiness?"

"Not now, somehow. I think there was, once, but not now. I see only sadness." For a time it was enough for him to watch her fingers as, thimble on her third finger pushing, she held the needle between index finger and thumb and drew the fine strands of colored floss through the interwoven threads of linen. Finally, he said, "Mayhap because you are not so close, you give to others a view of themselves that they, in their trip through the turmoil of life cannot see, so entranced are they by the multitude of incident."

He pushed himself back off the bench and vaguely tried to straighten his mantle, patting his side to be certain of the chalice. "Dame, I thank you. You do have a caring. Probably your God finds it best for you if you do not know how much."

"But your face, I have not even tried to succor your pain."

"Ah, but you have. Is there blood?" He reached up and gingerly patted the bruised patina of his face. Feeling the starting scabs, he said, smiling shyly, "I would have that water now, if it is by. I am to see Dame Averilla and I would be neat."

CHAPTER THIRTEEN

SECOND DAY

LATE MORNING, AFTER
CHAPTER MASS AND CHAPTER

I

fter chapter, the nuns scattered to their various pursuits: the abbess retired to her lodgings; the novices, overly solemn, scuttled to the west walk to study psalmody with Dame Petronella; and the obedientaries, like a flock of large crows, bent their heads together and paced the east walk, discussing Savette.

Dame Averilla slipped into the sacristy intending to hide her mind from those damning words of John the Mason during Terce. She would busy her hands with the service vessels that waited to be washed and polished and the linens to be rinsed.

Taking a piece of rough linen from a lower cupboard, she laid it reverently by the piscina. A jug of water stood ready on the floor. She lifted it up and allowed the stream to flow from the curved lip, but all she could see in the water's silver swirl were the sad eyes of John the Mason, and his huge hands beseeching her to bring Savette back.

Her eyes moved to her own hands. As if in a daze she held

140

them up. Healing hands. Ever since she had prayed over John the Mason with Father Merowald just months ago, people had come to her expecting miracles. Most of them had head injuries, as if she were versed in only one kind of miracle. First came a mother fiercely hugging a babe who had been dropped. Then a cotter from Cann was carried in; he had been kicked in the head by a horse. Finally, a father brought in his boy, who had slid on the ice and struck his head on a stone. She had been able to do nothing for any of them. She had placed her hands on their heads, knelt, and prayed, but naught had come of it. She had felt so powerful after the miracle that cured John the Mason, yet now she could do nothing. *Why did You let it happen the once,* she wailed in her mind to God, *if it is not to be at other times? I am so helpless. And they expect so much of me.*

A new thought sidled into her mind, and gently, as if holding a newborn chick in her palm, she observed it:

It is not yours alone to heal. Many die. All I cured died. I work in ways you cannot understand.

She nodded, and saw in her mind's eye Savette as she had been today, and watched the image change to the last time she had seen Savette.

"DAME?" THE VOICE HAD BEEN SOFT, but even so had startled Averilla concentrating as she was now on readying the church. Tentative and shy, like a young fawn, Savette had tiptoed around the edge of the rood screen. The maid wore a long gown of undyed wadmal and an over-tunic of misty heather blue. A shabby cloak trailed from her hand. Her hair dangled in two long blonde plaits from which glints of gold and wisps of brass escaped to curl about her face. She was pretty and slight and very tiny, with down-slanted, widely spaced eyes. Sprinkled liberally across her cheeks, marring her complexion, was a rash of youthful spots. Sensing Averilla's scrutiny, the girl raised her hand to her face

141

and picked at the scabs on her cheek.

Seeing her obvious distress, Averilla softened her voice and asked, "What is it, my child?"

The girl gave a deep reverence, untutored but still graceful. "I — Dame, I ... "

"Yes?"

"I am with child." A tear streaked past the purple bruises beneath her eyes.

Of course she is, Averilla thought. *Pale and with spots. Isn't eating enough cabbage.*

Averilla knew what was coming but would not help it.

"Have you pennyroyal or other herb that can ... ?"

Averilla stepped forward to place a gentle hand under the girl's chin. "Come. There is comfort in the south aisle. We shall not be disturbed."

As she sat on the tomb, a stray shaft of pale winter sun making ruby and midnight patterns on the tiles, the girl's mouth had trembled. "I was plighted, Lady," she started. Out from under the front of her tunic she pulled a long ribbon, from which dangled a ring of gold covered with tendrils and a tiny cabochon amethyst. "See. He gave it me, this ring, not three months since. 'Tis beautiful, is it not? Of such value that I thought he meant the words he spoke." The girl lowered her head.

"We were friends," she added after a moment. "From childhood, Dame. He was older than I by three winters; already sweating when I had but buds for breasts. He knew my brothers. Would come home with them and pull my hair or push me, and I was glad of the attention.

"The haying and harvest were early from the heat and from the drought. Some'ut after Saint John's day, if you remember. We were out early, before the dew had dried on the cow parsley beneath the hedgerows, with the birds in full voice and red poppies in the grain ... "

THE AIR WAS SOFT ON HER CHEEKS, and Savette was aware of her legs, newly long under the scratchy wool of the hot wadmal. It was her third year to rake with the women instead of being sent with the children to shake wooden rattles to scare the crows. Her brothers walked beside her, pushing each other and moving, always moving. When Todd slung his arm around Simon's neck and wrestled him to the ground, Savette stepped neatly around the roiling bodies, trying to seem unaffected by their play. She reached into the briar hedge beside them and plucked a wild rose to tie into her braids. By the time she had interwoven the stem into her hair where she could smell its sweetness, her brothers had run forward, jostling next to another young man who seemed unusually comfortable in his body. Beside him, her brothers appeared gawky, their Adam's apples bulging from slender necks, their feet and hands too big. The other youth had already grown the broad shoulders of a man, and his heavy neck was muscular.

Sensing her gaze, the young man looked back, and Savette saw with surprise that it was Jared, Todd's friend, long used to the freedom of their house, but this morning, in this light, surprisingly different. One of the women walking with Savette made a polite inquiry, then, about her father, Lovick, "'is leg. Painful with the cold comin' on, I wot."

Savette answered absently, her gaze fixed on Jared. He had left the roughhousing to the others, and, shrugging his jerkin to straightness, squared his shoulders.

When they came to the field, Savette took up her wooden-fingered hay rake. Sun on her back, chaff in her pores, she longed to look for him, to turn and see where he was and what he was doing, yet she wouldn't, not yet; a primitive intuition held her back, a visceral reluctance, like a wild duck in a mating dance. Everything around her seemed new: the soft smell of the green-tinged air; the cold feel of dewy grass on bare feet; the mist riding the top of the hill, and the brilliant red of the newly opened poppies.

He turned his head finally, as if called, just when she had allowed herself a glance. Their gazes locked. Jared lost his rhythm, trod on another's foot, and was good-naturedly buffeted for his clumsiness by the King of the Mowers, all full of himself, a wreath of poppies around the crown of his hat. Savette blushed and continued to rake, uneasy in the warmth and longing that had seized her body, eager to look at him again, certain that she must not.

Deliberately, circumspectly, she followed the women to that section of the field where they were propping the sheaves one against another. Her ears were newly opened to his every action: the rustle of the grass falling before the heavy hiss of his scythe; and the drone of his hone on the blade when he paused to sharpen it. Every part of her, it seemed, even the hairs on her arms and neck, as if singed by the chaff, could feel his direction. Like a weather vane dependent on the wind, controlled by it, existing for it, her body seemed hotter on the side that faced him. Savette forbade herself to look in his direction; knew that her not looking would somehow fascinate and attract him. An impotent shyness alternating with crass boldness controlled her every movement. She peeked in his direction. He had removed his tunic and was working with just a folded cloth around his waist and thighs. Sweat glinted on the lines of his muscles. Again their gazes locked. A scythe clanged against a rock, the wind rustled in the standing grain. A mouse squealed, and she watched a hawk grab it and, heavy-weighted, fumble off.

When the sun had reached its zenith, the great two-wheeled abbey cart came lumbering down the hill and out onto the field, pulled by the muscular red abbey oxen, their shoulders heaving, patient heads moving rhythmically above their gnarled legs. The women dropped the sheaves they were binding, propped them one against another, and went to stand beneath the old oak at the

144

side of the field. When the cart stopped, the men, tired from their swinging, clambered up to hand the food down to the women, who opened the bundles and spread out the great loaves of bread, the rounds of fresh abbey cheese, the cider from last year's apples, and the welcome barrels of ale. There were mounds of pies. Savette passed them out, their crusts streaked with gold where the onion filling had spread and bubbled.

He came to her at last, and late, as she was spreading out the leftovers. Hunger eased, the others sat in groups, or lay one against another, chewing fresh hay under the trees, the sun giving a too-bright greenness to the stubble. She felt his breath on the hairs of her neck as she stood bending over the boards. Deliberately, she didn't turn, wanting him to want her, knowing somehow that she must wait. Finally, he tweaked her plait. "Did you save any for an old friend?" he asked, the laughter tumbling below the sound of his words.

"Aye. But then, what kind of friend be ye? Always wont to pull my braids, have ye been. Hiding from me, too, I remember. And now it's a pie you covet." From under the linen cloth, she drew a golden round, redolent with onion.

He looked surprised and then laughed. "Waiting for me?"

"No." She looked at him archly. I — I thought they were gone, but ... " Her look belied her words, and she turned in embarrassment to the hedge to retrieve the stone jar kept there to cool the ale.

"I WAS CONFUSED THEN," she continued speaking in the aisle to Averilla. "He knew that I longed for him. I had had no experience of such things. I turned away. I knew not what to do. No one else seemed to mark the change in me, and yet I felt that everything had changed. I didn't look at him again for the rest of the day, but knew he was there, as if a cord bound our awareness one to the other. I found it hard to sleep that night, and tossed and turned with the heat of I then knew not what inside me … "

"Umm," Averilla noised dryly.

"The next day was the same, and the one after that. We spoke very few words, and I trembled to think that he felt not as I myself did, that he had no thought of me beyond that of his friends' sister.

On the third day, after a warm and dewless night, after we had turned the hay with pitchforks and spread it once again before shaping into cocks to be covered with hats of thatch, then, when I felt I could stand it no longer, he came to me."

"'Tis so much nicer,' he said, 'on the far side of the field.' I followed him and we sat, backs against the sheaves, the sweet smell of the cut grain sharp against our talk, the sound of the hedge crickets a sweet drone of underlying pleasure.

"There is a time at midday for rest. Many choose to nap in the sun, letting the fingers of heat take from their backs the coils of bending, letting the ale do its drowsy work, loosening them, one with his back against another.

"But I was not loose. I fidgeted. Jared felt the same, I think, for he scrambled to his feet of a sudden, went to the hedge, picked blackberries, and brought them to me. They held in their sweetness the warmth of the sun as he placed them between my lips. His voice was lazy, and he toyed with one of my plaits. He kept pestering me, saying that it caught all the sun of the morning and that was why I plaited my hair. I walked home that day in a cloud of wonder. Others, my father certainly, saw something, looked at me with an asking look. Next morning, Jared, too, seemed the butt of many a jest. I felt secure in his wanting then, felt no fear to look for him. Whenever I did, I found his eyes upon me, and we would stand thus, with the field and the wind and the being back between us, just looking at one another, wanting I knew not what.

146

"Toward the end of the week, when all was done and we sat resting at the edge of the fields, as had become our wont, he again probed me about unbinding my hair. 'Twill be like a dress,' he insisted. 'You need not wear any other garment . . .'"

She faltered.

"Oh, Dame, forgive me," she had said blushing. "I — I love him so." Two great tears had brimmed over her lashes and had dropped unheeded on her right breast. "He — he, I — you know how it went, I am sure. I mean," she had stammered, "you have heard the story before, closely spoken, and too-oft repeated.

"That night the bonfires were lighted and there was dancing, not just for the harvest, but for the feast of Saint John. After feasting was done and the benches pushed back on the meadow, chains of dancers swung between firelight and shadow. He was beside me before I marked where he was. I felt his hand on my back and felt myself ease into his touch as if wanting to be led. We spoke of the joy of the weather then, how it had not rained during the harvest, how the crowd was so great. Our tongues seemed tangled in meaningless words. He took my hand. 'Twas a feeling I had longed for, and as of one accord we ran toward a dance at the farthest bonfire, where the meadows run up against the fastness of the forest. I felt his breath as he muttered soft words against my neck.

"When the dancing was done and the sound of laughter muted, he drew his mantle around my shoulders and left his arm there . . ."

SAVETTE COULD FEEL IT, white-hot against her. A blissful languidness seemed to bind her and she sighed. He drew her into the forest, and soon, of one accord, they both stopped and she lifted her face for his kiss. His hand moved slowly down her breast, as if gentling a horse. A shudder trembled down her body. He placed his lips on the fine wool of her best gown down between the swells of her young breasts.

147

"…and then he gave me this ring. It seemed only right to me that he should. For days after that we took the proffered time, found places …

"After the harvest, though, by the time the cuckoos had gone …" Savette paused and looked down. Another tear had streaked her cheek and it was a moment before she had control of herself. "…he became dull with me and I saw him less and less. My father was angered that Jared had said naught to him. Simon, my brother, tried to confront him, but Jared as good as ignored him. I, too, met him one day, heading down Gold Hill with friends. 'Twas not the time to speak. It was as if a spear had passed through my body. What I knew was not what I knew. We had had one another to laugh with, and now I was as one apart, no part of him any longer. The cord that bound us had been severed, more swiftly and surely than had Robert Bradshaw's sword cleft it in twain. And then, and then I found that I was with child."

"Have you told him?" Averilla now remembered asking, knowing the answer, but forcing herself to ask.

"No. I—he—if he will have me no longer … I want him not. Nor his babe."

The sudden fierceness had drained Savette, leaving her face splotchy and washed with tears. She laughed harshly, and wiped her sleeve across her eyes. "And so, Dame, here I am. 'Tis a tale oft told, I warrant. The old wise woman Galiena is now gone. Some said she was a witch, but she would 'ave given me some'ut to rid me of the child. Now, I hoped I might persuade you. There will be nothing for the babe …"

"I can help you not." Averilla had hated the idea of killing the babe. In such dealings, as she well knew, sometimes the bleeding wouldn't stop and the mother was taken as well. It was dangerous. She had tried to persuade Savette. "Surely, you can find a father for your babe. Women of your age are few enough and of great value."

148

Savette's face had drooped into lines of stubbornness and hurt pride.

"Child, come." Averilla had said. "We shall pray on it," and she had risen and tried to put an arm around Savette's shoulder. The girl had shaken it off angrily.

Averilla now sighed. Carnal love. Foreign here in the abbey. The stuff of bards and the sunny nonsensical courts of France. "You must not use the convent to hide yourself from the strains of the flesh," Dame Petronella would admonish every new group of novices. "In spite of — or because of — the fact that carnal love is forbidden you, your lives will become more open to all the other loves and to the deeply satisfying ecstasy of placing the self within the might of God."

Even so, it was surprising how many of the nuns had something, some small kernel, that they cherished.

"Dame," the girl had brought Averilla back from her thoughts, "I have no way to care for a babe. Wist ye not so? Were I to bear a child, my father would have to pay, not only for the act, as if Jared had naught to do with it, but also for the babe. The child would have no father, and there will be a fine for that as well. And we will not have — the harvest was meager. We have no beasts. I can not bear this child. Understand ye this? Please, Dame. I know ye know of potions and tinctures and such. Help me, please."

"My child, my child, I cannot." Averilla had bitten her lip. "It is a burden, I know — "

"You know nothing!" the girl had spat the words as she stood up, tears again gathering, the back of her hand over her mouth. "I shall be beaten, and you will sit comfortably in your carved stall when you could have helped me. You will wonder why you did not help me, you with your talk of helping the poor. Well, remember, you didn't help me." She had run down the aisle and out of the oratory.

And I didn't help her, Averilla now thought, *and I do remember Savette. Oh, God, help me. I am guilty.*

2

"DAME?"

Averilla whirled around. She had been so focused on her memories that she hadn't seen Master Levitas outside the gate awaiting her attention. "Master Levitas," Averilla bowed her head in greeting. The old man limped closer to her as she stepped out of the sacristy to greet him. "Peace be unto you."

"And unto you." She raised her head to look at him, and her eyes widened in surprise. Something was very wrong. Not only was his cheek cut, but traces of dried blood were caked on his face, and his nose was purpled and beginning to swell. Though he was trying to appear calm, he was obviously agitated and askew; his peaked hat was gone, the careful, foreign arrangement of his hair had been mussed, and the embroidered hem of his tunic was muddied, silken threads dangling where pearls or precious stones had been ripped away. The one hand that clutched his cloak trembled.

"Master Levitas!" She took a step toward him.

"Forgive my interrupting your duties, Dame." He said it quickly, forestalling her. There was a flash of silver from the voluminous scrip concealed under his cloak. "Your chalice has been well mended, I think."

Averilla took the cup. "How," she asked, confused by his dishevelment, unsure how to proceed, and therefore sounding inane, "do you manage such a shine? Lovely."

"A powder, a red powder. I shall bring you some. A secret among us, but your aim, as is mine, is the glory of God."

"Yes," she said, meeting his eyes, honoring his skill and their past friendship, ignoring his distress.

As he relinquished the cup, she noticed that a blood-caked piece of linen was wrapped ineffectually around his hand.

"Your hand!" She fumbled the chalice. The lead-weighted cup slipped.

The injured hand shot out, fumbled, and finally caught the wide base of the chalice. "Dame!" he snapped. "I just repaired this cup. Please, be careful."

Averilla's eyes filled successively with anger, embarrassment, and finally amusement. She giggled. "I wouldn't want to deprive you of your work." When she glanced down, the wounded hand was again hidden in the wide sleeve of his gown.

This time, not to be sidetracked, she said, "Your hand. Please let me tend it."

Slowly, he stretched forth the hand from beneath his sleeve, and looked at it curiously, as if noticing it for the first time.

Heedless of his dignity, she took his hand and gently laid back his sleeve.

"It is filthy," she said. "At least, let me rinse it. If you leave it in this covering, it will fester." With cool fingers, she tugged at the edge of the soiled linen, inadvertently pulling it tight around the wound. He flinched. "If you would but hold your arm up to the neck of your mantle, your blood ... Your neck! Sir, did someone ... ?"

"Aye, Dame."

Had Master Levitas been in any state to notice he would have seen Averilla's hands hover motionless near his neck, would have heard her heave a sigh and say, with a stern note of determination, "We must go to Sister Cadilla."

She maneuvered him ahead of her out from the overhang of the rood screen. When they reached the narthex she asked, "How happened it?" They exited from one of the smaller doors beside the processional door.

"A cut. No more." He pulled at his mantle.

She nudged at his elbow to try to make him shuffle faster up the

151

gravel path to the infirmary. "Sister Cadilla will need to know."

His eyes were fastened to the gravel in front of him. "Know?" He looked offended.

"What instrument made the cut, Master Levitas, on your hand and on your face? It will make a difference in the salve she chooses."

He was silent. Finally, hoarsely, he said, "Youths. I was climbing Gold Hill. The way is so short, I came unaccompanied. They have been loitering around my shop of late. There have been occurrences."

"Disturbances?"

"Aye. Rocks and such like. Today I was pushed from behind and fell. I must have cut myself as I went down."

Master Levitas and Averilla descended the two steps into the cool of the infirmary. The familiar smells assaulted Averilla with remembrance. Sister Cadilla was bending over the brazier and fussing with a concoction in the iron pot. Averilla's nose identified vinegar and borage.

Cadilla looked up with a smile, which faded as her eyes darted from Averilla to the moneyer. A glittering slid behind her eyes.

"Dame?" she asked.

"Master Levitas fell and has been cut."

"Then one of his own kind must attend to him. 'Tis not for a Christian to attend a Jew." Cadilla turned her back and busied herself with aligning her salves and ointments.

"Saint Benedict," Averilla's voice was curt, superior to servant, "cautions us to be obedient one to another and to be host to the stranger."

Cadilla made no effort to conceal her disgust at the request, or her irritation at Averilla for disputing her authority, but finally, reluctantly and slowly, she turned to look at the hand. "Hold it out." She pulled his hand away from its position holding his cloak together.

"He took the brooch," he muttered, but Sister Cadilla was not

152

listening, merely scowling to herself as she unwound the piece of linen from the wound. She then poured water into a bowl, dipped a bit of burrel in it, and scrubbed at the injury. Master Levitas winced at the abrasive. "For Damasa, they said," he continued over the pain, but it was clear that Cadilla was still not listening. Narrowing her lips, she dipped a feather into the vinegar tincture on the brazier, and smoothed it into the open wound.

"Sister!" Averilla whispered, appalled at the use of the tincture, still so near to boiling. The skin around the wound reddened.

Cadilla lifted dark eyes to her former superior and said, blandly accepting the unvoiced criticism, "I know, Dame, that *you* would apply it cold, but I believe that it is the heat and the heat alone that strangles the evil humors."

Beads of sweat dripped into the goldsmith's eyes. He said nothing. His hand shook, but he himself seemed to have retreated from the searing pain. As they left the building, Master Levitas began to cough again. The fit that wracked his frail body was so severe that Averilla gently pushed him onto the bench outside the infirmary door and forced his head between his knees. When finally he could breathe again, she noticed flecks of blood on the scrap of linen with which he wiped his mouth. She glanced worriedly back at the infirmary.

"Will you allow me to bring you a draught to ease that cough?"

He looked at her for a moment and then said, "Aye, Dame. I will accept such from you."

3

WHILE AVERILLA WAS IN THE SACRISTY and infirmary with Master Levitas, Dame Edith, the abbey illuminator, was settling herself in her carrel in the north walk. She thought of the carrel as her "holt," for she, like the badger, was of a solitary disposition, and the enclosed nature of the wooden chair and table gave her a cozy comfort. She had confided this image of herself to Dame Averilla once, but the latter had seemed rather more confused than understanding and had only noted, "Indeed, both badgers and nuns do dress in black and white."

Edith now glanced up at the sky. As it had yesterday, a meager bit of sun was pricking its way through the mist and dragging itself over the open balustrade, but it was a thin light and promised little assistance. She felt an unreasonable irritation, as if the sun were eluding her on purpose. She sighed. She had so little time, what with the offices and choir practice and the obligatory nap, that when the light was bad she felt personally affronted.

The carrel Edith had been given, however, had the best light in the north walk. Her desk, a slanted plank of oak, sanded fine, was slotted into a depression on the chair bottom by an oak arm. The height and angle could be adjusted by means of stair steps cut along the length of the arm. Edith appreciated all the special allowances that had been made for her. *I really do,* she thought, *but I would that I had the light when I needed it.* As quickly as the resentment flooded her, it was gone, and a gulf of shame opened within her. Admitting it, she untied the straps that bound her little strongbox. *A sin to resent God's choice of light,* she told herself firmly and lifted out the gathering she was illustrating, a rush of blood reddening her cheeks. *A sin to be so caught up in myself when a girl has been brutally murdered.* "Mea culpa," she said aloud.

At the breaking of the silence, several scribes, in varying degrees of annoyance, raised their eyes from the formal rounded script known as Carolingian. Seeing, however, that it was Edith who was frustrated, they made mental allowances. The weary light bothered them as well, but, of course, Dame Edith was not only new to the scriptorium but did indeed have a gift. Small figures and leaves dropped from her pen with unbelievable swiftness,

154

decorating the manuscripts those same scribes had so laboriously copied.

As she deliberately slotted the inkhorn into the hole drilled
into her desktop, and peered at the nib of the goose quill, Edith's
mind moved with some humility from the dead girl — a girl she
couldn't imagine and a death she refused to see — to the book,
the "exemplar" that Master Hugo had brought with him from
St. Edmunds.

Often, those charged with decorating newly copied manuscripts
replicated the beautiful images they found in these exemplars
"freehand" or "by eye." Rarely now did they trace or "pounce"
the scene directly onto the new-copied vellum, for doing so ruined
an exemplar by making holes in it. Edith toyed with the idea of
copying by eye some of the illustrations from this exemplar, for
they were indeed beautiful, but the thought intrigued her only
momentarily. The fire of creation was already blazing new images
across her mind's eye, and she had to race to keep up with them.
The tip of her tongue slipped over her lips. Quickly, she gave a
final rub to the fuzzy-textured vellum with pumice, smoothed the
surface with chalk, dipped her pen, and allowed the ink to flow
into a little man climbing through the top of the twining vines
that formed the initial letter "P." Even to her critical eye, the man
looked real. A soft contentment from the immersed concentration suffused her thought.

She hummed the Gloria softly to herself, all her frustration
forgotten. *God with us — here, holding my hand — guiding it . . .*

Since charcoal and lead tended to leave grains on the parchment, she, as did most illuminators, used a pen. It slid deftly up
the edge of the page, a leaf here, a gnarl curling the tongue of a
leaf there. The gnarl seemed to draw itself in order to hide the
small flaw in the surface of the vellum where a tick had pierced
the animal's hide. The gnarl was a kind of blight; she had seen
such things.

155

Ugly, but nevertheless useful. God does use everything for good. Even blight. Why, oak galls are a blight, but ground, they produce my ink.

Edith's hand stopped. She saw the community standing in the warming room, after Compline, their hands in their sleeves. *They call it — this warming time before bed — they call it "recreation," but verily, 'tis not. Not the same at all as what I do. This is recreation. Showing again God's goodness in the world. Recreating . . . creating again. Only God can create; think the original thought. We merely copy.*

Holding in her left hand a small knife to catch any drips of ink that might accidentally slip from her pen, Edith resumed drawing, newly confident that the pen would move almost by itself. She only needed to hold it vertical to allow out of the nib what God willed onto the page. Often she found that she actually forgot what she had drawn, and the next day would be surprised and delighted at the images that stood revealed there, from her pen, but new to her eyes. "That Christ should so use me," she now murmured under her breath in a warmth of gratitude.

A small bell tinkled. Dame Edith's face again reddened and the pale-lashed eyes that looked vaguely like a rabbit's glowed. She had been hiding the thought of meeting the famous Master Hugo from herself since the abbess had made the appointment during chapter, but now she allowed herself full relish of the thought. She had been disappointed when the exemplar had been handed her; had hoped that it would hold some of Hugo's renowned work, but it had not. She had not seen his work, of course, but she had heard of it. The others in the convent had heard of the Great Bible that Hugo had illuminated at St. Edmunds, but they understood its importance only vaguely, like a dream half remembered. She, however, understood. She had, over the past years, queried various passing monks about the monumental work. One of them had actually seen it, and she spoke to him at length, learning how Hugo interrelated line and color, quelling the overly ornate borders of Anglo-Saxon decoration with strength of line and dominance of image. Now she, handmaiden of this abbey at Shaftesbury, would be able to meet, to look into the eyes of, the man who had seen such visions. It was beyond her most treasured dream. He had done what she could only imagine doing. Hands shaking, she rose and quickly hid the telltale tremble in her wide sleeves.

4

DAME EDITH WAS OUT OF BREATH when she reached the reliquary chapel, and seeing the other nuns clustered around the sculptor, she flushed in embarrassment at being the last to arrive.

Master Hugo stood in front of his makeshift table, so focused on what he was saying that he was lolling his weight against a pillar, his right leg cocked, his hand fiddling with a scorper. " ... so the three — " he continued.

"Ah, here is Dame Edith," said the abbess, interrupting him, turning her body from examining Hugo's slate to include the tardy woman. "Dame Edith is our illuminator." The abbess looked directly at Edith and then paused, caught by another thought. "We here at Shaftesbury are well endowed with those who try to catch the light of God in their work. Dame Agnes," here the abbess motioned toward another, rather haggard-looking, nun, "is renowned for her embroidery. The hanging above the altar ... "

Hugo bowed and his eyes narrowed, "The hanging above the altar is your work?" he asked the nun. Then, "It is indeed beautiful." A flush spread across Agnes' face and he was able to see, beneath lines of grief, her former beauty.

"For many years," the abbess hurried on, allowing Agnes to collect herself, "Agnes was chamberlain, our mistress of church work, as Dame Maura is now. The counsel of both in this matter of design is valued."

157

Hugo bowed as the others were introduced.

"Obviously I couldn't tell them," he would later relate, that as soon as I saw Shaftesbury I wanted to be away from its nowhereness. Nor," here he would smile ruefully, "did I mention that before I left Saint Edmunds I had been asked to come as soon as possible to Abbot Suger at Saint-Denis."

"My Lady, Dames," he now started, "with great presumption, I have already placed my thoughts on this slate. After I know what your wishes are, I will transfer these thoughts to this plaster with an iron wire." Hugo indicated the wooden form on sawhorses in which a bed of plaster was solidifying. "Now, however, before I show you what I envision, I would know your thoughts." His gaze was caught by a flicker of movement from the bird-like woman who had arrived flustered and late and was now lurking behind one of the taller nuns.

"One of them," he would continue to Levitas, "didn't know her name then, called her 'Innocencia' to myself. It was well that she was there — Dame Edith, I learned she was called — for without her, I think, I would have perhaps said those things that I told you I hadn't said. But she looked at me with the awe an apprentice reserves for a master. And that awe, perversely, kept me from those flurries of pride that ... " Hugo's words would trail off, leaving it to the goldsmith's understanding.

Levitas would nod gravely. "Our great temptation: to truly believe that what we do comes from our own hands, our own skill; to believe in our own vision."

"My understanding" Hugo now said to the nuns, is that you wish a reredos for this altar." He spread wide his hands. "I confess, I know little about this Saint Edward." Dame Agnes took a step toward the sketch on his slate and examined it with interest. "Now that I see this hanging, I wonder that you would wish to replace it with a reredos. Would you perhaps consider an altar frontal?"

Dame Agnes looked at him with such a confusion of emotion — her eyes huge, both beseeching and accepting — that he was forced to turn his gaze away from her.

There was silence as the nuns absorbed the multitude of implications that lay behind his words. A frontal for the altar. It was a new concept for them. He followed the thought, "Images are sometimes placed on the front of the altar and behind the body of the priest, so that the images themselves will not be easily seen and thereby encourage simple souls into idolatry. But indeed you have no fear of that here. I even placed scenes of the saint on the very doors of Saint Edmunds. The same was done at Hildesheim. The church has passed far along from the worship of wooden idols."

For some reason a few of the nuns seemed uncomfortable with that thought.

"If I may," Dame Maura said with confidence, "my vision — and I speak here only as one member of the community, not as mistress of church work — is that this panel, or series of three panels as you earlier started to indicate," here she deftly avoided the question of a reredos above the altar or frontal below it, "not be huge. This is but the altar at the shrine, and should be, secondary to both the high and nave altars."

Hugo raised an eyebrow. "I am glad of that, for else I should have had to find you a stone carver." He held his breath. "The three scenes I have here started to depict — "

"The martyr?" Dame Joan, a peg-shaped woman, interrupted enthusiastically.

Agnes raised her head from the sketch looking confused.

Hugo's heart sank, "Er, I had not — "

"That," the abbess interrupted her, "would be appropriate, certainly. It would enhance the pilgrim's focus."

"He would be at Corfe," Dame Joan was gathering impetus, "with the lady queen, his stepmother, who so foully murdered him. They could be talking. Over the fence..." Dame Joan trailed off.

159

"Apparently, Edward, King and Martyr, had not the qualities that lend themselves to portrayal," Hugo would give Levitas a wry smile. "It is a problem. How to portray the essence of goodness? Often we Christians use symbols: the eagle for Saint John, the ox for Saint Mark. They are not, as you Jews might presume, 'graven images.' Just symbols."

His eyes now lingered on the hanging. "Is this scene on the hanging with his mother the one to which you refer?" He cleared his throat to lessen any disparagement of Joan's suggestion and with a show of candor said, "Dames, I confess, because of the hanging I had not thought to depict the scenes of the martyrdom. I had thought ... "

The abbess was embarrassed for Joan, for her unwitting — the abbess was sure it was unwitting — ability to hurt Agnes by intimating that the story had been inadequately depicted in the hanging. The abbess said, "The reliquary is covered with symbols of the saint. And we have the hanging. Although this altar" she added thoughtfully as if it had just occurred to her, "stands within the shrine of the saint, the altar itself is, for the worship of God as we know Him — as Christ."

The group of nuns now moved to Hugo's slate to give a closer examination to the images Hugo had been working on since early morning. The sketch indicated three groupings, like grottos or chapels. Each enclosed a scene of the Passion, a scene indicated by a few sure lines.

"The longer they looked, the more mortified I became. Obliquely I began to see my presumption." Hugo would tell Levitas.

"It is only a sketch," he said.

"I see your vision," Edith's eyes sparkled with delighted recognition.

"As do I," Agnes' face softened as she caught Hugo's eye.

"Just the understanding of that one miserable woman made me feel justified," Hugo would later tell Levitas, referring to Agnes, still pale from her recent illness.

Joan, unable to fill in the scenes from the brief lines, looked bewildered.

Agnes continued softly, not just to Joan, though that was her intent, "It is masterful. The kiss of Judas to the left, the scourging to the right, and finally the crucifixion.

The abbess looked around. "I think we are in accord, Master Hugo. We would have it as you have indicated."

"So be it, Dames." Master Hugo said, looking from one to the other, but bowing finally to the abbess. "I will again ask for your approval when the detailed drawing is completed. But, I confess, I am still uncertain on your decision, frontal or reredos?"

They were all looking at the abbess.

"The altar is dedicated to God. But since the priest stands in front of it, it is rarely seen. Therefore, and because that was what the monies were given for, the design must be for a reredos." Here she looked at Agnes and said, "The hanging will be placed behind the reliquary, where the pilgrims can have the full benefit of it."

"A silver reredos will be very heavy," Master Hugo opined, "and for an altar of this size quite costly. The pieces of silver must be beaten thin, then heated and beaten into shape. It is a long process. I have seen something like at the cathedral in Basel, but that was a frontal and it was of gold."

"Perhaps we might discuss that, Master Hugo, if you would attend me in my lodgings sometime before Sext."

"Did you ask, my dear, what God wanted," Dame Aethwulfa would later ask the abbess.

The abbess would be curt. "No. I didn't need to."

161

5

AFTER AVERILLA HAD ACCOMPANIED Master Levitas as far as the outer court, she retraced her steps to the infirmary. At the door she hesitated. Cadilla was scrubbing vigorously at the pot that had been on the brazier. Sand littered the tiled floor. Sensing another presence, Cadilla turned, eyes black behind the light. Her voice came out a low growl, spewed from her insides with a nearly palpable venom.

"How dare you bring him here to me! I will not have such filth crossing my doorway. Jews murdered our Lord. If you care not for the poor ones who come into his evil sphere now, have you no concern for our Lord?"

Averilla narrowed her eyes.

Cadilla pushed nearer, forcing Averilla back two paces. "You think you know all about him, don't you? Look you then in the back of his workshop. Afraid to? Aye, I'd be afraid also."

"Sister, speak plain. I understand you not."

"Play not this game with me. You wist what has happened in the town by his hand. Or are you now too sanctified, spending all your days in the sacristy, your eyes piously lifted in yon great cliff of stone."

"I do know nothing," Averilla said after a moment, her voice cold.

"Ye wist well enough, though ye pretend not."

"Wist what?"

"About the child."

"The child? What child?"

"Nicholas, the miller's son. Gone missing."

"No!"

"Why say ye nay when 'tis so. He went into the forest looking for berries and has since not been seen. In June, 'twas. 'Tis not spoken of here. What means one English child to a Norman nun?

He was but the son of a miller. Of no merit except to his father and mother."

"Why speak ye to me with such anger? Have we not worked side by side many a year? Spent long nights together beside village beds? Why, you even saved my life."

"Because you will not see. You refuse to hear. 'Tis well enough known what they do. Jews will not eat the autumn-fattened pigs. Know you why? They have the succulent young children. Everyone knows. And now Savette."

"Sister! Do not even suggest that Master Levitas could do such a thing." In a hissing of skirts, Averilla turned and left the infirmary, slamming the door behind her. *Is there never a surcease from evil?* Her feet sloshed through the clods of slush. *How could Cadilla? Why?* In the distance, above the swelling grayness of the downs, the dingy gloom was being swallowed by yet another storm. Bent stalks of dried weed rose above white-clad beds. The black-gray lavender hedges were pillowed with leftover snow, and the apple trees had become nothing more than stark branches. *Do the villagers really think that?* A swirl of wings uprose from the cone-roofed pigeon house. Absently, she looked at it. On the roof a circle of birds were pecking, pecking at the neck feathers of one of their number. *Yes. That's what it is. The young ruffians in the market are just as bad. The many against the one. Do the villagers really think that? Throwing rocks at cats, tossing filth at lepers. This belief of Cadilla's is no more than that, the eternal pecking one at another. All-pervasive hate from nowhere. As Saint Paul says, "an amorphous coalescing of evil."*

Chapter Fourteen

Second Day

Mid-day before the sixth hour or Sext

I

After the nuns had left him, Hugo scrubbed his hands through his hair, giving him the look of a strange water bird, and then gave his attention to the plaster form. He could have worked directly from the slate, but it was chancy; there was too much opportunity for error. He needed to be certain beforehand of the placement of the figures. It was only a slight innovation he was now considering, but it intrigued him. The good thing about using a plaster form was that the scratch marks would fade and new ones could be superimposed atop the old without confusion. Behind Christ in the scourging, instead of a background without figures, he was intending an area that would depict those in Jerusalem going about their business unconcerned with Christ. In the crucifixion panel, it would be the horses of the centurions milling around the three crosses. Other sculptors had created similar tympanums, with hordes of "sinners" on one side of the judging Christ, and the "saved" on the other. Often in those tympanums all the figures were crowded together.

Depicting space around a figure? That was the problem. In the Kiss of Judas he would emphasize the men crowding Jesus. In that instance the whole point would be the crowd. With a start he remembered that he needed to attend the abbess in her lodgings. He hurried down the length of the oratory and through the great western doors.

"That oratory is beautiful," he would later tell Master Levitas. "Far more beautiful than I would have expected for a convent of women. And huge. Verily, an expensive undertaking. I had no idea the nuns could command such resources."

"Aye," Master Levitas would reply dryly.

Since he had just been thinking about it, Hugo paused under the tympanum, the three-tiered arch of carving that served to lintel the western doors. An unknown voice startled him. He turned. A priest was also looking up, but his gaze was directed at the twin towers that fronted the building. "Masons should have finished these towers before the cold set in. But you know these English."

Hugo turned. "What do I know about these English?"

The man was a priest, and by the fastidious look of him, the nun's priest. "That they're lazy, of course. We Normans have had the devil of a time getting anything done in this cold and godforsaken land. The Conqueror even had to bring in his own workers from Caen for the White Tower." The priest's voice drawled out the slow, affected Norman vowels. "This Last Judgment, though, is rather well done, I think. Must have been done by an imported sculptor. I've seen the like at Saint-Denis. Look at that movement." Hugo looked at the flowing robes of the various characters surrounding Christ. The lines of movement, more than the bodies or the scene, seemed to motivate the sculptor.

"It has a real flow to it," the priest continued. "Look at that hint of a knee under the robes." Hugo decided to say nothing. "A masterful bit of workmanship, I'd say, though I believe you have probably seen many such. Or created something like. You are, I

165

believe, the long-expected sculptor, Master Hugo."

"I am." Hugo forced a bow.

"I am Father Boniface, the nun's priest, lately of the entourage of Henry of Blois, the papal legate ... " The priest's monologue abruptly ceased on an intake of breath. A freezing drop of rain splatted on Hugo's neck, and he reached for the hood of his gorget as he glanced across the court to see what had arrested the man's attention.

An elderly man, ignoring Hugo and Boniface, ignoring everyone around him, was making his way toward them from the other side of the outer court.

Father Boniface furrowed his brow. "The audacity. What is he doing here?"

Hugo saw only an old man with a lichened-looking beard and rich robes in a mottled state of disarray. He glanced back at the priest.

The priest continued in increased agitation. "A Jew. What is a Jew doing in the outer court of the abbey?"

Now that it had been pointed out, Hugo, too, could see that the man was indeed a Jew. "They are everywhere, I suppose," he replied. "They were free to roam the sanctuary even during Mass at Saint Edmunds."

The priest was momentarily distracted from contemplating the Jew. "With Anselm as abbot?"

"Aye."

The priest couldn't take his eyes from the Jew. "Insufferable. Jews in a house of women?"

Hugo thought about the tract some of the monks had been reading at St. Edmunds, Isidore's *Tract Against Jews.* It seemed to be in direct conflict with Henry the First's charter protecting Jews, as well as being at variance with the monk's stated purpose of trying to convert rather than persecute them. The tract had caused much controversy.

"He's a Jew, all right." Father Boniface spoke through teeth clenched almost to grinding. "Just look at that conical cap. Keeps reason from their minds. Keeps them from acknowledging truth. Verily, I have better things to do than watch scum stumble through life."

As if their mutual disgust had solidified some bond between them, Father Boniface bowed to Hugo and started toward the gatehouse.

Hugo couldn't detach his eyes from the Jew. Nor, apparently, could Father Boniface. Hugo felt the priest still standing there, captivated like a bird before a snake. As if his thought had passed to the priest, the latter added, "Can't take your eyes off him, can you. That's the way it is, isn't it? Have to be careful not to get snared by their ways."

Disregarding everyone, or unaware, the man was continuing on his path across the courtyard. Hugo wove his eyebrows together and shook his head as he started for the abbess' lodgings, thus placing himself directly in the path of the oncoming Jew, forcing Master Levitas to make way for him.

As Master Levitas stumbled across the outer court, a few stray drops of rain splattered open on the gravel. He shivered himself deeper into his cloak, bending with the weight of the storm. "All that hate me whisper together against me," he muttered the psalm to himself, uncaring if any heard. The rain was drawing over him like a coverlet over a child, thick and cluttered and touched with gray. He felt alone and hidden. As he hunched himself along, he nearly bumped into someone. Since most who passed him took care to avoid touching him, Levitas looked up. He had never seen this man before. He looked away. For just a moment, his heart had lighted within him. He had hoped, had thought maybe, just maybe, it was one of his friends.

"But of course it wasn't," he would later tell Hugo. "Bitter, though, to have that momentary hope."

"Please ... " Master Levitas said, moving to the left to let the other pass.

"Watch out!" Hugo yelled and moved to his right, unwittingly maintaining the impasse.

Master Levitas swayed, and the man's huge hand shot out reflexively to steady him. Feeling the cold wetness of his cloak as the hand pressed it against his tunic, Levitas shuddered.

"Which way?" Hugo's irritation was clear.

"Of course I was surprised that you were speaking to me," Master Levitas would remember.

Not looking Hugo in the eye, not answering, Master Levitas passed to the left. As he continued through the outer court, he slipped on a pile of manure, wet and slick from the drizzle. He heard a crack, his ankle turned, and he crumpled yet again, catching himself with his injured hand. Pain zigzagged up his leg from his ankle and he looked at it numbly. He tried to rise, but the pain savaged him and he groaned aloud.

From a long distance above him, as if he were in a well, he heard another voice. "Get him out of here, carver. I don't care if you have to carry him. He has no place here."

Master Levitas felt himself taken firmly by the elbow, lifted up, and then hauled like a sack of beets along the path next to the church. He hopped as best he could, using the toes of his foot for balance. Few others were about; those who were made way for them. At the East Gate, without being asked, Master Levitas pointed down toward Gold Hill.

2

JARED CROSSED THE ABBEY DEMESNE FIELDS. The ridges were black and sharp against the snow that lay in the furrows, as if a cat had clawed the landscape. At the edge of the woods, the dried yarrow held pillows of snow, and eels of snow bedecked the branches. As

Jared moved farther into the trees, the snow became sparse. Periodically, he came upon the marks of deer's teeth on the trunk of a tree, and fallen branches seemed more obvious, clothed with ridges of snow. Near a beech, he saw the dainty track of the fox, but the prints soon disappeared in the bare spot under a fallen log. Gillingham Forest was no longer the place he had known in summer and fall. It seemed an entirely different wood. Every year it changed, and every year the change surprised him.

In his own life, too, everything had changed, literally everything. *What was black is now white,* he thought. *Finally.* The thought of Savette, like a moth around a flame, kept flapping against his mind, interrupting any other train of thought. *I cannot think on 'er. I cannot.* Nonetheless, he kept peeping into the locked box of his mind, until suddenly he could see only the color red mingled with a ghastly whiteness. Determinedly, he pushed it down. *The steward. It was Master Chapman 'as started the changes. Looking at me. At the end of the harvest. Sly at first.* Jared had been aware of a feeling, but had ignored it. Later, during the grape harvest, as he had hefted a basket of grapes into the wood-staved vats where the maids squished the slurry between their toes, he had turned to see the steward frankly observing him, eyes appraising. Clearly, Jared had been meant to notice, so he had gritted his teeth and bowed, close to mocking, just on the fringe of civility. Surprisingly, the steward had smiled.

Choosing to treat the scrutiny as if it meant nothing; as if the other man was merely interested in seeing to the crush, Jared had concentrated even harder on bantering with the girls and slicing through the cloying coils of Savette's gaze. He remembered the drunken sense of recklessness with which he had even flirted with Damasa, Master Chapman's own daughter, let out of her bower for the day, her plump calves reddened with the grape, her pale cheeks flushed with exertion. *Exercise be well needed,*

169

Jared remembered thinking, *spoiled, pampered brat she be,* and he had bantered with her brashly, despite her homeliness, and to spite her father, *who doubtless has great plans for her troth.* In essence, Jared had treated her as he did the other maids. She had blushed in answer.

That night, after too many draughts of the new ale, Jared had even taken her hand in the dance, so eager was he to avoid Savette. *Savette was like a weight tying me to a slavery of unending and backbreaking toil; she 'as kept me from entering the Church.*

It wasn't until the rains of December, and after Father Merowald had died, that Master Chapman had spoken. "The priest," the steward had said, hooking his thumbs under his belt, "had plans for you, I warrant." Chapman had looked levelly at Jared, eyes glazed as flint. "You aren't still seriously considering the Church, are you?"

Jared had been tempted to turn on his heel, but the man's look had held him.

"Now that the priest's not pushing you, there may be a place more suited to your, um, talents than the church. There are other paths."

Jared had stared back at this man with his wide nose and close spaced eyes. Curiosity prevailed. "Aye?" Jared had not looked away.

"There is another way open. You could take it. It's the way I took." Jared's eye flicked over the fine leather of the man's boots, the embroidery at the bottom of the long tunic. Master Chapman noticed the look and smiled. "I, too," he said, "was educated by a priest. But the Church was too, um, too confining. Particularly after Lanfranc."

Celibacy. Master Chapman is speaking of celibacy, Jared remembered thinking. Archbishop Lanfranc had enforced celibacy on the clergy. Jared had felt the heat rising from neck to face.

"In brief," Master Chapman had continued, "my needs were

for warmth of a night, in my bed, so I took the easy way. I rec-
ommend—for certes, I will make it possible—for you to do the
same. The knowledge you have, the knowledge that the old
priest poured into your head, is as valuable as, if not more valuable than, gold. Rare it is. Few have such learning, Norman or
English. During the time of Alfred the Great, it is said, everyone
could write. But 'tisn't the case now. Not the Roman script. Not
in Latin. Or English, though mostly it has to be in Latin. I write
for the abbess. And see to the other matters that the nuns can't
attend to, locked up and preoccupied as they are with the 'other
world.'" Jared felt a tremor of shock and excitement at the other
man's obvious sarcasm. "There is a need" Chapman continued,
"for someone to attend to such matters, not just for the nuns, but
for others in the county. The times have changed, but the Normans are still preoccupied with their horses and their battles.
Those who are adept as I—and you—can easily find a place.
The old king, Henry, took men like me. Made them his. He was a
wily old bastard, and knew where the power was." Master Chapman tapped his head. "He wanted men's minds. That, my lad,
is where the power now lies. Not in the Church, not in slapping
your sword against another's chain mail. It is here," and he again
had tapped at his well-cut hair.

"Not the Church?" Jared gaped.

"No. Wetting his plump lips, the older man leaned confidingly
toward the younger. "I have watched you. A life without women
is for a dried stick like that old priest, with no more juice in his
loins, not for a lad like you. You need a woman. Mayhap more
than one. It happens."

*Of course it did. Everyone knew that. And so what if you were
caught—a fine at the worst. King Henry had twenty bastards
or more. And look at his eldest, Robert of Gloucester. Not only
respected and rich, but in command of the armies of the empress
in this stupid war.*

171

"So, I suggest that you consider an alliance with my Damasa."

Jared's mouth dropped open.

"She likes you."

Ugly, pasty. Fat legs.

"You are kind to her."

Chapman's only child. His only heir. Has no other children, nor even any bastards.

"It would be no skin off your back."

Kings and queens did it all the time. Arranged marriages. For political reasons. Didna they say the empress 'ad been forced, when she was just a bit of a lass, to bed an old man four times 'er age—Holy Roman Emperor tho' 'e be. Then, when 'e 'ad died, even then she 'adn't got to choose, but 'ad to marry a lad, years younger.

"I could teach you what I know. You could take my place here at the abbey, or move farther along."

But there were others, weren't there, for Damasa to marry? Surely.

"The sheriff has need of such men, as will Stephen after this tiresome warring is done."

Mayhap there be no suitors waiting for her. Chapman is English. Of course. No Norman wants an Englishwoman of no beauty and small dower. Then, like thunder in his brain, it was clear to him. *He can't find a mate for her.*

"You could be trained. A clerc, man, not a cleric. An amazing amount of difference, that." Chapman had then made a circle of thumb and forefinger, sliding the forefinger of his other hand back and forth within the circle. "Start out as assistant to me, assistant to the steward of the wealthiest abbess in the land. Then ye'd be in the way of knowing people, Normans. Not a Norman yerself, but ye'd be useful. And rich."

Above all, rich.

172

The smell of Savette came to him as they stood there talking, and the memory of their lovemaking. A molten fire ran through his veins and shuddered down his body.

Master Chapman's gaze hadn't faltered, and he, as usual, missed nothing. "Damasa is knowledgeable. Understands that a man needs to have other ... outlets. Just give her an heir or two and she'll be happy."

Chapman would allow him mistresses?

"Of course, one needs to be able to afford those other outlets."

"I — I 'ave plighted my troth," Jared had blurted out.

Master Chapman feigned surprise. "For a good fuck? I 'ad thought better of ye, lad. Well, no matter. When you tire of her, I am sure that things can be arranged. I could manage a small ... "

"No," Jared had said, binding what dignity he had left around him. "I can't do that. No one knows because I — we — her ... " his voice had broken and he had not been able to continue.

"Surely she will want the best for you, boy. Merely explain it. She will see.

"She wants to marry."

"She will. She will. Just not you. And when she does marry — and plenty have certainly looked appraisingly in her direction — you will be in a position to make life easier for her. Something you couldn't have done," he pursed his lips and paused, "can't do without the right position. It is your choice, of course." Chapman had given him an oblique smile, nodded, turned, and left.

He could now, even with the early morning pain of her death, feel the rage that had then gripped him. *Why did she make me decide? Eve. She was like Eve. With her smile. Trapping me. Her smell. I was no more than a moth in a web.*

He had thought Savette had loved him, thought that she would understand and release him from his plight troth. Now, like the traitor it was, his body flooded his mind with images of Savette;

he saw the sun glinting on the soft down at the edge of her jaw; saw the curve of her mouth as she welcomed him.

He shook his head. It had been so easy to convince himself that, in his new position, he would be in the way of helping her. *Her and her new family. And her husband.* It made him feel ... large ... to think of what he could do for her. *Small favors to start. If her — their — children were sick, he could help. And they would continue to meet. It's done all the time.*

A hare poked its head out from a thicket of holly, but the wind was behind it. No matter how it twitched its sensitive nose, it could not smell him, could not understand the singing whir of the sling. It was over in a second, the rock arcing true. Only the smallest scream from the little throat. Jared picked up the soft, limp carcass.

All she'd had to do was to let go. Why hadn't she seen that? She didn't need to die.

3

BY THE TIME THEY HAD SLID AND CAREENED and sloshed their way down Gold Hill, Master Levitas was surprised to see the small flecks of soot before his eyes again. "Something's burning," he muttered. "But it is too late for Allhallows, isn't it?"

They came to a stop in front of a house with wide overhanging eaves held up by horizontal timbers, the branches of pollarded oaks, uncut and with bark on. Swinging above the door were the three balls of a moneyer and a sign painted with a unicorn, denoting that the man was also a goldsmith. In cities such as London or Winchester, the numerous mints were palisaded fortresses. Those holding the king's license were empowered to change the coins every few years in order to keep the value of the thin, malleable silver pennies constant. Here in Shaftesbury the moneyer's house was undefended — strongly built on a stone foundation and with a heavy iron-banded door — but nevertheless unassuming.

This is indeed my door, Levitas thought as he staggered against it. *Isn't it? Rebekkah will help me. No. Rebekkah is dead. Who is this man? Never seen him before. Someone Isaac knows? Mayhap. I should be polite. One never knows who it is one is entertaining. Why, Abraham entertained angels. This man has an unlikely appearance for an angel, but who knows?*

He looked sideways at Master Hugo and drew himself up.

"This is my home. I bid you welcome to it." After fiddling successfully at the lock, the goldsmith seemed exhausted. He pulled at the latchstring and tried to bow Hugo into the room, but his too-weak legs would not hold him even that far and he sprawled across the threshold, twisting as he scrabbled frantically at the doorjamb to hold himself upright.

The goldsmith's shop occupied the entire front of the house, the door opening at the uphill corner. There seemed to be no shutter that could, when opened, convert into a table for trade, and Hugo assumed that the goldsmith's clients were expected to enter the shop. There was one window — glazed, amazingly enough — under which stood the goldsmith's table. Next to that sat the small furnace, a cleverly designed fireplace set into the wall. Hugo had not seen its like for safety or for the cunning way in which the bellows were mounted at the goldsmith's left side. The "T"-shaped anvil was mounted on the table, part of which was covered in wax for creating small decorations to be affixed to the finished pieces.

A smell of damp mixed with a lived-in, unaired smell assaulted the two men as Levitas found the strong hand again holding him up. A fit of coughing shook him and he staggered toward the workbench.

"Broken, I am afraid," Master Levitas croaked, pointing to his leg. As Hugo knelt beside him another spasm of coughing sputtered out.

Irritated at this maddening Jew, at the loss of time, at the freezing rain, Hugo perfunctorily felt along the bones. "'Tis already swelling, for certes, but there is nothing spoilt. It can be wrapped. You could see one of the nuns?"

"No, no." Levitas' face was gray. "Not after this morn."

Hugo looked at him uncertainly, and then nodded. "As you will. I can do it well enough, I suppose. Have you linen? To tear?"

Hugo found a chainse or under-tunic hanging on a peg and started ripping the fine linen with a malicious energy, half enjoying the destruction. He felt gingerly along the bones and, as he started to wind around the ankle, said, "It isn't broken. I can tell these things. Have seen one that was." He watched the goldsmith's face, trying to gauge whether the wrapping was too tight, careful despite his eagerness to be gone.

The old man locked his jaw.

"It cracked," Levitas said after a moment of heavy breathing. "As I tripped."

"Cracked?"

"Aye. Heard you it not?"

"I assure ye, 'tis but wrenched."

Once the ankle was bandaged, Hugo stood to go.

"I have not" Levitas wheezed "a morsel of meat to offer you." There was a pause while he took a wheezing breath, "but if I might persuade you to tarry awhile, there is some wine."

Hugo gave a perfunctory nod. "I am else needed." He turned to leave.

"I must thank you," Levitas mumbled. "Your kindness. Very kind. If there is any way that ... "

Hugo hesitated. "It's nothing." He looked around vaguely and added, grudgingly, softened despite himself by the man's plight, "You are the one in need of wine and warmth. Have you a servant to help you?"

"No, I—I ... " Master Levitas shook his head.

Hugo paused, stooped to the hearth, and threw onto the embers a small bavin of mixed kindling. Seeing a flagon of wine on another table, he grabbed the first thing that came to hand, a huge silver goblet, and poured. Master Levitas tried his best to hold it, but his shaking slopped the wine all over his tunic and mantle. It took both hands, and Hugo's guiding, to raise the goblet to his lips. As he drank, the cup tilted and a tiny dribble oozed down his beard.

"You have succored a disagreeable old man. Why?"

Hugo looked at Master Levitas, whose thin lips were curved into an impossible smile of grief and irony, as if he hoped for one answer but fully expected another.

"Why?" Hugo held himself in and made a gesture of negation. "I know not. The priest told me to. You would not have made it." Grudgingly, he looked around. "If I had seen this afore," his arm encompassed the room, "I might have saved you for the sake of this."

"Ah." Master Levitas' face registered several emotions, finally ending in a raised eyebrow. "Though none would save me for myself, at least there is one who would save me for my work. I thank you."

The man's ironic gratitude nauseated Hugo, who responded through gritted teeth, "I'm sure you have seen better physic," and put his hand on the bolt of the door.

"Don't go."

Hugo paused, his back to the man.

"As you have saved me for the sake of my work, I will show it to you."

Hugo turned, curious despite the nagging appointment with the abbess. He had seen the workplaces of many craftsmen, knew of their tools, but this man was a true genius. Among the orderly tools were one or two examples of his art. Hugo looked curiously at another goblet standing alone on the worktable, seemingly near completion. He had heard, as had everyone, of the goldsmith, Matthew, who was creating an altar frontal for the abbey at St. Alban's. Hugo himself had seen the incredible work done under Abbot Suger at Saint-Denis in Paris. This goblet was all of that and more. It was filigreed, gilded, adorned with pearls and cabochon gems all over its base, lip, and handles. It was meticulous, painstaking, and glorious. The filigree alone...

Master Levitas' voice, now somewhat stronger, startled him. "The gold comes from coin, as you know, I am sure. Bezants hammered into sheets. Most of the silver, however, comes directly from the Rammelsberg mines above Goslar."

"And you, you... created all this?

"Does that seem so incredible to you? That a Jew can create?" He held Hugo's eye for a moment and then said, "Please to put it down, now. I am not up to rescuing more than one goblet in a day."

Hugo glanced at the goldsmith in surprise. "When you said that," Hugo would tell Levitas later, "I discarded all thoughts of giving you any further help. All I could think was, no wonder there was no one else to help you."

"Don't bother to deny it." Levitas said as Hugo replaced the goblet. "I know in what respect Jews are held."

Then, as if giving a lecture to an apprentice, and at the same time putting the goblet next to him out of harm's way, he changed the subject. "The real experts, of course, cut both cameos and intaglios and polish cabochons. I myself cannot. But since the Crusade, there have been more than enough cut gems — rubies, sapphires, emeralds, even turquoises — coming from the east to satisfy the open gorge of the West. They are brought through Venice."

Hugo crossed to the man's workbench, "I was so hungry after my travels," he would later explain, "for talk of shape and form and beauty, that I was ready to put up with anyone who would talk to me of them, even you. That and the fact that you were the most incredibly skilled goldsmith I had ever seen. Not humble, mind you," he would say with an oblique smile, "but..."

Hugo continued to finger the tools while he admired the finished pieces. There were the usual tools: tongs, the length of a forearm to stretch metal; hammers for beating it into shape, and four chisels, of varying sizes, for engraving. Saws, files, and another pair of tongs with cruel pointed ends hung by size neatly against the wall. Pincers, rasps, a chasing tool, and a scorper; all were there. Master Levitas seemed to be working on a piece that looked like golden ice and held in its depths the rays of the sun.

The older man interrupted Hugo after a moment. "So, you are to create a reredos for the altar in the reliquary chapel. This abbess is not only a gentle woman but a fair taskmaster. Most in the area are beholden to her. A commission in someone's memory, if I remember aright. The name "Master Hugo" was spoken of, and in great respect. I have not seen your work."

Hugo was still entranced by the piece on the workbench. He said, as if talking to himself, "Since you are forbidden graven images, how do you work for the abbey?"

"I do not create any images."

"I see. But some of these ... " Hugo picked up a lavabo with an image of Christ on it, "have images on them."

"I repair them. I righten them. I make none myself. What pieces I do make, such as that goblet with the beads around the rim, have no images." He added, the wine having plastered two round red circles on his cheeks, "The organum that made those beads is new. Have you seen one? It can make these gold beads as round and as perfect as, as berries. No, I make no images, you see, but designs. Even the people who inhabited these isles from the dawn of time bided by that rule, contented themselves with the swirls of infinite truth ...."

Hugo dismissed the comment with a shrug. "There is no purpose to those designs. They do not lead the viewer closer to God."

179

"Is that what you aim for? Is it not for your own fame that you create? Is it not to be known for what you have done?"

Hugo stared at the audacity of the man. "I couldn't believe you had said that," he would tell Levitas later, "after I had just saved — well, helped — you."

"Look at that goblet," Levitas said, oblivious to the insult he had handed Hugo. "It is meant for the Bishop of Winchester. Henry of Blois has the whole treasury of Winchester to draw on. Look closely at it."

Hugo had been doing just that. He now took it in his hands and walked to the light of the opened window. The cup was two-handled and wrought of gold on a gently curving foot. Around the conical base, various gems and pearls had been planted in an intricate filigree of beads and twisted wire.

He turned his head, his awe heartfelt, "This you made?"

No images danced around the goblet.

The other nodded. "But none shall ever know my name with it. Only that of the Bishop of Winchester. A gift from the nuns, but even that fact will be lost in time."

The base was shiny, but the lip was encrusted with jewels.

"It is magnificent." Hugo crossed to the workbench and gently replaced it. With your ability, why do you remain here? Shaftesbury is not ... "

Master Levitas touched one of the tools near at hand, slightly arranging it, his eyes pooled by sadness. "The abbey provides work, mostly repair, but often enough work of creation." His voice held a combined note of despair and resignation. "In many monasteries, one of the monks will be the goldsmith, having a shop near that of the abbey blacksmith for fear of fire. With a community of women, a rich convent of women, there is the need for a smith with my skills, near but not within the enclosure."

Hugo said, "I wonder that they chose not your skills for this reredos."

180

"The patron had heard your name spoken. And a work of that magnitude is not for one of my age. I am beyond that. I find myself breathing hard when using the bellows." There was grief in Levitas' words.

"As I was leaving Saint Edmund's," Hugo said, "another commission came to me. From Saint-Denis. I took longer than I had expected in getting here, and I would hate to lose the chance to be at Saint-Denis. You know how long it would take to mould a reredos? Such relief work is intensive. You have already a furnace and a workshop. I have my anvil with me, but no furnace, of course. I could work here with you. Would you be willing to help me?"

Master Levitas didn't answer at once, and in frustration, embarrassed to have opened his need to this man, Hugo said, "Well, anyrood, I shall take my leave of you. Your skill is great, but," he said raising an eyebrow, "I cannot believe that you take no pleasure in your creations."

The old man's eyes had lightened. They took on a faraway look. "A reredos of silver. It's been a long time since I had thought of a commission that large."

Hugo was heartened. Perhaps the man might take his bait. Carefully, he avoided mentioning the figures. "I have seen your candlesticks."

"Ah, yes. Of those I have pride."

"You should."

Hugo bowed again, just slightly. Later he would tell Levitas, "It was a bow for your artistry only, and in spite of your arrogance." Master Levitas would then reply, "But the arrogance was well founded, was it not?" Hugo would laugh. His hand on the door, Hugo now added, "I have an apprentice with me as well, a lad for the bellows."

"When I left your house that first time," he would later tell Levitas, "I couldn't believe that you were goldsmith and moneyer. You hadn't mentioned the moneyer part when you gave me all those fine words about graven images. Notice ye not that on every coin you struck, you struck a graven image of the king?

At first Levitas would be offended, and then he would chuckle. Last, he would say, drawing himself up on his fine horse, "But you see, it was not I who engraved the dies." Then it would be Hugo's turn to laugh. "And anyway, I changed very few coins in Shaftesbury."

CHAPTER FIFTEEN

SECOND DAY

MID-DAY AFTER NOON, SIXTH HOUR OR SEXT

I

nxiously, Master Hugo hurried up Gold Hill from the goldsmith's. Helping Master Levitas had deterred him from going directly to the abbess. Had he left enough time before Sext? He hoped so. Having recently experienced the administrative rigor of Abbot Anselm at Bury St. Edmund's, he was more than a little concerned to have kept such a woman waiting. Presumably—she had hired him, after all—she had heard of his work. Might not his fame grant him a certain leeway?

He thought about it. At St. Edmund's he had illuminated six full pages and thirty-eight initials in the Great Bible; no small accomplishment, as that Behemoth measured more than two and a half feet high by one and a half wide. Abbot Anselm had been horrified when Hugo, "this artisan, this carpenter, this workman," had insisted on traveling to Scotland for vellum that was smoother, softer, finer in grain. "Needs to be from animals exposed to severe cold." Hugo had had that kind of familiarity with Anselm. Both had been, at one time or another, in Rome; both understood excellence. Mayhap this abbess would also understand, and pay for, excellence. Mayhap, like Anselm, her thinking of Hugo as a mere worker would meld into something akin to admiration. Anselm had allowed Hugo freedom of mind and soul. Mayhap she would as well.

After the Bible, he had cast a beautiful little bell, and that had led, in the way of such things — to the completion of probably his greatest work — the casting of a pair of great bronze doors. There was a similar pair of doors in the Ottonian empire — actually those he had cast at St. Edmund's were copies, in essence, of those he had seen in Saxony — but his bronze doors were the only pair in England and were universally considered a marvel. Abbot Anselm had so wanted those doors. "You shall create for me some gates," Anselm had mused, eyes never straying from the illuminated pages of the Bible, "to show the cellarer why I pay you so much, to show him why I send you to Scotland for vellum, why, in a word, I put up with you. Never in this breath-stabbing land will they have seen such doors as you shall make for me. The doors shall be like those at Santa Sabina in Rome." Anselm had not seen those in Saxony. "But unlike those in Rome," Hugo had interrupted Anselm, catching the thought and bettering it, "which are of wood, these I make for you will be in bronze. The images I shall carve will never be blunted; will be graven forever in the minds of this people."

Perhaps Hugo might carve out with this abbess such a mutual respect, despite his lateness.

When Hugo finally puffed his way to her lodgings, the abbess smiled at him with genuine warmth and made no mention of his tardiness. She motioned him to one of three armed stools and, raising an eyebrow, said, "The dog is settling in well, I hope?"

He gave her a serious nod, and found his every anxious thought relaxing. "That he is, and the donkey, too, my lady. You have yet to meet the donkey, but I warrant you would find him a warm companion."

184

Her eyes became suddenly serious. "I would meet him. I shall make a point to so do. Unfortunately, I don't think I would be allowed to ride him. It seems that even though a donkey was good enough for our Lord, 'tis not good enough for the dignity of the abbess." She said it so dryly, and it had come so quickly that Hugo was taken aback for a moment. "Does that not strike you," she continued, "as somewhat strange, that my office should grip me with such tyranny that I am forbidden movement except by dictate, that I am bidden to assume those very trappings of which our Lord most disapproved?"

None of the monks Hugo had met at St. Edmund's had prepared him for this abbess — certainly not Anselm — and Hugo's eyes kindled at her chosen humanity. "Christ," he responded matching her irony with his own, "is always so pleased with the proper trappings of office."

It was Emma's turn to start at a dry wit. Her eyes widened and then she laughed, her head thrown back in real mirth.

Hugo allowed himself a wry twinkle.

"This dilemma," she continued after a moment, "is ever with me, and not a boon companion, like the donkey, but a devil I struggle against. She sighed. "It's insidious. Power can woo you into believing you deserve it; that the obeisances made are to you, not to the Lord you represent." She stopped and gazed over his head. He turned to look. A plain crucifix, made from two twigs lashed together, hung against the wood paneling. "I shall make a point at least to speak to the donkey. His name?"

"Bithric."

"Ah, yes."

Silence lay over the room. Both were comfortable with it. Finally, she placed a hand on one of the long account rolls that lay on the table between two intricate silver candlesticks. "I am in the embarrassing position of having to alter the terms of our agreement. It seems that you have been bidden here falsely."

185

Hugo looked at her levelly, a sliver of hope — and fear — igniting within him. "You do not require a reredos?"

"We do." She forced herself to hold his gaze. "But we can no longer afford the silver."

"Ah."

The monies that should have purchased the silver have been spent. It would — I cannot — I realize you have come expecting to use your skill in a medium worthy of it, and now ... " embarrassed, she faltered. "Our former abbess," she tried again, "spent lavishly in rebuilding the oratory. Vast sums. The monies needed for the building were far greater than our income. I had no idea. None of us had. We thought the money had come from her sister, Amabel of Gloucester. Or the king. It had not. Dame Joan, the sub-prioress, borrowed as the abbess asked her to, didn't question the abbess' needs. She couldn't have, of course; it would have seemed disobedient. In addition, we have forgiven our tenants much in tithes and rents. The drought, the war, the increasing hordes of poor — "

"Lady, I cannot work for free."

Abbess Emma sighed. "Of course you cannot. Nor do I ask it. What I ask of you, Master Hugo — what I must have — are suggestions for a less costly way of creating this reredos. Perhaps a less costly material? I would have the brilliance of your work. It is well heralded."

The room was silent. The bellow of a cow needing to be milked and the tinkle of a far-off bell floated up to them.

"Mayhap ivory."

"Lady," Hugo started, measuring his words, "be glad that the reredos was not to be carved in ivory. Although the men of the sea are finding more and more walrus on the vast stretches of northern ice, ivory is still very dear. You have perhaps seen ivory carved. It is beautiful used in the crozier of a bishop or in small pieces on the cover of a Gospel book, but a reredos? It would

186

take an enormous amount of ivory. The price would be a king's ransom."

Emma turned so he would not see her face. "We have a piece of oak."

Hugo could feel the grain of the wood under his hands, and, to his surprise, the feeling was not unwelcome; indeed his fingers itched for the feel of a fine piece of oak. "A piece of wood well carved is no disgrace." His eyes took on a foreign look. "There is a cross at Saint Edmunds that I carved, for the retro-choir. It is in wood. It was the first thing I did for them and was dedicated by Bishop Albericus Hortiensis. It is much revered, loved, even," he paused, coloring just slightly beneath the weather-worn cheeks. "I understand not why. Mayhap the agony the Man endured . . . " There was a longer pause. He cleared his throat and said, finally, "A wooden reredos could be gilded or painted later, or there could be inlays of silver if your bishop, your ladies, or your saint need such glory. I doubt our Lord does." Again Hugo colored, feeling as if he had presumed. He looked up to find the eyes of the abbess on him in consideration.

When she turned her attention back to the rolls of parchment, Hugo knew it was a moment of dismissal. She smiled as she looked up. "John the Mason can be found in the mason's yard between the north porch and the transept, or someone there will know where he is. It is he who will have Dame Anne's oak."

Still, Hugo didn't leave. He stood in front of the door, facing her. She raised her head to him, the look of embarrassed concern still paramount. "I would be less than forthright were I not to tell you that this need of yours allows me the sooner to get to Saint-Denis, where I am eager to practice my skills. I was restless with the length of time I foresaw with this your commission. Be not heavy of heart, lady; you have done me a favor I little expected and which shows me in no favorable light, perhaps, but so it is."

CHAPTER SIXTEEN

SECOND DAY

AFTER MID-DAY AT THE NINTH HOUR, OR NONES

I

After Hugo and Ralf had eaten a midday meal — dried pease pudding, cold boiled bacon, and oat bread — instead of entering the church, they entered the side yard between the north porch and transept, an area called the mason's yard, where they had earlier seen the men shouldering the rock. Despite a roof of rods and hides, the recent snow had made the ground in the rectangular yard into a morass of muddy ice and gritty puddles. John the Mason was not hard to spot, taller than all the rest, and he answered their arrival with nothing more than a curt nod and a bad-tempered scowl.

"John the Mason?"

"Aye, Master, and ye be?" He glanced warily at Tindal, who returned the look.

"Master Hugo. The abbess ..."

"Ah. Well met, well met." The mason wiped his hand on his leather apron and extended it to the carver, his eyes lighting. "Good to have ye here. Long anticipated have ye have been, and well heralded. I heard tell of yer treatment yester e'en. I apologize fer that. The maid we sought was found this morn, soon after daybreak, dead by the stream. She was a fair maid and well liked."

"I am sorry to hear it. I had hoped . . . "

"We all had. For the nonce, mayhap, least said the better. You have a need of me or my men?"

"Aye. The reredos for Saint Edward's altar? 'Tis to be carved in wood. Mayhap later 'twill be gilded."

John shrugged. "Ah, well. As the abbess giveth, it seems, so she taketh away. 'Twas a miserable harvest."

"Umm. Well, she offered me a piece of oak. Said you might know it."

There was a slight hardening of John's jaw.

Hugo tried again. "'Twas from the home farm; a staddle of great age, came down some past winter. Half of it has been aging."

John took a deep breath. "Aye, Master, indeed it is a fine piece. I had been saving it to replace a post that went rotten in the dovecote. Though, in truth, 'twould have been wasted there. I was loathe to use it thus, 'twas so fine a tree. You are welcome to it."

As the mason spoke, he led them farther into the yard, dodging between the men working on stone with mallets and chisels, and two sawyers hunched over a saw pit. He stopped beside a stack of timber.

At John's bidding, half a dozen men hefted out the piece of oak. When they had laid it in a cleared space, they all stood regarding the remains of what must have been a very old tree.

"It must have been huge," said Hugo.

Though the trunk was not more than eight feet in length, the oak, when whole, would have been at least three feet across. The main branch, still attached, angled off to a length of four feet.

John pointed at the squared-off end where the root should have been. "As you can see, it has no longer the widest part. Blacksmith wanted the root stump for an anvil base. The abbess gave no direction else."

"I could not have used the stump," Hugo said absently, eyes lighting as he scrutinized the length of barkless log. Few blemishes were visible. "I had little hoped for a piece so fine."

"As ye say, a staddle. From afore the Conquest, I warrant."

Hugo could feel Ralf's eyes on him. As John turned back to his men, Hugo whispered. "Staddles be trees left when all around be cut. I'll only need a big slab from one side of the center, and two smaller slabs from beside it."

John nodded. "Just the one side, lads, is all 'e needs. This side o' the core."

"Two feet wide for the big one; less for the others. About so long," and Hugo held his hands about a yard apart.

John relayed the order. "Master, if there be naught more … " Already the men were settling the log for splitting. Hugo nodded his thanks and John hurried back to the center of the yard.

Two men clambered atop the rootless trunk to position the wedges. Ralf stood fascinated as they drove wedges in along the half tree. "They call this cloven work," Hugo said. "Not sawn, but cloven. Like the devil's hooves."

With a rhythmic series of blows, the men forced the wedges deeper and deeper. The sound of it was much like a musical scale, the notes mounting higher and higher, until, with a sudden flat drop, the tension was broken and a large piece was split off the core. "Never want to carve wood from the center, lad. Core tends to expand and contract with moisture, ye wist, and then, when what ye're carving dries, pop, an arm or leg falls from your carving."

Hugo advanced toward the slab. Measuring with his hands, he said, "Here be all I need," and he drew with his finger where he wanted them to slice off the piece he wanted with the adz.

190

WHEN HUGO AND RALF RETURNED TO THE CHURCH, few sounds disrupted the quiet, which absorbed even their gritty footsteps. A door reverberated hollowly as it closed, but the silence merely rippled with a hiss of movement as another opened. Then, once again, a lone voice arced over a note. Like spring rain, other voices embroidered a veil of sound around it.

Nones, Hugo supposed. He seated himself at the bottom of a stone pier and motioned Ralf to stay where he was. *Wood. Back to carving in wood again, like a peasant before a fire. At least it will be quickly done, and my fine tools will not be harmed — at worst, dulled.*

Tindal, beside Ralf, trampled out a spot on the floor, turning three times around before plopping down, his eyes slowly drooping shut. *There is something about these women,* Hugo thought, watching the light slash amber pockets in the stained glass. *Didn't think they'd be this way. Truth to tell, never thought about them much at all.* An image of Dame Averilla followed that of the abbess across his mind's eye. *Strong, that's what they are. Comfortable in themselves. They fit their bodies.* He smiled. *How could praying make you comfortable in your own body? Particularly when celibacy allowed only half a life?*

He fixed his gaze again on the small altar in the saint's chapel, trying to fit in the shapes he wanted to carve there, trying to watch them emerge. As the music eddied around him, he remembered a font he had once seen. He wanted to try to create movement above this altar of the nuns, an undulating continuity of images. He felt a buzz start in him, like that of a bee, just beneath his breast. It was a long time since he had been given such a freedom in creation. These nuns were going to let him do just what he wanted.

"Takes patience, lad, this art of carving." Hugo whispered as the nuns filed out by way of the abbess' door. *Why am I trying to teach the brat?* The words had seemed to just dribble down his chin before he had even thought. "It's a question of taking away. Some might make a study piece, a practice piece, to show where the dragons be." Ralf's eyes widened. "Not real dragons, lad. Problems, ye wist, errors ye might make, but I be well versed in such doings."

They watched as several men lugged the slabs of wood up the aisle to the chapel.

"Well," Hugo mused, peering at the grain, "if it had to be wood, nothing could have been better than a great hunk of oak, hard and dense and readily cut." He ran his hand over the slab. It had not been planed, and ridges, the fibers of the wood where it had parted from itself, made a pattern. "'Tis called the 'grain,' lad, of the wood. Always carve with the grain. Or try." Hugo flipped open the flap covering the tools. "Need to be able to read the grain," Hugo continued softly, aware of yet another file of pilgrims coming up the side aisle behind Dame Celine, "to anticipate the need to change the method, the tool, or the tool's angle. Always run the tools with the grain. When ye have to cut across the grain, make cuts lightly and with a razor-sharp tool.

"After ye have the design in yer mind," Hugo moved over to the plaster, "ye try to match it up with the piece. Now this piece be shallow, not much more than a handspan. I can carve, ye see, but not deep. Those in the south of Italy, where the pope is," Hugo watched Ralf's face for some spark of recognition of any of his words. "Well, no matter, I worked there for a bit."

Ralf's face remained blank.

Why am I talking like this to him? Have done since this morn. Hugo shrugged. *Doesn't understand a thing I've said. Nor is he interested.*

After more than two hours of quiet, the only sound the gritty movement of the pilgrims and the patter of their muttered prayers, the only light that of muted cloud shadows against the floor, Hugo looked up from his work. For the past hour, Ralf had been handing Hugo exactly the right tool, only needing to be told once the name. Hugo now chose a thin "V"-shaped tool. "Called a 'veiner,' this is, or a 'fluting tool,'" and swiftly he started to scribe a series of running cuts. "Just to get the outline in." He worked quickly, placing a line here, a squiggle there, "to make sure that it squares with the shape and the size of the wood."

"Call this 'bosting out.' Then more running cuts for the detail with the ... ?"

"Veiner," Ralf said obediently, his elbow on the end of the bench.

"Aye." Hugo gave him a considering look. "Or ye can call it a 'paring tool.'" An idea passed through his mind and he straightened, giving full attention to Ralf. "Place 'em all out for me." When that was done he added, "Pick 'em up one by one and tell me their names."

Ralf parroted off the names, stumbling now and again, and then stopping altogether mid-row. Ralf held up a long, curved gouge.

"Aye, I haven't told ye that 'un. That be different. A longbent gouge, for bottoming off the background. That next be a spokeshave. Aye, handle that 'un with care, 'tis very sharp, like a razor. Used to pare off bits of waste stock. And those be rifflers," he pointed to rounded files, "for planing off inner curves."

3

DAME AVERILLA AND DAME JOAN had stood obediently, like two stranded ducklings, in the mason's yard, watching with increasing degrees of dismay as Dame Anne's oak was further split. After Master Hugo had gone and the men had removed the pieces he wanted, John the Mason came over to them, taking in the heavy aprons draped over their habits, and the white linen protecting the ends of their sleeves.

Trying very hard to keep his face straight, he said, "When the abbess told me that she was wanting the rest of my staddle for a reredos in the choir, I fought with her, ye wist, as I wanted to use this side of this great tree in the dove house. Truth to tell, I had wanted it all, but ..." he lifted his hands in mock despair, trying to induce in these two some release of the palpable tension surrounding them. "So, we — she, actually — decided that the two of you will work with that which be left. Master Hugo took what he needed." This last was spoken over his shoulder as he led them into a relatively quiet space at the rear of the yard, tucked under a thatched overhang. "I wot the abbess understands little of what she asks of you, so I decided that you two will saw into lengths these two large pieces." He motioned at two large chunks of wood.

Between the two pieces lay a saw, a thin sheet of iron held between rounded handles of wood, straight teeth gleaming along the edge. "I had the saw newly sharpened." John continued handing them an as yet unrecognized gift, for he liked Dame Averilla. Dame Joan, formerly so bossy, seemed to have turned as mild as a lamb after the events of the fall. He smiled to himself, knowing that they little knew how frustrating a dull saw could be.

It was a huge piece of wood and Averilla's heart misgave her. Joan bit her lip.

"We are to saw that?"

"Aye. Into lengths."

"What will they be used for?"

"The abbess said she would have it for panels in the frator. Perhaps carved, later."

The task seemed insurmountable.

John turned and left them to it.

A look of fear passed over Joan's face. She was short and round

194

and given to the joys of the table. Her skin was pale, with the texture of a very smooth cheese. She shook her head. "I have never worked with my hands. For that we had servants. Here, in the abbey, mine has been the province of study and the account rolls and—"

"And rules."

Joan looked up, a flush of anger forming along her cheekbones. "Aye, Dame. Rules are oft needed for those in the community who seem to think they need them not."

It was Averilla's turn to look angry, "Which end do you choose?" Averilla asked, trying to sound forgiving, but managing only a surly growl.

"Whichever you do not want," Joan replied sweetly.

"Well, then, we shall each take the side closest, and switch when we tire. I know not how—despite my Englishry, I've never done this afore, either," said Averilla, faltering. She glanced toward the men in the yard, but none seemed to be paying any attention to them.

"Oh, really," said Joan, pinching her lips. "I have heard it told that you know how to do almost everything, that your old nurse would take you out and teach you all the woodland lore..." Joan paused, looking at the stump, tapping it with her hand, "or," raising an eyebrow, "if you didn't know an answer, you could just..." and here, Joan, not daring actually to say the words, raised her eyes and steepled her hands in a look of pious supplication—"and then the answer would come."

"How dare you?" Averilla growled. "You were the one who trafficked with a witch, nearly bringing a sister to her death..." Averilla's eyes were trembling, her hands shaking.

Joan took a step back. "I didn't know..."

"Nor did you pause to think."

There was a silence between them. Both sensed that to go further would leave nothing unsaid.

195

Finally, Joan sighed. "I think it would be best if we just try to get this done. We are never going to agree."

Averilla nodded, "Should we ask one of the men?"

Joan took a deep breath. "I think we are meant to learn — together. I think the workmen have been ordered not to make it easier."

Averilla looked over at the men and nodded. Bending over, she picked up one of the wooden handles, surprised by the weight of the saw. Joan lifted the other side, and together they managed to place it atop the block of wood. Their first attempt at moving the saw gave them an inkling of what they were up against. The metal would not catch; they were too short to be able to get any leverage.

Joan glanced around. A pile of stone, dressed for building, was stacked nearby. She motioned, and together they hauled two of the blocks over, so that they could stand above the wood to get some purchase.

"I think that when one pulls, the other must push."

"Then you push toward me first."

They tried, but the blade bound, making a mere scratch on the surface.

"Mayhap just guiding."

"Which one of us guides?" Averilla's upper lip was already beading with sweat.

"You said," she guided it as Joan pulled it, "that you have never done any work like this."

"Not I," Joan snapped, but they were managing the beginning of a small indentation with a little sliver of sawdust on the top of the log. Averilla pulled and Joan guided. The blade bent again.

"Too much pressure."

"What I was going to say ... " this time Averilla guided, but again the blade bent. "I am no better than you are at this." She jerked her end of the saw up and out of the furrow. "I was going to say

196

that I cannot imagine that the abbess has ever done this, either."

They worked for a few minutes, stalling, binding, and then, finally, when there was a small furrow, easing into a rhythm. After the stops and starts, the success was so refreshing that before they knew it they had sawn two inches. Averilla stopped, wiped her brow, and looked over at Joan, who was forced to stop as well. Joan's face was red and her wimple was askew, but she had a look of determination about her that was somehow endearing.

Joan raised her eyes, saw Averilla's half-placating look, and breathed deep. "I shouldn't have said that ... about your nurse ... or your prayer. I—I still don't think. I am too quick to judge." She made a halfhearted smile of camaraderie.

Averilla nodded. Surprise and shame left her speechless.

She put her hand back to the saw and waited for Joan to get her grip. After another few pulls, Joan stopped. Averilla looked up. Joan was waiting, but her look was unreadable, not judging, just giving Averilla a chance. The longer Averilla waited, the worse it was going to get. "I ought not have said that about you. It is not my ... place."

Another two inches.

"Remind me, Dame," Averilla said, lifting a hand from the wooden handle and looking at the blisters starting across the redness of her palm, not daring to catch Joan's eye, "what this has to do with Christ?"

Dame Joan was gritting her teeth. "He was a carpenter?" she panted.

"That may be why he spoke ... in short sentences."

"Because he had no breath left."

Averilla dropped her end of the saw, leaving it wedged in the wood, and flopped down onto the dressed stone. "Do you suppose we have to finish the whole thing? Don't you think we have bonded enough?"

There was an unusual glint in Joan's eye. "Aye. But the abbess

197

would have us finish this task and I am determined to so do."

"I admire that in a nun."

Joan giggled.

"Your wimple is askew."

"When you are quite finished with describing my habit, come back here and help me finish. If you haven't noticed, I can't do it on my own."

Averilla sighed, pushed herself to her feet, and resumed her place. "Are you sure you don't want to rest? You seem a bit red."

"She said to finish—"

"You need to rest—just a bit—perhaps splash water on your face."

Pushing the saw, Joan replied, "I used to be so precise in following orders. Mayhap now, instead of following the abbess' order to finish, I will go to the wellhead and get a dipper of water."

When Joan returned, Averilla, realigning her hands on the saw and pushing again, said, "I think that you were really right about the rules. I ended up in much more trouble than I would have imagined the breaking of a few—"

"No." Joan pushed back, her face grim. "I was too inflexible. Benedict commands moderation."

Having waited all day to find out, Dame Aethwulfa asked the abbess that evening, "Did your experiment work with the two recalcitrant dames?"

The abbess allowed herself a self-satisfied smile. "When I left them, a bit before Vespers, they were halfway through the second piece. Their hands were bleeding, but both had affixed a wood chip to their girdles. 'The order of saw,' they told me, their eyes alive. Yes, thank you. I listened for guidance as you suggested. It seemed an absurd trick to play on them, but yes, I think it worked."

Chapter Seventeen

Tuesday

Before Vespers, about four o'clock
in the afternoon

I

The shadows had lengthened when a long and mirth-ridden laugh clattered into the silence of the oratory. Hugo started, startled, and his hand slipped, just a fraction, but enough to slice a crooked gash into the side of the arm he was carving; not just any arm, the Man's arm, our Lord's arm, lifted in healing over the missing ear of the servant of the high priest. "'Sdeath. What in the hell?" An interior thunder surged through Hugo, blinding him, and he flung his chisel toward the creation-numbing disturbance.

They weren't hard to find, rolling on the floor of the transept just beside the foot of the north pier. They hadn't even noticed the thrown chisel. Ralf was giggling helplessly as Tindal licked his face, hands, neck, and eyes with the loving intensity of a bitch cleaning her pup.

Hugo grabbed Ralf by the hood of his tunic and hauled him up, hand under the boy's chin, heel pressing gaggingly at the

199

small nub of his Adam's apple. Then he heaved back his rage-bent hand, to stifle the giggle from the red mouth, to squash the swiftly receding glint from the gilded eye. In the instant it took his arm to retreat, something grabbed it, vise-like, piercing as a sharpened dagger. Blunt pain ground up along Hugo's bones, and he jerked his head to see what held him. The steady yellow eyes of barely tethered ferocity glared back, and from deep within the depth of his chest, Tindal growled. Hugo yanked and twisted his arm, releasing, in the process, his hold on Ralf. The iron pressure increased, sharp incisors tearing his flesh.

"No," Ralf's voice cracked. The yellow eyes wavered, unsure. Again the boy's command, his voice stronger now, "Down." With a nimble grace, Tindal lightly let go of Hugo's arm, the saliva still tying the two together. Tindal sat, eyes still locked on Hugo, the menace implicit.

Hugo, like a cat, self-justifying, bent to pick up a stray splinter of wood. "Don't ever," he said, "startle me like that." The words were vomited from deep within him, spewed one by one as if it hurt to utter them. He stomped back to his workbench and slumped on the stool, fists dangling. "The arm of Christ was ruined," he would tell Levitas. "The focus, the one place on the whole panel that couldn't be hidden or touched up, ruined. I thought I would have to, at the very least, rework the whole panel." Now he sat there rubbing at his slathered skin, absently noticing the blue-black dents slowly welling with blood. "And I would have hit Ralf hard enough to deafen him," he would continue.

WHEN HUGO'S SISTER, PASTHEEN — everyone called her Pasha — when Pasha's cardinal had called Hugo south to Rome, he had taken the commission gladly. It was in Rome that it came to him that other people didn't seem so consumed by their work as he was.

Pasha had laughed about it with him once; she a woman of the world and, as was common in Rome, spoken of as a "friend of the cardinal," a cardinal whom Hugo deliberately chose never to meet. That day, Hugo had been explaining to Pasha that it was important to him to be on time. "A matter of honor," he had said.

She had turned abruptly from pouring a cup of wine and then laughed aloud, "On time?" she had hooted. "You? On time?"

He had drawn himself up stiffly, wrapping around himself whatever dignity an older brother has left in the eyes of his younger sister. "Yes," he had said. "I am never late for an appointment. It really is a matter of honor."

Seeing that he was serious, her eyes had mellowed. She took a sip of the wine and let it settle on her tongue before saying, "Perhaps you are." Instead of saying more, she had moved the dish of olives, redolent with garlic and oil, a little closer to him.

From then on he had watched himself from afar, as if he were someone else. It was true what he had told her; he saw that he was on time for his appointments with those seeking to buy his work or to commission it. He saw also that he was not so particular with regard to other, more personal, engagements. Why, he had just barely managed to arrive back in England to see his own father before the man died. It had seemed at the time only a few days since he had last seen the old man. "It's been two years," his brother had spat as Hugo caressed the leathered skin of the limp right hand.

With consternation, Hugo had mumbled, "I—I didn't notice the time. My work..." But, Hugo found, he did lack consciousness of time. Even though they were both in Rome, months would go by between his visits to Pasha. "I was working," he would excuse himself.

One memorable time she had given him another long look and said, more than asked, "You lose yourself in it, don't you?"

201

He had known that it was true. He often found that he had forgotten to eat as he sat carving; that without knowing he had done so, he would have lighted candles and lamps, sometimes placing them in queer corners or high shelves to cast light on what he was doing.

"It obsesses you." She alone had understood him, and she alone accepted him for who he was without blame or recrimination. It was a gift she had given him, this knowledge of himself, this recognition that when his mind was entangled in creating, the creation itself usurped all the rest of what made him a man.

The worst part of remembering it now was that it hadn't bothered him. The finality of peace, the aloneness, the lack of interruption had seemed blessed.

Oh God, he thought now, *help me with this boy. I cannot seem to keep myself from doing that which I don't want to do. Let me not drive this boy away.*

2

AS THE BELL RANG FOR VESPERS, DAME AVERILLA stood next to the laver, her face, hair, and arms dripping from the wash she had just given them in the trough. Dame Helewise tapped her on the shoulder. Surprised, Averilla justified herself to the younger woman: "I am afraid I badly needed a wash after my time in the saw pit."

"I am to tell you," returned the newly professed nun, her open face showing some concern for her former superior, "that Dame Alburga has prepared the church for Vespers, so you are not to worry." Averilla raised an eyebrow as she toweled her hair with the rough wadmal that hung above her place at the tin-lined trough. "And that Sister Cadilla asks that you accompany me to Lovick's house with these." Helewise opened her scrip to reveal two wax-covered pots. From her time in the infirmary, Averilla knew what they contained.

"The abbess excuses us from Vespers?"

"Dame Helewise nodded.

"Seems odd that Sister Cadilla comes not on this errand," said Averilla as they slipped out the postern gate beside the main gate and hurried down the Bimport.

"She said that Dame Aethwulfa required her," Sister Helewise responded. "But being from the town herself, one would imagine … " Helewise left the comment hanging as they drew near Lovick's house.

The two hesitated before entering. Harsh, grating sobs spilled through the doorway. Townsfolk crowded the smallness of the cottage. Like a hive of bees, they whispered, mumbled, and crooned to one another with an anger and shock against which Lovick's agony crashed like blows on an anvil.

As the nuns entered, those in the rear parted. Averilla made her way to the bier, knelt on the packed dirt, and waited. Finally, Lovick lifted a ravaged face, his jaw set in a line that softened when he saw the tears brimming in her eyes.

"May we help prepare her?"

Lovick looked at her as if she were speaking in a foreign tongue, and then shook his head. "Nay, Dame, though I thank ye. The women of the town … " and here he gestured vaguely at bent forms quietly watching and tending to small duties, "have had the honor. Their last gift to the dead child."

Averilla nodded her understanding. "We have brought some balsam and oil of rose. The abbess sends them. She was a good maid, Lovick Borack's-son, and will be sore missed."

Averilla finally looked down. The girl looked peaceful, and no smell had started; the cold water and January weather would have helped. The women had washed the body and laid it in a linen shroud from which only the head and chest with the crossed arms could be seen. The deerskin, which would be sewn tight before the burial and after the Mass, was folded beneath the linen, making a kind of nest. The girl's lips were blue, but other than cold, her face held no expression. *Had there been any expression when she was found? Probably, and probably erased by the kindness of these women or the dissolving of the rigor.* Averilla looked for the ring. Neither hand wore the ring Savette had shown her, nor did any ribbon nestle along the hollow of her neck. *Savette showed me a ring. Where did it go?*

Averilla turned to one of the women. "How happened it?"

"They wist not. Her clog was off, and her beating paddles nearby. Mayhap she slipped on the bank, or caught her foot in a root, hit her head and drowned."

Averilla leaned over the girl. The bruise where she had hit her head was on her temple. It was jagged, and washed clean of blood, but with the blueness of swelling beneath it.

"Dame?" Hearing the voice with half her mind, Averilla turned. One of the nearer women bowed awkwardly, her coif slightly askew. Averilla knew her: she was the wife of the man who slaked the ponds. Elfgiva was her name, after the English queen and another of the saints honored at Shaftesbury.

"There do be other bruises." Elfgiva kept her back to Lovick and spoke in a whisper. "Poor mite bashed her head. 'Neath her hair in the back be a great hole. 'Tis covered by the hair. Cleaned it be, 'cept for tiny bits of gravel. Seemed mean-spirited to bother Lovick with more misery."

The woman went on in Averilla's hearing but not into her consciousness. *A great gash on the back of the head? More likely that killed her than the gash on the temple. If it had, then how had she hit her head both back and front?* Averilla furrowed her brow. "In the back you say? A great gash?"

"Where?" The voice was an anxious rumble in Averilla's ear.

Averilla hadn't noticed Simon's presence next to her. *Did he hear Elfgiva.*

His voice was hoarse. "On Savette? Another gash?"

204

Averilla said, "Aye. In addition to this on her forehead."

While speaking, Averilla gently lifted the girl's head as if smoothing the hair, and probed a gaping wound that yielded its spongy matter to her touch. "Aye, 'tis true." She wiped her hand, surreptitiously on her scrip as if looking for more unguents. "On the back of her head."

"Two wounds?" Simon whispered, barely able to speak. "Front and back? How can that be?"

"Unlikely a second, grievous wound in the back of her head, a killing wound from a mere slip and fall. I wonder if perchance this be other than a mere slip on the bank."

"What are ye hinting at, Dame?"

"I wot not." Averilla rose awkwardly from her knees. Taking Simon's arm, she moved him out of Lovick's hearing, toward the back of the house, where the beasts were penned in a byre. The smell of cow was warm and clean after the cloying closeness of the front room. "Savette showed me," Averilla whispered to Simon, "a ring that she wore on a ribbon about her neck."

Simon looked startled. "What ring? I ne'er saw such. It must have been hidden. Was it under her gonelle?"

"Aye."

"Think ye she was robbed? That this is the work of the outcasts from the forest?"

Averilla shook her head. "I know not."

The women were gently anointing the body with the unguents she and Helewise had brought.

"I would rest easier knew I that she had placed the ring I saw elsewhere."

"You think she was pushed and it was stolen?"

"Mayhap."

"That would explain it, outcasts who wanted the ring. With winter on the verges, there is little eno' for those in the town, much less those in the forest."

"Mayhap. Wist thou whence came this ring?"

"I never saw it, know naught of it. Mayhap our mother?"

"There was no young man who could have given her a token of affection against the day of betrothal?"

He looked confused. "You think mayhap it was not outcasts, that there are others who would have hurt her?"

Averilla made her face bland. She could not reveal the secret of the babe. Not yet. "Because there are two wounds, I suspect that it was no misstep that took her life. Until we know where the ring is, I will wonder if it be not the cause of her death."

"Who would care other than an outlaw?"

"Seems not like, but perhaps one of the women coveted it, was at odds with Savette, or sported mischief against her."

"But, Dame?" His face crumpled into a rictus of unshed tears, "How could such a one have an enemy? She war," his lip trembled, "she war light, and spring and pure like — like the brook. The lads all loved her. Everyone did." His previous self-control settled back on him with the speculation. "The lads all saw that light in her, like a moonbeam it was. She was just coming to the time of betrothal. There was Jared paying her court this summer, but 'twas no more than calf-love. It would not 'ave done for a betrothal. Fader would not 'ave had it. Though he be friend to Todd, Jared be slippery, ye wist, like an eel, ne'er to be relied on past his own willingness. Fader was waiting for it to cool, and cool it did during these last months. Jared wants more, I wot, than the life here. Like his moder, he wants more. I have seed him taking note of others."

"And after Jared, there was no one else for Savette?"

"No one. Some tried, but she was like a bitch in heat that won't settle for any other. Aye, she was grieving Jared's loss, but it would have eased in time. We war as glad."

"If it were Jared's ring, Simon, that she showed me, I would rest easier knew I it had not been taken."

206

"We can look through her things, little though they be. Won't take long."

Averilla watched as Simon started searching through the barrels and pottery jars that held the grains and flours away from mice and worms. Soon, one of the women asked her a question about the laying out, and Averilla was distracted from Simon's search.

Awhile later, Simon came from behind her again. "Naught to be found. I looked in all the places she was wont to go. Even the midden in the back, and the pen for the pigs." Averilla had already known that from his smell.

Averilla said nothing for a moment, then said, "I bid you send someone to fetch the bailiff. I think it would be best if Robert Bradshaw saw these gashes, to decide for himself. Probably the ribbon just frayed, but it is gone. If there be outcasts with evil intent, we need to know."

Chapter Eighteen

Tuesday

After Vespers, near Sunset

I

It was misty as Jared made his way back across the fields, the hare hanging from his belt. The smoke that had already started to rise from the cottages was tipped yellow from a setting sun barely able to lance rays between black and gray clouds. The water of the fishponds was purple with the waning light, and Jared's feet squeaked with the chilled snow of evening.

As he topped the rise on Tout Hill, he saw Todd and a few others heading down the High Street toward the blacksmith's. Their arms dangled heavy, and they seemed deep in conversation. He didn't want to see Todd — they were probably heading to the carpenter's, where the 'town coffin' was kept, used and reused on the day of burial for those too poor to afford one of their own — but he did want to see Savette, just to make sure.

A scrap of black cloth fluttered on the door of Lovick's house. Two men from the garrison, one on each side of the door, stood alert. *Too late to turn. They've seen me. They suspect something. He licked his lips.*

"Bailiff called?" Jared asked, nodding at the door. The men looked at him skeptically. Unsmiling, one said, "Some'ut amiss. Bailiff's with the lady abbess, so Tom came in 'is stead."

Amiss? Jared frowned, then bent under the lintel to enter. The room seemed dark to him, dark and alive with the smell of perfumed water and oils.

Her body. Savette's. And his babe. She who had been was now being prepared to become a rotting mass of… bitter, hot vomit surged up his gorge. He stumbled back out the door, turned, and retched, tears filling his eyes, cold sweat starting.

There had been the sound of mourning when he first entered the house, but by the time he reentered, his every step fell into an eerie and hostile silence that lay like smoke between him and the bier. Jared glanced around. Two nuns stood to one side. He thought one was Dame Averilla. Father William sat on a three-legged stool beside the old man. Lovick himself was rumpled and stale with strain. His red-rimmed eyes peered out blank and bewildered, childlike in surprise and a mute, animal agony. Tom stood on the other side of the old man looking grim. Savette, though, lay composed. He'd seen her thus, in the slanting afternoon light, after the harvest, but this, this wasn't she, somehow. Not Savette. Someone else. Like, but not… He shook his head to rid it of the image. It wasn't she.

2

As soon as Vespers ended, Dame Edith hurried over to the north chapel.

Oh, Lord, why now? Hugo thought, his head still hanging between his knees. *Can't they just leave me alone?* He remained seated, eyes on the floor. *Maybe she will just go.* She *whoever it is* stood for a moment behind him. He sighed and rose, trying to compose an ingratiating smile, fishing for polite words to feed her.

209

When he finally turned, he saw, to his relief, not just any nun, but "Innocencia." He bowed slightly. "Dame Edith, I believe."

The red rose over the alabaster of her face in a broad and swift flush. "Sir, I meant not to disturb your concentration. I know how precious are your times of carving."

He tried to smile; knew it was probably a grimace. "It is no trouble." *And actually,* he surprised himself thinking, *it isn't. With this nun.* His smile relaxed a little as he added, "I had hoped you would come."

"I?"

"Aye. I would have your counsel on this that I have so presumptuously started." He turned back to the carving, sure, matter-of-fact. Edith moved close, her residual shyness replaced by interest. She leaned forward, the better to see in the sallow evening light, then glanced swiftly around the walls of the chapel and up the piers. "You need more candles," she snapped. "Particularly as evening falls, and probably during the day as well. The few windows in here are so obscured with color that it must be impossible to work in such light. I shall have it seen to."

He smiled at her intensity.

As she returned to examining the carving, her face assumed the mien of an astute housewife bargaining with the fishmonger. Eyes darting, she studied first one aspect, then another, comparing, judging, voicing funny little words now and again. "Ah, yes," she said finally. "I understand now even more fully. What a remarkable construction. Can you accomplish it?"

He smiled. Here was an honest assessment indeed. "I hope so, Dame. I too would like to see it accomplished."

With a sigh, he turned to examine the beginning of the carving. Unconsciously, instinctively, his eye traced the ghost lines he had etched onto the third panel, studying the relationships of mass to mass, height to angle, curve to curve, weighing, sorting, judging. The mutilated arm continually drew his focus, as a sore

210

tooth draws the tongue. The arm, not just any arm, but the arm of Christ, extended, with ultimate compassion, over the head of the servant of the high priest. *A man with no ear. Cut off by Peter's stupid and heedless act.* Dame Edith said nothing about it. She didn't seem to see it.

Hugo scratched his beard, pretending to study the carving. And then he looked at it, really saw it with new eyes.

Maybe it isn't so obvious after all. Maybe not entirely without redemption. Might be able to make it right. His eyes narrowed. *That arm, the Lord's arm. Not so bad, actually. Had it been a trifle static before? Not that most people would notice, but maybe it had been a bit, well, limp.*

"When I work, I draw but small images, mere tremblings around the letters, the better to make the words have meaning. I — I know not what it is that comes to my hands, or why."

He turned back to her, interested despite himself. "You illuminate Psalters for the abbey to sell? Is it not so?

"Oh, no sir, not to sell. The aim of this labor is quite different. The meaning of the words in the Gospels is a changeable thing; it changes for each of us with our growth and understanding. 'Tis, I imagine, like seeing a star, or — or a crystal." Her face furrowed with enthusiasm. "Every side of it gives a new reflection. I saw a crystal once. When you looked from one side you could see through it, and from another, things were transfused with light and so transformed, that, well, you understand. So what I draw, perchance without comprehension, may bring new insight to another in the community, mayhap not even in my lifetime, mayhap some unknown down the ages shall see my small scratchings and by them come to understand that needful thing that she knew not before."

Hugo leaned back against the chapel wall and crossed his arms, concentrating on her words and thus forgetting to pay, through word and stance, the deference due her.

211

"So your drawings and," he motioned to the windows, "the glass, even my carvings, are intended to increase the understanding of a particular passage? Is that it?"

"Yes! Yes and no. Or," here she blushed again, "or only part. You see, ofttimes we will take a word, one word, from the Gospel, and think on it for many hours. To hear the passage being read at Mass is not the all of it. We try to hear only one word from the passage, or perhaps a whole phrase; something that leaps out to us that we had not understood before."

"Is it different each time?"

"No, not always. An individual spirit might perhaps tangle with one word for many years, until the meaning becomes clear to her, or an understanding meant specifically for her journey of faith becomes bright. It is different for each of us, but as I work, I try to create crystals of possibility that can open the prayer more fully for each of us."

"For understanding?"

"Not only understanding."

"Then what? Is there more?"

She smiled at his question, a soft intimate depression of her eyes. "That, sir, is the great secret. It is not understanding alone that we strive for. Were it only understanding, were we only exercising the brain, it would be a dry exercise indeed. No, it is a oneness for which we strive, a putting of ourselves inside the heart of God. The peace of such resting is bliss; some would say ecstasy. It is that which keeps us here day in and day out, and for each it is different." She held out her left hand to him and, with the right hand, pointed to the slim gold band on the fourth finger of the left. "We are brides of Christ in the intimacy of our relationship with Him. John speaks of it in his Gospel, and it is indeed true. The unencumbered bliss of being with, or in, our God." She paused, thinking. "It is this peace that helps us to become more than we ourselves alone can be. It is the oneness with God that enables

212

us to love even those who are rather unlovable. Answers come to questions we didn't even know we were asking. Oh, sir." She blushed and pressed her hands against the heat of her cheeks. "I am talking more than I have in a year. Forgive me." Edith ducked her head and started to back away.

"No." Hugo reached out a hand but stopped short of touching her. "Wait just a moment. Your drawings help this communion with God?"

"That is my hope. It is our presumption. Some in our community have certain images that they keep in their stalls," she gestured vaguely toward the choir, "or in their places of sleeping, in the dortor. These images help them to slide quickly into thoughts of God. One may cling to an image for her whole life and it seeds her meditation."

The deep tones of the great bell, Dunstan, thundered from far above and to the west of them.

Edith started. "I must go." She turned toward the choir, but, seeing something on the tiles, bent to retrieve it. "How lovely," she whispered. "Where does this go? Where does it fit?"

Hugo frowned. "What?" he said, and crossed to where she stood by the pier. She held in her palm a bird, just lifting its wings for flight, carved with enormous skill, the few strokes catching the essence of the effort to lift free.

"I did not carve that."

"The lad is very talented."

Hugo glanced over at Ralf, sweeping with more than his usual concentration. "Er," Hugo said and lifted the bird from her palm, "so it would seem."

3

THEY ALL WATCHED AS THE EMOTIONS crowded one after the other across Jared's face. He took Savette's cold, limp hand, and, holding it tenderly, like a bird, bent as if to kiss it.

Always the smooth one, Simon thought, and scowled.

But Jared stopped mid-bow. His brow furrowed, seemingly in real consternation. He held Savette's hand away from him, examining it. There was a scrape on it. The women had noticed it, like the head wound, but assumed it was the result of the fall. Sensing his agitation, the woman closest to him put a hand on his arm. He shrugged off her restraining hand and shoved Savette's unresisting hand toward those crowded behind him. "This? What's this? A cut. See ye?"

"Poor wight," the women crooned to calm his close hysteria, "perchance broke her fall . . . "

Tom, lips curved in a jagged line of loathing, strode around the bier, impatience tugging at his temper. He caught Jared's upper arm, his grip fierce, yanked the younger man back, and in a grating whisper said, "'At's eno', boy. Have a care for the old man."

"No. No, look." Jared struggled. "At her hand."

Tom ignored him and continued to try to pull Jared away from the bier.

"The lad's right," another man muttered, crowding closer. "There do be some'ut on her hand."

Tom stopped and bent close. "Aye." Then, more slowly, pondering, "Aye. 'Tis not a bruise, I think. Too clean, not jagged from a rock." He took the hand. "Be a cross, or like enough. Carved onto her hand." The line of the cut was clear, washed cold and blue, but it was there. It wasn't just a bruise or a scrape.

As those in the room elbowed closer, craning to see the cut, Todd pushed open the door to the cottage, accompanied by those others who had gone to the carpenter's. Propping it open with one shabby booted foot to make way for the coffin, he absorbed the altered atmosphere and looked around, bewildered, not sure exactly what had changed. Laying the small end of the coffin on the sill of the opened door, Todd glanced warily toward the corner where Lovick still huddled.

"Wha?" Todd's voice was hoarse.

"Come 'ere," Jared lifted the slight hand, little bigger than that of a child. Those in the cottage made way as Todd pushed through. "See. We thought just a bruise, but 'tis not. Some'ut else." Todd bent to look and then turned toward Jared. Jared held his gaze.

But it was Simon, not Todd, who shouldered past the nuns and grabbed a fistful of Savette's hair, yanking her head from the bier. "See this," he snarled at Jared, lips over teeth, and pointed with his chin to the back of her head. Caved in, the back of 'er 'ead is. Go ahead—look at it. Put yer hand in. Feel what used to be love, and—and … "

Jared dropped the hand and tried to back up, but the crowd held him where he was.

"What's a scratch to such as this? How came ye to see that was a scratch when no one else did? Were ye going to tell us of this great gaping hole, too? Swine. Had to make sure, didn't ye, that she was good and dead. So ye bashed in her head." He wrenched the head toward Jared, trying to push Savette's hair into his hands.

Jared jerked back, the stronger of the two. Heaving, his eye-teeth bared in a wolf snarl, he growled, "I had 'na cause to kill her. Ye know that well. But more than that, why would I carve a cross onto her hand? Why would I profane the body of a dead woman? There is no point. If ye be too crazed to believe my love of her, at least believe my love of Him. That ye all have long known to be true."

No one later could remember who first spoke it. Someone in the crowd whispered into the silence, "Bloodsucker." And then louder, until it could be plainly heard, "The Jew."

215

Jared's jaw hardened. From somewhere came the hollow words, "Remember? That babe in the forest a time ago?"

"Aye," grudgingly. There were nods.

"That be the Jew, from another. "They do that."

"So what was there to keep 'm from pushing 'er?"

"The Jew 'a pushed her?"

"Came back later—for the blood."

"Maybe took it already. From the cross on her hand."

"Aye."

The black scrim of anger roiled from grunted questions into bellowed threats.

"Not here," Father William bellowed, his voice surprisingly loud. He glanced at Lovick and thumb-gestured toward the door. The muttering subsided as the men self-consciously shuffled their way to the door.

When they were gone, they left a hollow silence. Lovick looked around at the priest and the women, bewildered at the sudden exodus.

"Some think the Jew may have murdered her," soothed the priest.

"Master Levitas?" Lovick's voice was querulous.

"Aye. The symbol on her hand. See, 'twas drawn with a knife, methinks," the priest continued patiently.

"But I thought Jared," complained Lovick, unaware of Jared's nearness. "Why would the Jew?"

"Murder? I know not. 'Tis said by many that they," the priest jutted his chin in the direction of Gold Hill, "that they, er ... " Having a hard time bringing the words up, he looked over at Dame Averilla for help. Averilla found her hand over her mouth in appalled consternation. She shook her head at Father William, bowed, and together she and Helewise left. Finally, he spewed the words out in a croak, "that they eat Christian children and virgins. Suck their blood."

216

Jared, ignored after his initial discovery, blundered outside to retch again, violently, against the side of the house. A rib-sunken cur sidled over and sniffed. Jared stumbled past it, wiping his mouth. At the sound of voices coming from the Bimport, he veered, eyes now hard, fondling in his pocket the brooch he had taken from Master Levitas.

4

WHEN EDITH LEFT, HUGO CRADLED the sparrow in his hand. Thoughtfully, he laid it beside the panel. As he retrieved the linen dust sheets, he reexamined the arm of Christ.

Hadn't really been the hand of a carpenter. Not before. And now, with that gash? He lifted his own arm, slowly turning it before his eyes, seeing it anew. It was rounded. The skin, pocked with hair, was laid over a strong intertwining of muscles. *The arm of a carpenter. An arm of used muscles. A strong arm.* He hadn't thought of Christ that way before. *Certainly the Man wasn't a starving or emaciated leper. A strong man, a workman.* The gash he had sliced with the chisel was now a line of muscle that mirrored the muscle in his own arm.

Made right by God. Hugo rubbed his forehead. *Stupid. Heedless. God, forgive me — the boy. I—I almost hit him, could have killed him. Lord have mercy.*

A refrain trickled into his mind. "Burnt offerings have no value to me, but a humble and contrite heart." *Yes, well.* He rubbed his arm and looked around for Ralf.

The sweeping had stopped. The tools had been wiped with oil and aligned, their sharp edges facing the same way. Ralf sat beside the pier, tense, eyes wary; stone itself.

"Come 'ere, lad," Hugo said gruffly.

Ralf approached hesitantly, avoiding Hugo's eye. Tindal followed close, eyes vigilant.

"Glad you brought the dog," Hugo said, rolling the pouch of tools.

Ralf shot Hugo a startled look. As no words followed, he pretended to scrutinize the panel with much the same intensity and focus as Edith had. His paused to finger a rough protuberance marring one of the hooves of the centurion's mount.

"Ye wist some'ut about carving?"

Ralf flushed. "Aye. Only animals, though: cows, pigs, horses, and such. Did a badger once."

Hugo uncurled the fingers holding the sparrow. "This bird?"

Ralf hesitated. Hugo could see it. Trying to choose. Which answer did Hugo want? Ralf looked down. "Aye."

"Myself, I was never much good with horses, or animals of any kind, actually. Ye see the problem of that hoof. My difficulty is," he turned from the panel and pointed to a place on the plaster, "I've a passel of horses in this center panel. Behind the cross. Behind the Christ. Horses all over the place. Here, here, and here. If I try to carve 'em, I'll spend more time than I want. They won't come out right." He jiggled the carved bird in his hand. "Not like this sparrow."

Ralf assayed a glance at Hugo's face.

"You might try yer hand at one o' these horses," Hugo continued. "One toward the back."

Ralf didn't answer. His ears flushed and he fumbled his hand along the chisels. Hugo nodded. "Mayhap this 'un here at the top," and pointed to the partial silhouette. Ralf glanced over once more, picked out two of the finest chisels, and aimed his sight at the panel. Ralf's eyes never wavered—for him, Hugo had already left.

Is there anything valuable in the act of creating? Hugo wondered. *Maybe Dame Edith is right: I am engraving images and my pride is in them. I would 'ave killed the boy for pride in my own creation.* Hugo pulled up his hood, pushed open the door

218

of the north transept, and slipped out, heading for the loft above the stable. *Best leave him alone with it. I'd just meddle — tell him what to do.*

5

EARLIER, DAME AETHWULFA HAD LOOKED at the shadows playing on the walls and known that it was time for Vespers. She had been enclosed for so long, she didn't need the bells. But, she thought, as Dunstan boomed out over abbey and town, *Ah, there he is now.* It gave her a feeling of comfort; the regularity of it. *The absolute consistency. No, constancy. That was it. Really that was the most important of the vows that Benedict granted to us. Constancy. In this world of change, one can rely on the constancy of the community. One can rely on the others to remain in the abbey, to abide by the rules. Or to try. They would always be there to live with; to grow with.*

Her musings were interrupted by the soft whish of the infirmary door. *From the village?* she wondered. All of the nuns would be hurrying toward the abbey, walking past the laver or down the long walk of the north cloister. Dame Averilla would have lighted the candles. *I would like to see Dame Averilla; talk to her.* The old lady felt a tinge of sadness. *Mayhap, when the sorrow of leaving her duties here has worn off. Mayhap then it will not be so painful for her to come here.*

"Sleepest thou?"

Dame Aethwulfa's eyes flew open as a cool hand caressed her brow. "I must have dozed off, my lady, for I thought I just heard Dunstan —"

"You did just hear Dunstan. Well, a bit ago. Vespers is still being sung. I —I must deal with something terrible: Dame Averilla just told me they are accusing Master Levitas of killing Savette. There is so much I must do. There is the bailiff to tell and — dear Master

219

Levitas, I fear ... "

Aethwulfa's eyes narrowed. Every nerve of her being had been twanged by the desperate words just uttered. She tried to keep her voice noncommittal. "Vespers is being sung and you are ... ?" She couldn't finish the question. Inconceivable.

"Here with you."

You think I need you, The old lady thought. *But what you really need is God.*

"They can sing the office without my presence. Surely the community became quite competent at so doing all the years Cecily was so often entertaining."

And you don't hear the bitterness in your voice as those words issue from your lips, do you? Surely you can see how shocked I am.

"I need your counsel, Dame. I feel lost."

"You have another to turn to."

Emma disregarded the words as if they meant nothing.

Chapter Nineteen

Tuesday

Supper and evening collation

I

Supper was always a sparse meal, particularly in winter, when provisions were scanty at best and the cook's temper testy because of her inability to provide adequate nourishment. This night, as they stood before the laver, pulling their towels from the hooks assigned to them and washing in the water from pitchers, Dame Petronella muttered, "They say in Canterbury that the water flows through the laver, is pumped into it." Petronella's brother was at Canterbury and she was rather proud of the fact.

"But they have running water, Dame, a stream from which to pump water. We do not." Dame Alburga hated to be reminded of any fault in their foundation.

The nuns filed into the frater in order of precedence, and the nun assigned to read for the week mounted the steps to the pulpit raised above their heads. Currently, the readings were from the desert fathers; there was a certain humor to those writings that added zest to the meager meal. The servers placed a trencher of bread before each nun and then ladled a hearty pottage of beans, lentils, and winter vegetables onto it. There was a rather disappointed silence as they all looked at it and waited for grace.

Into this silence the first rumblings from the market made themselves heard. Low at first, no more than a passing cart, but then louder, fraught with something brutal and frenzied, the rhythm frantic.

From the head table, the abbess loudly intoned the grace and then deliberately sat down and signaled the reader to begin.

2

As HUGO LEFT RALF IN THE SILENT CHURCH, the long shadows of the brode hall melded together into that gray opacity that is neither night nor day. Cooking smells came from the guest hall, and he felt his stomach rumbling, but past the guest hall he could hear someone yell, followed by a roar of massed voices. Curiosity overcoming hunger, he squished across the muddy graveyard and out the east gate. Already, several torches had appeared, lighting the sweaty faces and gleaming teeth of a mob swiftly coalescing ˋ like mercury in the market square. Someone was shouting from the steps of the guest hall, face red in the firelight, eyes squinted, teeth bared. Hugo turned, the better to hear, but the wind, fiercer now, shredded the words. Catching his neighbor's eye, Hugo raised an eyebrow.

The man, probably from the garrison, sword at his side, scratched his beard with his eating knife and, mumbling around a slice of half-chewed apple, pointed toward the steps with his elbow. "Simon says 'twas the Jew."

It was like a blow in the stomach. *The Jew? Master Levitas?* Hugo, mystified, stepped closer into the crowd, his presence accepted by those around him as if his differences, so apparent just days ago, had now become familiar.

"My man." The voice was a woman's, low and slightly tremulous. "My man went on the Crusade. Gave his life to kill the infidel. What difference be there? What difference I ask 'tween this here Jew and those infidels. Might as well get rid of the one here first."

"Hark ye to the words of Abbot Bernard, Bernard of Clairvaux." An older man tried to temporize. "Says we are to save 'em."

"So they can kill more?" It was the woman, hands cupped around her mouth. "Ye can gi' him *your* babe."

"How else to convert them?" The man's voice was lost in the clamor.

"The same youth on the steps grasped back the crowd's attention. "I've seen 'im, I 'ave. The way he looks at women. Smiles. But we know as what 'e thinks. Bet 'e was the one 'as took the babe killed in the wood. Blood sacrifice."

"I say we hang 'im. Taken money, 'e 'as, from 'ose as 'ave worked for it on the land. Takes what is ours."

"Took my sister." It was the youth again, and despite his rage his voice cracked.

That's where I've seen him before, Hugo thought. *It's the man who attacked me at the alehouse, brother to the maid who was killed.*

"Aye, that 'e did, took her and raped her, ye cain be certain o' that."

"Killed her with one o' them sharp instruments he does 'is gold with. Gold's not eno' for one o' his sort."

The light and the hate flickered like a wildfire, burning in one and then leaping across the blackness to catch a neighbor. Hugo shivered.

"I say we take 'im!"

"Aye."

"Gi' 'im a taste o' 'is own."

They're accusing Master Levitas of killing her. Is it possible?

"Er," he nudged the woman next to him. "Who are they talking about?"

"Oooh. You've not heard? A maid, Savette by name, went missing night afore last. Or was it two nights ago? Be that as it may, after the hue and cry and all, they finally found her, they did. This morn, it was. Dead and blue with a great hole under 'er hair. By the washing stream it was, half in it, you understand, with a cross carved on her hand. Must' a been the Jew. Who else would 'a done such a thing?"

"Master Levitas?" Hugo asked again.

"Aye, Levitas, the goldsmith. And moneylender. Isn't any in the town don't owe him. Even the nuns. Great sums they say. Squeezes us dry. And now he 'as killed the lass."

Hugo stopped listening. *Why does this shock me? What do I really know about Levitas?* Then, like a trap sprung in revulsion against itself, he clenched his jaw and threw the thought away.

Nodding to the woman, pretending to be interested in what Simon was yelling — "Look, he's started again," — he stepped backward, sidling toward the Market Cross. Hugo had heard once before of a mob like this one, whipped into the rabid froth of madness. He had heard of it when he was a lad at Hildesheim. Crusaders against the Jews. "Too easy," he whispered. "Way too easy."

The man-at-arms stared at him, and Hugo realized he had spoken aloud. The man's look was half curious, half hostile.

"Too easy for them," Hugo amended, deliberately vague. "Death comes too easy." The man, thinking Hugo meant the killing of children, returned his gaze to Simon atop the steps, a froth starting at the corners of his mouth.

Hugo turned, and, as fast as the steepness of the slope would allow, hastened to the goldsmith's shop. He rapped, then without waiting for a response ducked through the shadowed doorway. Not only was the door unlatched, but one of the shutters had a hole in it. *Not there before,* he thought.

Cold gripped the room. There was no fire, nor had there been one. *Probably since after I left.* The ashes smelled. Master Levitas was methodically bending and lifting pieces of silver and gold and tools from a safe hollowed out underneath his workbench. These he was placing into calfskin bags, counting aloud to himself in guttural Hebrew. Three rocks lay in the middle of the floor. The glazed window had been broken. There was a rock beside Levitas on the bench.

"Levitas," Hugo whispered. Levitas continued with what he was doing, unaware and dazed. "Levitas! They're blaming you." Hugo grabbed a sleeve and shook. "Hear ye them? That howl? For you, man. Calling you a bloodsucker."

Levitas studied the hand on his sleeve. The eyes that rose to Hugo's were black and distant. "Aye."

"There's a mob up in the market. I've seen its like. You must flee. Now." Hugo tried to grab the bag.

Levitas brushed aside the hand as one would a fly and continued filling the bag with gold and jewels.

"Come." Hugo felt as if he were four years old, trying to persuade his mother to do something. "There is no time for this. Not even what we have. They mean to kill you."

The eyes that finally turned toward Hugo held a vortex of sadness. "My work," he said and held up a chalice of silver-gilt, of such beauty that Hugo was momentarily mesmerized.

Hugo grabbed the shrunken shoulders. "You can't take it. It's too heavy. You cannot drag it with you."

Levitas held stubbornly to the chalice.

Hugo looked wildly toward the back of the shop for a hiding place.

"Naught back there but the well," said Levitas following his gaze.

"The well. That's it. We'll throw the bag in the well," Hugo tried to tug it from Levitas. "We'll come back for it, I promise. Leave

225

something, just a bit, in this store-cave. They will think you took the rest with you."

A little spark moved behind the Jew's eyes. Taking advantage of Levitas' momentary uncertainty, Hugo grabbed the sack from the moneyer's listless hand and dropped it in the well. *Why am I doing this, risking my life for a man I don't know, don't even like very much? Admire his work, but...*

There was a dull slurping sound as the bag hit the water. When Hugo tried to grab the chalice, though, Levitas resisted, with a strength Hugo didn't think the old man still had. "God gave you to me," he grunted. "Someone who understands me, what I do. A man who does far better work than I could ever do. I will not see such talent destroyed."

Levitas raised his eyes and said, "There is that." He examined the safe-hole as if he had never seen it before. "Ironic, you must admit." He dropped the last calfskin bag into it and pushed back the iron lid. "A Christian saving a Jew!" and he turned the iron ring to lock it. "Second time."

While Levitas' hands were occupied, Hugo grabbed the chalice and tossed it into the well. He crossed himself. "Forgive me, Father," and then turned to peer through the hole in the shutter. No looming bodies were silhouetted against the torch flames scattered atop Gold hill. Roars and howls, though, had increased. Flames rose and scattered into the hovering mist.

Banging the door open, Hugo half dragged a limping Master Levitas across Gold Hill to the postern door on the buttressed abbey wall. Some part of his mind remembered it. A slim dwarves-door it was, bolted with a stout hanging lock. Hugo pulled from his belt the scorper he had snatched from Levitas' worktable and started to claw at the lock.

Master Levitas, finally comprehending where Hugo was intending to lead him, drew back. "No."

"The nuns can protect you," Hugo grunted as he tried to pick

226

the lock. "Sanctuary," he growled, "is your only hope."

"It's the drains."

Hugo was able to get the scorper full into the rounded hole but it would not turn any of the plates.

"The drains?" Hugo repeated, focusing only half his attention as he drew his hammer from the loop at his belt and smashed the lock.

Master Levitas had gone chalk white. "It is forbidden. Unclean. Desecration. I cannot."

Finally, Hugo understood. This was not a back door to the abbey park as he had thought. He was preparing to take Levitas into the drains that carried all the abbey refuse somewhere.

Hugo clutched the collar of Levitas' cloak and spat words into the older man's face. "Dammit, there is no choice. God'll understand." As the brocade under Hugo's hand started to tear, a skin-hungry howl rose from the market. The old man slashed one glance up the hill, pulled up the skirt of his robe, and ducked through the low door frame. When they were inside, Hugo tried to close the door, but with the slope of the hill and the broken lock, it dangled obstinately open. He kicked at the tunnel floor, but there were no rocks with which to prop the door closed. In frustration, he pulled off the strap that held his hammer, and with a savage thrust of the scorper pierced the leather, forcing it over and around the bent piece of iron on the door. The other end he tied to the door frame. It was not secure, but it would keep the door from swaying inward for a while and giving them away. With the door shut the crack of light disappeared. Hugo put out a hand to his right. The walls were moist and clammy, slimy with the muck of time. Master Levitas moaned, "My ankle . . . "

"Come on, man," Hugo hissed. "No time for that," and then he turned around. The space seemed more open in that direction. Strange to be able to hear and feel the openness when he couldn't see it. Maybe it was the echoes.

227

They hunched along the tunnel for a few yards, following with feet and hands the path as it wound deeper into the hill. Soon, they made a turn and came abruptly to a dead end. Hugo's heart beat with irregularity. He patted the surrounding walls.

There has to be a door. Why didn't I grab a torch? Higher, we need to climb higher. It's a hill. It has to go up.

As Hugo turned back to tell Levitas, his foot hooked on a protrusion. He nearly fell, but caught himself by bracing his hand against side of the tunnel. "What the ... " He felt around with the toe of his other foot.

"What? What?" Levitas sounded near hysterics.

"Stubbed my toe." *A ring? Oh, let it be a ring!* "I think it's a hatch."

On hands and knees Hugo scrabbled through the mud and clay and thick gunk around the protuberance. Teeth chattering around his words, Levitas said, "We—we have to go on." His fingers plucked against Hugo's back. "Have to hurry. I—I can hear them. They will—"

"Stop it!" Hugo pushed Levitas' hand away. "The entrance. I think I've found it. It's on the floor." With his forearms, he brushed away enough muck to feel around the edges of a rusty hatch cover, then clawed at the dirt under the edge of the ring until finally he managed to free it. There were no hinges to the iron lid, and Hugo needed all his considerable strength to push it far enough to the side to expose the hole.

3

The mob's hatred had quickly flamed into frenzy.

"Second time 'e's killed."

"'E might do it again."

"Hungry fer blood."

"Afore 'e does it again."

"Gold be at 'is house."

"Should 'na be allowed to keep it. Not the gold. Profit from the deaths of babes?"

"Let's at 'im." Torches made from kex — dried stalks of cow parsley — filled with waste flax appeared from nowhere. With hate-sanctified authority, the mob marched down Gold Hill, their feet making the sound of waves breaking, ill defined at first, but soon stomping into synchronicity and coalescing into purpose.

Alone among the others on the hill, the Jew's house was unlit. There it stood, flagrant, a flag to their anger.

"'E's gone."

"Fled, most like."

"Or hid."

Although they had weapons at hand and the beat of anger armed their souls, even so, the mob hesitated to enter the house. The gesture was hard to see, and later none could remember who had made that first move; just a small move it had been, like the flight of a sparrow half seen from the corner of an eye. That insignificant motion communicated itself, and as one, the mob charged across the open space of the road and into the house. Those in the lead shouldered the door open. They needn't have. It swung easily inward, and they stumbled across the high threshold. The second wave tripped on the first, but, prodded by greed, they scrambled upright and then paused.

Later, the abbess would be told that women had been among them, and her lips would freeze into a line of anger, disappointment, and dismay.

"It is human," she would wail to Dame Aethwulfa, but..."

4

THE FETOR THAT CAME TO THEIR NOSES from the opened hatch was overwhelming. It rose like a live thing and clung to them and to the upper tunnel like pond scum. Hugo shoved his arm against his nose. Levitas gagged and retched until a bout of coughing shook his body like a dog mauling a kitten.

God, 'tis going to be tight going down into that drain. Hugo tried to breathe.

"I'll go first," Hugo said as Levitas' coughing fit finally subsided. "My boots are the heavier." He slipped down and after a moment found a precarious footing. He reached up to help Levitas.

Levitas plopped down onto the floor of the upper tunnel and scooted over to the opening. "Can't bend anymore," he grumbled, thrusting his legs through. Ruthlessly, Hugo tugged the dangling legs down and into the drain tunnel. Levitas' coughs became another spurt of retching. When finally he could breathe, they had both found footholds. Hugo felt with his feet. "Should be a conduit running down the center," he mumbled.

"Shush."

"What? You think they can hear us?"

"Mayhap."

"Here. Here it is." Hugo's voice dropped in disappointment. "But it goes down, and we must go up."

"We might go to St. James, Cann."

"No. Sanctuary. A well-defended sanctuary. Your only hope."

To the left of them, the channel veered slightly uphill toward the abbey. There was very little water to carry the muck away, just a slow trickle.

"Uggh," Hugo said aloud. Once again his boot slipped in the ooze and he felt the wrench in his groin. Breathing loudly around the pain, "Center's too slippery. Choose a side. Hold to the wall. I'll take the other."

"I am on the left," Levitas' voice was muffled through clenched teeth and the cloth he held to his nose.

The drains were about four feet in diameter. They had to crouch. After his first skin-crawling touch, Hugo felt the walls sparingly and only when he had to. They climbed slowly through the dark. The conduit ran at an angle away from Gold Hill, and therefore wasn't nearly as steep as the hill itself. At last the shaft leveled out.

Must be under the graveyard by now, Hugo thought.

When it seemed that the stench could become no worse, the tunnel they followed was joined by another, and the smell became unbearable. "The necessarium," Hugo hissed, then vomited what little was left in his stomach.

Levitas' reply was unintelligible, and then he, too, vomited. It seemed he couldn't stop, and Hugo, careful of the now clogged center drain, reached over and half-pulled, half-carried the frail Jew until they had staggered far enough away from the confluence that the air became barely sweeter, as water dripped from the ceiling and trickled down the walls.

"Springs." Hugo muttered. "Thank God."

"Yours or mine?" Levitas croaked, and Hugo was so surprised at the unexpected humor that he bellowed a guffaw and for a moment they were both bent double laughing. "Who would 'ave thought," Hugo hiccuped, tears running down his cheeks, "that any sane man could laugh here and now?"

"Just who was it called you sane?"

When at last they started up again, they came to another intersection, and Levitas, strangely lighthearted croaked, "Never thought garbage—the rottenness of a kitchen—would seem welcome."

"Which kitchen, though?" Hugo could feel himself tiring. His voice, even to his own ears, sounded like a whine. "Abbey or almshouse?"

"What matters it?"

Hugo found himself unaccountably irritated at the man's good

231

humor. "Matters little, I suppose," he growled. "We'll try for the almshouse."

"Why?"

"It's farther from the main gate."

"Drain seems to be getting smaller?" Levitas' voice had finally lost its strength.

"Close. Too close." Hugo was feeling frantically for another grilled exit.

Hearing the waver in his own voice, Hugo thought, *I am far worse than he is*. He took a deep breath, trying to think it through. Then he whispered, saying the words aloud to make his mind function, "Have to clean the drains. At some point they have to clean the drains. Should be another grille. Somewhere."

They continued. *The drain has to stop.* Everything inside him recoiling at the slime, Hugo again gingerly patted at the sides of the tunnel. His hand crunched on a horizontal. *A rock?* His fingers crabbed along it. Not just one rock, a wall. They had come to another bending. He hoped. "Mayhap a fork." He smoothed the stone. The wall was solid.

"Levitas?" his voice, even to him, seemed high. "Is the wall solid on your side?"

"Aye."

"We have come to an ending," Hugo said through gritted teeth, trying to swallow his terror. He patted as high on the ceiling as he could. "When we entered, the grille was above the tunnel." He could feel no bumpy knob jutting down. "There must be another inlet, some way to clean and flush. They wouldn't leave it all to the springs. Would they?"

5

By the time Ailred, a turner by trade, a maker of wooden cups and plates, had squeezed into the house, there was little room for movement. The legs of the overturned workbench blocked the doorway, forcing him to remain half in and half out of the door. Some of the men were busy filching tools from the shelves and workbench. Most, however, were overturning the furniture and pounding on the walls, looking for the gold and jewels.

"Mun be here."

"Took it, hisself."

"Couldn't take it all."

"Then where be it?"

"Strongbox."

"Aye? So where is it, then?"

Because of where he stood, it was Ailred who first noticed the ring in the floor near the overturned workbench. No one had ever observed it in the usual course of business; ordinarily, the ring and lid were hidden beneath the bench, the floor rushes, and Master Levitas' feet. Ailred fiddled with the ring, turning it this way and that, trying to unlatch the lid. Soon, the men were jostling each other to help him, trying to be the first.

The women in the mob had immediately headed to the inner room. There was no hesitation. All those words about dead children were just so much chaff. They knew as well as they knew their own houses what the inner room, and the loft as well, contained. Though ostensibly trying to help in the search for gold and jewels, they were looking for Rebekkah's chests. The first box they came upon was of wood and covered in red leather. The hasp was easily unlatched. Revealed within, among the pale blue folds of Rebekkah's mantle, were their memories of her: Rebekkah picking her way through the market, shielded by this very mantle, its impractical blue declaring to all who saw her that Rebekkah needed never worry about such things as soil or tears. Greedily, first one, then another caressed the wool of the mantle, Flanders wool, soft-woven and banded in heavy embroidered silk — work that most of them might themselves have accomplished had they the fine silken thread available to them, and the time. Two of them at once grabbed at it with their scratchy fingers and splintered nails. Fiercely silent, the two glared at one another and tussled over it, their eyes locked until an indrawn breath beside them distracted them. This one, relinquishing the mantle to the other two, had dug deeper and come upon the belts, ribbands, chainses, and gonelles that had been neatly folded with lavender tucked among the silken gathers. Rebekkah's two long-sleeved gonelles, fashioned of silk and designed in lines that grazed the breasts and hips and hinted at the waist, lay on top. The chainses, tunics meant to be worn under the gowns and next to the skin, were filmy, fashioned of linen of such thinness that it seemed woven of cobweb and mist.

"From the Holy Land, that be, or to the south," one of the older women said. Another nodded and looked through the folds. "Gaza."

Near the bottom, Rebekkah's pigskin needle case held several sharp needles of steel — to the women an incredible treasure. "Probably from Damascus."

Resting on the bottom, wrapped in linen, was a belt of golden braid, its round buckle embellished with two cabochon emeralds.

While most of the women were transfixed by the chest, another, unable to get near it, came upon Hannah's little box, with the small pleated shift on which the maiden had so carefully labored. Two gonelles, different lengths for different ages, lay beneath, again carefully folded, with lavender and linen tucked here and there in between. "Linen! The waste of it!" Hannah's spring-green gonelle had lacing up the sides of the bodice. A sigh escaped from the lips of the woman holding it up. The daisy embroidery on

234

the hem and sleeves still shone with the rich shimmer of silk. Yet another woman, sharp-eyed and quick, snatched away the leather belt, painted and knotted, before the first realized it was meant to accompany the dress.

6

"Master." Levitas' voice was close beside Hugo. "I am the taller. Let me." Levitas had already started methodically tapping on the arched roof near the place Hugo had given up. From where he stood, Hugo whiffed Levitas' gasping, hunger-soured breath; he could smell the acrid stench of terror.

"Patience, patience," Levitas muttered. "I think I've found it. It's … right … above me. Yes. It's iron. Rusted. But … a grille. With … a … "

Hugo felt his hand pulled upward, where his fingers just barely reached a cold metal bar. A flake of rust dropped into his eye. "There must … be … a hatch cover … above the bars … to keep out the smell," Levitas panted. "Need to push it off." He looked at it a moment longer and then bent over, his hands braced on his knees, his voice unaccountably firm. "Step on my back." Hugo clambered onto Levitas' back and tried to slip a hand between the bars. His fingers fished upward, struggling to get enough purchase to push the grille aside. He tried to rock it, levering first on one side and then the other.

"Use the scorper," Levitas' voice was harsh with exhaustion. Obediently, Hugo sliced all along and above each muck-encrusted, rusty bar. Finally, with a prolonged squelch, the lid above the bars started to lift. A crack of slightly less dark gray slotted from one corner. Scrabbling his fingers around the lip and between the parallel bars, Hugo scooted the lid off the grille.

Hugo stared at the size of the revealed hole. "Smaller than the other one." Trying to keep the terror from his voice, he added.

"I can't fit. He looked at Levitas' hands, now interlaced into a stirrup. "I — I can't fit. The opening is too small. I won't make it through. I'll stick."

Levitas, puffing, again bent his back. "Well, then, at least push the damned grille off."

Hugo remounted and again raised both arms. The grille was worse than the lid. He strained, took a deep breath, and gasped, "Lift me higher." Levitas gave a final heave, culling strength from he knew not where, arching his frail back like a cat in terror. Hugo, on top of him, bent his neck so the full breadth of his shoulders acted as a fulcrum on the iron bars, levering them from the rust and the muck that glued them in place.

It was too much for the old Jew — Levitas staggered, wobbled, and finally collapsed. Hugo, his support gone, arms windmilling, ricocheted against the wall and landed, his whole body atop Levitas', straddling him like a lover. They lay there, the muck around them, wheezing the labored breath of exhaustion. Finally, Hugo rose to his knees and reached out a trembling hand to Levitas. "Hurt?"

"Nay. Just old. Lift me up when ye can. My strength be on the wane."

Hugo pulled Levitas to a sitting position, and the old man propped himself again onto hands and knees. Then, one leg at a time, he stood. Hugo, still squatting, intertwined his fingers, and Levitas, both hands on Hugo's shoulders, lurched one leg into the finger-stirrup. With the ease born of his great strength, Hugo hoisted Levitas easily up and through the hole. Levitas grasped the far edge of the grate and lay heaving upon it.

"Think ye," he whispered when he had regained some breath, "that the abbess knows of this lack of... attention to cleanliness?" Hugo, hands on his knees, bent over for breath, eyed the spindly shanks that still dangled before him. "I am sure... she will be dismayed... to hear of it," he panted in response. After another

236

longish pause, Levitas said. "I cannot heave myself further."

Hugo, head still lowered, crabbed over to put his shoulders under the other's feet. He raised himself from his crouch until Levitas began to struggle forward and away. Then, raising his arms like one of the jugglers at the Michaelmas fair, Hugo grasped Levitas' feet and thrust them up. The old man was through. There was a long silence. Hugo could see nothing, but finally heard scraping.

After a moment Levitas' head peered down. "Now," his voice was stronger, "take off your clothes. My hand is reaching down." Hugo froze. Levitas slapped the side of the grate like an irritated schoolmaster. "Hand me your clothes."

"My clothes?"

"Your shoulders are too wide. You said so yourself."

As if in a dream, Hugo took off his heavy belt and passed it and his hammer and tools up to the goldsmith.

"If I stick ... I will never ... get out ... alive." Hugo's voice was muffled as he shrugged out of his jerkin and tunic.

"Don't breathe. Let your breath out. All of it. Make your chest narrow."

Trying to obey, Hugo drew in a huge breath.

"Out, Out! Not in." Hugo exhaled. Holding onto the breathlessness, he jumped, grasped the edge of the hole, and with one of his huge hands on the lip, his other shoulder lowered as well as he could, inch by inch hauled and squirmed his sweaty — *thank God for the sweat — feel like a greased pig* — body through. When his second rib had reached the top of the opening, he gasped a breath and, feeling the increased constriction, a sudden panic seized him.

"Exhale, exhale," Levitas hissed.

Terrified, Hugo let out his breath, braced his forearms on the floor above him, and, grazing the skin off his midriff, writhed his hips and legs up and out, falling exhausted on the rim.

The room they had erupted into appeared to be a cellar or

237

storeroom. *Almshouse or abbey?* Hugo didn't know and for the moment didn't care. He lay on the rim, tamping down the claustrophobic terror that had gripped him for those last moments, then tiredly reached for his jerkin and braes. Clambering into his clothes, he drank of the wine-must, damp-oak smell that pervaded every corner. There was as well a cider essence from apples, and a pungent earthiness wafting from the baskets of onions and leeks. After the drains, even onions smelled ambrosial. Shrugging on his shirt, he noticed piles of stacked wood.

"I think there are stairs over there," Levitas said, interrupting Hugo's thoughts. The old man had started to crawl toward a corner where a staircase could just be made out.

"Must go to the kitchen," Hugo muttered, groping into his jerkin.

"Just as well," Levitas grumbled. "The stairs are the only way I'm going to be able to stand." He sat on the first stair, backed up to the second, grabbed the railing, and hauled himself upright hand over hand.

When they had both reached the top of an extremely narrow stairwell, Hugo carefully creaked open the stout door. Scraping the floor slightly, it swung inward to reveal an alcove. "Scullery."

As if in confirmation, a pot clanged.

Standing directly across from them, gaping in alarm at the moving door, red hair slightly tousled, was the lad Hugo had passed on the first day, the lad who had been helping the shepherd. Hugo put his finger to his lips, and the boy's startled "O" widened into a grin.

A rustle of steps platted from somewhere behind the boy, and the light increased subtly from the left.

"Odo?" a woman's voice.

Hugo flattened himself into the shadow of the door.

The boy turned, and his answering mumble was unintelligible. As Odo moved farther into the distant room in answer to the query, his voice receded. The woman's answering laugh sounded pleased.

Hugo let out his breath in a hiss. The light from the woman's cresset became a shadow, and they heard a door bang farther off. Hugo crept across the scullery and peered through the arch into the kitchen. Ahead of him stood another door, which was both bolted and barred. "Has to be an outside door," he whispered. No light slatted through the shutters. "Night, finally. Outside, we'll be invisible."

Hugo tiptoed toward it, Levitas right behind. Two steps from the door, something squished under Hugo's foot, and a sawing yowl erupted from beneath him. Taking advantage of the noise, he threw the bolt and swung wide the door. Fresh air. There was no sound of the mob. As soon as they were through, Levitas pulled the door closed behind them.

Just as silently, it reopened. Hugo felt the puff of indrawn air against his legs. He whirled, hammer raised, shoving Levitas behind him.

Chapter Twenty

Tuesday Night to Wednesday Morning

Between Compline and Matins,
around 11 p.m.

I

After Compline, pleading the unfinished tasks that had piled up while she and Joan were sawing the logs, Dame Averilla retreated to the sacristy. She was bone weary from the unaccustomed physical labor, as well as from the fatigue brought on by the unrelieved tension. *But I need to be in the church.* The sounds coming from outside the gates had mounted as the night wore on, and they scared her. *Those from Lovick's house have told others and gathered them into a mob. A mob. After Levitas.*

A shiver ran up her spine as she puttered aimlessly around the choir.

"Christ be with me," she muttered under her breath as she replaced the marker in the Psalter, slightly adjusting the great book on its stand.

"Christ within me." She closed the small wrought-iron gate to the sacristy.

"Christ beside me." She noticed that she had not put away the goblet from the morning's Mass.

"Christ before me." It was gold, of course, a modern piece that Master Levitas had repaired some years earlier.

"Christ behind me." She shook her head. "Christ to win me."

Levitas created things, too. The great candlesticks, of course, and rings and fairings. The girl's ring. "Christ to comfort and restore me." *Master Levitas couldn't kill Savette. Wouldn't have. Who would have a reason to? Not outcasts — they wouldn't come that close, and the ring wasn't enough to murder for. Besides, it was hidden. Savette said Jared had plighted his troth, then changed his mind and didn't want to marry her. Because she was pregnant? Surely that isn't enough for murder. A pregnant woman is a boon. Means more children for the cold years of age; sons to work the land, pay the tithes and the rents...*

Averilla stopped, her hand on the gate as she thought.

What did she say? That Jared didn't want to marry her? But Savette was besotted with him. Could Jared have another plight troth? Not unheard of. He was indeed handsome. That must be it. Had he used Savette and discarded her because he had found someone else? Suddenly, the memory surfaced. She was with Master Levitas in the infirmary; he was talking over the pain of the hot tincture. *'They took the fibula. Said Damasa would like such a brooch.'* Averilla's eyes opened wide. *Could Jared want to marry Damasa? And Savette wouldn't release him because of the babe?*

She must tell the bailiff. She would send the porter. *Robert must be told before Jared can flee.* Averilla fluttered down the three steps from the rood screen to the nave altar and halted. *I can't send the porter. Not now, not tonight, with that horde outside. Abward is needed to protect us. And he needs to watch for Levitas. If that is a mob outside, Levitas may seek sanctuary.*

Frustrated, feeling confined by her habit, *I could go. Dress like*

241

a lad, as I did before. And thus disobey. Again. No. I can't disobey. Lord, I can't. Please. Can You? Averilla remounted the steps to the sacristy. If God wanted her to do something, he would make it possible without disobedience. *I must stay here. If Master Levitas should knock for sanctuary . . .*

2

THE MEN IN LEVITAS' SHOP WERE STILL dealing with the ring in the floor. One of the masons — not John, the master mason whom Hugo had met — raised his hammer and, with liquid strokes, destroyed ring, latch, and mechanism. There was an indrawn breath as the lid was lifted, and then a pause. Knocking heads in their eagerness, the men peered deep into the goldsmith's safe-hole, and then hands, nails rimmed with dirt, knuckles enlarged, hairy and worn, scrabbled into the well, clawing at one another, grabbing and clenching until someone grasped a corner. They hefted the small box up and onto the floor. Most of the "hoard" that lay inside was used coin waiting to be re-minted, although a small store of semiprecious stones nestled in a calfskin bag. Ailred, he who had noticed the iron lid on the floor, managed to hook his forefinger and thumb onto the bag. Before any were aware, he slipped it out of the box and into his scrip, and slowly, furtively, backed out of the shop. Keeping to the shadows, he slipped between two houses and was gone.

"E must 'av took all the rest, the chalices and so, with 'im," said one, slipping a handful of coins into his pocket.

"Or hidden it somewhere else," said another.

"Taken it with him. Sure, 'e'd take it."

"Have to find 'im. Get what's ours back."

Casually tossing his lighted torch onto the pile of chips beside the hearthstone, Bayard, Jared's older brother, who had never gotten along with the reeve and lived with them no longer, winked at Wulfere. "Too bad, in't it, that the shop caught fire?"

"Aye, that it be," agreed Wulfere, tossing his torch onto the bavin, the larger tinder beside the chips. "Just vanished in smoke, that shop did. Course, iffen there be any gold in the walls, it'll be in the ashes. When the fire cools."

"Mayhap the goldsmith won't be inclined to get his hands dirty."

"Don't imagine 'e will. Iffen he lives. Murderer and all."

One of the women was just short of the inner doorway when the flames started across the floor. Screaming, "Fire!" she scuttled like a crab, dragging behind her the red leather chest, which wedged itself in the legs of the overturned workbench. Grabbing the chainse she held in her other hand with her teeth, she hefted the trunk over the projecting legs. "Goldsmith was long gone by then," she would later tell her grandchildren. "And didn't take it with 'm."

By the time the last woman had pulled the bedding from the bed and was struggling with the pallet, "but down-filled, imagine, goose down" through the door, the fire was inching its way into the inner room. There was nothing to encourage the flames, since the recent days had been wet, but there is an inevitability about fire, and the mob watched from the wall on the other side of the road, waiting for the satisfying climax.

One of the smaller men, Tumbert, a fletcher, with the clever, long-fingered hands needed for making arrows, noticed the crack around the postern door through which Hugo and Levitas had made their escape. Having stopped to relieve himself against the wall, he saw that the door, a familiar door, one he had walked by numerous times as he ran down or plodded up the hill, was ajar. He wouldn't have noticed it at all had he not been standing right there. "Lads," he cried as they stood watching the fire. "He went into the drains. Through the postern."

"He never." Several men turned, crowding around the broken

lock, swiftly pulling out the restraining leather loop.

"Sanctuary." The word was breathed out, almost whispered.

"Scum."

"Aye. Christianity be not good eno' for the likes of 'im. Won't accept our Christ, oh, no, but will sure eno' take the good o' it. Try to use our God's church for sanctuary. I say 'e don't deserve it."

"'Taint right."

"But the nuns will gi' it to 'im."

"Aye."

"Soft hearts."

"And 'e'll slay 'em in their beds."

"Aye. Unless we find 'm first."

"Through the drains?"

"Nay, lads. Wait. Why should we?" Bayard's smile held a wily knowing. There be only one outcome for those drains. But we don't have to put up with that stink. We can walk plain as day into the church."

"Our church."

"Aye. Our church."

"Not 'is.

Like gnats they swarmed upward, movements jagged, erratic, and hungry. Warin, the night gatekeeper, warily opened the grill. A multitude of eyes glittered from the reflected fire of the torches. "Want to go to the church," said Bayard. All Warin would tell the abbess in his defense, eyes wide in innocence, was, "I wot not but that they wanted to pray, milady. For Savette." Her reply would be curt. "And had they been masterless men, would you have opened the gate to them as well?" "Nay, milady," he would answer with perfect candor. "These men I knew. It be their church."

Warin opened the gate.

They entered the church through the door in the mason's yard; the one some of them had earlier noticed when Father Boniface

244

used it. It alone remained unlocked, mostly because Abward had not known it had been opened.

3

AFTER HUGO LEFT HIM ALONE IN THE CHURCH, Ralf stared for the briefest moment at the outlined figures Hugo had ghosted into the center panel. Hugo had started carving the right-hand panel, leaving the other two bare but for the nearly invisible outlines. It took Ralf a moment's thought as he examined the static areas beside the main figures; these, the lesser figures, and animals, were mere hen scratchings waiting for being.

Ralf considered the chisels he held in his hands, running his fingers over their smooth wooden handles. It was neither lack of confidence nor misplaced sense of inadequacy that stayed his arm. Ralf had a naive certainty in the power of his hands, the cocky sureness of youth. The talent had always been with him, lightning from his fingers. When he pictured a figure, his hands could somehow find it in the wood. In the face of this panel, though, he felt an unfamiliar sense of awe: this was no plaything for a neighbor child, nor some frivolous fairing intended for wooing a maid on a midsummer night; the intention was wholly different. Until he had come into the vastness of this holy place, he had had no reverence for God—fear he had had, but not reverence. Now, though, his being had been creased by the shimmering light and the silver notes that washed the great vault. The nuns' obeisance and reverence had changed the tenor and purity of his gift. An unused humility now delayed him. These women had a poignant vulnerability and a sanctity that cloaked the oratory in peace. For them, for their love of God, he wanted to do his best, and so he hesitated.

Feeling awkward, as if he were acting a part, he mounted to the altar and dropped onto the cushion laid before the rail. It was his first real attempt at prayer, his first recognition of the magnitude of God. It was, as well, his first recognition that this beauty that swirled like a whirlpool into the depths of his being was a gift beyond measure from a being beyond comprehension. His use of this gift must henceforth be an expression of his thanks, must be his prayer forever.

Further introspection was beyond him. What Ralf prayed was without words, and even this prayer was so foreign to him that it felt like nettles on his skin, so, thankfully and with haste, he shed the prayer, and rose to immerse himself in the reality of steel and wood.

Ralf dug into the oak with sure, even strokes. Time evaporated. Ralf's whole mind stood captive to the being-ness of horse. Hugo had delineated a multitude of horses: horses with legs outspread as they tried to throw their riders; the backs of horses, the sides of horses; horses nipping at flies on their hindquarters. Ralf's mind eagerly seized the images as they rose from the surface. They were as likenesses mirrored in a pool at midday, ever clearer as the rays of the sun lengthened. As Ralf's chisels eked out the superfluous, gouged and dredged and scooped, a hoof received a small chip, the muscles glistened on a flank.

As his hands were bringing certainty to the silhouettes, part of Ralf's mind mused on the riders. They were men, soldiers, although now mere traceries, standing in their stirrups, mailed feet down-pointing. Should he further incise the creases and outlines Hugo had intimated? He hesitated. Hugo had mentioned only horses ...

Suddenly, baying voices splintered Ralf's reverie. The bellows of bloodlust glazed his mind with unforgettable images of black depths and charred interiors. Dropping the chisel as his vision slivered into shards of fear, Ralf slipped under the rail surrounding the altar, slithering like a newt around the front and into the niche carved behind and beneath it.

246

The mob burst through the little door from the mason's yard, the flames of their torches dancing grotesquely on the piers. Willies, ghosts, and phantasms made of smoke and ember rose from the flames and twisted into the blackness. The men headed directly for the candles lighting Ralf's work.

Seeing the panel and the chisel on the floor, "He's still here!"

"The carver? A friend to the Jew?"

"Aye. Seen 'em together all this day."

They thrust their torches into every shadow, and finally found Ralf cowering beneath the altar.

"Where be they?" Bayard grabbed a tuft of Ralf's hair and dragged him out into the light.

He couldn't speak.

Ignited by his own fury, Bayard shook Ralf so his head wobbled back and forth on his neck.

"Wh — wh — who?" Ralf finally managed to stutter.

"Yer master and that son of a whore, Levitas. Where be they?"

"I — I dunno. I dunno."

"We saw 'im just a bit ago in the market. Then he disappeared. Into the drains, like as not." The man's fingers dug into Ralf's skin. "Planning to take sanctuary. We know they're here. Where be they hid?"

"I — I..."

Bayard drew his hand back to smash his fist into Ralf's nose. "I said, where be they?"

Before the fist could connect, Tindal had coiled and thrown his full weight against Bayard's arm, a back-throated growl thundering from his belly, his fangs sinking deep as he tore into the flesh.

"Dam'ee. Get 'im off." Bayard dropped Ralf and pummeled Tindal's snout, as another man rushed forward, beating the matted fur with his torch. The charcoal smell of burnt hair rose as the fur sizzled. With a howl, Tindal fell back, but flipped into a crouch.

247

Head lowered, lips raised in a snarl, he again flung himself across the space. The men stumbled back, fending him off with torches. In a fit of spite, because a mere dog had defied and bested him, Bayard picked up a hammer and slammed it against the top of the middle panel. The curved arch splintered off, leaving the upper edge, intended to portray the crucifixion, jagged and broken.

As they swirled through the nave, Bayard put his hand out to stop the others and pointed through the grille to the rood screen. "'At be 'is work," he growled. Statues of gold and silver were mounted into niches of the stone screen. Despite Father Boniface's efforts to get them moved, the great candlesticks still stood on either side of the altar. Of gilded silver, they had been modeled on those in Gloucester and given to the former abbess, Cecily FitzHamon, by her sister, Mabel of Gloucester. Centered on the altar 'fair linen' was the treasured reliquary.

The men absorbed the implications and, as if drawn, their thoughts teemed together. Bayard took tentative steps through the grille and up to the altar, becoming bolder as he felt the others behind him. One of the shadows to the right of the altar suddenly moved. Dame Averilla, puffed like an angered hen, eyes narrowed, veil billowing like wings, screeched, "House of the Lord," and then, snatching one of the huge candlesticks with both hands, swooped down on them. Because of the massive weight, she could only drag it and then heft it in a semicircle about her, but no bitch defending her brood could have carried a heavier weight of anger. Her eyes alone were fearsome. "Get ye hence from this sacred place," she howled. Her rage was palpable, and the men bumped into one another as they skidded into headlong flight. "Harm ye one splinter herein and the vengeance will be that of the Lord."

"I confess I was consumed by rage," she would tell the abbess.

"There *is* another instance of such fervor for the house of God," the abbess would reply, more perplexed than judging, amazed

248

that any person, especially a woman, could manage to lift one of the candlesticks. "It took two of us to move them," John the Mason would remark years later to his grandchildren, by which time the story had become myth.

Averilla dropped the candelabrum and, her skirts kilted, sprinted after the scurrying men. She was surprised to find herself accompanied on one side by the slapping of ill-fitting shoes and on the other a panting shadow. One of the fleeing men looked over his shoulder and redoubled his pace. Averilla, unarmed, was surprised that she alone should occasion such terror, until she too focused on the panting shadow and recognized the reality of Tindal's square muzzle crinkled into a ready snarl. When she overcame her rage, Averilla realized that the other shadow was Ralf, who was armed with two sharp tools. The three reached the north door, which hung open. The men were partway across the outer court. "Abward," she screeched toward the gatehouse, but already its door was opening and she could see Abward's heavy form lumbering down the stairs.

"Dame!" Ralf's voice barely managed to penetrate the onrush of shock. He pulled frantically at her skirt. "Dame! The windows!" He pointed back into the church. She looked up and saw light pouring through the stained glass, creating a riot of color where only the blackest night usually settled.

Hand to her mouth, Averilla whispered, "Fire." From the edge of the porch she could see by the fire's jerky light the outline of the guest hall, billowing smoke rising from Gold Hill behind it. "Fire!"

With Ralf's help she pushed the north door closed, but her hands were shaking so hard she couldn't slot the pieces of the lock — cast in the shape of a man's elongated head — into one another, and Ralf was too short to manage it. "We'll have to leave it."

Acrid smoke came in through the louvers of the lantern tower, and jerky blasts of light splatted against the windows as Averilla,

249

Ralf, and Tindal stumbled back up the north aisle. "Fire," she said, strangely bewildered, and at a loss. "It is fire. Oh, God, help us. Please, send rain. If it be Thy will. *What am I doing? I can't just slam the door and hope for the best. I have to tell the abbess or Abward. Ralf. I can send him to Abward, tell him to ready the abbey for fire,* her mind went on, seemingly without her conscious direction. *I could, as well, send the boy with a message for the bailiff. Can I send him out into this maelstrom? Not a boy alone, certainly, but with the dog? Boys can slip where men can't, and Tindal will be there.*

"Listen, Ralf," she broke off her thoughts and bent her lanky from down toward him. "I need your help."

Ralf puffed himself up. "Aye, Dame." They had reached the north chapel and, still listening, Ralf grabbed another chisel and slotted it into his belt.

"Go to the main gate. Tell Abward of the fire. He will know what to do. Then go to the castle. Tell them as well, and also tell the man at the gate that Dame Averilla sends for the bailiff, that I must see him now."

"Aye, Dame." Nodding to Tindal, Ralf said, "C'mon, boy." Together, Ralf and Averilla pushed open the small north door, and when boy and dog had slipped through, she closed and re-bolted it behind them.

Now, she thought, *I must ready the church for Matins,* and, hearing a little giggle, knew that she was very close to hysteria. *I won't have time to tell the abbess before Matins. But what if she doesn't come down?*

4

O𝐃𝐎 𝐒𝐓𝐎𝐎𝐃 𝐒𝐈𝐋𝐇𝐎𝐔𝐄𝐓𝐓𝐄𝐃 𝐀𝐆𝐀𝐈𝐍𝐒𝐓 𝐓𝐇𝐄 𝐅𝐀𝐈𝐍𝐓 𝐋𝐈𝐆𝐇𝐓 from the door of the almonry kitchens. Relieved, Hugo drew in a breath and re-slung his hammer, then as quickly squatted, as Warin sauntered by, finishing his evening rounds of the abbey.

"Edge. Dark," Odo mouthed, pointing to the path at the edge of the park, and the three of them crouched along the side of the almonry, keeping to the shrubs and the shadows. Every footstep, every crackled leaf, slammed into Hugo's awareness as they crept across the path to the uphill side of the dovecote. Hugo would have gone on to the downhill side of the little building, where the slope of the hill would provide further protection, but Odo pulled him back. "Slippery," he hissed.

On the church side of the dove house, the inner court was laid out in front of them. Drifts of light filtered from the clerestory windows of the church. Hugo grabbed Odo's tunic and pointed. "They're in the church," his voice hopeless even in a whisper. "No sanctuary."

"The castle," Odo's whisper was usurped by the rage of the mob as they erupted into the inner court. "The bailiff'll harbor you," he shouted.

Seeing the terror start in Levitas' eyes, Hugo growled in disbelief, "A Jew? Ye think the bailiff'll rescue a Jew?"

"Aye." Odo was firm. "I know him. Besides, there is naught else."

"Is," Odo continued as he led them alongside the dove house and veered right at the almonry, " ... a secret gate ... on the other side of the orchard."

The going was tough. Clods of dirt, broken for the winter rains, but slippery with ice, tripped them. Levitas tried to muffle his racking coughs, but they came out in spurts of spray. At the wall to the Bimport, Hugo peered into the shadows. The wall looked impregnable. Odo loosened a few rocks from the base, revealing a slight hole. "Used to steal fruit," he said without diffidence. "Al'ays been 'ere."

Hugo's confidence broke, "Others might 'ave used it."

"Mayhap. I wot not. Ne'er seen any other use it," Odo winced

251

as he shifted from foot to foot, his impatience obvious. Finally, almost whining, he said, "Master, 'tis the best I can do."

Sighing, Levitas sank to his knees.

"I cannot be caught with you," Odo pleaded, his eyes rolling like a calf at the slaughter. "My moder—I am all she has."

Hugo nodded, then, realizing that Odo could not see him, said, "Aye, lad, we understand. Go with God. Our thanks are with you."

"At that moment, the sound of the chase, wind-driven, soughed toward them. With fear-born ease, Levitas wriggled through Odo's hole; Hugo, feeling his strength wane, followed.

"God go with you," Odo's disembodied voice floated up from the other side of the wall, followed by the finality of chinking as the rocks were replaced.

5

RALF DARTED ACROSS THE OUTER COURT OF THE ABBEY, hugging the shadows. The closer he came to the wall, the clearer became the shouting and turmoil. He deliberately slowed his pace, sauntering unconcerned toward the main gate, where the porter, body pressed against the lachet, looked through the grille at the Bimport.

"Er," Ralf tapped Abward on the shoulder. The porter spun around, terrified, believing that some of the mob had remained inside and were ready to stab him in the back. Seeing it was only Ralf, he scowled to cover his embarrassment.

"What d'ye want?"

"Needs fetch the bailiff. For Dame Averilla."

The man peered at Ralf suspiciously his eye flicking back and forth to Tindal.

"Oh, aye. And why's she not sending me?"

"Said you were to prepare wagons and caldrons"

252

"And why is that?" Abward had had it with this pompous little brat, apprentice or no.

Casually, Ralf pointed. "There is fire on Gold Hill."

The porter's intake of breath as he turned toward the east gate was audible even over the sounds of the mob. He slid the bolt toward the main gate, and, as the sally port inched outward, Ralf and Tindal slipped through.

It was easier than Ralf had expected. No one paid him any notice—curious boys were everywhere. Most who passed him were too intent on their own pursuits to pay any heed to another boy, and none noticed Tindal slinking through the shadows.

6

FROM WHERE HE SAT AT THE HIGH TABLE IN THE CASTLE, elbow cocked over the back of his great chair, a flagon in his hand, Robert Bradshaw listened to the men around him. Tom had returned from Lovick's and was telling Robert of the strange cross carved into Savette's hand.

Robert turned to Tom. "So, they think it was the Jew."

"Aye. Naught else makes a rood o' sense now, do it?"

"I'm not so sure." Robert sighed. "I have found naught against Master Levitas. And there is Jared still to account for."

"Dunno, bailiff. Jared seemed right woeful, 'e did."

"Robert!" His wife's voice reached him over the muffled reverberations of the men. Mavis never raised her voice. She was screeching. Mavis never ran. Now, skirts uplifted, heedless of the dogs fighting over a bone, and a babe, someone's babe, peeing in the rushes, she was flying toward him, panting, "Fire."

All who heard her silenced themselves. "Fire!"

The word stretched itself out into a hundred different visions, slotted itself into the various consciousnesses, and each person scrambled. Somewhere. The women started pulling at fabric: pallets, blankets, coverlets, any loose textile that could be carried, and ran for the well. In the keep, they jostled for place near the wellhead, eager to dip and wring. The bucket made a reeling twang as again and again it fell into the water and was raised.

Men, the ostlers, and beaters, and those whose function was both less and more than fighting, grabbed baskets and panniers, pulled horses already wild-eyed with the smell of smoke, and harnessed them to carts that others were loading with every leakproof container they could find. Without orders, they opened the gates and rumbled down the Pilgrims' Lane, past St. John's and St. James, to the streams and fishponds.

Within the hall, only the men-at-arms stolidly waited for orders. Impassive amidst chaos, they alone stood, ranked around Robert.

"Whose house?"

Mavis, still out of breath, looked up and shook her head.

"The Jew's." Robin, the man-at-arms who had been with Tom at Lovick's house to see about Savette, had followed Mavis into the hall. Though Tom had returned to the castle when the mob streamed into the marketplace, he had left Robin and a few others to keep a watch. Robin had stood and listened as Simon fulminated. He had observed unmoving outside Master Levitas' house until the first torch was flung. Then, leaving the others, Robin had come running.

"Not the abbey?" Robert wanted to be sure.

"Nay. Nowhere near to it."

"Only the one house?"

"The goldsmith had already fled."

Robert scanned the hall. "Edbert! Take the carts down to the ponds."

Robin interrupted, "Already gone, sir."

"Well done. Tom? Take men to the Jew's. We'll get water from the nuns. They've a well and plenty of pots. By then those who've

254

gone to the ponds should be on their way up Gold Hill." In some instances, Robert would have stayed where he was, a rallying point for the men, but something still pinched at the back of his mind. "Edbert? You and Mock and Peter are to stay here with Mavis and those already on duty at the gate and on the walls. Someone needs to be here to care for the wounded," he added, his eyes holding those of his wife.

"I wanted them to know," Robert would later tell Mavis, "that I wasn't protecting you while other men's wives were down fighting the fire."

"Oh, aye." She would lean over and kiss the back of his neck. "Yet, Robert, can you understand that I choose to believe that the care of us is so much a part of you that ye wist not where it leaves off?"

7

IN HER LODGINGS, ABBESS EMMA LOOKED UP from the rolls and rubbed her eyes. She had missed Compline; it was time for Matins. Apart from the witness of Peter the Metalworker, she could find no entry that proved Master Chapman was taking their monies. Drawing one eyelid over the other to ease their dry scratchiness, she became aware of the musty smell of old smoke. *Had not the warming-room fire been carefully extinguished? She wouldn't smell smoke from the warming room at this corner of the cloister—it would blow the other way. The kitchen? It was after curfew. Could there be a fire in the kitchen? Or drifting up to her from St. James?*

Not wanting to believe it, she crossed to the door and opened it out onto the stairs.

The sky was alight with mad, erratic devils of flame. She had seen fire like this when she was a child. She didn't even want to think about it; the gnarled, blackened fingers of the old woman who had worked in the dairy, the frenzied pounding of the horses against their stalls. *Fire.*

"Oh, God, help us!" The words came aloud, unbidden, and she tasted their foreignness in her teeth, finding once again the bridge between herself and her Creator. She laid her thoughts onto that fragile pavilion that again seemed to exist.

There was no answer; needn't be one. She felt the presence, the comforting being-ness beside her: that which made all things well; which negated pain and fear and loss. Even this fire, in light of the reassuring presence, seemed inconsequential. She needed to deal with the fire. No. She needed to be there with the community. *Where have I been? What has possessed me? How can I have left my sheep? I am as bad as David when he went looking for Bathsheba.* The Bible was very clear on that. When kings were supposed to be in the field battling evil, he was sitting at home, restless. Instead of praying with her flock as she was supposed to be, she was here, trying to force the accounts into some kind of order. *Why? I don't need proof. I have what I need. The only thing I need know is that Chapman is not honest. I have known that for months. I am misusing my time, trying to be perfect, when all my nuns want and need is a good shepherd.*

She fled down the steps, feet tripping on her underskirts until she grabbed them into a bunch around her knees and sped through the slype to the south door. From where she was, it looked like all of Gold Hill was aflame. The wind — *there would be a wind* — tugged on her veil. She ignored it. Veil and wimple were torn from her head. She grabbed them, letting go of her skirts, and tugged open the south door. *Why is this door not locked?* The sound of voices, not voices of panic, but voices raised in praise, floated to her. *They were singing. The office had gone on despite the fire. They must have seen it, smelled it.*

When Emma burst through the rood screen, all eyes turned toward her, faces expectant and very frightened, then shocked as they took in her appearance. *They think it a Viking raid. And yet their courage ...* Emma smiled. She looked young and vulnerable, her head crowned with a tumble of fabric. Dame Alburga alone ignored the interruption. She neither glanced up nor disrupted the circuit of her moving arm, and her voice was constant, intoning the psalm, allowing — as she had been taught — absolutely nothing to distract her from the duty of the office.

Emma quieted her hands and paced to the abbatial chair.

And so the office concluded, with the addition of the abbatial voice for the closing antiphon. Most of the nuns — surprised and shocked by her appearance — felt comforted nevertheless. All was right with the Lord. Everything was as it should be. The abbess was back in her chair. As the Apostle Paul had said, nothing could keep them from the love of God, not principalities or powers, not the heights nor the depths.

8

As soon as he had wiggled through the hole in the abbey wall, it was clear to Hugo that they had misjudged, and that their pursuers had returned to the Bimport. Shadows and torches flickered, by Hugo's reckoning, very near the main gate. They limped across Magdalene Lane and crouched into the shadow of the first house they came to, but it was too late. As they scuttled along the Bimport, Hugo's foot crunched on a patch of unexpected ice.

Someone unseen but very near drew a breath. Then, "'Ere. I've found 'em." Like ravening hounds, there came the indrawn breath of twenty throats, "Aarrggh."

The mob, all arms and teeth and eyes, crashed into them. Hugo felt himself pushed, lost his balance, and went down. A foot slammed onto the bones of his hand.

Like the skeleton of the last leaf on a tree, Master Levitas twirled and staggered under multiple blows, until, forced to his knees and forearms, he curled, like a hedgehog, into a ball, and fists smashed into his spine, his elbows, his right ear.

Knowing their quarry, the mob quickly passed over Hugo, leaving him to heave himself onto hands and knees. Instead of backing up, he crawled toward where he thought Levitas must be, at the center of the thrusting mass. "I couldn't believe it myself," he would later tell Levitas. "Risking my great abilities for your miserable, scrawny hide." Unable to squirm between the bent legs, Hugo fingered out his hammer and clubbed at tendons, toes, and the backs of knees. Little by little, he gained ground, as one after another staggered out of his path. When he finally found the bloodied goldsmith, Hugo, mindless of his own pain, heedless of the hail of blows, shrouded the frail body of the older man with his own. Someone howled; wouldn't stop howling. A red-hot pain ricocheted through his ribs. All sound seemed to waver. Hugo thought he heard words, growled from high above him, "Leave him be."

But they didn't. Hands pulled at his hair. Someone grabbed his arm and pried the hammer from his fingers. Sweaty hands twisted his arm into a hammerlock.

Then, Hugo stopped hearing.

CHAPTER TWENTY-ONE

WEDNESDAY

LATE NIGHT, AFTER MATINS AND LAUDS

I

obert plunged from the hall into the keep, heading for the fire. An ill-dressed assortment of men followed, buckling on swords and tying the leather thongs on their chain mail. The wind was pushing fans of fire sideways from the fire-boxes. Looking up, Robert shook his head. "God's blood! The wind." Grimly, he pulled his nosepiece down, stuck his foot into the stirrup, and mounted.

As the great gates swung open, a tearing howl seared the night sky. Robert led the garrison at a half-trot directly down the Bim-port and into the edges of a mob. The mob was not at the fire, as Robert had expected, but milling around between castle and abbey. He had no time to stop to find out what they were about. "March right through 'em," he yelled. His men closed ranks behind Robert's horse as, head tossing, heavy feet pounding, it crowded and pressed against the thrashing bodies.

Even with the threat of the horse and the garrison in their midst, those crowding the street moved neither forward nor back, but roiled and thrashed like fish after chum. As Robert closed on the center, he found not calm, like the eye of a storm, but turmoil dense and angry, and he felt the first tinges of apprehension. "Unsheathe your swords." Neither his words nor his voice of command were enough to pierce the rage-driven haze of hate. Few in the mob stepped back, but those in the center, a many-armed tangle of fury, rhythmically kicked and pummeled away at an inert form.

Who? What?

"Jew lover!" The words were spouted up at him on a gob of spittle.

Did the goldsmith have the guts to run for the castle? Robert clenched his jaw and spurred his horse a few steps farther in. There at the center, one man — *Bayard?* — flailed up and down, a cadenced arc of loathing. *Beating something — no, someone.* Grimly, Robert leaned down and slapped Bayard aside with the flat of his sword. Bayard whirled and looked up, teeth bared, a mad lack of recognition gleaming red in his eyes. Quick as an adder, another — *Simon?* — aimed his eating knife at the vein running down the chest of Robert's horse. Before Simon could realize his intention, the point of Robert's sword had nicked his ear. As the sword traced a red arc down his neck, Simon lowered his knife. A third man, unheeding, still pummeled at *a dead man?* "Leave him be." Robert growled, his voice brooking neither thought nor disobedience. Grudgingly, the third man rolled over and rose, wiping the blood dripping from his jaw.

On the icy gravel between Simon and Bayard lay a rumple of clothing, arms and legs curled protectively. *Around something? What? Gold?* A heavy hammer lay beside one of his hands. *Hammer. Not the goldsmith. Master Hugo?* Robert signaled with his mailed fist, index finger upraised. Two of the garrison elbowed forward and pulled the man off the ground by his hair, wrenching a limp arm into a hammerlock. Despite the swollen eyes and the blood, Robert recognized Master Hugo. Beneath him was revealed what

Robert at first took to be a mantle or cape, but there was heft to the fabric, and there were hands clasped around what looked like gray fur. *The goldsmith.*

"Be Master Levitas."

"Him, too." Robert was curt. "Pick him up." The men-at-arms looked at one another questioningly, hesitating, and then two or three of the younger ones put their hands under the body and lifted, much as one would a coffin.

2

RALF SPRINTED ALONG THE BIMPORT. The crowd around him moved randomly, some going toward the castle, some toward the fire, their movements jerky and excited. Followed close by Tindal, Ralf squirmed among them like light through water. As he neared the castle, the groups seemed to center and coalesce around the houses, but so intent was he on wending his way through and between their legs and bodies, that he paid no heed to the increased sound and knotted crowd. At the castle gate he pounded until the grille was opened. To the nose-plate behind the grille, he shouted his message.

"Message to the bailiff from Dame Averilla."

"Aye. And I'm my mother's auntie."

"Nay. 'Struth. Dame Averilla needs to speak to the bailiff."

"Yea. No one comes in or out without the bailiff's orders."

"No. It's not like that. Bailiff needs to see Dame Averilla." Ralf was jumping up and down in his frustration.

"What is it?" Another nose-plate peered out and down at Ralf. "Lad," the second voice said, not unkindly, "Bailiff's gone, see? Turn around." As he turned, all the hairs on Ralf's neck rose, and his memories enveloped him in an all-consuming fear that made water run down his leg. With no more than a muffled gasp, Ralf turned and ran, the dark shadow protecting his side.

261

3

HALTINGLY, THE MEN-AT-ARMS MADE their way back to the castle, supporting Master Hugo, carrying Master Levitas, forcing their way through a jostle of people who still grumbled and spat.

When they reentered the keep and the hall, Robert's eyes sought the calm gray eyes of his wife. The men lay down their burden. He said, "Do what you can."

Then he and his men quick-stepped back out the gate and down the Bimport. A glow spattered against the height of the church, outlining in black the lantern tower and seeming to flame through the slits of its louvered windows. *Worse than I expected,* Robert thought. From astride his horse, he used his mailed fist to hammer on the gate. "Open up! Warin! Abward! Fire!" Immediately, the gate swung open, first the sally port, then the full portal. *Of course. They've already seen the fire.*

Abward was ready. Near the wellhead stood carts, harnessed and loaded with great cauldrons that ostlers and stableboys passing leather buckets were filling in situ.

"The mob broke into the church." Abward's voice was toneless.

Robert swallowed his shock. "Any damage?"

Abward allowed himself a twitch of a smile. "Dame Averilla was readying for the office. Scared 'em away, she did. Chased 'em right out o' the church and called to me."

"Ah."

"We herded 'em onto the Bimport. 'Twas she 'as saw the fire first. From the Galilee porch. Sent the boy to tell me to ready the carts and such. 'E ran off to tell you of it."

It made sense that Averilla would tell him of the fire. Robert frowned. "Odo?" he asked.

"Nay, Bailiff. 'Twas the carver's apprentice. Ye wot, the scrawny one?"

Robert took a step toward the church.

Abward lifted an eyebrow. "Still at prayer, they be. Matins."

"Ah."

The fire was contained on the far side of Gold Hill. Neither the abbey wall nor the guest hall had yet caught. All through the market and down Gold Hill, figures sped this way and that, carrying buckets and yoked pails. The sky was brazen, as with mad, twitching bursts, the thatch on Levitas' house was consumed. Not everyone was helping. Standing with his back to the park wall, a low-browed brawny fellow fingered his trousers. Next to him, a slattern without wimple, hair falling into her eyes, grinned in ecstatic abandon. Robert narrowed his eyes. Sensing his scrutiny, the woman turned and stared back at him, in no wise cowed by the might of his armor, the sword at his side. *Is that Enid?* he wondered, recognizing the old woman. *More's the pity.* He held their eyes until, as one, the two started to climb back to the market, where they melted into the crowd.

As Robert and the armored men watched, the house downhill from the goldsmith's caught. At first just a few red-blue embers fell like autumn leaves, then larger flames, the size of rats, bit into the thatch. Flakes of reed, lath, and encrusted amber corkscrewed against the charred sky and then dissolved. Robert picked out Tom's form on the roof, along with the few men he'd had with him, frantically laying wet blankets on the thatch. *At least the carts from the laundry got here,* Robert thought, and pointing an ironclad finger, he sent more men to help Tom. *That house might be lucky.* A small alley separated it from Master Levitas',

With a sudden whoosh, the Jew's house was completely engulfed. Great branches of flame rose into the air. There was a tremendous crack and the roof timbers collapsed into themselves. A sigh rose from the onlookers. Tongues of fire rose even higher into the tangled clouds of acrid smoke. The heat was a wall against them.

On the second house, despite the alley and the blankets and

263

the buckets of water, new runnels of fire licked at the thatch. Here and there the supporting beams were exposed. A third house was starting to sprout nests of embers under the eaves and in the thatch. Robert shook his head in frustration and glanced uphill. The house above the goldsmith's hadn't yet caught. He was surprised. *The wind?* He licked his finger and held it aloft. *Aye, the wind. Good for something, at least. Night wind is a down-valley wind. It'll keep the flame from spreading upward. Thank God. Spare the abbey, at least till morning.* Robert was about to send for more water when a drop spat on his helmet. He looked up in perplexity, thinking for a moment that a bucket had been miscast. Then, *Rain? By the cross, 'tis rain.* He crossed himself and waited as the drops, large and heavy-weighted, started to beat down, slowly at first, then more quickly, becoming sharp and pronged, until, no longer isolated and individual, the wet coursed down in a heavy sheet. The spark-charred beams, all that was left of Levitas' house, sizzled in the wet, while the flames chewing on the second house cowered, hissing under the onslaught, and sending up irritated clouds of smoke and steam. A ragged cheer came from the third house, unseen behind the screen of wind-borne smoke and rain.

With the threat gone, Robert shrugged his shoulders peevishly. He hated rain in his armor and the thunder of it echoing around inside his helmet. It was clammy and cold, and imprinted every link of the chain mail through the leather of his jerkin and onto his skin. Completely irritated, Robert signaled to his men. "Wain, Hadrig," his voice rose over the confused shouts and the rain's hiss. "Keep watch that none disturb the ashes. I'll send replacements after Prime." As he passed the main gate of the abbey, it occurred to him that he should probably make certain of Dame Averilla's message, but he was wet and irritated, and she most likely wanted only to tell him of the fire.

4

By the middle of the night, during Lauds, the abbess was chanting her responses reflexively. Dominating her being was the frightening awareness that someone — someone close in space or time, she didn't know which — was in the shadow of death. *Aethwulfa? Or is Christ's passion still calling me? A Jew? The killing of a Jew? A man beleaguered for doing what was expected of him? No, mayhap not that. But one soul is in need of God's help, and can't pray on his own. Dear God, be with him, whoever he is. Let him feel your strength. Stand beside him.* Her voice rose higher on the words of the psalm as her mind prayed beneath them. *Someone is in trouble, Lord. Has need of your solace. Oh, God With Us, be with whoever he is. Guide him and give him your solace. I ask this in the name of your Son, Jesus Christ.*

Chapter Twenty-two

Wednesday

After Lauds, late night, early morning

I

aster Levitas and Master Hugo lay like so much debris in an unused corner of the great hall of Shaftesbury's stone keep. Hugo had lost consciousness; a lapse, he would later tell himself. He was roused by a serving girl offering water from a dipper. He drank, ashamed to find himself dribbling half of it down his front. He looked around. *At least they didn't put us into the cage. What can the bailiff plan to do with us? He — they — the whole burgh thinks this man beside me killed the maid. And babes before that.* Hugo glanced over at Levitas. *Man doesn't have the strength to hold up his own head, much less grapple with a strong girl. But why am I risking my life for this old man?*

He wiggled a tooth with his tongue; finally releasing it, he spat it out. He could barely see from his left eye. Fear coursed down his spine. With his right hand he pried open the upper eyelid, shut his right eye, and focused on the huddle of women in the center of the room. He could see. *That's all right, then.* That was his fear: the loss of sight, second only to the loss of his right hand. He flexed it. Thank God that whoever stepped on his hand had stepped on his left. *The left will recover.* He looked at it. Already it had swelled to the size of a cow's udder with full teats hanging down. *Not as bad as it might have been.* He was hurt and bruised, but nothing was angling out of place, like poor Levitas' arm. He tried moving his legs. *Ache, but that's about it.* He spat. No blood, or just from the tooth. Having saved it for last, dreading it, he tried to take a breath. A fiery pain ripped across his chest and echoed down his groin. *Not even a deep breath,* he thought ruefully as he hunched himself into the pain, enduring the fire while it dampened into a dull ache. *My lungs? Oh God, not my lungs. Mayhap just a rib.* A wave of nausea overtook him. He retched. Nothing but bile and the water he had too eagerly taken dripped from his lips. With a groan he righted himself.

Turning his head so he could better see Levitas, he tried to discern whether he was still breathing. *Unconscious, but...* He caught the eye of the guard standing over them. The man looked away, scowled, and spat. *Can I move Levitas?,* Hugo wondered. He didn't know how much freedom would be allowed. *Are we prisoners, or are we being protected?*

"Can I move him?" he mumbled around his swollen tongue.

"Mistress be comin'." The man gestured with his chin, obviously disgusted that "the mistress" would care for them. Hugo glanced over to where a woman in her middle years, the matronal wimple white and neat around her face, was heading toward them. She wore a tunic of blue over her long-sleeved gonelle, and the color of the tunic, plus the cleanliness of her wimple and the impressive bunch of keys dangling from her girdle, declared that this woman was probably the wife of the bailiff. A leather scrip and several rolled lengths of linen were tucked under her arm. She moved with efficiency, but her deep gray eyes were full of concern. Hugo relaxed. *Such a woman wouldn't be married to a harsh man, a man devoid of justice, would she?*

She glanced briefly at Hugo and then knelt before Master Levi-tas, clucking her tongue. Hugo leaned over to look more closely. Levitas was more bloodied than he'd feared. Blood still oozed from cuts that were clearly deep. "At least not spurting," he heard her mutter to herself, her hand just barely touching Levitas' pulse. His body was twisted at an odd angle.

"Mistress, can I help?"

"Aye. Pull him toward your lap." She gave the man-at-arms beside them, who was studiously observing the hearth fire across the room, a look of disgust. Levitas' arm, the one that had seemed out of joint to Hugo, was at an awkward angle, and when Hugo grabbed at it and tried to pull, Levitas moaned.

"Nay, not his arm," she sounded irritated. "Just help me get him so he's lying flat." Together, Hugo leaning over and favoring his left arm, they tussled Levitas fully prone.

"Cedric, have you a knife?"

Cedric produced it. With swift, competent strokes Mavis slit the heavy fabric of the goldsmith's tunic. "If we set the arm now — here, pull on his shoulder while I — Cedric, I need a flat board to splint this with — pull on his arm."

Cedric looked for a moment as if he might disobey, but seeing something in her eyes, he shrugged and slouched off.

"When I say pull, you pull your end, and I'll get the ends straight. Be he right-handed?"

Hugo shook his head. He didn't really know, couldn't keep his thoughts straight. He tried to lean his weight onto Levitas' left arm, where she had indicated, but with only a usable right hand, his left couldn't steady him sufficiently.

"Better the pain now ... "

Hugo's fingers were becoming numb. He could feel them slip-ping off of Levitas.

She was speaking in half-sentences while she worked, taking

deep breaths between. There was a grinding feel, a tremor up the bones, as she pulled. Hugo's hand slipped off the arm and he fell onto his shoulder, over Levitas. She pushed Hugo off and propped him upright.

"Hold on for just a little bit more," she said, mopping her brow with her sleeve. "Mayhap Dame Averilla will come, but ... "

Hugo thought he knew what that "but" portended.

Mavis unrolled a length of linen, bit into the edge, tore a slit, and made of the end two small, attached strips. When she was done wrapping Levitas' arm onto the piece of wood, she tied the torn ends together around the arm, neatly tucking in the flaps.

Her probing fingers played down Levitas' chest, again clucking a patter of dismay. With the unwilling assistance of Cedric, she wrapped more of the linen tight around Levitas' body, and then looked with miserable eyes at his head and the bloodied ear. "This—this—I cannot—there can be little hope for him."

"He coughs," Hugo said.

"Well, he will not now, I wot. The body forbids it when the ribs are broken. But if that be so, he must be propped up, so he can at least breathe. The stuff in his chest will make it harder to heal, particularly if he cannot cough it up. Levitas was like a sodden leek without spine or strength, and she ended up bolstering him into a sitting position at the "V" of the corner, furs and blankets tucked around him.

Finally, she turned to Hugo and examined him as one does a horse before purchase. "They tell me you covered him with your own body," she said, an appraising look in her eye. "Had ye not, I wot not the old man would now be alive."

"If the bailiff hadn't come as he did ... " Hugo left the thought dangling.

"Aye, Robert is a good man," she said. "And fair." Then, with a last look at Master Levitas, she concentrated on Hugo. In her capable voice she added, "The two louts as brought ye here said

269

as they thought, from the beating ye were given, that ye, too, might have a broken rib."

"Aye, but … my hand." His voice was a whisper as he held it out.

She muttered to herself as she looked at it. "More … probably splinted."

While she wrapped and splinted his hand, the two louts flopped a pallet on the floor next to him, and with no more honor than they would give to a sack of flour, lifted him onto it. The straw felt amazingly soft. Knowing that Levitas was now in good hands; that there was nothing more he could do, Hugo retreated into his pain. All he wanted was to be left alone. He was vaguely aware of being eased out of his boots and hose, until only his shirt was covering him. Two of the younger serving maids were tending to him, and their hands were soft, like the fluttering wings of some shy bird, as they wrapped linen around his chest, tendering him a respect and honor that he didn't feel he deserved, patting furs and coverlets around him. With surprise, he found he was shaking and his teeth were chattering. A tear welled, and he shut his eyes so that they wouldn't see it. He felt like an old warhorse being groomed.

Mavis' voice, overloud, as his parents had been when he was drifting off to sleep as a boy, pierced his unconsciousness. It took effort, but he opened his eyes. She was holding out a piss pot. He raised his eyebrows. It was the last thing he'd had in mind. "Before ye go off to sleep, I need to see if there be any blood in the piss." And she turned her back to him, signaling the maids to do the same.

He obliged; she peered into the pot, and, with a little noise of satisfaction, handed it off to one of the girls. To Hugo she said, "Ye be a fortunate man, for despite the kicks to yer back, yer interior took little harm."

Again, Hugo felt his eyelids droop. *Levitas. That's it. It's all right, Levitas,* he cast his thought to his friend. *She'll take care of you. Strange,* he thought again, *that I should care.*

2

THEY TRANSFERRED MASTER HUGO and Master Levitas as soon as Robert returned to the castle. "You can't mean to move them," Mavis, aghast, snapped at her husband. Then, more softly, closer to his ear, she begged, "Robert, it might kill the old man. And he cannot be guilty—I do not believe that he could have murdered that girl."

"Nor do I, Mistress, nor do I, but we can't keep them here. I have to at least try to keep Master Levitas alive until a trial, and I fear that more damage might come from keeping him here than from moving him." At her incredulous look, he said, exasperated, "The men of the burgh, my men as well, believe him guilty. For his own safety, and to care for his wounds, if any can, I must send him, and the carver as well, to the abbey."

They hauled Hugo up roughly, and forced him to stumble out into the keep. Levitas, however, was carried outside, where he was heaped into a cart, his bottom down, his ankles sticking out like so much kindling.

As the first streaks of dawn pierced the heavy cloud cover, the castle gates rumbled open. The crowd was still massed outside, light from the dimming fireboxes reflecting in their eyes. A square of men surrounded the cart and accompanied them the short way down the Bimport. *Why do we need an escort? Surely it is just a short way.*

Nothing happened at first. The troop slushed methodically toward the east. Behind the horse and cart, two from the garrison were propping Hugo up as he stumbled down the Bimport. He couldn't keep his thoughts straight. *The horse is pooping, right there in front of the cart. Couldn't it wait?* But *he* hadn't

271

waited. He had jumped so easily into the drain. What could he have been thinking? He didn't even like the man. *The pain in my head. And my side?* Hugo tried to put his feet under him; tried to ease his shoulders where the two men-at-arms were pulling on his shoulders. *Can't they see the bandages?* He wasn't even properly dressed. Shoes on haphazardly. *I know the number of my ribs just as God knows the number of—of what. Can't remember. Knees are all right. I'm glad my knees work.* The mob was keeping pace with the men-at-arms. Hugo tried to crouch. *I am a coward. I didn't know that.*

The mob couldn't reach Levitas in the cart, so they wouldn't let Hugo go, circling closer as they neared the abbey gate. A hand snaked between the guards and pulled hairs from Hugo's beard. "Saved 'im didn't ye?" Another hand struck at him, just grazing the hurt rib. He could smell the sudden acrid fear from the men guarding him.

"Jew lover." A fist smashed into Hugo's face, and he crumpled, arms suddenly slack.

The men-at-arms circled closer to the cart. "Ye be worse even than the Jew. At least he was born to it. Ye choose to betray our Lord."

A rock clanged against the steel of a helmet. "Dam'ee." The man beside Hugo staggered against him.

"Leave 'im be." Hugo heard a slap as one of the men-at-arms struck someone with the flat of his sword.

"E's right." It was another voice, weaker than the first. A kick came from the side and caught Hugo's shin.

A voice, Hugo didn't know which of the men-at-arms it was, but a voice of command, albeit slow and drawling, said, "Ye might as well leave 'im be. We won't 'ave 'im with us much longer."

"I didn't want to." Hugo mumbled. "He's rude."

Another blow came from the right.

"Break it up." It was the bailiff's voice.

272

3

AFTER THE REBUFF AT THE CASTLE, Ralf, Tindal beside him, ran back to the abbey. Fear and slats of rain enveloped him. Seeing the mob at the gate, he waited in the shadows, and then slipped through behind a cart and a troop of men-at-arms being harassed by the mob. Even when he had gained the security of the outer court, he sidled into the earth-smelling shadows of the ewery and the brew house until he could scramble up into the stable loft. He didn't expect to see the lump of Hugo's body, yet he had hoped. Some long-held breath deflated when he failed to hear the familiar sputtered snoring.

With the pummeling sound of rain on the roof came an awareness of the snorting and stamping from the animals below. The smell of wet smoke was everywhere. *The horses are scared. They hate fire and smoke.* He slid down the ladder to the stable floor, gathering splinters from the rough rungs. Going from stall to stall and patting the outstretched noses and upraised heads, Ralf crooned softly to them, "Somer is a'komin in, the birdies sing too-whee." It was tuneless, disjointed, and repetitive, but it was the only song he knew.

His memories seemed to lunge at him from the shadows and the writhing spurts of the dying flames. The night in his village, the screaming of the horses as the houses had been torched. When he had first smelled the smoke, in the oratory, he had tried to hold away the agony of remembering by working feverishly on the panel. Then, Dame Averilla had needed him, and it took all his concentration and cunning to avoid being caught as he ran to the castle. But all that time the memories had lurked behind his eyes. Now the animals needed him. He could concentrate on them. They glanced at him as he passed, stamping and whickering in their nervousness. A few kicked at their stalls.

Old Wat, mending harnesses, always puttering, muttered to himself. At first Ralf thought the old man was speaking to him, asking about the sounds. But then, as there were no pauses, Ralf decided Wat was merely cursing and grumbling to himself or the horses or perhaps to God. *Maybe Wat knows,* Ralf thought, *talking like that to God.* Whatever Wat was doing, it was comforting to have him there.

Where was Hugo? Had he been hurt? The howls from the market seeped through his tune. Someone screamed nearby, and the redness of the memories burst through. Flames were devouring his mother's soft white flesh. He could see the swords and ... he whimpered. A wet nose nudged his hand, and a wet tongue lapped his face as he bent down. Ralf clutched at clumps of fur as, gently, soothingly, the great dog offered his neck to be squeezed, his warmth as comfort. Nearby, Bithric, tense with the smell of fire, whinnied in his stall, calling boy and dog to him. Duty warding off fear, Ralf loosed the dog, grabbed a handful of hay, and began methodically rubbing Bithric's soft flank.

4

THE MEN-AT-ARMS, THEIR DUTY ACCOMPLISHED, thrust Hugo against the opening main gate of the abbey. He grabbed the grille for support, but was pushed off the gate with such force that he stumbled face down onto the gravel. The gatekeeper walked past, kicking gravel.

With Hugo stumbling along behind him, the bailiff carried Master Levitas from the cart into the inner court and up the stairs to the guest lodgings next to the abbess' rooms. "You yourself carry him?" The abbess stood at the head of the stairs, Dame Averilla beside her.

"I carry Master Levitas myself," Robert growled in response as he reached the top stair, "because I trust myself. And I trust you."

A solemn look passed between the three before Robert continued into the opened door of the guest's lodgings.

"I thought it best," the abbess would tell Dame Aethwulfa, "to put the goldsmith in one of the guest chambers, the one next to mine."

Dame Aethwulfa would look shocked. "But that chamber is for the king or—or some other great noble."

"Nevertheless, I have so done. Sister Cadilla has too many in the infirmary to keep both Master Hugo and Levitas there, nor would it be proper. The guest hall is too … open. Since Sister Cadilla needs Dame Helewise's help in the infirmary, Dame Averilla will tend to the two men."

5

DAME AVERILLA FOLLOWED THE ABBESS and the bailiff into the guest room and watched as Robert settled the beaten and woebegone men. Blood still oozed from Master Levitas' ear, his arm was a bloodied mess, and she feared the gray tinge to his lips. Master Hugo seemed in great pain. And both men reeked.

Robert looked up to find Dame Averilla's eyes upon him. He passed his hand over his eyes and seemed to be trying to focus his mind. "Dame, you sent for me, I think?"

"You never came."

"No, I … " Robert softened his voice, "I thought you meant me to know of the fire?"

"But could you not have stopped on your way back?"

"As I say, I thought it was the fire."

"Dame." There was a new note of command in the abbess' voice, and Averilla recollected herself. "Perhaps if you were to leave this chamber and speak to the bailiff elsewhere?" It was not a question.

The bailiff and Averilla moved outside, the wind cutting into their faces. "I'm sorry," she said. "We are all overwrought. What I wanted to tell you of is Savette's ring."

"Aye."

Overriding the weariness she heard in his voice, she said. "This murder is not the work of that old man. Old men don't do such things. They haven't the fire."

"Dame, I understand your kind feeling—"

"No." Averilla interrupted. "It is not that, albeit that is true. This killing is not the work of a Jew. It would be a blasphemy to him; to Jews, blood is a blasphemy." She paused uncertainly. "I think—how can I explain it? What was done to Savette would be against all—all the rules that are important to them. In a way that it is hard for Christians to understand, Jews abide by laws, not just the Ten Commandments, but other laws as well, tangling laws that would make such a killing not only an indecency but unclean, an abomination."

"I only know, Dame, that there is much talk of his murdering her—as well as others."

"Aye, but 'tis only talk."

"Mayhap the Jew just pushed her."

"No!" Averilla was becoming strident. "Why would he so? What merit him that?" She gave an exasperated look at Robert and continued. "Don't you see? I have known the old man. I have seen his works. I watched with him as his wife died. 'Tis not who the man is. He—he is honorable. Has lent to the poor he knew would never repay him; has lent to us, but has not asked for our plate in return . . . ."

Her fierce protestations broke through Robert's negligent acceptance. "By the rood, I, too, know the essence of the man. But, Dame, what matters our thought? He must be tried, and most here believe him guilty and are eager for his blood."

The wind blew her veil over her eyes and a warning flake of snow wandered down. She was shivering. "I—I came to know something."

276

Robert narrowed his eyes and gestured toward the stairs. With anyone else, certainly with most of the other nuns, his patience would have been exhausted. But, tired as he was, implausible as the coming rationalization might seem, to Dame Averilla he would listen. "It is cold. Tell me in one of the parlours."

Together they pushed open the door and entered the dark room. Before they had time to enter, she turned to him and blurted, "Jared gave Savette a plight troth. A ring. Of Master Levitas' fashion. She showed it me, yet no longer does it rest around her neck, nor the ribbon it hung from. I saw them both myself, and not long past."

"Aye. I can believe it," he said slowly. "The two favored one another. I saw it myself. Not just a heard-tell. But that proves not the goldsmith's innocence. The ribbon and the ring could have been lost in the stream, slipped under a rock." Robert's head pushed forward, like a tup's in the spring preparing to battle. "I say not that Jared might not have broken a troth. He could have. All his life he has kept just this side of trouble. It would be in character. But why kill her for a broken troth? And why make the sign of the cross on her hand?"

"I know not. But he might have." Averilla felt stubborn.

"For a ring?"

"Not just for the ring. She was with child."

He shook his head and furrowed his brow in annoyance. "Dame! That is not a killing matter, more a matter of rejoicing. A child is a boon."

His eye rested on her as he thought. Slowly, he refocused, saw her, really looked at her.

"Dame," he said, his left eye narrowing, "you know more, don't you?"

"I believe that Jared found another woman to marry. He was avoiding Savette not because he had tired of her, as she thought, but because he could wed another who had more to give him."

"So you believe that this other maid — and not the Jew or an outlaw — pushed Savette?" Robert was pacing in circles, his brow creased into a look of astonishment. "Not Anne. She is plight troth and there would be no advantage. Nor Mary. There is no one else his age. There is Damasa, but — "

She made the slightest of movements.

"Damasa? But Damasa has not the bloom that lightened Savette. She ... is rich, but has no other suitors. And Damasa has not the energy to kill. Her humors are — are ... " He shook his head in frustration, his sentence unfinished.

"Nay, I meant not that Damasa had killed Savette. I meant that Jared killed Savette because he had plighted troth to Damasa and wanted the ring from Savette. It came to me early this morn. I know not why, as all else was on my mind, but I heard, in my mind, the words of the goldsmith as Sister Cadilla was tending to him after the attack by Jared. Master Levitas remembered one of Jared's friends saying that Damasa would much enjoy the goldsmith's brooch."

Robert covered his look of astonishment with one of speculation. "Tom told me that Jared's eye had strayed, but I little credited it. Thought it was a love spat. There would be small reason to trade Savette for Damasa."

"She is the steward's daughter. And she is rich."

"Ah." He turned for the door. "I shall look into it." With his hand on the lachet he said, "I shall send word on the morrow. Whatever I find."

Chapter Twenty-three

Wednesday

Prime, at daybreak

I

Soon after cockcrow, Robert rode back down the Bimport, ignoring the mob still gathered around the abbey gate-house, all too aware of the wet, charred smell that overlay the town, the motes of ash on the grimy snow. He knocked at the two-story house of the steward and was shown into the hall. When he asked for Damasa, the maid looked surprised, but hurried to find her mistress.

Damasa's was a pasty face under lash-less eyes. If she felt any surprise at Robert's coming, she did not show it. Her eyes glittered an irritated lavender, but revealed nothing more than surprise at Robert's intrusion into her morning. With a muttered greeting, she led him through the hall and into the solar, a fashionable new kind of withdrawing room where the women of the household could evade the burly masculinity of the more public hall. The steward's house boasted not only this solar, Robert noted in surprise, but also the glory of a fireplace built into the wall. *I don't remember hearing of this,* he thought, eyeing the stone structure. *How has Master Chapman, I wonder, come by such wealth? And*

*why has not this new plaything been heralded more broadly about?
'Twould seem he little wanted it speculated on. It might be worth
a word to the abbess. If her steward—?*

But not this morning. Damasa cleared her throat to get his
attention. He looked at her, noting that her hair lay in two long
plaits, brown and dull, albeit intertwined with silken ribbons
the color of her gown. *Surely her hair had not grown that long.
Could she be using horsehair entwined with the ribbon?* His
wife, if he remembered rightly, had told him that women did
such things. The reasoning was beyond him. But even he could
see that her gown was of a fine fabric, though the lumps of fat
about the waist pressed against the cloth, and her flesh moved
on its own as she walked. *At least she is up and working,* Robert
chided himself, though at such a frivolous matter as embroidery.
She was accomplished. He could see that. And accompanied: a
serving maid hovered uncertainly by the fire.

"Bailiff?" Damasa's tone was peremptory. She made no attempt
at mouthing a mannerly courtesy.

"I will take little of your time, Damasa." His use of her Christian
name was deliberately disrespectful. She flashed him an arrogant
look before stabbing her needle into the cloth stretched across the
hoop of her embroidery frame.

"I need your true answer to a question." Her eyes were suddenly as opaque as a pond on a cloudy day. He turned his back to
her, holding his hands to the fire. "Easy enough to find the truth,
should you ... misspeak." He waited, letting the tension mount.

"What is it you want to know?"

He turned, the better to gauge her reaction, then asked, "Are
you plight troth?"

Even though she regarded him with deliberate disdain, she
couldn't hide the question that stirred behind the frigid eyes.
"You dare ... ?"

I have my answer he thought. *Elsewise, lady, your tongue*

280

would be the less arrogant.

"Aye," he said instead, and let the one word lie between them. She sighed and bent her head over strands of ruby wool. Her needle, he noticed, was motionless.

"I am." The red came from above her breasts and splotched her skin. A little smile that she meant to look demure played at her lips.

"I have heard it spoken that Jared Reeve's-son has bid you to wed. Is it so?"

"Aye."

"Did he give you a plight-troth?"

"That can be no business of yours."

"Mistress, heard you the crowds last night?" Robert's voice was patient, yet exasperated, as if explaining something to a particularly dull child. "Master Levitas, the goldsmith, is suspected of murder."

Her relief was palpable. "That can be of no interest to me."

"I am here because I have been told that perhaps you might have been given as a plight-troth a piece of his work." She looked at him with a slight hesitation and then pulled a ring from her finger.

He inclined his head and reached for it. She curled her fingers. "I will treat it with care, but I need to show it to Dame Averilla at the abbey."

Damasa clung harder. "What can she need this for? Surely the abbey has many pieces of the goldsmith's work."

"I will send it back to you," he said, taking her hand in his and uncurling, one by one, her smaller fingers, "with one of my men." He placed the ring in his scrip, bowed just slightly, turned, and then paused. As if he had just remarked it, he said, his back to her, "The brooch you wear, was that also a gift from Jared?" He turned in time to see her put her hand over it protectively.

"You have your piece of the goldsmith's work to see that that

281

evil man kills no more innocents. That is sufficient. You may leave me now."

2

MASTER LEVITAS REMAINED UNCONSCIOUS through the night. He had vomited twice. Averilla had had to raise his head to keep him from breathing it in. His lips retained their bluish cast, his pulse rate was alarmingly high, and it seemed to her that he couldn't move one side of his body. "But we can't really know until he regains consciousness," she would report to the abbess. The leaking of blood from his ears had ceased as soon as Robert had lain him on the bed. The alarming bruise on his head had blued and purpled with the morning.

Hugo had been placed on a pallet on the floor. He awakened after Prime to find Dame Averilla still with them, her eyes carrying the faraway look of prayer. Hugo's hand remained on his chest, where she had placed it the night before, telling him, "It will ease, somewhat, the pain. You have cracked, perhaps broken, a rib. He dimly now remembered her worried mien at the linen strips Mavis had wound around his chest, and looked down now to see if his memory was tricking him. She smiled. "You refused at first to wear the sling. Quite adamant you were. You told me that you would never wear it when you were working."

"And what did you say then?"

"I told you that the pain in your chest would be severe for longer."

"And then?"

"You lost consciousness from the pain in both your chest and your hand."

As if it belonged to someone else, Hugo lifted his left hand to examine it. Dame Averilla removed the linen strips that were binding it to the splint, and they both looked at it in some horror.

282

During the night, the hand had swollen to twice its normal size, and the colors were deeper blacks and brighter blues, mired within a jaundiced yellow. He tried bending his fingers, but they moved as little as a string of sausages. He laid it back on his chest. "At least it is my left."

"I am sorry, she said. "I can give you no poppy. I fear for your chest."

Laboriously, he levered himself into a sitting position. Wavering at first, finally he stood, albeit leaning against the wall. "I need to tell Ralf where I am. He will be worried."

Dame Averilla gasped and put her hand to her mouth.
"Dame?"

"I—I sent Ralf to the castle last night. To fetch the bailiff."
"When?"

"Last night."

In the midst of—of that chaos?"

"Aye."

"Did you see him return?"

"I—I didn't think of it."

"You sent a child..." Exhaustion overwhelmed him and he plopped onto a stool.

Averilla said, "From what the bailiff told me, I think Ralf made it to the castle. Mavis would not have allowed him to come back."

The look he gave her was black. "No, I imagine not, he snapped. "She has children of her own."

Averilla lowered her eyes.

"All the more need for me to find him."

"You are not able."

"I shall go. My clothes?" She pointed to a pile. He looked aghast at the assortment.

"They were what the novices could find. Yours ... smelled."

"The drains," he growled.

283

Dressing was exhausting work. Hugo was forced to allow Averilla to help.

"Why don't I send someone?"

"Dame, he is my responsibility. I—I care."

"But you are ..."

3

CURSING THE HYPOCRISY WITH WHICH he had had to treat Damasa, cursing her grasping control, Robert strode back down the Bimport. It was after Prime. Was it before Terce? He hadn't listened for the bell.

"Dame Averilla," he said to the portress, and she walked him through the outer court, to the abbess' lodgings, where, with a sign, she indicated he should wait. When Averilla finally emerged, she seemed worn and haggard. Robert realized that she, too, had been up all night.

They bowed.

He took the ring from his scrip and held it out. She moved into the light and turned the ring this way and that, noting the intertwined leaves and vines encircling it. "Yes," she said. "I believe this is the ring she showed to me. I wonder if Master Levitas ever makes two alike?"

Robert had wondered also. "I can ask him."

She shook her head.

"You will have me informed if there is any change."

"I will."

4

ABLE TO LIMP DOWN THE STAIRS only by leaning his weight against the wall, Hugo had finally agreed to allow Averilla to find an ostler for him to lean on. He and the ostler crossed the outer court at an angle, Hugo panting and stopping every few feet. *Ralf must have heard the mob. Then Averilla sent him to fetch the bailiff? Did the mob catch him and beat him, and blame him for my friendship with Levitas?* Hugo shook his head. *Lord, please, no. He took care of himself in the forest; mayhap ...* He tried to thwart the recognition that was writhing slowly into his consciousness. A fiery pain stitched from his side to his bowel. *Lord, forgive me. I left him. Don't let me have lost Ralf, too.* With a suddenness that surprised him, his knees misgave him and he plopped onto a mounting block. With unexpected kindness, the ostler forced his head between his legs. Though various feet passed into his view, no one asked or showed any interest. *They still despise me.* After a long time he rose, and, leaning even more heavily on the man, stumbled the rest of the way to the stables. *Lord, let him be there.*

When he reached the stables, Hugo thanked the ostler.

"Dame Averilla 'us al'ays good to my moder," the man said, and without a smile or a bow, turned and left Hugo leaning against the doorjamb.

Hugo heard the boy, the dog, and the donkey before he saw them. Ralf was still crooning a counterpoint to the animals' nervousness. It was peaceful. Hugo stood just out of view. A weak slat of sun lighted the smoothness of the boy's skin. Tindal's thumping his tail against the side of the stall in greeting alerted Ralf to another presence. Wide-eyed, the boy bolted into a standing position, clutching a pitchfork. Seeing Hugo, he loosened his grip on the fork and started to tremble. "Wha, where?" Ralf asked, allowing his terror, unable to articulate any further, eyes round in fear.

Hugo reached out and awkwardly patted the boy's shoulder, drawing him close so he could lean on him. "Aye, lad, 'tis all right now. Help me over to a bench; I'll sit and tell it."

Ralf fell asleep next to Hugo, elbow pillowed on the dog's flank, head lolling. Hugo's eyes slid across the splintered boards

285

to Bithric. The donkey, sensing a gaze, turned liquid eyes toward Hugo and twitched an ear. Hugo's thoughts, as always, turned to the comfort of his work. *Grace. Humility. It was to a donkey that God gave the honor of carrying His Son.* Hugo smiled to himself. *I will put a donkey among all those horses Ralf is carving.* Later, noticing the donkey, Levitas would tell Hugo, "You know your Christ and his donkey? Not just chance that he chose a donkey. Old tradition for Jews—Solomon came to his crowning on a donkey. Or mule. I think they viewed it the same."

Unable to do anything more, Hugo too started to nod off, the smell of the hay comforting. *Like a summer's morning,* he thought. The warmth of the animals and the motes in the sunbeams were better than a tonic. *Or is scent more robust in a late afternoon? Are things sweeter broken? Is everything? Is that what I feel? Levitas will know.*

As he sat there, eyes drooping, Hugo drowsily watched a spider lift itself, tendril legs waving, across the roof beam, trying to evade the larger spider following it. The harrying pursuit reminded him of the mob of yesterday. The mob was still outside the main gate, still spewing molten hate against Levitas. He had been all too aware of them as he crossed the court. *Against me, as well,* Hugo thought with certainty. *If he lives, Levitas will have to flee. He can't stay here. But where can he go? And with whom? Can't go alone. I little trust the men from the garrison. Too close to the thoughts of the mob. Like as not those men'd leave Levitas on some track and return to Shaftesbury swearing that they'd met a band of outlaws. Fought as hard as they could, they'd say, but...*

So I—the boy and I—will have to go with him. Wherever he decides to go. The decision made, Hugo forced his battered body to rise, waking Ralf in the process.

"You'll have to help me, lad. I'll need to lean on you to get back to the abbess' lodgings. Levitas. He is hurt. Needs me. Can't expect the nuns to be with him all the time. Have the offices to

286

sing. Most folk think he killed the girl, so 'tis best if someone is with him."

Nodding sleepily, Ralf stood.

5

HUGO AGREED TO WATCH OVER LEVITAS as best he could. Even so, Averilla was uneasy about him during the day, and scurried back and forth between her duties in the oratory to her patient in the lodgings, to ascertain that nothing untoward had occurred.

Late in the afternoon, surprising everyone, Dame Edith came forward to alleviate the toll on Dame Averilla.

"Master Hugo's work is important," Edith said, with the look of a lover seeing the beloved with eyes of wonder. "I would do anything to help him complete what he started."

When Averilla and the abbess looked dubious, she continued, straightening the room and making a place where she could both sit and be near Master Levitas. "Mayhap it does not happen thus to you," — this was addressed to Master Hugo, who had returned, and whose eyes she had shyly avoided, — "but when I work, if I am not able to get the thought down right away, sometimes I lose it."

She said it with such pathos that it was suddenly clear to Emma and Averilla why Edith, whose carrel was so close to the oratory, was often one of the last to enter it for the Divine Office.

"I have spent years in the infirmary, so you know that I can care for them." This she addressed to Dame Averilla, but as if to convince the abbess, she added, "When he feels able to start work again, Master Hugo can relieve me during the offices. He will have to stop work then, anyway." Edith looked down and then said, voice low. My hands cramp in the cold of the cloister. 'Tis much warmer here, so I, too, will be better able to work."

It seemed a happy solution, so Dame Edith was detailed to relieve Dame Averilla and watch for the first full night.

Chapter Twenty-four

Thursday

Terce or mid-morning

I

lthough his left hand looked peculiar and his breath was shallow, by the second morning after the fire, Hugo insisted that he felt well enough to view the panel. When Edith had relieved him, he hobbled across to the oratory, leaning heavily on Ralf, to assess the damage, very aware of his ribs and his left arm in its sling. Dame Averilla had warned him, but nothing could have prepared him for the ravishment of his work. A gasp of anguish burst from him when he saw where Bayard had lopped off the top of the panel.

Letting go of Ralf, he crumpled onto the foot of the pier and looked from the horses Ralf had carved, with their perfection and vitality, to the splintered destruction that was the top of the panel. Tears coursed down his cheeks. *I care nothing for this panel,* he thought, bewildered. *Why am I crying?*

As he elbowed the tears off his face, he was horrified to find the abbess and Dame Alburga making their way toward him, hands tucked into their sleeves, their breath a faint haze of smoke against the black cold air of the nave. At the edge of the chapel they stood beside Hugo and surveyed the damage. Ralf was lugging the other two panels over to the altar, to prop them in front of and on either side of the injured one so Hugo could better assess the damage.

After a long silence, the abbess said, "It occurs to me ... " Her voice was reflective, her eyes affixed to the panel in order to allow Hugo the time he needed to rise, and to further collect himself, " ... that I was in error in preferring a reredos to an altar frontal. I am now quite decided. I like these panels as they are now, placed in front of the altar." Her eyes shifted from the hanging above the altar to the panels and back again. "It has troubled me, you understand," her voice retained the slow, thoughtful cast, "the moving of the hanging on which Dame Agnes labored so long. Now that I see the panels in front of the altar, I am convinced that this placement better reflects the Eucharist, which occurs upon it."

"But Margaret de Huseldure?" attempted Dame Alburga.

"Margaret is a very wise woman."

"Alburga was slow to understand that I was trying to relieve Hugo of his pain at the loss of the top curve," the abbess would tell Aethwulfa.

The latter would nod and then remark, "Tact, my lady, was never Alburga's strength, now was it?"

As they were speaking, Hugo, too, shifted his eyes back and forth from the panels to the hanging. Because they had been intended to go behind the altar, with the curve intact, the panels would not have fit in front of it. Now, however, as only one of the horses, the top one, had been completely destroyed, ironically, the destruction drew the observer's eye more forcibly to the centrality of Christ. Hugo furrowed his brows. He turned to Ralf. "I'm sorry lad, I would have liked to have seen that horse. Was it fine?"

Ralf did his best to look noncommittal. "I'd ne'er afore 'ad a chance to 'ave my work — 'toys' — admired, so if it's one horse more or less, I still be honored."

Hugo turned to the abbess. "You may be right about the relation-ship of the panels to the altar. I saw such altar frontals in Saxony. The priests will not always be standing there in front," he continued nodding slowly, "so mayhap accidents are not always so bad."

"We might put it else," the abbess countered. "We would say that anything done with evil intent can be put right by God, if we but allow it."

2

BECAUSE THE NUNS WERE TO HELP Father William with Savette's funeral mass, Averilla kept three of the novices with her in the sacristy after Terce. The sound of the funeral cortege could be heard coming from the High Street. "Here," she said, "take these." To each of the novices she handed a basket of candles. "Remem-ber. Go slowly. Keep your eyes on one another and try to match your movements. Sister Mavern, when you light the candles, be dignified."

She followed them through the rood screen and into the nave, placing the censor and a stoup of holy water in front of the rood screen.

As the clergy and mourners entered the north door, simultane-ously the abbess' door opened to admit the nuns, their pace solemn, their heads down, their hands nestled in wide sleeves. Instead of halting somewhat back, as did the rest of the community, the twenty-six novices continued on toward the nave altar. Each young woman bowed to either Sister Cantile or Sister Theodosia, and was given a candle, which Sister Mavern slowly and deliberately lighted. *Too slow,* thought Averilla, fretting. The sonorous voice of Dame Alburga broke the shuffling silence with the first word of the antiphon, "Dirge," and the cortege with the bier moved forward between the line of nuns. The bier was made of two long poles topped by crosspieces, and upheld the coffin. The bearers, cloaked in unrelieved grimness, placed the bier between the lines of candle-bearing novices.

When the funeral mass had ended, Father William removed his chasuble and handed it to Dame Averilla. He then turned to cense the coffin and sprinkle it with holy water. As smoke rose through the perforations of the censor, Averilla saw again in her mind's eye Savette's burnished curls and anguished eyes. As Father William droned the absolutions and the antiphons of forgiveness and deliverance, Averilla and Sister Theodosia smoothed and folded the embroidered white pall in on itself, until the heavy silk was nothing more than a pale blanket atop the plain wooden coffin. This pall was one of the abbey's best, and had been deliberately lent as a symbol of respect from a community of virgins to Savette, another virgin. Averilla made a little moue of justification to herself as she laid the pall across Theodosia's arms, to be taken and placed in the sacristy. *The fact that Savette was no longer a virgin hardly mattered anymore, did it?*

The crucifer and torchbearers were the first to exit the church, and as soon as they stepped out of the north door, the candles fluttered sideways and flickered into charred wicks. During the burial office, the skies had again mottled themselves into a wind-driven mist, which served to further isolate and separate the mourners as they trudged through the half-frozen slush to the graveyard. The gravediggers were already there, waiting for them, seeming to emerge like ghouls from the stinging drizzle. When the last of the mourners had arranged themselves, coughing into the quiet, Father William again swung the censor in wide arcs, censing the ground and sprinkling holy water over the splotchy grasses. The passing bell, soft-toned Michael, started its solemn tolling, and the nearer gravedigger, a somber man with a widow's hunch, handed his spade to Father William in order for the priest to carve a shallow trench in the shape of a cross. Then the actual digging began. Crunching through rocks and occasional bones, the spades again and again entered the earth, while the nuns drearily intoned the seven penitential psalms as if trying to cover the sound.

We can't seem to keep together in this, Averilla thought, as the voices in the back echoed those closer to the grave. The six bearers placed the coffin lid on the ground, and tilted the coffin so that the small bundle of deerskin tipped into the open grave. Even before it had fully settled into the small pool of water that was forming at the bottom of the pit, across the silence a bewildered cry was vomited from a deep well of grief.

"Aaiirrgh! Nooooooo!"

Lovick? Todd? Despite herself, Averilla looked around.

Jared!

Where had he come from? He was struggling toward the front. Hands grasped at him. He shrugged them off and threw himself into the hole, tumbling awkwardly onto the crumbled bundle of leather, where he started trying to claw the lacings apart.

Tears streamed down his face, and he blubbered incomprehensible sounds, "Mine...Noooo. You can't. I haven't..." No one moved.

Jared, seemingly deaf to anything but his grief, had torn open the swaddling, revealing to all the face of the girl, bluish-green in the dreaming of death. Seemingly unaware of the blue lips, the cold stoniness, he held Savette's head tenderly between his two open palms, devouring her features.

3

AFTER THE BURIAL, THE ABBESS KNELT at the nave altar. She needed counsel, but since she felt it rude yet again to bother God, she had come to Saint Edward. He knew about betrayal. She had anticipated a comfortable chat with "the beloved saint." Instead, she found herself seeking again the succor of the Almighty. Without a conscious recognition of her own need, the strength that she sought flowed into her. *My God, my God. You know that chapter is like to be as full of distrust and fear as is the town. The hatred of Master Levitas will be heavy on them.* She shut her eyes, and allowed herself to drift. As if stung, her lids again opened to see a watery sunbeam gilding Edward's reliquary, the reliquary refashioned by Master Levitas. Master Levitas, dear Master Levitas.

4

BY LATE AFTERNOON OF THAT DAY, a faint tinge of color had massaged Levitas' cheeks, and his lips had lost their blue tinge. Finally, during Vespers, when only Master Hugo was with him, Master Levitas stirred. "Caaan't."

Hugo was so startled that he jumped, and then knelt beside the bed. "Oout. Oout. Oout."

Hugo shut his eyes in a grief that surprised him. *Levitas, don't leave your senses. I have just found someone who understands my work, and have I now lost you?*

Hugo opened his eyes. The black melancholy eyes of the Jew were turned toward him, beseeching. "I," Hugo said, a tear trickling down his cheek, "can't understand you."

Later that night, alone with Hugo, Levitas spoke again. After the initial words during Vespers, he had kept his eyes on the ceiling, his body unmoving. Hugo had forced himself to recognize that, though the body of the man was alive, his brain was in all probability not, and the open eyes saw nothing.

"Thank yooou," Levitas said, moistening his lips, his voice cracking with disuse.

Then he was quiet, sipping obediently of the willow-bark tea Dame Averilla had left for Hugo to spoon to his lips. After a few impotent sips, the goldsmith again lapsed, but this time into a deep sleep.

Chapter Twenty-five

Friday

Prime, or daybreak

I

It was not until the third morning after the fire that the bailiff was allowed to see Master Levitas.

"You may try to ask him," Dame Averilla said, when the bailiff again asked to see the goldsmith. She led Robert back up to the guest lodgings. "He has said nothing this morning, but Master Hugo said that he spoke a little last night." They entered without knocking, and Dame Edith looked up, startled, so engrossed had she been in her work that she had not heard their steps on the stairs.

Levitas was coughing in his sleep when Robert touched his shoulder. The old man looked terrible. Where his face wasn't purple from bruising, cuts and scrapes blistered into great black scabs. Levitas woke with a start and tried to say something. His whole body shook with a hoarse hacking, and Robert watched as Dame Averilla helped him to sit up. The old man shook his head and waved her back as he tried to suck in a breath. Averilla was not to be deterred. She forced Levitas' head between his knees and gave his back a series of thumps. When he had managed to expel a large glob of phlegm, she wiped his face with a cloth and laid him back down.

The old man turned his eyes on Robert. *There is sense in those eyes, and fear,* Robert thought, *but no shame. And great depths of grief. God help him; the loss of his wife, the desertion of his friends; and now, now this embodied hatred.* "Master Levitas? We needs talk, you and I."

The left side of the old man's face lifted in what must have been meant to be a smile, but managed only to separate one of the scabs into a fresh flow of blood.

"The mob still wants your blood," Robert said, choosing his words with care. *Will you understand this?* he wondered. *And more, will you understand that I am convinced you couldn't have killed her?*

Levitas finally responded, "Aaaye," and lifted both hands, barely off the coverlet, in a gesture of resignation.

"So I must find who killed the girl. Without that, there can be no safety for you." Robert took the ring out of his purse and held it out. Master Levitas was too weak to hold it himself, so Robert rotated it in front of his eyes, between thumb and forefinger.

"Your work?"

Master Levitas gestured for it to be brought closer, and pointed to a mark on the underside.

"Your mark?"

Levitas nodded.

"Do you remember whom you made it for?"

"All aaare uniiii." It was too much. He paused to sputter and then gulped in air.

Baffled, Robert looked at Dame Averilla.

Levitas shook his head, fatigued by his inability to speak. "Luuve."

"They are given for a unique love?" Averilla asked. "So each is unique?"

The old man nodded.

"So, no two are the same?" Averilla wanted to be sure she understood.

Robert was more impatient. "Do you know whom this ring was made — ?"

"Jaaareeed." The answer was given even before the full question had been asked, as if the goldsmith knew that it held the key to his freedom.

"You are telling me that you sold this ring, this very ring, to Jared Reeve's-son as a betrothal ring?"

"Aaaye."

Looking at Levitas, seeing the fleeting half-smile the memory had brought to the old man's eyes, Robert curled his fingers around the ring and withdrew.

2

WHEN ROBERT AND AVERILLA EXITED the sickroom, as if of one accord, they paused. He held his lips in a bitter line for a moment and then said, "You are sure Savette wore this ring?"

"I am sure."

"So I must needs tell the abbess."

"Aye."

"The sooner the better."

"There is something new about her, a firmness that I noted not before. She will not like it that the reeve's son is accused.

"Mayhap you underestimate her," Averilla said, and, bowing slightly, went down the stairs.

As he stood on the landing, Robert felt the full strength of the wind curling up from the downs. He held his cloak close, and thought wryly, *This wind, if nothing else, will force me inside.* He knocked on the door next to that of the guest lodgings. When Sister Clayetta finally appeared, he followed her in, his spurs giving a male jingling.

He noticed a sadness in the abbess as he entered. The twinkle that usually hid just below the surface seemed damped.

"Master Levitas — " he started.

"Dreadful business," she cut off his words with a weary gesture. "He was never guilty, was he?"

He marveled. Was there nothing in this town that passed without her knowledge? Her immediate knowledge?

"No, my lady."

She rose, paced to the fire, and stood looking into the red-gold depths of the newly burned coals. Then she turned her gaze, very somber now, back to him. "I have been so preoccupied this past week, with our Lord's death."

"Milady?" The bailiff was at a loss to know how this was connected to Master Levitas.

"He was a Jew."

The comment surprised Robert and frightened him. *Christ a Jew? Jews are the companions of the infidel. Jews killed Christ. If it hadn't been for the Jews ... Everyone, even the smallest child, knew that. He had not ever thought of Christ as a Jew. Christ's heritage was an accident. Wasn't it?* He knitted his brows and said, tentatively, "Aye."

"The persecution of them goes on and on and on — "

"But surely, lady, sometimes the cause is just."

"Whose cause?"

"There are stories of children who have been killed. Mayhap not here, but ... "

She gave him a long, searching look. "I cannot make my mind see those who abide by the law and the prophets doing such things. We really don't know, do we?"

He was silent.

The abbess continued, "There is a slurry, I believe, of mingled motives in all of us." She stopped and looked at him before con-

297

tinuing. "The Jews are rich. People are indebted to them. There is envy. The proximate cause is not the cause. The envy here has boiled to a fester. It would burst."

"Er, yes."

"Today, the honor is given us to help this wretched and beloved man. Just how do we do so, Master Bailiff?"

He said, "Their blood lust is up. Like dogs chasing the hart. Those in the town believe that Master Levitas killed Savette. No one will ever be able to convince them else. There can never be peace henceforth between him and them."

"So, you are telling me that the townsfolk will always believe that it was Master Levitas, no matter what might be proven?"

"Aye."

"And no matter how fair he has been to them over these thirty years or more, they have forgotten it all?"

"Aye. The hate is like a virulent disease."

"He is very old to start anew."

"There will be gold and silver, of course, to be found in the ashes. Men from the garrison are standing guard to prevent the good townspeople from relieving him of it."

"And he will need it to continue his trade, and to travel. To France?"

"I would so advise him?"

"You have not spoken of this with him."

"Not without your leave."

"Then, when it is appropriate, do so. He is not yet well enough to hear it. And when you do, tell him please, that I realize that the abbey is much in debt to him. We shall pay enough of what we owe so he shall be able to again ply his trade immediately where e'er he may choose. To carry all of what we owe would be dangerous. We shall send the balance of it with a safe carrier when he is settled. And tell him, as well, that we shall be happy to send two" — she glanced at him for confirmation — "from the garrison

298

with him as far as the channel, for protection."

Robert sighed. "I believe that the sooner he is well enough to go, the more chance he will have to remain alive." He bowed curtly and turned toward the door.

The abbess stopped him. "Bailiff? Know you who killed her?"

"Aye." He stopped and turned back slowly. So now it had come. "It was Jared."

"Jared?" Her face took on such a look of despair that he thought she might cry.

"Aye. Jared Reeve's-son. I am sorry, milady. They were betrothed, Jared with Savette, though they had told no one. It was well and truly expected, after this summer's ... um ... happenings, that they would wed. But he had seemed desultory in his attentions to her of late. Few remarked on it or took it seriously; more noticed by the women of the town. My Mavis went on a bit about it. Now it is said that there may have been a child fathered. Probably they fought at the stream. He pushed her. We do not know. But the ring, the plight-troth he gave to Savette, was gone from her body. Dame Averilla had seen the ring herself around the girl's neck."

"Dame Averilla," Emma's eyebrows shot up. "How does she so manage to get into the middle of these things?"

"That, my lady, I know not. By the evening, Savette was dead. Very soon thereafter, the same ring was given, again as a plight-troth, to Damasa, daughter of Master Chapman."

"Is that so? Really and truly?"

"It is." Robert shook his head from side to side, whether in negation of his own words or in negation of the human race, even he wasn't sure.

299

AFTER RETURNING THE RING TO DAMASA, Tom had reported back to Robert. "Late the next day, the day after the death it was, that Jared came to her, Damasa, and offered her the ring. She was coy-like with me," Tom had continued, "but I buttered her up with honeyed words. She hadn't put the two things together, the hue and cry and her betrothal ring. Well, who would? I didn't ask her if there was blood on it."

"Oh, good man."

"JARED GAVE DAMASA THE RING THAT VERY NIGHT?" The abbess had needed to be told.

"That very night."

The abbess took a deep breath. "Master Chapman again."

"Again, my lady?"

"Master Chapman has not been entirely forthright in his dealings with us."

"I had wondered about that. Very soon Jared will be in the castle."

"You think he will not flee?"

"As you have mayhap been told, a cross was carved on the girl's wrist. No one had noted it until Jared pointed to it. That was what made the townsfolk think it was Master Levitas as did the killing. Nothing has been said else, so Jared still thinks he is safe. Pretends to believe like the rest, that Master Levitas killed her."

"You think Jared could have carved the cross in her hand."

"I think it was more of a happenstance that took the look of a cross; however, I would warn you, my lady, that though I firmly believe Jared to be guilty in this, I think the county will not find him so. They will not believe it was of a purpose."

"Could it have been?"

"I know not. Lady, no one ever knows that. Sometimes I think

300

not even the murderer. The human breast is well and fully able to fool the hands that the head supposedly controls. The hands do the bidding of the heart, and the head is unaware."

3

LATER, WHEN HUGO ENTERED the oratory Ralf was there before him. As he pulled the door of the church to, its swishing sound was quickly overrun by a startled cry and the noise of something breaking. The frustrated cry was familiar to Hugo, and, frightened for Ralf, he gimped up the north aisle, favoring his sore foot. He reached Ralf just in time. The lad's arm was raised as if to slash at the frontal itself, like a man about to stab his lover in a fit of passion.

"No!" Hugo's shout echoed around the vault, startling the pigeons that sheltered in the louvers of the tower and sending them flurrying outside. He grabbed at Ralf's arm, but the boy wrenched himself away, tears sheeting his face.

"Look at it," he blubbered. "Look at what I have done."

Hugo looked and was assured of the safety of the panel.

"It's awful," Ralf insisted, his chisel clanging onto the flags.

Hugo viewed the horses Ralf had carved with the sense of awe he had felt before when observing Bithric. It was more than just anatomy that Ralf created. Hugo had always had trouble getting the musculature of horses right. He knew that. But here was an aliveness, a reality, a love, that he himself had never been able to catch. The morn after the fire, he'd understood something new about Bithric, but Ralf's love of beasts, his empathy, called out from the panel to the viewer with a transparent vulnerability. Ralf had handled the tricky body movements with a grace Hugo hadn't believed possible.

Hugo saw at once what had caused the boy's fury: a gash, like his on the arm of Christ, but this wound had cut off a piece of hoof. The bit lay on the floor below the panel.

Ralf was menacingly quiet. Hugo turned and examined him. With a sigh of relief Hugo saw the frustration ebbing. *He'll be all right. His eye still hopes.*

"Have I ruined it?"

"Have you ruined it?" Hugo mused, "No, lad. The hoof be bad enough for what it is, but it don't ruin the whole. See," and he motioned with his right hand, "we can make it into a rock, as if the hoof was behind it, a kind of intaglio." Ralf looked bewildered. "Ye'll see. Have to be able to take our mistakes and kind of pray, ask God to help us see what else they can be. And then—"

"Snail," Ralf interrupted, energy replacing lethargy. "Not a rock. It's a snail." Hugo glanced at the hole. The shape did look more or less like a snail, albeit quite a large one. *Well, there's no reason it shouldn't be a snail. There's undoubtedly an arcane symbolism these religious put to snails.*

"The snail," Dame Edith would later tell him, her interest piqued, is born from mud and feeds on it. It symbolizes the laziness of sinners because it eats what is in its way."

"You see. 'Tis not ruined." Hugo said now. "But, lad, would ye have gashed the panel?"

Ralf thought for a moment. "I didn't want to, but my—my..."

"Don't ever harm a piece of creation. You work with God when you create. 'Tis a great gift he gives you, this power of His in your hands. You must never defile it. The talent inside you is unique. I—I couldn't have done this. I do other things, but your talent is yours alone, God given. You must harbor it and cherish it. God has never seen this image of His creation before, and he is excited by the love and purity of your gift. Through you, others will be able to see His handiwork. Never, lad, never destroy what God has wrought."

4

CHAPTER WAS RESTLESS. *How can one group of women be so very noisy?* Averilla wondered. It was the commotion of minds ill at ease, like the scurrying of small creatures in the forest.

The voice of the abbess interrupted her thoughts: "Dame Averilla, you know of the matter that transpired in the village during the past days ... "

Averilla stood. "Many of you have probably heard that Master Levitas has been accused of the murder of the maid Savette." A sigh, almost a wind, hissed along the rows of attentive women. They knew, had all heard. "It now appears," said Averilla, and recited the events as she knew them, from Savette's appearance in the herbarium to the present.

"The accusation of murder now lies on Jared Reeve's-son." There was a gasp. The bailiff thinks that Jared, not Master Levitas, took the life of Savette. Master Levitas, as you are aware ... " There was a rustling, a palpable unease among the sisters, " ... has served this abbey truly and well for more than thirty years.

"I could tell by the rapt attention they gave me," she would later confide to the abbess, "that this was what they yearned to hear. I felt like a bard, or worse, a gossip. But when I started to tell them of the travails of Master Levitas, it was as if a wall, a hedge of thorns was between me and them."

"Yes"

Averilla had darted a look at her superior. "There were too many coughs, and no one would meet my eyes."

"The bailiff thinks ... " Averilla continued, the antagonism of the chapter breeding within her a strange hesitation, " ... that because the feeling against him is so widespread there can be no bridge over this breech, even were Master Levitas and the people willing to attempt such a reconciliation. Men from the garrison have scratched whatever gold and silver they could from the cooling

303

ashes of Master Levitas' burned house. The gold will give Master Levitas the wherewithal to journey. He—he is to be sent away. Master Levitas must start anew." Averilla fell silent against the impassive looks. Blinded by tears, she sat down.

When no one rose, the abbess allowed the silence, trying to dampen the anger that burned like a light behind her green eyes. "Before my installation," she would tell Dame Aethwulfa, "the old bishop told me that my will could always be done, my will alone. But he also told me that if I forced my will against that of my flock, an illness would break out like boils in the body religious, until it finally coalesced against me."

This will not do, the abbess thought, measuring her words. "Dear sisters, Master Levitas has done much for us; things that ... " she shook her head as if to rid it of an unwelcome thought. "All we need to do is glance around the oratory. As I told you our debt to him is immense. Before he leaves we must repay him with our own plate. That is all we have."

There was a hiss from the back of the room, sibilant into the jumble of irritated minds.

The abbess' head came up like that of a hen over her brood, and her eyes sparked into the towering anger she had tried to repress, into one of the rages that had been wont to afflict her early years in the convent.

"Show yourself." With surprise she saw herself lash out. "Who is it that has such enmity and a coward's lack of courage?"

A raven's call wavered into the shocked stillness. The strands of community seemed woven thin across the warp of individuality.

The silence lengthened further, like sap down a tree, until Sister Fayga, one of the lay sisters, rose to stand formidable and unembarrassed, her wrinkled hands roughened with the chaffing and chilblains of the barren seasons and her years in the laundry. "My lady."

The abbess inclined her head. The two red spots in her cheeks still flamed. She did not speak, even the nothing words of acknowledgment, for fear of what she might, in heat, say.

"There be a restlessness here among us, my lady, with these here actions, despicable actions, not only in the town, but here in the abbey. No, 'twasn't me as hissed at yer words, but I speak for many of us, choir nuns too, that 'ave no truck with what yer about. Goes against sense, it does, and what we've been taught all our lives here."

Emboldened by the sound of her own voice, Sister Fayga took a step forward, the better to see the whole room and to assess the mind of the abbess.

The flush in Abbess Emma's cheeks deepened. "An argument is still a kind of communication," she would later justify herself to Dame Aethwulfa. "The communal respect must allow for this — this rupture and tearing, if the community is to grow."

"First of all," Fayga now continued, "that there frontal is to be made of wood. Not all of us here agrees with you, though I be the only one to say it. We know that it be yer choice and all, about the cost of the frontal. There's some as would say that 'tis unseemly to reward our saint, a saint who has performed miracles and done well by us, with a miserly panel of wood, no better than what be carved in the cheapest peasant hut, be Master Hugo famous sculptor or no. 'Tisn't the best he can do, that be the point. And out of wood! Money, good money, was given to cast it in silver. It should be cast in silver. 'Tis only honest."

Fayga took a deep breath and started in again. "And then there be the matter of the plate. To take the plate, the plate dedicated piece by piece to God for his glory or to Saint Edward. That be stealing. Now, I know that I swore to obey, but that was assuming—"

"Assuming nothing," Dame Osburga, the new prioress rose, her accents soft, cultivated against those of the other.

"Dame." The word lashed across the intervening stones. "Oh, I

305

knew," The abbess would later continue to paint the scene for the old lady. "I knew indeed that Osburga was only trying to defend me. It has always been thus, even since our days together in the novitiate. And indeed, there it was necessary. I was shy, scared of my own shadow, coming from a barren household in the fens, with a mother overwhelmed by sickness and a father morose, and so I needed Osburga to defend me."

Until recently, Aethwulfa would think with a sense of satisfaction, like a mother seeing her babe finally walk, but she would let the abbess continue.

"So, sometimes Osburga still tries to protect me."

The abbess' voice as she turned to Sister Fayga was fully controlled now, and soft. "Sister, please continue. Though I may not agree with you, you have every right to be heard."

Hurt, the prioress lowered her eyes and sat down.

"As I was saying," here Sister Fayga couldn't help but cast an offended glance in the direction of Dame Osburga, "we will obey you, but I think this is the wrong ride. There be plenty o' money in the treasury, I assume, with the dowries from all these new Norman babes as we keep sheltering behind our walls, and the tithe barn in Tisbury is full, I know. So there is money to adorn the saint, and I, for one, think we should." She paused, guileless, then continued darkly, "There are those who would hate to see him leave us, Saint Edward, that is, bones here or no. It has been known to happen when the proper respect, the respect due, was not paid to a saint."

Sister Fayga would have continued in this vein, but the abbess held up a warning hand, her eyes soft, feeling Osburga and the other obedientaries stiffen at the unsaid but believed superstition. "I understand your concern," she said as Fayga sat down, satisfied, "and might have held it once myself. But though our saint has helped us, helped the pilgrims by interceding for them, we must never forget that the only true intercessor is our Lord Jesus."

She paused to let the point sink in. "I—we cannot begin to understand how He has arranged it all, but He was clear, most clear, that the 'sick and the friendless and the needy' must come before the things of this world. The glories with which we adorn our oratory help the heart and mind to praise God, but these adornments are secondary.

"And ye are saying that this Jew," Fayga rose and spat out the word like a stone caught in the porridge, "that this Jew is one of his sheep?"

"He said, 'I have other flocks.'"

"Jews had their chance; had Jesus among them, walking with them. And they murdered Him. Foully. As they now murder our babes. He deserves nothing from us. He has his life, doesn't he?"

The temporary calm in the chapter house flailed into chaos. Numbers rose to be heard, a flurry of black cloth, pinched faces.

"Silence!" Dame Petronella could always be relied on.

"And we obey her as if we were still in the novitiate," Dame Alice whispered to Dame Averilla.

"I am not sure on this—this Jew, one wise or the other," Dame Petronella continued. "'Tis not for me to discern. That is why we elected the abbess. We each chose, each of our own free will, to obey. The abbess now, her arguments have merit, backed up with the words of our Lord. So I must follow her. I have vowed so to do. Since none of us, on our own, can know the mind of God, we listen to His words and follow those whom we believe might be able to discern more, those we trust."

"In this particular case," the abbess said, lifting again the burden of her office, "Master Levitas is sick, friendless, and needy. As for being a Jew, Christ was a Jew. We all kill Christ; every time we sin, it is another nail in the cross. Our brother, the saintly Abbot of Clairvaux, has spoken on that matter, and with authority. Our actions must be those that lead others to Christ, not drive them away."

307

Most of the heads in the chapter house were bowed. "They didn't like to hear that," she would tell Aethwulfa, her face taking on a haggard look.

"As for the murders, Master Levitas had nothing to do with those. The bailiff has assured me that another is responsible. I should say no more on this issue. It is a matter for prayer and for God. I expect you all to file back into the church and there listen to the mind of God. I will use our treasury to help Master Levitas in any way that will be to his advantage. I would very much like your counsel on how this is to be done, and I would like your acquiescence to it. Father Boniface will read us something enlightening. We shall pray and then return."

5

Since Father Boniface had taken no part in the funeral mass, had not been asked to take even the smallest part by *that illiterate* Father William, the abbess had asked him to read to them as they meditated.

He strode into the choir to the opened Bible. A passage from the Old Testament had been marked for him. He started to read:

> Those who squander their bags of gold and weigh out their silver with a balance hire a goldsmith to fashion them into a god; Then they worship it and fall prostrate before it; They hoist it shoulder-high and carry it home; They set it down on its base; There it must stand, it cannot stir from its place. Let a man cry to it as he will, it never answers him; It cannot deliver him from his troubles.
>
> —Isaiah 46:6 – 7

After the reading, he raised his head and waited, trying to look into the eyes of each. A short homily, she had said, only a word or two. A momentary panic raced through his mind. He couldn't think of anything to say. They were all looking at him now, staring with those vulnerable eyes, none realizing his frailty. He had to say something. *They are starting to look panicked, starting to stare, as if there is something wrong. As if I can't speak. I can, of course. Not like Zachariah.* He opened his mouth.

"We expect," he said, "when we hear this lesson, for Elijah to give the widow what she needs. We expect him to take care of her. He is, after all, the appointed, the wealthy prophet. And yet that is not what happens."

What am I talking about? Why am I saying this? My tongue is running away with me. These aren't the words for this lesson. Words. Not mine.

"She," his tongue continued without him, "the poor and humble in spirit, she is ministering to the rich. She gives everything that she has, and gladly, from what we can tell. She gives all of her pittance to the one who has much more than she has."

He stopped. He didn't know what else to say. *What did I just read? What did I then say? Did what I say come before — or was it after — what I just read?* With a look of panicked confusion, he turned and sat down.

When they filed back into the chapter house, the women were even more confused than they had been. The Rule of Saint Benedict stipulated that the least of them be asked her opinion first when a great decision was to be made, so it was the smallest and youngest of the novices who was asked to give her opinion. "Mother," she started slowly, finding confidence by keeping her eyes on those of the abbess and not moving an inch from her lowly place. "Jesus gave to his disciples twelve baskets of leftovers after He had fed the five thousand; one basket for each man, just as Saint Benedict stipulates that each of us shall have no more and no less than one pound of bread a day. So, when we give away our plate and treasure, in the end we will have more than if we hoard all our resources." She sat down.

There was a long silence as they tried to understand what she had meant.

Finally, the abbess said, "Er, yes. Thank you, sister."

When it seemed polite, another, a professed nun, rose, "From the treasury?"

They all knew what she meant.

"Pieces of plate?"

"Just the coins themselves?"

"But how will he carry them?"

They finally worked it through. It was decided that when Master Levitas was well enough to travel, John would be called from the stable to accompany Father Boniface and Dame Averilla down into the crypt to the treasury.

6

"JARED REEVE'S-SON," Tom had not been happy about having to arrest Jared. For as long as Tom could remember, the reeve had protected the townsfolk against the steward. It didn't sit right with Tom to arrest the youngest son of the reeve. Jared was out with the sheep all day, so it wasn't until sunset that Tom found him at home, shrugging off his old sheepskin. "In the name of the abbess, I charge you with the murder of Savette, daughter of Lovick and Anne his wife." Tom's voice was sure but impassive, his eyes opaque.

"The thing about it was," Tom would tell his grandchildren when it was all over and everyone knew how it had come out, "Jared got all white around the gills. He looked shocked, as if he hadn't been the one as done it. I wondered right then, I can tell you, and so did most of the lads, but there was the thing about him being plight-troth to another, and with the ring as was taken from the first girl, so I did as I 'us told. Not happy about it, but

310

what was I to do? Orders is orders, eh?"

"C'mon lad," Tom had said. "Get it over with."

7

LEVITAS WAS LOOKING BETTER; there was no doubt about it. Dame Averilla had forbidden him movement. She had slathered his head with an ointment of comfrey, and he was expected to take a tea made from a combination of anise oil, primrose root, and thyme several times a day for his cough, as well as a tea of mille-folium, which, she assured Hugo, was good for a blow of iron or a strange swelling on a man's head. While Hugo was working in the oratory, Dame Edith was assiduous in making the old man inhale a medicated steam and placing evil-smelling poultices on his chest.

But now was the hour of Compline, and Levitas had only Hugo with him. He leaned from his bed to caress the small head Hugo had started to whittle from a piece of kindling.

"Miii."

Hugo shot him a questioning look.

"Wiiife."

Hugo raised an eyebrow, "This looks like your wife?"

"Ummm."

Hugo held it up so the old man could better see it. "Mayhap thoughts can be delivered from one to another, like wind or ... breath or ... "

Hugo felt a strange fluttering right around his heart. Slowly, with effort, the older man reached up the one hand he had tended to favor. Hugo pushed the little carving into it. "Let me finish it, shall I?" Hugo reached to take it away, but the old man's fingers tightened. Hugo smiled. "Well then, you shall keep it."

"I have often wondered, my friend," he said aloud, "as I've watched the bees in a swarm, if we are quite as separate as we imagine. Or,

311

like them, are we part of a greater pattern, part of each other in some strange way that defies thinking or knowing?"

There was a silence between them. With a turn of the head that had become habitual as he sat with Levitas, Hugo looked over to find the battered face swathed in tears, the little carved head held awkwardly between thumb and forefinger. Perhaps it was the weakness that was making Levitas so vulnerable, but his words were the words of impotent pain. "Miiii fault."

Hugo's eyebrows veed into a mask of incredulity. "Your fault? What is your fault?"

"Hannaah."

"Your daughter?"

"Aaaye."

"What rubbish. The lass was mown down by someone else, some Norman brat riding through the market. You told me so yourself."

"Not thaaat." Master Levitas leaned over, his chest spasmed in a drawn-out cough. When Hugo had managed to slide the old man back onto the bed and Levitas had regained his breath, he said, "God's anger."

"God's anger at a child?" Hugo bellowed.

"Naaaay. Aaat meee."

"God's anger?" he repeated with even more force. "Can you sit there and tell me that you think she died because God was angry with you?"

"All illness ... result of sin ... no atonement."

Hugo hit his head with the palm of his hand, got up from the stool, and paced his anger around the room, muttering to himself, "Pigheaded, obstinate, obdurate, blind ....

Levitas stared, flabbergasted, his tears drying.

"You say you believe in your God. You say that you abide by the law," Hugo turned suddenly, nostrils flaring, "and yet you sit there — lie there — and conveniently forget the first words of those very commandments. "I am the Lord thy God who brought you out of the land of Egypt. What kind of God do you think that is?"

Hugo broke off, obviously perplexed as how to put it clearer.

"When weeee sin ... pain helps us see — burns us clean."

"What kind of God would kill an innocent child because her father didn't follow some obscure rule? Verily, only a truly wicked god, not one who would accompany his children through the wilderness. Jesus said — "

"Ah. Jesus."

"Yes. Jesus. He came for that very reason. You Jews were too pigheaded to understand what God was saying about Himself. God doesn't inflict pain on us. Or sickness. That's why Jesus healed. Couldn't help but heal. His love translated into healing to make us whole, body and soul. Loved us. Only a loving God would have brought his people out of the land of Egypt. You know your Latin. That's what 'salvation' means, it means 'healing.'"

"Yoouu know nothing about ittt. How dare yoouu?"

CHAPTER TWENTY-SIX

SATURDAY

I

With Dame Edith looking after Levitas, Hugo was able to fully concentrate on the frontal. He had managed to reshape the center panel, *The Crucifixion,* despite the mob-mad damage to it. With Ralf's nimble connivance, the horses at the top had been slightly repositioned. The right panel, *The Kiss of Judas,* was also finished; only the left panel, *The Scourging of Christ,* needed finishing touches.

Levitas' long healing gave them time; time for considered shapes and rounded figures that seemed to be held onto the background only by the most tenuous of threads. Hugo gouged deeper and deeper, rounding each arm, trying to get behind each finger with his chisel, so that the characters seemed to be bravely trying to free themselves and again and again allow the scene to be replayed.

Ralf pondered the slashes and striations, so dogged and, well, fierce — there was no other word — of his master before questioning them. "This panel is to be deeper — in the cuts?" Ralf's voice was tentative.

"No." Hugo's voice was gruff. "I'll go back."

Ralf waited, anxiety glooming his mind. Finally, he brought

himself to ask, hesitantly, almost hoarse with the phlegm of fear, "My horses?"

Hugo's hand stayed, the chisel inches from the head of the Savior. He turned, his eyes softening. "Nay, lad. Yer horses be as they be. I have in mind figures I saw long ago that I would turn these more lightly spun figures into. It was in a land east of the French. Many things were there created that just now seem to have captured my mind. 'Twas there — if you would know — that I saw the first bronze doors. Wouldn't have thought to have created doors at Saint Edmunds had I not first seen 'em in the Saxon lands. Watched the men at their foundries; saw how it was done. Thought I could impress the monks at Saint Edmunds with the newness of my vision, a new vision, one they'd not seen afore."

"So those images — on the doors — were deep cut like these?"

"Those doors, and my doors as well, had soft figures, merely lines etched on a scene, barely there, except the head or another important part of the body would emerge, as it were, from the background. Pointed out the meaning by intensifying the importance of one part. 'Twas the altar frontal I saw made under King Otto that changed my mind. Every figure was almost whole, almost standing free of the background. That was my inspiration for this work. I would have this altar frontal be the same, so the mind can capture the scenes in all their pain."

"What land was that? Hep it a name?"

"Aye. I recollect not what it was, but the kings were all named Otto and lived some'ut after the great King Charles was made Holy Roman Emperor. But that was long ago, when I was a young man.

Every day, while Hugo relieved Dame Edith, Ralf and Tindal would sit and listen to the nuns. Not being able to see them through the thickness of the rood screen and the choir walls gave the sound an ethereal quality, and Ralf let his mind travel down its vagrant paths as his hand nestled itself in the winter fullness of

Tindal's coat. The feeling it gave him, this echoing sound, wasn't that feeling of oneness with God that he had felt the night of the fire, but that would return — at least he hoped it would; it seemed to for the nuns. For the time being he was content to know that such peace was possible.

Ralf was growing. He no longer had the half-starved look he had come with, and he would speak now with confidence, if not to anyone else, to Hugo. He had wanted to put a bird in the frontal, had tentatively suggested it.

"'Twouldn't be right, inside Pilate's house, now would it, inside and all?" Hugo had said, turning to the boy, his scorper raised. "And not at night with the kiss of Judas. Can't rightly see it on the cross. Do ye not remember, 'And when he was on the cross, outside, darkness covered the earth'? Heard those words since I was a babe in arms."

Ralf found himself surprisingly and impertinently persistent. "The Holy Ghost could be there, couldn't He — er, It? — well ... well, until Jesus went away."

"Hasn't never been done that way."

"But why couldn't we do it that way? Even if it hasn't been done." Slyly, the boy added, "Ye've made changes. Proud ye were of them, showing the backs and fronts of the horses — not just side on."

"That was technique," Hugo had replied somewhat testily. "I didn't tamper with the stories. And it's never said that the Holy Ghost was there when He was on the cross."

"No. Yet they're supposed to be one — Father, Son, and Holy Ghost. So wouldn't He be there?"

Hugo had had to think a long time on that one and then it hit him. "Nay, lad," he said softly, sure of his ground, magnanimous in his righteousness, "Remember, Jesus said when He appeared to them after He'd risen, He said, 'I will be gone but I will send my Spirit to be with you.' And that was a new thing. A Spirit always

316

able for us to touch, to be with."

"But the Spirit was with him when John was baptizing Him, wasn't He?

"Aye. It says so there, and that was a new thing, d'ye see? 'Twasn't al'ays like that, and that's why the writer makes a point of it." Having seen that Hugo needed to concentrate, Ralf had gone on with his work, muttering sotto voce, just the freedom of rebellion starting to creep into his tone, "Someday, when I am carving with my own studio, well, then..."

2

It was known that Jared was accused and Master Levitas exonerated. None of the people truly believed it. The few times Hugo had gone outside the abbey, he had been glared at as he passed. Now and again someone spat or threw a spare rock. These gestures weren't completely wholehearted, for the cloak of the abbess clung to Hugo's shoulders, so none dared commit a truly egregious act against him.

Most believed Levitas had bewitched Hugo. "Why else would he help the goldsmith?" they'd ask each other. "The county won't convict Jared, nay matter what the abbess believes."

"She be a good woman, but she be off in this. Just look at the carver. Had been a sensible man afore 'e met the goldsmith. Now mumbling to himself and haggard."

As he strode across the inner court now, Hugo did indeed mumble to himself, "There is no other way. The old man can't go by himself." Then, thinking of what Pasha would say if she knew that he'd taken on not just a boy but an old Jew, Hugo laughed aloud.

The truth was, Hugo was flowering inside and didn't quite know how to cope with it. "First the brat and now a Jew. A Jew."

It was Hugo who had forced Levitas to stand and to take his

317

first steps. He it was who took him to the privy. The first time, Hugo had had to prod. "Where's yer pride? No Jew allows himself to dirty his clothes." From then on, the old man grudgingly, groaning, complaining all the time, allowed himself to be needled into walking farther each day.

"But the cough?" he asked. "Isn't there ... ?" Dame Averilla thought Hugo was behaving like a new mother with her first babe.

Dame Averilla used the same tolerant, patient tone with Hugo that she used when a child wouldn't sleep, "Aye. There is a chance of the lung disease. That's why you need to walk him. Remember to pound him on the back, with his head over the side of a bench." In addition, there were the various teas and some evil-tasting potions that managed to loosen the phlegm that collected in the old man's lungs.

"Whyyy dooo this?" Levitas had asked, after one methodical pounding on his back by Hugo.

"I went to a great deal of trouble to drag your battered old hide out of those drains. Think ye I mean to see all that work go for naught?" Hugo had smiled, an unused softness lighting his eyes. As he improved, Levitas gained the breath and the words to complain of his treatment. "You enjoy it."

Hugo responded, rather gruffly, cornering his emotion, "You understand my work."

Every day, Sister Mavern, now assigned to the kitchener, climbed the stairs with a thick bean soup, which Hugo would force by spoonfuls through the old man's lips until it was all gone. Levitas started to improve.

"Just all of a sudden," Dame Edith murmured.

"But then, Dame Averilla is there," Sister Mavern pointed out to the other novices, and they crossed themselves. Despite her failures in healing the wounds of Savette and others, the novices still chose to believe that Averilla's hands held a magical healing

318

power. "It was an injury to the head of the Jew," they whispered one to another. "Just like John the Mason." They would nod and raise their eyebrows. Infected by their faith, the cook worked extra-hard on the soups. "If he be still alive, after all that's 'appened, well, then it be the will of God, I wot, and so I need to do the best I can as well."

On this morning, after applying to speak to the abbess, Hugo was conducted to one of the parlours by a novice. Abbess Emma entered as she always seemed to, without sound, the door opening on a gift of wind. He bowed.

"Master Hugo."

"Surely she knew what I needed to say." Hugo would later muse to Levitas, "She seems to know what I intend to do before I myself have parsed it out."

"I would accompany Master Levitas." The words were out even before the customary greeting.

Her head cocked, just the tiniest bit. Then she nodded, "Yes. I see," and nodded again to herself.

Before she could form more words, he stumbled on. "I trust not these times. And the men from the garrison have little love for him. With my presence they dare not just, just ... " he couldn't say it.

She finished for him, "Abandon him somewhere and tell the bailiff that all was accomplished, that he was safely delivered? Or better still, that they were set upon by a band of masterless men. They fought fiercely, but ... " her eyebrow arched.

"Aye" He looked at the heavy leather of his shoes, unseeing. "The frontal will be finished. Enough."

"My spirit is fully rested that you do this good deed."

"I don't do it for the — the sacrifice of it. Be not misled."

She raised her hand to stop his words. "I am not. I think I understand." She smiled. "Like all the rest of us, your motives are a trodden mixture of self and those acts you do for the love of God, or because He tells you to."

"It is better thus, this sword's edge. At the beginning I was making the reredos for myself; praise, fame, even perhaps adulation. Being with you," Hugo's hands included the community, "a new understanding has crept into my seeing and into my thinking. The glory of each bigger commission no longer drives me. When I started long ago in Hildesheim, I wanted to share what I knew of God. I lost that. I can't explain it.

"And so mayhap even I," he said with a touch of bewilderment, "will learn to love my neighbor. No. No, I can only promise to try to recognize that he is there. That I can promise without fear of lying."

She grinned. "Start by loving someone whom it is impossible for you not to love." He looked at her inquiringly. "Mother, father, brother," she noted his jutted jaw and added, after a pause, "or son."

Hugo's head came up like a cock's and his eye softened.

"Aye. When I found Ralf, he was starving. He needed me, or someone, to help him survive. I had no choice."

"Were you carving then?"

"No. No, I wasn't. I was coming here."

"So you were able to think on him and notice him."

"Aye, so I did. Is that it? The attention?"

"We love what we give attention to."

3

AFTER HIS CONVERSATION WITH THE ABBESS, Hugo tinkered with the frontal, altering a line here, a slash there. Only when the tension inside him became intolerable could he force himself up the stairs to tell Levitas.

"The abbess and chapter have decided that," he started, then started again. "They, they wish, the people—well, they agree with me. There is nothing more to be done about your safety but move you," Hugo managed. Then he added, rather more bleakly, "Where can you go? Have you thought?"

"Whaat eelse could I think on?" Master Levitas' speech was much better, but still rough.

"Family?"

"No one." Then, as if his answer was too rude, even for his speech, Levitas added, "Bruuther ... was killed. Never married. No cousins." Then, in a spurt of clear speech, "We are a family who do not often breed. As you know, my Rebekkah has been dead these last years." He stopped, paused, and when he had mastered the emotion, finished the sentence. "And my Hannah —"

"Well, then," Hugo interrupted, "we —"

"We?" Master Levitas turned stiffly toward Hugo, still favoring his injured head and neck, his look one of bewilderment.

"Yes, we. My work here is finished. I have a commission at Saint-Denis, as I told you, and Abbot Suger knows my work. It would be a good place for you, as well. We might even take the cowl, you and I." Hugo's eyes twinkled as he watched Master Levitas' face contort — from disgust, when he thought Hugo was joking, to amazement when he understood that Hugo really intended to accompany him, to overwhelming joy at this token of their friendship — to appalled amazement when the suggestion of becoming a monk registered.

"Er, I guess you wouldn't want to actually become a monk, now that I think on it." Hugo amended.

Hugo had spoken. It was done. Inside he was quaking. *What did I just say? Go with him? No! I don't want to go with this man. Suffer his hardships? Why then, do I leave my work for a stinking old man?*

"Yoouu don't need," Levitas interrupted Hugo's silence, the edges of his mouth curved in the pretense of a smile, "prooove yoou are a Christian."

Hugo's face contorted into several shards of expression before he burst into a great bellow of laughter, pounding Levitas on the back and almost doubling him over. Wiping the tears from his eyes he sputtered, "You—you'll see what a good time I'll have suffering. With just a little bit of tutoring, see if you too don't become a martyr."

"If yoou 'member, I—taste maartyyrdom. Not aaagree with me."

"Then it is settled," Robert would later remark to them when discussing the plan, "the sooner you go, the better. We will send two from the garrison to accompany you to the channel. And, of course, you do have the dog." Robert would add dryly, "I understand he is worth two of the garrison."

"Has trouble holding a bow," said Hugo, and raised an eyebrow at Levitas.

CHAPTER TWENTY-SEVEN

MONDAY

I

No work had been engaged in on Sunday, *except for that which I do in readying the church for the services,* Dame Averilla had thought, her emotions by then quite threadbare. By Monday morning, Sunday night's rest seemed only to have made her more irritable, and the thought of being accompanied by Father Boniface into the crypt in search of partial payment of their debt to Master Levitas seemed untenable. *I hate letting him know where we keep our treasure, how much we have.* The stairs, built into the north tower, led through a tiny, well-barred, and heavily locked door. Cleansed by the open air of the recent rebuilding, the crypt itself hadn't the musty smell of age and decay that pervaded the reaches farther in, but it was still and empty. *Like Christ's tomb and His death, and the stories Nan told me when I was little.*

The stout arches beneath the choir and the narthex were the very oldest parts of the oratory, fashioned as support for the Anglo-Saxon church built by Alfred the Great. Father Boniface was fascinated. He meandered along behind her, examining with the eye of an artist, stonemason, or sculptor, the patterns of stonework. The little chapel that enclosed the treasury was recessed from the length of the crypt, and lay, Averilla suspected, under the nuns' graveyard. She pushed against the sturdy gate with both hands as she turned the key in the rusted hanging lock. This chapel was seldom used any longer, and there were no hangings or linens on or about the altar. Father Boniface lowered his torch to examine the fretwork. Averilla bit her lip. Tamping down her irritation, she said, "Originally, we kept the reliquary here in the crypt, in imitation of St. Peter's tomb in Rome. But since Saint Edward had not originally been buried on this site, and since the pilgrims ofttimes find the stairs a trial," she motioned behind them, "with the rebuilding of the oratory we moved Saint Edward up to the chapel in the main church."

On the right side of this crypt chapel were several unremarkable stones of greensand, unnoticeable from inside the chapel and unmarred by hinges or the grease from constant use. These stones were light, being only pieces of facing, which, as Averilla removed them, revealed another door, this one not only of strong planks, but secured with several intricate locks and bolts. Pulling up a huge ring of keys hanging from her waist, she fitted them one by one into the locks and unlatched them seriatim. The hasps were rusty from the pervasive moisture of the greensand, as were the iron bars that bound the door. Three hasps, three iron bands, three locks. Father Boniface hovered — "Hadn't expected … Quite a clever … " — and gasped when the door swung inward to reveal to his hungry torch the watery gleam of silver and the sherried light of gold. Knowledge of the treasury, however, was information that the Customary ordered be revealed to the nun's priests. Averilla had procrastinated at bringing Father Boniface here, but because of the Rule, she had been obliged to so do.

"This," Averilla spoke softly, explaining, "was a cave." She was scanning the shelves for pieces appropriate to the need, her mind more taken up by the task than in communicating to the priest. "We have appropriated it to hold the bulk of Saint Edward's treasure. Here are stored pilgrim gifts, memorials, our own plate, and the bulk of the re-minted coin Master Levitas has saved."

"It won't do to take anything given to the saint," she muttered, her eyes abstracted. "Our own plate? A piece Master Levitas himself wrought?"

Verily, I hate to give up any of it, she thought, and again bit her lips, this time hard enough to hurt. *Greed. Pure greed. Forgive me, Father.* She glanced at the priest. He was transfixed; the sheen of gold glinted against his eyes.

"No wonder I was reluctant for his company," she would tell the abbess when she returned the abbess' set of keys, each of which went into one of the locks. The third set was held by the cellarer. "If he could have gotten away with our plate right then, I think he would have."

2

RETURNING FROM THE CRYPT, Averilla pushed open the door from stairs with her left foot, cradling the wrapped bundles. When she and the priest entered the outer court, one of the numerous men-at-arms moved aside and Averilla saw a little band of travelers standing ready to depart. Hearing the crunch of feet on the gravel, the travelers turned and she realized who they were. The change was enormous.

Dame Petronella is wrong, she thought. *Clothes do make a man, just as the coif makes me a nun.*

The travelers were neither Jew nor gentile; merely weary travelers, pilgrims on some vigil of their own. Had her arms been free, she would have put her hands to her lips to cover the twitching of a smile.

Master Levitas was no longer. The black eyes peeped out from under a gray hood and gorget that covered his shoulders. Over it he wore a cloak of a short and grubby length. *No more the fastidious and embroidered silks for him. Probably has fleas, too,* she thought. *Where did they find that cloak? Snatched off one of the wights in the guest hall, I'd wager.* His legs rose pitifully thin in loose braes of a dun wadmal, with brown hose pulled saggingly over. The hose were cross-gartered with rough strips of grayish cloth. The dirty boots looked cruelly hard. *Never before,* she imagined, *has he been so clothed.* His beard had been pushed into the thong-tied top of his shirt, and only one who had seen it could imagine the length and luxuriousness hidden within. *A real "hair shirt,"* she thought, repressing a giggle that threatened to bubble into laughter.

Ralf, Hugo, Tindal, and Bithric were there, too, looking as they had when first they entered the forecourt, looking now as if they were meant to accompany the old man. Turning, the bailiff smiled at her and motioned for one of the men to take her bundles. She approached the little band and, to cover her emotion, patted Bithric's flank. Blinking back tears, she handed Ralf the one bundle she still carried. He hefted it up into the woven panniers on Bithric's side, daring the donkey to refuse the burden. Bithric, as if sensing the moment, merely glanced back at Ralf and let loose a long stream of pee.

"Master Levitas?" she forbade herself a smile at his discomfiture.

"I — I — I am no longer ... welcome." Sensing the fullness of her emotion, he smiled wryly and added, "Master Hugo would have cut my beard. I ... refused. I am ... descended from Abraham, Isaac, and Jacob." Of all the words Master Levitas said, the last three came out pure and even.

Finding her voice, Averilla managed, "We recognize that what we now send with you does not fulfill our debt. The abbess feared to make of you a target for outlaws, so, when you have arrived wherever, she bids you advise us where to send the remainder." She turned toward Hugo. "You accompany Master Levitas, is it so?"

326

Hugo swallowed. "We are glad to keep Master Levitas company. We travel to Abbot Suger of Saint-Denis. I have another commission. After that, if he has no more need for our skills there, we are sure to find work in the town of Limoges. Or elsewhere. There are sure to be plenty from whom Ralf can learn when he has outstripped our knowledge. I had not thought to be given the gift of an apprentice, crotchety as I am, but ... " Hugo busied himself with something on Bithric, hiding his own feelings, "we must proceed before the day lengthens further into night. We await only a letter from the lady abbess giving us introduction of Master Levitas to the reverend abbot."

Master Levitas had been hoisted onto his horse. "Master Bailiff ... " he started, but was taken with a fit of coughing. When he could again speak, Levitas leaned over so as not to be overheard. "Miii hooome. The well. Chalice. Gold. Send Chalice. Blois. Gold for you. Grateful."

"I—" Robert's brow furrowed. He looked to Dame Averilla for translation.

"There is a chalice," she said, "that he threw into his well and which he would have you send to Henry of Blois. It should be entrusted with a secure courier. He is giving you a present of the rest of his gold."

There is no need, my friend," Robert said, coloring. "But I thank you most heartily. You will be sorely missed when this madness has cooled."

When all was ready, Averilla stood with Robert as the little cavalcade trotted through the main gate. Two horses had been given to the men. Ralf was left to lope alongside with the dog. No trace remained of the sad, thin waif Ralf had once been. The wind pulled at Averilla's skirts, but there was no sound from the mob that waited on the Bimport. It was not the blood they had desired, but at least they had had their will, and the Jew was gone, or soon would be. *And where,* thought Averilla, as the gate slowly

327

closed, *will folk now go for rings and fairings?* But she knew the answer. The void would be filled. Still, she would miss these men. A tear traced its snail path down her cheek, and then another. She didn't bother to wipe them away.

As she turned toward the guest hall, the bailiff at her side, she asked, "Jared?"

"He will be tried. But their heart will not be in it. Even I think he did not mean to kill her."

"Mayhap. But he didn't mean not to. He was thinking so of himself. No thought for her."

"Yes."

"She was nothing to him." Averilla's voice was fierce. She could still see the pain in Savette's eyes. "Just a thing. In the way of his desire."

The wind blustered, pushing against them as they moved, of a mind, to the wall beside the guest hall and above the park in order to catch a last glimpse of the travelers. They were in time. Already the little cavalcade had, like milk and cream, separated into distinct groups. The men-at-arms strode before and after, distancing themselves from those they accompanied. Master Hugo, astride an abbey pony, seemed both awkward and uncomfortable. Master Levitas, however, sat with surprising ease, despite his broken arm, atop a most beautiful animal.

Averilla started. "That's the abbess' palfrey! Master Levitas is riding the abbess' palfrey! There must be some mistake."

"Do you really think so?" The bailiff kept his eye on the travelers, his tone bland and uninflected.

Averilla turned to look at him and caught just the hint of a smile twitching in the corners of his beard. She sighed. "No, I suppose not. The palfrey was a possession, wasn't it? And because, 'Go and sell all you own ... '" her voice trailed off.

"As you say."

"See you any sign of Ralf?"

"There." Robert pointed with his black-fingered glove at a clump of trees, and Averilla watched as Ralf emerged onto the clods of the freshly plowed field, chasing after Tindal.

"Chasing crows?"

"I think not."

Tindal, rear in the air, forepaws on the ground, egged Ralf forward, then leapt high. As they watched, the boy stumbled and fell. The dog hesitated mid-stride, flipped, and landed next to Ralf, his absurd, thin dog legs pawing stiffly at the sky, the boy nuzzling his neck.

"He's happy, I think, and lucky," said Averilla.

"It's an adventure. A chance. He has more than Jared had."

"More talent?"

"Different talent. No, Ralf has more people to care. He has two, where Jared, by the end, had no one. Lost both his mother and the old priest."

"He has his sister Cadilla."

"Dame, am I wrong? It is my understanding that now she must put God first."

3

"IT MIGHT HAVE BEEN BETTER TO BE CAUGHT by the mob than to ride this beast," Master Hugo grumbled.

The pony cocked his ears backward.

Master Levitas grimaced at the thought, "Be careful ... what yoouu say."

"You intend to take the donkey across? Even after this generous gift from the abbess?" Master Levitas patted the neck of the white horse.

"Aye," Hugo answered the first question, eyeing the horse with envy. "She gave you the horse, but as I am to send back the pony, I will need the donkey to carry my tools. Anyrood, I have grown fond of the donkey. I might not find another beast with whom I can bluster so well. I talk. He listens. It's a good arrangement."

<h1 style="text-align:center">4</h1>

WHEN THEY COULD NO LONGER SEE the scraggly little band, Averilla and the bailiff returned to the church. Perhaps it was merely that that was where Averilla was meant to be and the bailiff was accompanying her. Perhaps he, too, felt the need of solace against the ennui of this unsatisfactory ending.

They drifted up the north arcade and into the transept. The panels had been attached to the front of the altar.

"And now he won't be here to receive the gasps of awe, the congratulations," Averilla muttered after a moment. Robert was silent. His eyes darted from the carving to Averilla, and then reattached themselves to the people and horses on the panel. "I have never," he breathed, seen the like of this. It is as if it was happening here in Shaftesbury." He leaned down. "As if we are seeing it from just a bit off, from the castle tower or — or the top of the church. But see, look," Robert's finger traced the line of a building behind the central figures in *The Scourging of Christ.* "Surely that is the guest hall. And there, behind, that is the view from Gold Hill. I never knew that such could be done. Real people in a real place, and moving.

Averilla, too, squatted to better view the piece. "Oh, Robert." The Man in all three panels is a Jew, and not just any Jew, but someone very like Master Levitas. Not as he is today," Averilla continued, expecting Robert to follow her line of thought, as she knew from the old continuity between them that he could, "or as he was last week, but as he looked when he first came. Remember? Years ago it was. Not so young, I guess, but ... "

"I do not suppose that Hugo knew, even guessed at, what he was doing," Robert said slowly, meditatively. "He couldn't have, could he?" The circles around Averilla's eyes seemed to have darkened as she bent on one knee. "It is a judgment Hugo has rendered here. Of us."

Robert's face was grim. "I do see it," he said as she rose, "but he didn't know what would happen when he started. How could he?"

Chapter Twenty-eight

Tuesday

After supper and before Compline

I

t was two days later that the first whispers came to the abbess' ears. As the winter had sagged into itself, the fire in the warming room had become more and more frequented during the pause between Vespers and Compline, when recreation and talking were permitted. The leisurely strolls through the cloister garth of the summer twilight had long ceased. The black-robed forms were now wont to scuttle for the warmth of the hearth, where they could thaw their hands or sit companionably, enjoying one another's peace. Often, two or three would speak softly about some housekeeping matter, or about the queen or empress or family outside the walls. The abbess was wondering where Master Hugo and Master Levitas were to sleep this night, sending an unspoken prayer for their safety, when the solicitous voice of the novice mistress broke into her thoughts.

"Dear child," — they were all "dear children" to Dame Petronella, but most particularly "dear" were the current crop of novices — "how doest that finger?"

"It festers, Dame. See." Sister Theodosia good-naturedly held up her injured finger. "Haste as usual has made me suffer." She peeked sideways at Dame Petronella, half-teasingly, laughing at her own frailty, for Dame Petronella was forever trying to slow them all down.

"As well it should," Petronella snapped.

"Always the novice mistress, you are." Dame Osburga, the new prioress, smiled at Petronella's concern.

"Aye, that I am," Petronella puffed up, ready to defend her ministrations and her mothering.

Osburga held up a hand. "Nay, nay good Dame. You know we all love your concern. Jealousy is snapping at my innards. Would I had someone to take such care of me." Dame Petronella was peering and scratching at the angry and swollen finger. "Mayhap a thorn embedded?" And she looked at Theodosia sternly. "To the infirmary with you. Now, when Sister Cadilla has finished saying Vespers with the old dames, and there be none from the town craving her care. She needs must draw this thorn and cleanse the place with bugle or loosestrife before the humors take it."

Theodosia bit her bottom lip and withdrew her finger, holding it between the folds of her habit. "No need, Dame. Really. It—it soon will heal."

"Sister Theodosia!" The old lady, momentarily speechless, glanced at the abbess for support, and then continued. "The Rule bids us, as well you know, insists that we obey any instruction given from one to another."

Theodosia, the abbess noted to herself with surprise, *is on the verge of tears.*

"Dame, forgive me." Theodosia mumbled. "I mean no disobedience. Indeed, I have gone to the infirmary. Yesterday, after Nones. Sister Cadilla said 'twas naught, that I was ill counseled to trouble her with such an—an insignificance."

The wind that had been absent during the last two days could now be heard whistling through the silence that followed Theodosia's words. Very carefully, no one looked at the abbess.

"Aye. Cadilla is worried." Dame Osburga said neutrally.

"Not herself." Dame Averilla was quick to defend the woman she had worked with for so many years.

"Jared is her brother," Dame Edria added.

"The youngest in the family."

" ... and she was professed when he was barely a lad."

" ... but she always had a soft spot for him. Remember ye how she always pressed Dame Averilla to be allowed to take the simples to the village."

The abbess sighed. *Jared is Cadilla's brother. Of course. How can I have forgotten? Mea culpa, mea maxima culpa.* She looked up from studying her hands to find that all were watching her.

"There were the accounts." Dame Osburga's voice was soft, conversational, spoken into the fire. "And Master Levi."

Emma also looked into the fire. *I have been so preoccupied — overmuch preoccupied — by the debts. Worried. Money, coins — graven images indeed. "Render unto Caesar." Osburga's words are for me.*

"We have all been sore distraught," Dame Osburga continued. "All of us."

Osburga tries to relieve me of guilt, but I should have remembered! So entangled was I in worldly goods that one of the souls entrusted to me ...

"I — I don't understand." Theodosia's petulant voice interrupted the abbess' musings.

"Sister Theodosia," Abbess Emma's voice was pitched low, "It is perhaps by most forgotten. I certainly had — much to my shame — but Sister Cadilla is sister to Jared."

"Jared?!" Sister Theodosia had come from north of Lincoln and had yet to learn all the interrelationships of the nuns. "Blood kin to the man who stands accused of the murder of Savette?"

334

"Aye." Emma said, pulling her shawl about her as she bowed to the assembly and moved to the door.

2

As she traversed the inner court to the infirmary, Emma bowed her head against the newly risen wind. So it was in looking down that she noticed a patch of snowdrops at the edge of the infirmary garth, each white petal cradling a green spot with such a deliberate regularity. She stopped. *Oh, Thou, who thought to create such beauty for our cheer within these months of bleakness, give to me words for Cadilla,* she prayed, *of peace, and comfort. Oh, Lord, it would be Cadilla, of all those You entrusted to me! And I—I have so little understanding of her. She has always stood so proud. So jealous of her status. It has been difficult to like her. Even for me. And I, of all people, should understand, half-English as I am. But others here are half-English. We have been able to adapt. Why has not she?*

Emma halted in mid-step, as if a giant hand barred her way.

Is that indeed so? You are equally English? The voice in her mind was gentle, but firm. *Raised Norman, were you not?*

She knew it was true.

Indeed, of more importance, your father was Norman? Given by the Conqueror titles, lands, men, and beasts. Cadilla's father was, well, you know little of Cadilla's father, except perhaps that he is a fine reeve to you. You have no idea what it was like to be stripped, as he was, as were others like him, of everything. Forced to work as a slave on land that had been his for generations.

Emma shook her head. *Surely not a slave.*

A serf. Is there such a difference?

Emma again shook her head. *No difference. No difference at all.*

She knew that. And knew even more. That even here in the

convent, Cadilla was relegated to the status of lay sister. Servant. Whereas Emma...

"So ashamed," she whispered.

The infirmary door seemed heavy as Emma pushed it open and descended the two steps into the soft flickering light emanating from the wall niches. As she glided toward the "T" end of the building, she noticed that Dame Aethwulfa was not asleep. She hadn't been to see Dame Aethwulfa that day. She'd had a tendency, every day since the fire, to put the visit off until the last possible moment, sometimes, as she had today, forgetting entirely. *How awful,* thought Emma, *to have to wait and to have the one you are waiting for not come! How could I be so cruel?* She bent over the bed to straighten the coverlet. The few wisps of gray hair lay matted on the linen, and Dame Aethwulfa seemed — *dirty?* The old dame's eyes were rheumy, and a fetid sweet smell and an odor of urine — *Can this be?* — issued from the bed.

"Aethwulfa?"

"My lady." The old lady lifted a veined and gnarled hand in the direction of the abbess, and her eyes turned toward the voice.

"You have not been cared for."

"There is something wrong, my lady. For me ... " she coughed " ...it does not matter. But for the others ... if there be others here ... I — I do not see well."

"There are still Dame Maud and Dame Aethelia."

"Ah. Well, then ... Sister Cadilla, lady, is sore troubled. I can do naught for her. She comes to me rarely, and when she does, she is abrupt."

"Where is Cadilla now?"

"In the kitchen, I presume. She came in, not long ago, from the outside. She smelled of chamomile."

Emma looked up. Cadilla was indeed there, standing in the transept, where chapel and kitchen intersected the long hall that was the infirmary. Perhaps she had heard the soft smack of their lips as they whispered, or the faint rustle of the wool habit on the tiles.

A lost sheep, she has become. Emma thought, seeing Cadilla anew; really looking at her. *Her wimple is mussed, and a stain lies 'neath her chin. What kind of shepherd am I?*

Emma motioned her to the empty benches that stood awaiting the sore toes, the coughs, the unmanageable stomachs that were Cadilla's province.

Though Emma sat, Cadilla remained as straight as a furrow. Emma ignored the disobedience and blundered in as best she could. Her voice was low. "I have greatly erred; trespassed against you. I—I remembered not your kinship to Jared."

"Lady," Cadilla hissed fiercely. "He did not do it."

Emma was surprised at the vehemence. Cadilla's eyes gazed straight ahead, and she clenched and unclenched her hands. "He is sinless. And you have let the Jew go free. Didn't his kind kill Christ? And now my brother will pay for the Jew's sin."

Emma tried to keep her voice even and calm. "You would fain go, I know, to minister to your father and brother. Surely they have need of your kindness just now. And nourishing food. I shall send Dame Averilla here to watch Dame Aethwulfa."

Cadilla's eyes opened in surprise, then as quickly narrowed with suspicion, and, at the mention of Dame Averilla, jealousy. With a cursory nod, she started to turn her back on her superior. Realizing, perhaps, just how far she could push the abbess, Cadilla made a shallow, almost mocking, reverence.

Emma sighed. *Enough of empathy. What Cadilla needs now is a bit of obedience.* "I expect you in the oratory on the morrow for every office. Do not miss a one. You need them now. Shall I send one of the novices to accompany you?"

"Nay, lady. These tracks I have known since babyhood. What harm would come to me now that the Jew is gone?"

337

Chapter Twenty-nine

Wednesday

After Terce, or mid-morning

I

he abbess' court, called the Curia D. Abbatissae, was assembled every three weeks on Wednesdays. The steward had, surprisingly, decided to try Jared in the Curia D. Abbatissae instead of the Curia Legalis Feodorum Baroniae, which the bailiffs of all the other barony manors were required to attend. As he stood in the great hall of the gatehouse, waiting for the trial to begin, Robert vaguely wondered why the steward had chosen one court over the other. It didn't trouble him much. It would become clear in time. The ways of the steward could be relied on to be wily even in the most straightforward of circumstances. Certainly, though, something didn't feel right. To be sure, the steward hoped to gain in one way or another. Could he still want Jared for Damasa? Impossible. Robert's brow furrowed as he reviewed the interplay of events over the past few days.

As Sergeant of the Hundred, Tom had held the inquest on the body in Lovick's house early on the day of the funeral. The gashes on Savette's forehead and the back of her head had been declared not the normal result of her fall or of a misstep on a slippery rock. Murder most foul had been the opinion. The avowal of Mary — Robert's own child — that she had seen Jared with Savette the very afternoon of the death and in the very location that the body had been found, cast suspicion on Jared. But it wasn't until the ring — made by Master Levitas, and, according to Robert, identified by its maker as intended for Savette — had been taken from Damasa that Jared had been hauled from the castle to the "cage" in the cramped, stench-filled dungeon beneath the keep.

A prickle of unease caused Robert to flick his eyes repeatedly around the hall. Unlike the ancient shire and hundred moots that had been held in the open at places like Modbury, the Hill of Speech, increasingly the abbess' court was convened inside. With its huge overhang and buttressed upper story, the hall of the gatehouse could hold and shelter most of the borough. The room was lighted only by the watery shafts that managed to sneak through the shutters, and it reeked of unwashed bodies and dirty wool. An overlarge crowd clung to the corners of the hall and ranged out the door and into the courtyard. Robert pressed his lips together and glanced balefully toward the front of the hall, where the twelve, the "county," who would decide Jared's fate, milled importantly.

When Master Chapman entered, he nodded to a few, ponderously fitted himself into the one chair, and steepled his fingers under his chin. As was usual, he would serve as presiding judge in the place of the abbess.

Responding to a nod from Master Chapman, Robert cleared his throat in order to start the presentment of Englishry, a tedious formality, but necessary in establishing that, despite her name, Savette was indeed, English, as was Jared. Norman law assumed that only Normans were important enough to murder, and the murder of a Norman could only be heard by one of the King's justicers. So it was important to decide that this inferior court could hear the case.

Robert was partway through the wearisome genealogy when the

tenor of the crowd increased from bored whisperings to excited hissings. He paused and looked up in time to see Jared being jostled through the press. Jared's face had aged. He had been in the cage for only two days, but looked as if he had been beaten and scourged. Yet Robert knew he had not. *Interesting.* Jared's eyes were red-rimmed and crevices that belonged to a man of three-score years scarred his cheeks.

At the conclusion of the presentment of Englishry, Robert nodded to Todd, who was standing toward the front of the room with his father and Simon. Todd stepped forward. His face was redder than usual, his jaw jutted.

"I am not acting out of hatred or malice or wrongful covetousness," he glowered, hammering the words of rote with an iron-hard purpose. "I accuse Jared Reeve's-son of killing my sister Savette." Todd looked over at Robert, not sure now how to proceed, uncertain what he should say, just how much further to go.

Robert moved into the open space between the crowd and the county and asked, "Think ye that this was done by Jared with malice aforethought?"

Todd looked at Robert as if he had lost his wits. "Ye saw her skull, the gashes both front and back, the one on the back the size of a peregrine egg. Couldna ha' happened on her own. Not front and back both. Nay. 'Tis clear eno'. Jared pushed her. And hard. And then left her ... " Todd's voice broke, " ... left her there all the night. Ha' she na' been dead afore, she would 'a died from the cold and the blood. Lying there in the bushes with nothing to comfort her, no warm hand ... "

Todd brushed his forearm against his eyes. His supporters stood behind him, grim-faced. To a man they were those who had searched for Savette, who had been at the stream when she was found.

John the Mason was the first to swear: "In the name of Almighty God, so I stand here by Todd, in true witness, unbidden and unbought, that as I saw the dead Savette with my eyes and heard with my ears the bailiff's child, Mary, declare that she had seen Jared with Savette a little while afore Savette was killed, I pronounce with Todd that Jared Reeve's-son did most foully murder the maiden Savette."

The others spoke one after another, changing the wording here and there occasionally, but the sense was the same.

Robert waited for a moment after the last had spoken. The county was intent, fascinated, definitely not above the voyeurism of morbid curiosity.

As the words of his old friend pounded away his life, Jared's stance became more and more defiant.

Robert looked at him directly now and saw pain. "Jared Reeve's-son, what say ye to this charge?"

In a clear voice, jaw clenched, straining his body against his captors, Jared shouted into the silence, so that even those crowded outside the hall could hear his scorn. "By the lord, I am guiltless both of deed and — and instigation of the foul murder with which Todd Lovick's-son me charges."

Robert scanned the crowd for an oath-helper to stand with Jared. None appeared. *What did I expect,* Robert asked himself. *Jared has never been oathworthy. Not only are Mary's words cast against him, but who would vouch for any oath given by Jared? They all know him; have known him from birth. Why, even as a lad, Jared had stolen the pies from the windows and poached the birds from the forest. They all know it.*

A movement rumpled the outer edges of the crowd. Slowly, the reeve, patting a back here, moving an elbow there, pushed his way to the fore. When he reached the front, he took his place beside Jarred, legs wide apart, hands hanging at his sides. "By the Lord," the reeve said, giving emphasis to the words, "the oath is pure and not false which Jared swears. I have asked him. He has told me true."

The room was silent. One or two in the front row turned to look behind them. No other oath-helper came forward. Robert took a deep breath. *The word of the reeve is worth the swearing of four lesser men. The pity is,* Robert thought despite himself, *no one will believe him. The sacrifice he makes in coming to Jared's defense will rebound to his hurt. Next harvest, for certain, probably sooner.* Robert raised his eyebrows. *By this recognition of his seed, he forfeits mayhap all the hard years of trust he has labored to earn. Can only hope they will understand that as a father he loves his son; this son, the apple of his eye. Bayard has become no more than an idle drunk, and Cadilla is lost to him. A tragedy indeed.*

Unsmiling, Master Chapman gave Robert a curt nod.

Robert stepped back out into the middle of the room and went through his whole presentment. He questioned Tom and the men-at-arms; took their pledges. " ... Had Savette been found by the stream?' Were there gashes on her body? Had the ring been made by Master Levi? For Jared to give to Savette? Had it subsequently been given to Damasa? ... " When his presentment was completed, Robert, carefully avoiding a look at the steward, ended with the ancient formulary, " ... which was done against the peace of God and of the abbess and to which ... "

A commotion beside the open door interrupted Robert's monologue. Those nearest the door seemed to be making way for someone short, wearing black, the black of a nun's veil.

A nun? Robert asked himself. *The abbess? Surely not!* Finally, she turned and looked at him fully. *Sister Cadilla?!* Robert glanced at Master Chapman and saw reflected his own look of impatience. *Jared's sister. This would make a mare's nest of an already difficult situation.* The townsfolk continued to give Cadilla place, and she moved easily within their empathy and between their bodies.

When Sister Cadilla reached the front of the room, she glared at Robert for a heartbeat of silence before opening her mouth.

Then she closed it again. *For certes,* he thought, she means to plead for Jared's life. He rubbed above his mustache. *Might as well wait it out. It is to be expected. A family never thought one of theirs could be guilty.*

Master Chapman straightened in his chair, leaned forward, and cleared his throat, "Sister," he said finally, "mayhap we can find you somewhat to sit upon while we search here for the truth."

There was a flicker behind her eyes, and a bitter smile hovered at the side of her mouth before it, too, was roughly extinguished. "'Twill do ye no good to search for the truth, for without my say *ye* canna' know the truth. That be betwixt me and the good God." Then she laughed, not the high, hysterical laugh Robert had expected, but a laugh speckled with disdain.

The steward's brow furrowed in the quick anger for which he was known, and he opened his mouth to speak.

Overriding any sound he might have made, she continued, "For you see, 'twas I as killed her."

The sudden silence that followed Cadilla's words dissolved into a hissed intake of breath followed by squeaks and rumbles of surprise. A look of disbelief crossed the steward's face, and Father William, taking a step toward Cadilla and laying a hand on her arm, said, "Sister, you are overwrought, let me ... "

She shook off his arm with an angry growl. "Fiend'll take me hinder soon eno'."

Robert saw Jared's face flush with worry, understanding, relief, and then — *hope?*

With a peculiar glint in his eyes, the steward finally found his voice, and surprised Robert by saying slowly to Cadilla, "We will hear you, Sister, in courtesy to your veil and love for your God."

"Jared ... " she started, and then, surprisingly, stopped, as if now that it had come to it she was at a loss for words.

"Speak of only those things that will absolve him, if that is your intent."

"Oh? Oh, aye, ye'll have what ye need." Then she moistened her lips, and, fixing her eyes on one of the webs drooping from the timbers of the ceiling, started to recite, as if telling a story to the young novices in the infirmary. "'Twas the night that she, Savette, I mean, went missing. Jared come to me. During Vespers it was. 'Light down and welcome, brother,' I said. I remember because I was well pleased to have the company. I'd been uneasy all the day, the willies creeping up my spine. He, though, he would have none of it. His eyes were wide, and he was white, I can tell you, with the fear of Mother Church on him where it had never been afore. 'Come, sister, now,' he says, and grabs for my arm. 'And bring your scrip.' I looked at him then, and something told me that what he had to say I didn't want any else to hear. As I followed him, he told me what had happened. He had pushed her, he said, in anger, and she had fallen and was bleeding. Dead, he thought." Here, Cadilla shifted her eyes, not to Robert, as he half expected, but to the face of the steward, and some look passed between the two of them.

Does he know? Did he know what she meant to say? Is this his doing? Robert's eyes narrowed.

"Continue, Sister," Master Chapman said. "You have our attention."

"He loved her. Ye wist that. There was no discretion between them. All during the harvest. But, well, that's as may be, and not a real reason for marriage. And so, he had taken his troth elsewhere. That was it. And she wouldn't let him go. I knew her well eno' to know that." Cadilla shook her head, and a look of sorrow passed fleetingly across her face. "But we — we of English stock, we don't have time for such blather. Jared needed to make his way, needed to breed with the best he could. And the offer 'ad come. To marry Damasa." She waited then, expectantly, for a buzz of recognition. But it was old news. One or two of the county exchanged glances, seemingly surprised; most just looked a bit

344

grimmer. Robert looked again at the steward, who maintained his composure. Locked his jaw. That was all.

"But, as it happened, he had not killed her. I followed him down to the ponds. Kept my counsel. They wouldn't miss me at Vespers, stashed in the infirmary as I am with only the old dames and those as are too sick to notice. I have a certain freedom. I saw the moment of it. Led to it, by angels or demons, I wot not. I found her, all right. We found her. Lying in the water with that gash on her head. She had crawled up onto the bank. She was alive. Jared gave a cry and was ready to fall on her as ye wist a lad will do, but I sent him on. Told him not to come to me to ask about it."

Robert's gaze shifted fractionally to take in Jared's face, and mirrored there was all the confirmation he needed. The lad was nodding, relief erasing the lines that had charted his face.

"After a moment of struggle, ye wist, Jared left us," Cadilla continued. "I had said some'ut that sent him back, reminded him of what he was about. And so he went. Looked back, 'o course, but what could he do? Told him I'd take care of 'er, or some such.

"When he had passed the bend in the stream, I looked to her. She was lying there bemused, but awake and half sensible.

"I had brought simples in my scrip, and took her head in my lap and soothed her brow. She knew nothing at first. It so happens. There is a time where the wit tries to sort things out, asks the same question over and over. At first she remembered not what had passed. I thought it best to leave it be.

"And then, well, 'twould 'ave been better had she stayed so, witless, but, she did na'. Her eyes, they opened wide, and now they had sense.

"'Cadilla,' she says, 'help me.' She grabs at me, ye wist. I hate to be grabbed. Pulled her off. But she was clinging. Like ivy she was, twining around on me. 'Ye have a greater strength with him,' she said. Or some'ut of that sense. 'Have me, he would, I know that. If you persuaded him.'

"I shrugged, 'Ye can have the babe.' I told her. 'Naught wrong wi' that. And Jared can find the babe price.'

"'No,' she cries. Screamed at me, the hate rising in her face, her teeth bared.

"'Don't ye understand?' I asked her then. 'Everything that should be Jared's by right 'as been taken by the Normans. Our brother at least has some land to 'is name, but that was by marriage. Our father has given his sweat and life for the good of the land, but it is no longer ours. Ye can give him naught. With Damasa and his learning ... well, with Damasa, Jared will have the rights and the gold, and who knows to what he may not rise? 'Tis an opportunity and he mun take it.' That is what I told her.

"'His rights! His freedom! But what of mine? We have the same English blood, he and I. Both have the same oppressor. I will stop it, Cadilla,' she said, barring her teeth. 'I promise you. He gave me a plight-troth. This is not just a babe begotten behind the hay.'

"'Tho' it was,' I said. She could na' play me the fool.

"'No,' she says. 'Begotten only after a plight-troth given. Never before.'

"'Never before?' I asks. 'I may be a nun, but I saw the two of you ...'

"'Mayhap he told you not,' She was cross in her words. 'But there was a plight-troth between us.'

"'Your word against his.' I says. 'Your father gave no bride price to mine.

"'Matters not. I had a ring. He gave it me, I tell ye.'

"'Show me, then, this ring,' said I.

"'I canna. He ripped it from me.' And here she opened her fist. Her muddy hand had been clutched around a silken ribbon.

"'That is a ribbon,' I said. There is no proof here. Just your word that there be a ring to it. Which I believe not.'

"'What care I whether or no ye believe my words. The old Jew made the ring, and he knows for whom he made it. Well known,

346

he is, for his truth and righteousness, and iffen they believe me not, his word will weigh heavily with the abbess. She trusts Master Levi. And Cadilla,' she says here, her face in mine, 'I will go to the abbess if I needs must.'

"'So be it,' I say. I lifted up my simples then and started back. Not four steps had I gone when the fiend caught me. I wot he climbed out from under the bridge and put in me such an anger, such a hatred as I had never before known. I turned.

"She was kneeling now, where I had left her, watching me with such a look that no longer was I myself, but in the time it takes to swat a fly, like a berserker I was on her, tearing at her hair. We rolled a bit then, beside the stream. She got up and tried to run, but her sense was still not her own, and she wobbled and fell over backwards. Unknowing — mayhap I just let myself be led — but before she could rise again, I was on top of her, my hands on her throat and hers on mine. I forced her head, shook her, pounded her head against a rock. I wot not if I knew the rock was there. Mayhap I did. The sound of it brought to me what I had done, the blood on my habit, on my face, on my hands. I sat there for some moments, not knowing.

"Then, when sense came back, the fiend used that very blood on my habit to spirit me on. In the form of a cross the blood had spattered. That brought to my mind the face of the Jew, and of a sudden I knew the path that would rid Jared of both Savette and the Jew, both together. For without the Jew, there was no remembering, no memory of the plight-troth, and no blame to light on Jared. That I feared more than anything. 'Twas no chance of life in her by then. I took my knife and carved a cross on her hand.

"Then? Then I dragged her washing basket and beating paddles deep into the bushes, where none could see 'em, and climbed back to the infirmary. 'Twas a messy business, all told, for there is much blood in the head. But folk have come to expect the odd stain on my habit, and black is a hiding kind of color. Even so, I needed to wash it out afore it stiffened. I kept the ribbon," — here Cadilla unclasped her fist and dangled before them a silken ribbon slashed with brown stains. There was a gasp. — "in case it should be later questioned. I told Jared, o' course, naught. And 'twas for the best, as it turned out. The first he knew was when he heard the hue and cry. So his grief, when he saw her was as real as was his surprise."

She stopped as abruptly as she had started. Robert had been watching Jared. The lad's head lay awkwardly in his hands, and his dry sobs could be heard across the room. No one moved.

Master Chapman masked his feelings well by touching the tip of his jeweled dagger across the fullness of his lips and watching Cadilla through slitted eyes. When he spoke, his voice had lost none of its command. Out of the depths of defeat, his plan seemed to have arisen like the phoenix: Jared was once again his; his daughter was assured of children; his line might continue. He looked over at the county where they sat along the bench, with all the trappings of leather boots and silken tunics. "My lords?"

The oldest among them stood, a man of venerable years, his hose wrinkled around spindly knees, his eyes guarded, hard, and full of years of stern command. "We will discuss this further amongst ourselves. It seems not as simple a question as we were wont to believe. We will recess."

The hall solidified into a mist of blurted comment and conversation. Though the assembly had been speechless during the moments following Cadilla's words, it now gave vent to its anguished horror. The twelve burgesses leaned into one another, those on the rear bench craning forward, the eyes of those on the front bench unseeing as they concentrated on the remarks whispered into their ears from behind.

Unwillingly, Robert's eyes sought the face of the reeve. First the man's wife goes mad and dies. Now this. *And the reeve is a good man, a fine man. None finer.* Robert thought of Mary and

Clement, his own two children, and could not imagine the agony that must be searing the inside of this man. And there was nothing anyone could do. The reeve stood with a stillness that was unnatural, his eyes inward, his face ashen.

After an unsatisfyingly short time, the oldest burgess again rose and cleared his throat.

"My lord," said the steward.

"It is our considered opinion that the evidence of the nun leaves questions. *Qui bono?* Who profits? In this it would seem that the young man would still profit, and she would not. She doth protest to the contrary, but mayhap she would do all in her power to save the life of this unsavory scamp, her brother." The thane's face became, if possible, even grimmer. "No, Master Steward, we are unconvinced of this nun's guilt. It seems unlikely that she would have it in her to do such an act, whereas her brother would be both strong enough and well-enough motivated." He turned to Robert. "You, Master Bailiff, must provide us better evidence of her guilt, must prove to us that she and she alone did indeed kill the maiden. Elsewise we must assume that her love for her kin, for her younger brother Jared, prods her to assume his guilt.

CHAPTER THIRTY

WEDNESDAY

MID-AFTERNOON, OR BEFORE NONES

I

he abbess always hated it when there was a trial other than the usual dispensations of nuisances. She had seen Cadilla enter the gatehouse. *That, at least,* she thought, *is to the good. How can I not have been aware? The camel and the needle.* She imagined Cadilla's face as it would look now as she stood next to Jared. No, between her father and Jared. *Does she hold his hand? Her placid face would lend solace to the miserable scene. He didn't mean to kill.* Emma was sure of that. *Can Cadilla understand? Savette and Jared had been so besotted. No, there was more to it than besotted. There was real caring. Even I saw such looks pass between them.* Emma fingered her pectoral cross and peered again out the window, only this time she saw the bailiff striding across the inner court. *To me, of course.*

Deciding that it must be an emergency, she opened her door, swept past Sister Clayetta, and hurried down the steps. Robert would have spoken immediately, but she held a finger to her lips. Nothing could be so important as to disrupt the silence of the cloister. He bowed cursorily, and she read irony in his eyes before she turned and led him into one of the ground-floor parlours.

"Lady," he blurted as he shut the door behind him, and before he had given her a chance to seat herself. "Cadilla has confessed to murdering Savette."

Not aware of moving, Emma sank onto the bench. It was as if a thunder bolt had gone off in her head, a burst of light. "God help us," she whispered.

Firmly gripping her cross, Emma saw the horror and confusion in Robert's face mirroring what must be on her own.

"How know you this? How comes such a wicked thing to be told out?"

"She confessed, my lady, to the court, to the steward. Told how it was done."

"But," Emma felt like her mind was moving slowly along an icy path, across a pond covered with flat sheets of ice, trying to comprehend all the various shards of crystal that seemed to be piling themselves one atop another to form a stalactite. "How had she time? Wh—Wh—When? Why?"

"To save Jared. So that he might marry Damasa. The steward's doing, I warrant, and yet he shall be free of the taint."

Emma heard the chill of disgust in Robert's voice. *He has never liked or trusted Master Chapman, but I thought... what did I think? I don't know anything anymore.*

"When could she have?" Her mind still grappled with the original question.

"Damasa?"

"No, Cadilla. When could she have — have killed her?"

"After Jared pushed Savette. Here's the plain fact of it. Apparently, he went to Cadilla for help after he had fought with Savette. Together they went down Laundry Lane. Savette was still alive. Cadilla then sent Jared away, and ere he was home she had killed Savette. She showed us the torn ribbon that had held the ring. But, my lady, whilst that question is grave, another lies deeper and is far

351

more murky. The county believe it possible that Cadilla is herself innocent, but confesses to the deed in order to free Jared."

It is possible, Emma thought, and with a sinking feeling, knew it was.

"And," Robert continued grimly, "what makes that possibility seem probable is the fact that Cadilla cannot be tried by the steward."

Emma's face fell as she recognized the tangled skein that Cadilla and Jared seemed to be manipulating.

"Could Cadilla? Could Jared? Could two villagers be that devious? Can they possibly know that because Cadilla is a religious she must be tried by a church court?" Emma rose and started to pace the room, back and forth, wrapping her hands around one another over and over again, as if trying to find a place to put them. "It is not possible. They wouldn't know that a church court would be more lenient since Wulfstan's edicts. Why, I only know because one of my brothers ... well, no matter." Emma put her hands to either side of her head.

"You could give her the ordeal of the consecrated morsel?" Robert, Emma knew, was trying to be helpful.

"But how can that help? She has already confessed."

"Mayhap the consecrated morsel will force her to state that her confession is untrue."

"But then why would she need to be tried? And even if she were to be tried, whom would she go to? Bishop Roger is still in prison for treason to King Stephen."

Robert nodded. "And even if the bishop is released," he mused, "as I hear may happen, he will be little eager to bring to trial a nun who has killed a, an English maid."

They looked at each other silently for a long moment. Then Robert opened his mouth, "The crucial question remains unanswered, my lady: Can Cadilla have actually bludgeoned another woman to death, an innocent? In cold blood?"

"I cannot conceive it. Do you think it possible?"

Robert looked at his lady with a warm compassion in his eyes. "My lady, I would that it were not possible, but in my work I have seen things that I would not have believed had they not been before my own eyes. It is possible, very possible, you see, that she would sacrifice herself for her brother's life. She seems fierce in her hatred of the Normans; seems to bear a lofty grudge for the loss of their family lands."

"You, too, could heft such a grudge. But you do not."

"No. But I do have a job with you, my lady."

"Just so. If I understand this aright, that was exactly what Jared was aiming for. It is what I had considered giving to him myself before all of this happened."

"For certes? With his background?"

"I had thought that under the reeve's hand his youth would be blunted, that over time he would mature into the likeness of his father."

"Yes." Robert went back to the earlier thought. "It is one thing to commit a murder by accident, as Jared seems to have done; quite another to choose to do it aforehand."

Emma was suddenly suffocated by the thoughts tangling in her mind like a cat in the weaving spindle. She could not speak of it anymore. She needed to be alone with these terrible thoughts, to face the horror of them and to try to sort them out. This evil came so quickly on the heels of that other, which had so savaged Master Levitas. Were they one and the same, was there a miasma of hatred hedging them in here atop the mount? "I need time to pray on this," she said. "Have the steward dismiss the court, or has that already been accomplished?"

"Nay. They await your counsel."

"I have none so swift. The matter rests heavy on me. Speak to Dame Alice about a place to hold Sister Cadilla. It cannot be within the castle. It just cannot. We have some punishment cells

353

for miscreants, though little used. So, Jared, it seems, may go free."
Their eyes met as they tasted the rank gristle of that thought.

Robert raised an eyebrow, bowed, and left.

Emma was past noticing anything except the whirlwind in her mind. She sank to her knees there, in the middle of the floor, and the tears sheeted down her cheeks. *My Lord, my Lord,* she prayed. *Help me in this. I am witless. What shall I do? How can I help her? If she be not mad, she must hate her own hand. But how can she face You with such evil in her heart?*

Emma shut her eyes, cleared her mind, and allowed herself to sink into the dark-lightness of God. It came to her then, in a still, small voice of thunder, not in words, but in a fullness of knowing. Cadilla must be reminded of the remission of her sins; she must be made piercingly aware that Christ had taken these horrendous sins of hers upon Himself in his agony. Without that knowledge, self-flagellation and self-hatred would gnaw away at her soul, feasting on her spirit until it withered into a seedless husk. Cadilla must be reminded that one of the reasons — a selfish reason, but one that mankind understood — for the death of our Lord, was that this was the only way a sinful soul could regain its trust in God. Else, like Adam and Eve, the soul, knowing its own evil, would hide from the Creator, would flee and cower and dissolve like chaff in the wind. The sin was paid for, and needed only true grief and repentance from the sinner.

2

EMMA WAITED FOR THE INTERVAL between Nones and Vespers to go to Cadilla. Darkness was falling with the swiftness common to winter nights, and, as she hurried down the north walk, it seemed to Emma that the purple shadows held in their darkness the reality of the crouching monsters sculpted onto the pillars of the cloister walk. As she passed the path to the infirmary, she felt a strong urge to visit Dame Aethwulfa. *Dame Helewise will be caring for all the old ones, with compassion and skill, but e'en so I need to look in on her.*

The infirmary was again in order. Emma noticed that it smelled sweet, and smiled to herself, seeing that Helewise had put dried lavender in the cressets, banishing the sick smell, but abiding by Dame Averilla's rule against rushes.

Dame Aethwulfa watched with her bird-like eyes as Emma came to her, stopping, as was her wont, to say a word to the others. "I had hoped you would come," Aethwulfa said before Emma could even pull up the stool. The old lady turned her head so that the wisps of white hair were haloed by the muted light from the chapel cressets. "We have been told."

"About Cadilla? Who? Why? When had they time?"

"That matters not. I have kept a matter of import from you."

Emma felt truly bewildered.

"Cadilla did kill Savette."

Emma's brow furrowed. "How know you that? Why told you not me?"

"No one asked. It was not my place. I have no proof."

"Then why say you it is so?"

"Because I saw her washing out the blood." The old lady lay back on the pillow to regain her breath. "I know it was the day of the death, because that night I heard the hue and cry, and then, of course, the next morning she was found.

"It could have been anything that she was washing. Anything."

"She tripped by my bed on her way back into the infirmary. You had left the stool in the aisle, and the lamps were not yet lit. She thought I was asleep. I close my eyes when I want my prayers not to be interrupted. Cadilla muttered, and righted the stool, pushing it close beside my bed. A little later, when I wanted to move, I put my hand out for balance. I felt something wet. I

355

held my hand to my eyes. It was blood. And of course we heard the washing. There were several trips to the well. And the wool of her habit smelled wet for days."

3

EMMA HATED THE PUNISHMENT CELLS at the best of times — small, airless chambers within the gatehouse, locked and ill lit — but in the darkness at the end of a winter's day, they were fearsome. She put her hand against the wall to steady herself in the gloom; the only torch was at the door of the passage. She took a deep breath and knocked. There was an intake of breath, audible even from outside the stout ironbound door, followed hesitantly by a whispered "Deo Gratis."

Emma unhooked the key hanging next to the door and turned it in the hanging lock. The cell was pitch-black, shuttered from the outside. Emma left the door ajar so the torch in the corridor could shed light into the cell. There was a bed and a chamber pot; that was all. Not so much as a coverlet, and it was both cold and musty, freezing from the winter and from a shard within Cadilla herself.

Emma stood inside the door, hesitant. Cadilla rose from the bed where she had been sitting, her face defiant *or scared?*

Emma took a step, "Do you hate God?" Emma herself was surprised at the words that issued from her mouth.

Silence.

Emma let it lie there between them, where it stayed for a long time as their minds groped, grappled with it.

Finally, "Mayhap."

"The Jew?"

"Aye."

"Savette?"

"Aye."

Silence again. Dunstan tolled above them. *As long as that,* Emma thought.

"He ... He ... " Emma didn't know which "he" Cadilla was speaking of. " ... took it all. From us. Stiff-necked, hard of heart."

"Master Levi?"

"Nay. Him. God. They couldna 'ave done it without Him."

"And left you without."

"Wouldn't speak to me. Not as He does to the others."

"Do you listen?"

Another silence.

Finally, Cadilla shook her head.

"Then perhaps you should begin." The abbess moved closer, but hesitantly, as with a wild fawn. "I — I myself have just learned to listen." Seeing no answering look in Cadilla's eyes, she decided to leave her with that thought. She said, "I will have a coverlet sent you, as well as food, for I imagine you have not eaten; food and a cresset and a small brazier for heat. I charge you, Sister, to spend your time listening. God is there, I promise. He is waiting for you. I suggest you open the door. This is your only and last chance, lest you go unshriven to your doom."

And what if she does listen? Emma thought as she strode back across the courtyard hunched against the ever-present wind. *What do I do then?* Passing again through the slype and reentering the shelter of the north cloister walk, she paused. The cloister garden was now merely a refuge for cold stalks, brittle stems, and sodden leaves.

Sacking already covered the delicate plants; the flower beds had been mulched down, and the beloved roses that surrounded the statue of the Virgin cut back. *I could send Cadilla to the bishop. That is my duty, I suppose. And then? Then he will find her guilty, of course. After all, she has confessed. But did she really do it, or is she confessing to save Jared? Cadilla well might do something like that.* Emma could imagine it. *It will only be worthwhile if, and only if, Cadilla can see what she has done and truly repent. But how can she if she has achieved what she wanted, if she has succeeded in helping Jared? Is it my job to take that away from Jared? Will that make Cadilla more aware of what she has done? Does she need to be aware? My Lord, please help her to see what she has done. She hides from You. She ignores You, defies You. If you need me to be of help to You, show me the way. Please.*

4

FATHER BONIFACE HAD VEILED HIS EYES when the abbess told him of Cadilla. They had been in a downstairs parlour. "My dislike of that man is such," Emma would later whisper to Dame Aethwulfa, "that I don't even want him in my lodgings."

"Sir priest." His head had shot up at her words, like a hooded hawk smelling blood. "You have heard, I am sure, of the maid Savette of the village.

"Yes, milady. Killed by the Jew."

It was her turn to look startled.

"No. No, the bailiff found that Master Levitas was not the murderer. He suspected that Jared Reeve's-son had pushed Savette in a quarrel over a plight-troth."

"Indeed."

"You have heard all this, And still believe it was the Jew?" She paused, giving him a level look. He had the grace to flush, but barely. *This is hard, Lord. Help me in it. He is going to make a mess of it.*

"Whether it was the Jew or a quarrel among the serfs matters little to me."

"Sister Cadilla has since confessed to the murder."

"Sister Cadilla?"

So he hadn't heard.

His astonishment was real. "Killed the girl?"

358

"So she says. And made it look as if it had been done by the Jew."

Emma couldn't stand it anymore, and turned her back to him as if she were looking for the bench to sit upon. "She needs to be offered confession and absolution."

"But she hasn't been tried by a church court."

Emma turned back slowly. "She has confessed. What more can the court find? Howsoever, the further resolution of her case is not of your concern. An immortal soul is in need of your guidance...."

He opened his mouth as if to say something, ran his tongue along his bottom teeth, and suddenly bowed to the abbess. "I shall go to her immediately."

If Father Boniface had thought anything about the buildings squatting on the far side of the gatehouse, dwarfed by it, he had supposed they were for some class of animal—pigs or goats or sheep. He fumbled the key in the lock and pushed in the door, which scraped up dirt from the earthen floor.

He looked with distaste at the huddle before him. This moment held everything that was abhorrent to him. The room smelled of mold, despite a brazier and cresset still burning. There were cobwebs in the corners, and, overriding all, the distinct pungent smell of mouse. His lip curled in distaste.

Sister Cadilla seemed entirely unaware of his presence. She was sitting, head hunched over her knees, on the pallet under the window.

He cleared his throat.

Her eyes shone briefly as she blinked at the light from the door and scrambled to her feet, lowering her eyes.

He stood by the door, a black figure towering in the light. "I have come to hear your confession."

She glanced at him, and her gaze became conscious. She returned it to the rushes on the floor.

359

"I confessed in the court."

She is defying me! She, who should be grateful that I am here to offer her salvation from the fires of hell.

"Kneel, woman, and make your confession!" His voice lashed across the room with a violence that seemed to force her to her knees. He turned his back to her, as was required by the needs of the confessional.

"Forgive me, Father, for I have sinned," she croaked the words to the straightness of his back. "I — I," the sobs struggled past her throat. "I didn't mean to do it."

"But you didn't mean not to." His voice took on an edge of malice as he whipped around and gripped her chin, forcing her to look up at him. He had never felt, never grasped at, such power before, had never dared to. Even though it was only over an insignificant woman, something in him swelled and grew, and he watched it with a new feeling of satisfaction.

"Since you didn't mean not to kill her, your sin is the more wicked. Not only did you kill her, but you treated her like a dog. You failed to even recognize her humanity."

The thing inside of him glowed and amassed substance. Within himself he reheard his words, delighting in the firmness in his voice, the authority and sureness it held. He was a priest! Finally!

The small voice Father Boniface tried not to hear tried again: *Help her. You can, now, before it is too late.*

By the time the words seeped into his consciousness, Cadilla's eyes had rolled back and she had toppled sideways.

Pick her up, the still voice said. *Give her the touch of your hand. Give her absolution.*

Instead, he looked down on her and started across to the door. With a hand on the latch, he sniffed. *It's gotten worse,* he thought, *the smell of mouse is even more pungent than before.*

She has repented. The voice was now merely an echo. *Give her My absolution.* He pulled the door toward him, but it was

360

stuck in the dirt on the floor. He tugged harder. Like a bubble, rising through the golden thing of power within him, the Word struggled up and out of him, his voice low and quiet and resonating with the depth of truth. "Your sins are forgiven."

Entirely unaware of what he had said, Boniface gave a last yank on the door and slipped out.

5

THE NEXT DAY, WHEN EMMA CAME to the cell door, the fire-basket beside it was unlighted, and it took a moment for her eyes to adjust to the darkness. The door was not only unbolted, but unbarred and unlocked. In rising panic, she pushed it open and peered inside. The cresset had gone out, as had the brazier. If anything, the cell was darker than the hall had been, but she could make out Cadilla's form, hunched on the floor, her arms on the bed, not lying prone and not kneeling, but both.

Cadilla looked around, surprised and mazed by the abruptness and scraping sound of Emma's entrance.

"The door was unlocked?" Emma was puzzled.

"And you feared that I had flown?" Cadilla smiled bitterly. "Where would I go? Who would have me if I am cast out from my town, my community, and from my God?"

There is change here.

"My lady, I bid you sit."

Emma hesitated, then crossed to the bed and sat so that the kneeling form was at her knees.

"I have spoken to God, as you bid me. Well, listened, really. We had been estranged, He and I. I had thought that my little elf bolt, and then Saint Edward, I had thought that if I had faith in them 'twould be enough." She made a sound of gagging under her breath. "I didn't understand that power can't come from things, from mere bits of stone or the memory of saints. I didn't

361

understand ... at all. 'Twas a horrible sin I did. My lady, He would not have me to Him. No, that is not true. He would have me. I would not go. Nor could I. I didn't feel worthy." She made the funny sound again. "Until now. In the depths of the pit I have dug with my own hand, now I understand. Because He explained it to me. That his Son, His own dear Jesus, had taken my sin. There, there on the cross." Cadilla was gazing at the wall beneath the window as if she saw something there, as if ...

"See there, He is bleeding for me. See. See the nails in His hands and those slashes in His sides. They were for me."

Emma turned to look, a frisson of terror climbing her spine. She turned back to the glazed stare, wanting but not daring to put her hands on Cadilla's head, shoulders, or hands.

"And that crown on His head. That was for me, too. And I, I who as a child used to cower from one thorn in the tip of my finger, who would fain not go to the brambles with the others for the thorns, and yet He, He had a full crown on His forehead, piercing His brow. They pushed it in." Cadilla turned to look at Emma, her eyes beseeching, full of pity and grief, not seeing Emma at all. "Did you know that? So the thorns would pierce His flesh. And they scourged His back. I saw it, lady. He showed me. Well before He died, He showed me. Before He went to the cross, showed me the gashes on His back. The scourge was not just a whip. Oh, no. For me He endured more. There were pieces of iron tied on the ends of the whip. And not just one tail was it, but like the root of a tree, many tails tied together. For me, He died. Such love. I thought I killed for love of Jared, but now I know I did not. He loved her. I wanted the best for him. I told myself that I did it for love, but now I know what love is. It is what Jesus did for me. For me. So that I could crawl to His Father. So that I could stand afore Him in all my sluttishness. And the Father does understand. This I know. For He told me. And He is a Father with a Son to Him, so He understands. I can't go yet. He is with the

362

Virgin. See, see there in the hall, inside, by yon window? You can see the light of Him. But He will bid me approach and I can tell Him. I will practice if you will." Cadilla crabbed yet closer to the abbess and put her hands in a steeple, willing Emma to enclose them in her own. After a moment's confusion, Emma placed her own long fingers around Cadilla's, whose face was awash with tears, like river water over a rock. She licked away some drips and then, in a firm voice began, "In spite of everything, Your Son, dear God, has died for me. See, I can speak to Him for all that, because of the one who is hanging there. I can speak. He died for what I did. I see now the wrong I did. The pain He had to suffer because of it. But for that suffering I can come to you. I had a father once." Her eyes became inner-focused as she hunkered on her knees. "A strong man. He used to take me on his shoulders, he did. And I could see then to the heavens, I could. He was quiet then, but there was a glint in his eye far back that promised a smile later, or a treat. He was reeve, ye wist, and if he was given honey from a new hive just found, he would give it me. Ofttimes there was no reason for the smile, just his love for me. I am not fair. Never was. Sturdy, more's the pity, but enough so I could follow him on his haunts. He was everywhere, ye wist, with the sad and the lonely, even binding wounds when it was needed. He would sit for hours at a fire, just letting out the airs of anger that had settled on an old man. But then," Cadilla's eyes became more troubled, "but then he — his eyes lost their shine somewhere. I looked, searched the house, but it had gone. 'You are too big,' he said, 'to follow me about. Stay with the maids or help your moder,' and so I did.

"Then they fought, he and she. She wanted more, ye wist, than he could be, more than he could give, and she fixed on the lad, fixed all her love on him. 'Twas a terrible birth, and so I think the more sickle for her. They were no longer man and wife together. There was no more of the shaking of their pallet of a night, but

363

a cold freezing came between them and pervaded our house, so that it made me shiver when I entered, like a bleakness of a winter wind with no hope in it. She kept at him, ye wist, worrying him like a dog does with his bone, and every night she would strip a bit more of the meat of his manhood from him.

"The property had gone, you see, that had been in her family for generations. Orchard Farm was there no longer, given to one of the king's men, and Fader could do no better than be reeve. It was enough for him somehow, the joy in helping peace to brew in the town amongst enemies. He fed on that. But not she. One night she threw her best bowl, of a pottery glaze, 'twas, yet she threw it at him, and it shattered, and she screamed that it mattered not, for everything else had gone, too. She blamed him, ye wist, for the steward had showed him a way to riches, a small bending, the steward said, of the shares of barley that go into the barn at Tisbury. But he would not. 'Your honor,' she spat at him, 'will make us starve. The nuns care not about us, about how we have naught on the table of a bad winter's e'en. They will not know or care in their luxury.' But he would have none of it. 'Who am I,' he had asked, 'without my honor?' She never forgave him that.

"She soon died, but not until she had given me the skills she knew, whether I wanted them or no. And it is strange, indeed, for I did not at first. Took no pleasure in it and for many a year it was a tedious duty. But I took those skills and now am glad, for she had transferred to me her knowledge, and it became for me the way I could be of worth.

"But all those years, over and above her fights with my father, over and above her goading of my skill, she doted on Jared. The favored one. When he did wrong, it was called a mistake that he had done. When he taunted any of us, he would hide behind her to avoid our spitting wrath. She died wanting. She wanted...

"So I am a step-daughter of God. Like my father, I am God's step-daughter, and as such I would suffer the fate reserved for those who murder." Cadilla sighed. "Only in dying can I atone for what I have done; only my death will avert the vengeance that else needs be taken between families, Savette's and mine. God died for me, sinless. I have sinned. It is little enough that I die for it."

Chapter Thirty-one

Wednesday

Mid-afternoon, after Nones

I

Snowflakes sifted down in slow arcs onto the uplifted branches in the garth. Flat-topped shrubs now had snow draped across their wiry surfaces, and inappropriate frills of snow trimmed the veil on the statue of the Virgin. Emma hurried past, oblivious of the silent beauty, through the slype and up the stairs to her office. She lowered herself into her chair and immediately ached to rise again and pace. Instead, she folded her hands and waited. *I will not allow him to see how weak I am. Dear God, am I doing the right thing?*

There was a perfunctory knock, and Sister Clayetta, face impassive, opened the door to admit Master Chapman. Making a deep bow to the abbess, the old lady closed the door, murmuring, "The steward, my lady."

"When he arrived in your office?" Dame Aethwulfa would later ask, eyes bright with questions.

The abbess allowed herself to rise. *An advantage.*

You need not an advantage of that sort. Truth is your stanchion.

366

Emma accepted the rebuke with a smile. *I asked You in as counselor, and now You are here more often than I had ever dreamed possible.* The thought widened her smile.

Master Chapman saw the smile and returned it. "You sent for me, my lady." He stood, feet insolently apart, one hand behind his back, the other tapping idly at his left foot with a whip. "'Twill be easy now that the wretch has confessed..."

"He was portentous again, and ponderously solemn," Emma would say to Dame Aethwulfa.

"...and, of course, she will hang," Master Chapman persisted, "or would you rather..." he lowered his voice in feigned inquiry.

"He rubbed his thumb against the knuckle of his forefinger," the abbess continued to Dame Aethwulfa, "as if the rope of her hanging were then passing through his very fingers."

"...would you rather I sent her to the bishop?"

"The audacity! He assumed I knew nothing of canon law. I gave him a look."

"Of disdain?" the older woman would ask.

Taking Emma's silence and her furrowed eyebrows for confusion and implied assent, Master Chapman added, "You will need me, as well, to prepare the necessary letters of explanation and confirmation, and to..."

"None of that will be necessary. I myself intend to handle the matter."

Master Chapman raised an eyebrow.

Emma said. "This matter is more serious, Master Chapman, far more serious than you seem able to comprehend. It is not a matter of a mere sentencing. One immortal soul weighs in the balance." Her eyes shadowed into the darker green of a black opal, but her gaze remained steady, and for the first time in their interview Master Chapman took note of the change in her and felt a finger of unease. The drumming of the whip stopped.

"I summoned you here with no intention of discussing Sister

Cadilla. No, I would discuss with you, Master Steward, the only thing that need concern you: your part in this."

"In all things, as you, my lady, must be well aware, my only concern is the good of the abbey."

"He blustered and bluffed. I had had an inkling of his true nature before — taken on faith from a heard-tell. Finally, however, I could see him for myself. It was as if a skin had been removed from my eyes. That man had the audacity to judge Cadilla!"

"Is it?" Emma asked the steward now, her voice ominously soft. "In all of this, your only concern was the welfare of the abbey?"

"Of course."

"I am aware of your manipulation of Jared."

"Ah." He paused, slightly off balance. "In sooth, 'twas but a matter of choosing a worthy replacement to succeed me. It takes time to train a good steward, and —"

"A good steward?" she interrupted. "'Tis a concept worth examining. A good steward looks first to the interest of his master. Your interest in Jared? I trow that was but a snare to secure a husband for Damasa. An unbroken stewardship for the abbey? Nay, Master. Your intention, I fear, was to ensure the health of your get."

"Dealing with him wasn't as hard as I had thought it would be," Emma continued to the old prioress, "from somewhere I found —"

"From God, perhaps?" the old lady would whisper. "It is a strength we all have if we but ask. Heretofore you had seemed reluctant to lean your full weight against Him."

"You offered Damasa to Jared!" Despite her resolve, Emma's eyes flashed. "You deliberately severed a plight-troth. The words spoken in the marriage sacrament, 'those whom God hath joined together' ought —"

"They were not yet married, my lady." His voice was irritated.

Emma held him with her eyes. "Not to mention the matter of Dame Joan."

Master Chapman turned his head, just a fraction, like a hawk smelling danger.

"I bear a great feeling of rancor toward those who ill use my nuns, who deliberately manipulate them against their own loyalties. Dame Joan is not strong. You knew her weakness and cast it against her; further, you stole from us." Emma's voice was so low, her lack of passion so disarming, that it wasn't until she uttered the last words that Master Chapman's eyes passed from caution and into a studied calculation.

"My lady, you are a hard mistress. The recompense for my duties is paltry, my skills great. I needed to supplement —"

Her hand rose in a preemptory sign of cessation, which, had her eyes not held a new authority, a commanding presence, he would have ignored.

"Were all this betrayal not enough, you had the impudence to encourage me to leave my flock at this time of turmoil in the abbey, not to mention the anarchy brewing throughout the land, to go argue with the king about a piece of land. I know not what vile machination you intended in my absence, but such a temptation I take as a personal insult. You will leave us."

Master Chapman started to turn.

"By 'us'," Emma's voice was icy, "I speak not only of this room, but of the entire abbey."

She kept her green eyes hard and unwavering. "So much agony has resulted from your little piece of greed. In this place we try to live as the Lord has commanded us. It is not always easy. Love can be pushed into a crooked path. You did so with Joan. Into another crooked path strayed Agnes, then Dame Averilla, and now Sister Cadilla. The fester that you have become must be cut out forthwith. Were you to be tried before the county, I am not certain you would be convicted, nor be punished with more than a sharp fine. But the abbess gave you your position, your house, the very clothes you wear, so the abbess can as easily take them

369

away. You, Master Chapman, are dismissed from this burgh, and dismissed from your duties to the Abbey of Shaftesbury. You shall be escorted to the edge of the demesne, where you shall be sent away, cast into the darkness you have brought upon yourself. I have no fear that you will manage to roll over this disgrace and come up again, having fabricated lies and deceptions to justify your actions. It matters not to me what you say as long as you are gone. Your daughter, Damasa, having been, as far as I can see, no party to your deceptions, will be given the choice to accompany you on your journey or to stay here as a lay sister, where she can be trained to whatever suits her. I intend never to lay eyes on you again. May God have mercy on your soul."

"My lady! It is deep midwinter! Snow is on the ground."

She did not falter. "The bailiff will help you to bundle up such belongings as came with you to your present position. And some others. I have asked him to be fair in the division of property, for indeed you have given us service. But, since I am unsure how far your perfidy has seeped, we will not be overgenerous. I would imagine that you have tucked away for yourself some sum that will sustain you and yours. I shall not inquire into that, for I doubt very much that the truth would be forthcoming. I should perhaps have your tongue out or your hand off, but I have no taste for such violence. I think this dismissal will be enough penance to assuage the wrong you have done us."

"You will regret this."

"I was most surprised," her eyes would be round as she spoke to the old prioress, "mayhap justified, that after all he had done, he should have such presumption to even respond, much less to strike out at me."

"Like a snake, my dear, he was mortally wounded and knew it."

"'No, Master Chapman, I think not." Emma found herself saying. "I would far rather have the stumbling advice of a man

370

I can trust, than a brilliant man whose words slither around me, waiting to strike where I am most vulnerable. Leave us."

As his heavy boots clattered down the stairs, she raised her eyes to the plain crucifix on the wall. *You do provide the words. Why did I question? I am in the palm of Your hand. But, oh Lord, this has been a lesson most sear. I would not have this pain of Savette's death on my soul. Poor, dear Savette.*

2

THE EXHAUSTING TUMULT OF THE LAST MONTH had taken its toll on all the nuns. They were quieter, each tending to her own pursuits, her own prayer life, none having the will or inclination to dispute in chapter or scrap during recreation. It was as if the snow had silenced them as well as the countryside and given them a needed peace. The beams, black and tilted, all that remained of the goldsmith's shop, no longer infused the air with the flavor of scorched wood and charred thatch, for the cloying scent had been erased by the snow.

Dame Averilla found herself fleeing to the sacristy whenever she could, as if that little workroom beneath the rood-loft was a cave that could give her shelter and protection. No longer able to rely on her disapproval of Joan's actions and activities, she had come face to face with her own iniquities, and the self-knowledge made her feel naked and vulnerable, like a snake having shed its skin.

The night of Master Chapman's departure, shortly after Compline, Averilla was puttering in the sacristy, taking more time than she needed, relishing the dumb busyness of her tasks. She was startled by a sliver of the full winter moon as it brushed her face. It felt as if a man's hand were slowly and lovingly caressing the edge of her jaw. "I gloried in it, Mother," she later confessed. "I thought of it as the hand of God."

The abbess would give the troubled woman a lopsided smile.

371

"Daughter, what you imagined is not wrong. He is yours, you know. Your husband. By the receiving of this ring that your wear on your fourth finger, you took Him and renounced all others. If you imagine His hand on your face, so be it. There are times in this life of austerity that an incomprehensible joy steals upon us from the wonderful love affair we each have with our God. For that is truly what it is. You have given all you have. You share your deepest thoughts. So ... He lets you see Him in new ways, every day. And increasingly you will glory in the tumbling love and ecstasy that is between you."

The moonbeam was transitory and after a moment hid behind one of the leftover clouds. Averilla, feeling honored and loved beyond any deserving, resumed her rubbing of the silver-gilt candlestick.

Chapter Thirty-two

May 1140

I

The abbess delayed the onerous but unavoidable trip to the king at Winchester for as long as she could. The missive in which King Stephen had again claimed the abbey lands in Wareham had been received in January; however, the spurring of armies all through the late winter and early spring made the thought of travel, for a woman, much less an abbess, untenable. In addition, Emma successfully convinced herself that, with the unsettling nature of Savette's murder and the necessary role of the abbess in the liturgies of Lent and Easter, her rightful place was with her nuns.

Thus it was not until late April, when the roads again became passable, that Emma felt she could procrastinate no longer. But events outside the sheltered walls of the nunnery had taken a course of their own. Not only had King Stephen been betrayed at the battle of Lincoln, but he had been captured and imprisoned. The Empress Matilda's uncle and ally, the Scots' King David, had arrived in Normandy, and Geoffrey de Mandeville, constable of the Tower, had gone over to her side. By late May, therefore, Empress Matilda was at Westminster, discussing the details of her coronation as England's queen with the Archbishop of Canterbury.

Because Shaftesbury's abbess was a baron of the realm, she was expected to attend the coronation and then give homage to her liege "Lady." The community deemed it wise that Emma make use of her presence at the coronation to reaffirm with this new monarch the abbey's rights to the lands at Wareham. The ties of Shaftesbury to Matilda's cause were strong, but "it would be prudent."

As Emma's leave-taking approached, she became unusually testy, even refusing to consider riding in a litter between two horses, which would have proclaimed her station.

"Since the task itself is bound to be loathsome," Emma said firmly, "I intend to enjoy the journey."

"She becomes more and more difficult," Dame Alburga mused with surprise, as the community stood in the outer court bidding Emma Godspeed.

As usual, Dame Petronella expressed her thoughts. "This is the first time that she has had to deal with the consequences of giving her palfrey to the Jew. The animal had a very comfortable gait."

"It was she herself who chose to give it to the goldsmith," Alburga snapped. "I myself think it was an absurd and unnecessary extravagance. Such a valuable animal for the likes of him."

"It was generous of you to give your horse to the goldsmith," Dame Aethwulfa had said mildly when told of the gift, reminding herself, but not Emma, that exactly because such attachments impeded concentration on God, monastics were forbidden them.

In mid-February, however, Dame Anne had found for Emma another mare. "We misjudge Dame Anne," continued Dame Alburga now, admiring the gentleness of the glossy chestnut standing placidly, one foot cocked, switching her tail against the early flies."

"Of course we do," snapped Dame Osburga, her fear of being left in charge of the abbey overcoming her usual mildness.

"We never do see Anne's mind, do we?" Alburga continued,

374

unwilling to give up this new insight. "She covers her thoughts in words."

Dame Osburga gave a wry smile. "That she does."

On that rainy day in February, the farmer from near Motcombe had, in some apprehension, brought the new mare into the outer court. Dame Anne had been aghast. The animal was filthy.

"Could na' stop her, Dame," the man said, as Anne hesitated to take the lead rope. "She would roll. Down in the muck near the fishponds."

The abbess, however, had been undeterred by such fastidiousness, and had approached the mare, not only smiling, but making little horse sounds, nickering and waffling in a very un-abbess-like manner. Seeing Anne's surprise, Emma had grinned and said, with the mischievous look of having gotten away with something she ought not to have, "I asked Ralf to teach me. We spent an entire day in the stables."

"In all fairness, it must be said that she did acquiesce to the silk habit," protested Dame Helewise now, trying to still the envy that gnawed at her at the thought of the journey that lay before the abbess, with its imagined delights and the blissful freedom of wayfaring. For the foreseeable future, Dame Helewise would be in charge of the infirmary.

The silk habit, which Emma would don for her audience with the empress soon to be England's new queen, had been a bone of contention. Half the nuns bidding Emma God-speed secretly believed she would never wear it. The habit had been made for the former abbess, Cecily FitzHamon. At Cecily's death, the elaborate thing had been carefully packed away, for Emma, newly elected to succeed Cecily, had protested the extravagance of the silk and had refused to wear it.

"But for an audience with the empress," Sister Clayetta insisted to her mistress, breaking her chosen reluctance to interfere in the life of the abbess, "you must wear it."

Even Dame Averilla agreed. "You wot well, Mother, how those at court are awed by such things. Why, the doorkeepers might not even let you in, much less the empress listen to you, without these trappings of power." Averilla had paused and then added with a moue of repugnance, "I hear tell that the empress is at the palace of Westminster with, of all people, King Stephen's brother, Henry of Blois, Bishop of Winchester. Well, we know how that man savors such trimmings of a high and lofty birth."

This "trying on" of the silk habit came as close to the complicated robing of a queen that most in the convent would ever see. To this duty the obedientiaries bent themselves, persuaded that only the pressure of their combined wills would be enough to convince the abbess of her need to wear the luxurious thing. Dame Celine bundled the heavy silk over Emma's head and arms, slipping it past her body with oiled ease, while others tucked and sewed, adjusting it to her frail frame.

"There is not much difference between their figures," said one, a needle in her teeth.

"A habit is a hiding sort of garment," said another, standing back and regarding a seam with satisfaction.

Cecily's habit had been woven of heavy silk, and gleamed. Fur lined the sleeves; wimple and veil were likewise of silk, although of a much lighter weave, and the whole thing rustled as Emma lifted her hands in self-mockery. The habit exuded Cecily's peculiar sea-fresh scent so overwhelmingly that Emma murmured, "Verily, I don't belong in this." Then she added, more soberly, "In sooth, it is as heavy as this burdensome responsibility. I've half a mind to send the habit to Winchester on its own. It has no real need of me inside."

When the habit was fitted to their satisfaction, Dame Celine motioned Dame Averilla forward, piping, "And now, Mother, the jewels."

Emma's look of appalled dismay was so naked that they all laughed.

"At least this time, in going to the treasury," Averilla said, brushing a stray cobweb from her veil, "I had not the cumbersome breath of a nun's priest on my back." The abbess smiled, but vaguely, her eyes censuring the mocking.

Averilla unrolled a black silk case on the table to reveal the fortune nestled within.

Emma was aghast. "I had forgotten."

There was a large chain, cast of great loops and swirls of gold, more Celtic than the modern ornaments that had become fashionable since the time of William Rufus. "I don't remember this," Emma had looked around bewildered. "I should have thought Cecily would have worn it—for something."

It was Dame Averilla who answered, her face red with shame, "Mayhap Cecily knew that Joan would have insisted that such a treasure be sold. For our debts."

Emma paused, gave Averilla a long look of approbation, and then, nodding, donned the heavy chain. "For the nonce, mayhap it is as well that she did not sell it, for I fear our liege lady, and certainly King Stephen's brother, will be impressed by it."

Dame Averilla held out the pectoral cross. "To hang from the chain."

"I remember not this, either."

"A gift from King Canute? On his final visit?" suggested Dame Osburga.

"I am sure Cecily wore it," offered Dame Petronella, dubiously.

Great cabochon diamonds and rubies caught and swelled the light.

"Why do we even possess such an extravagance?" Emma asked peevishly as the cross was attached to the great chain on her shoulders. "It swallows light." On the third finger of her left hand, next to her betrothal ring, they placed an emerald ring—"Another ring?" — that rivaled in size the signet ring of office. On the fourth finger of her right hand someone thrust a dark sapphire — "It's too loose!" — and on the second finger a kidney-shaped white pearl, "wondrous to behold" and "of great price."

"Indeed," said Emma, clenching her jaw and standing still, like a child waiting to be dressed in a shirt not of her choosing.

For today, for the start of her journey, Emma wore the slightly frayed habit of heavy wool that had been hers since her solemn profession and which embarrassed certain of her nuns by its shabbiness. "But you must admit it is cooler in this heat, and certainly more appropriate." The silk habit had been safely tidied away in a leather-bound box along with "the necessaries" a person of stature traveled with to make the journey comfortable. All of it was now bundled into the wains with food delicacies and the extravagant gifts the abbess would tender at the various convents along her route. Most of these necessaries, like the habit, had been stored away since Cecily's death, and the novices who had been dispatched to unearth them had been awed by the softness of the down-filled bolsters, the gem-encrusted goblets and knives, and the magnificence of the tapestries and bed hangings.

"From the Holy Land?" the smallest of them whispered in awe.

"Tapestries?" Emma had been appalled.

"I shall reside with nuns. I shall have no need of such."

"Oh, Mother." Dame Averilla had been exasperated. "Why say you nay? Everyone travels with such things."

But the abbess was no longer interested in the argument.

"She is probably just testy."

"Disturbed by being away."

"At Westminster there will be little time for prayer and private meditation.'

Indeed it was the lack of this needed solitude that was stinging like a thorn under her skin. It was so disturbing that Emma had remarked on it to Dame Aethwulfa.

"I have not been out in the world... since ere I entered. Westminster is a city. I can hardly imagine it. And the oratory will be different. It makes me feel vulnerable. Naked. Will I be able to pray?"

The old woman had given Emma a long look, and then, motioning with a gnarled hand at the niche in the infirmary transept, had said, "Saint Edward could accompany you if you have need." Brow furrowed, Emma had risen to peer at the small niche. Softly she said, "I had forgotten about him. Completely. In the old church, when I was a novice, I used to creep into the dark of that back corner when I was homesick, and he would give me comfort."

"We all did."

Emma turned around, surprised. "Verily?"

Memory lightened Aethwulfa's eyes. "Aye, verily. And so 'tis an unexpected solace for us bound to the infirmary to have him with us. But," if Emma had been watching, she would have noticed Aethwulfa fortify herself with a breath, "I seem to remember a portable altar that Cecily used to carry Saint Edward when she traveled."

"Cecily? An altar?"

"There was more to our flighty abbess at the end than many knew."

"Dame Averilla was again dispatched to the treasury, this time with instructions to seek the portable altar. "It is thin and of wood, closed to the center."

"Aye. I've seen it tucked in the corner. Wondered what 'twas, but never thought to open it."

"'Twas dressed as a peasant for travel."

The box Averilla returned with was of oak covered in leather, oblong and quite dirty, except where the dirt had rubbed off on her habit. She dusted it with a dampened cloth quickly offered by Dame Helewise — "I wanted to keep her from using the hem of her habit." — and struggled to slip the hasp from its hous-

379

ing. Helewise again forwarded herself. "May I?" and without waiting for permission the younger nun pressed a small circular knob, which allowed the hook shaped hasp to be pushed out of its guard. "My mother had one," Helewise muttered, and stepped back.

Emma put out her hand and slowly lifted the left flap, then, more hurriedly, the right. Their awe made no sound. The interior gleamed, shooting sword thrusts of light back to the windows of the setting sun. Each side flap held three round lunettes depicting, in blue and green and turquoise enamels on a background of gold, six chapters of a story.

"Like the stories in the stained glass."

"Exactly."

"In gold."

"I think they refer to it as 'copper gilt.'"

"Why not all gold?"

"The enamel needs too much heat for gold, I think"

Revealed by opening the side flaps, and to which the flaps were hinged, the central portion was scalloped gilt, framing an empty recess with a place for a statue.

"Do you think it originally held Saint Edward?"

"Saint Edward fits."

"I think not. I think Cecily put him there on her own," Dame Aethwulfa emerged from her reverie, her face taking on a stern sadness. "I think it must have held our crystal cross."

"Our altar cross? The one on the altar in the choir?"

"It would fit."

"You see," the old hand reached out to caress one of the scallops and then pointed, "the lunettes are all scenes from the life of Christ."

"So she removed the crystal cross. Removed it to grace our altar?"

"Um."

380

"So she could carry Saint Edward with her?"

"Mayhap. It belonged to her."

"It did? Whence camest it?"

"From King Henry. A gift when Cecily was installed as abbess."

A more thoughtful abbess returned to her lodgings. At the request of Dame Aethwulfa, Emma had shooed the rest of the nuns out of the infirmary. "Of what did Aethwulfa speak to you?"

Averilla had waited until their second day of travel before the audacity of the question sprang from her lips. Emma gave her a long look and responded slowly, "Of kings."

2

Later, when the abbess and her companions had been home a long while, Helewise asked Dame Averilla about the journey. "The wayfaring—what came to you with new freshness?"

"It was the birds," Averilla smiled at the memory. "I had not realized how I had missed them all these years. We do have birds in the garth and the orchard and the walk down the park, but it was the sound of them of a morning, chattering and chastening, bursting from the boughs together in a flutter, swerving through the air, barely missing one another in flight, lighting atop each other ... " realizing what she was saying, Averilla blushed.

"And the smell of green. I had forgotten the color of spring. That piercing green, the poignancy of it—heartrending. We came upon a dell of bluebells under the beeches. The beeches themselves seemed clothed in a fog of green as they stood knee-deep in the bluebells. It was a scene such as I had forgotten."

On the way home the road was white with the dust from the to-ing and fro-ing of pilgrimages; the grasses on the verges creeping into the trees were yellow. "I remember a cottage with a swayback thatch, and white smoke rising into the air."

381

WHEN EMMA AND AVERILLA REACHED Westminster, the abbess was not kept waiting for an audience with the empress. The empress' coronation as England's queen was to take place after Midsummer's Night. Rumors were rife on the streets of Westminster, and although many made obeisance to her habit, Emma could see that the city was still unsettled. It was said to be worse in the city of London itself.

Emma entered Westminster Hall just after Vespers, when the summer sun was finally setting. The chief glory of King William II, the banqueting hall was an awe-inspiring building. More than sixty feet wide and two hundred forty feet in length, massive timbers upheld its roof. The great beams of the doorway and the soaring height of the room dwarfed the small figure of the abbess. She had chosen to enter alone, her several vassals, and the other nuns, Dame Averilla and Sister Clayetta among them kept some paces behind. The black silk of her habit gleamed in the candlelight, and drew all eyes to the alabaster of her face, the emerald of her huge, lustrous, slightly slanting doe eyes. In that moment, it was the simplicity of the habit, not the jewels, that made Emma appear beautiful. The diamonds and rubies of the pectoral cross did, however, rise and fall with her breath, and so reflected, "Perhaps for that one time alone," the brilliant lights of the room. The dignity of her stance and its ingenuousness were enough to halt the concert hum of the various conversations. The last to look around was the empress. She had been deep in conversation with a man who looked to be a merchant, elegantly arrayed even so. The gestures between them seemed angular and curt, and the color on the empress' cheeks was high, as if the words had been brusque.

The empress rose—it was unheard of—and descended the two steps of the dais, both hands outstretched to greet this abbess, one of the most powerful barons of her realm.

"She had been informed of my arrival."

"Abbess Emma," she said, smiling with more charm than she was reputed to have. "Lady, we welcome you and have been informed of the reason for your visit."

"There are rumors" a courtier whispered to Dame Averilla later at the banquet, "that the empress, did, before her marriage, succumb to Stephen's smiling charm. It is also rumored, with malice, I suppose, that the real reason behind this tedious war is not the crown of England, but the fury of a woman scorned."

That thought, well known to Emma, was briefly behind her eyes. "It gave me a feeling of power, that thought did — to my great shame — that she was so wary as to stand for the welcoming of me. Such, too, gave me strength."

"You had the charter with you?" Aethwulfa could see as if she had been there the fire baskets and brackets of candles, their light shimmering against the rich blues and reds and golds of the court: tunics and bliauts banded with jewels, trailing sleeves so long they needed to be knotted to keep them out of the rushes, and the ridiculous pointed-toed shoes that had come into fashion with William Rufus.

"That I did."

Emma's hands were demurely hidden in her sleeves when she entered the room. As she advanced to give the empress the deep reverence due from vassal to liege lady, she withdrew from her sleeves the rolled and ribbon-bound charter.

The face of the empress tightened, just fractionally, taking on a slightly haunted look.

"My lady, how well you look. The hearts of Shaftesbury are and have been with your cause, as well you know. The empress nodded in recognition.

"I come, my lady, in defense of a charter that has mistakenly been assigned to the moiety of the king. This is the charter in question. It clearly grants the tithes and thirty acres of the demesnes of Richard de Stoclaro of Wareham to the Abbey of Shaftesbury as part of the dowry of his daughter, a nun of that place."

Matilda flicked her finger, and two of her ministers went to look at the charter, gravely unrolling it before Emma, who kept her finger on the edge as if to hold it up. There were too many stories of charters having been stolen and destroyed. It was well known that most of the hundred charters that had reiterated the promises made by Henry I to his lady wife before their marriage had strangely disappeared.

"I thought it wise not to allow this charter to slip from my fingers."

The old prioress would always like hearing this part. Or she said she did. Emma told it to her over and over again, before finally realizing that the prioress was having her rehearse it, not because the prioress herself was losing her memory, but because Emma needed to firmly grasp the lesson it held. Emma had finally learned to give credence to her power of reason and to ignore her fears.

"I reminded her that we badly needed the salt fish from Wareham; that in accordance with Benedict's Rule we must partake of salt fish. I explained that these particular lands were necessary as we had traded our other holdings in Wareham when asked to so do by William the Conqueror."

"The charter," the minister's voice was hoarse, as if the spoken words stuck in his throat, "is not forged, but signed and sealed and dated. The witnesses are known."

"He actually intimated that it might be forged?"

"Aye. But the court was there."

Watching.

Her vassals were standing behind the abbess.

Matilda gave in with surprising grace. "Madam, we are glad of your presence here for our crowning, but you should have no fear that we are of the same stuff as our cousin, Stephen, who is known to give and then take away. As I was just telling my Lord of Winchester in a discussion about the bishopric of Durham, when I make promises, I abide by them. These, our clercs, shall note it.

"Luckily, all these witnesses are here present, who will remain to sign their names." Emma bowed to take the sting from her words.

On the days of waiting—for of course it took time, "wasting time"—the abbess took the opportunity to meet with various prelates. "I needed their advice about Sister Cadilla," Emma would tell Aethwulfa.

What she heard only confirmed what Emma had suspected: Cadilla was English. "I spoke to a young man who had been in the service of Archbishop Theobald, one Thomas à Becket, knowledgeable about laws. He took the fact of Cadilla's Englishry to be of prime importance. As with Savette, the law of the land takes no notice of deaths of the English, be they man or woman. 'Even were Canon law paramount,' Becket told me, 'according to the precepts set down by Archbishop Dunstan, there is little that the Church would want or could do with her. The Church would rather leave it to God. And her conscience.'"

"And so we left Westminster," Averilla recounted to the surrounding nuns, whose interest had flagged after the details of dress had been recounted. "The abbess was tired and hot and the smells made her gag. The river is no more than a sewer. It was auspicious that we left immediately, for after Midsummer's Eve all London rose up against the empress."

"But wasn't the abbess supposed to be there for the crowning?" Dame Helewise was persistent.

"We sent word. The abbess really did feel ill, of the heat. By the time the word reached the empress, she had far more to think about than the affairs of an abbess."

"So, it seems Stephen is again our king," the abbess had added glumly, coming up behind Averilla. "But the trip was not entirely for naught, as I received the advice I sorely needed."

5

WHEN THE ABBESS RETURNED from Westminster, the chapter meetings became slightly fractious, the community finding itself uneasy with something new in her being. It was hard for them to put a finger on what had changed. "She takes it for granted, I think, that we will agree with her."

"Mayhap going to court turned her head. She begins to think that she is to rule us."

After a while, the community gradually adjusted, and managed to return to the old ways of viewing her. Despite her newfound backbone, their abbess was apparently still the holy and humble woman they had always known.

Thus they were unprepared when, on the Thursday following her arrival, the "affairs of the house" were broached in chapter and, instead of listening, she said, 'My sisters, I bring again for your consideration this worrisome matter of Sister Cadilla." Movement in the room stopped. "I have wrestled with my concern in this, as I am sure have all the rest of you. And she has been in our prayers. While I was absent from you in Westminster, however, I spoke with several bishops, including the papal legate."

This was indeed news.

"We are unlikely to receive any definitive answer about Cadilla from Bishop Roger or the justiciars of the crown. The former would be lenient, give her time to repent; the latter have no interest in the loss of an English maid because of her Englishry. Nor, if you remember, did the county find Cadilla accountable for the murder."

Sister Fayga rose.

The abbess held up a hand, motioning the lay sister to wait.

386

"Sister Fayga, just a moment. Were Cadilla found guilty and hanged," the abbess continued, "Lovick, the one most offended against, would have no redress. Cadilla herself looks forward to a death by hanging, but what would that profit ... anyone? It would not bring back to Lovick his daughter, nor provide him with a hearth in his old age. So, I suggest to you, my dear sisters, that Cadilla be punished for her anger, her rage, and her failure to restrain herself in the all too understandable love for her brother that forced her to seek not the will of God, but her own. I suggest that she be denied the surcease of pain that death purports to bring. I suggest that part of her days be given to Lovick for as long as he lives; that she be required to care for him, and prepare his food, speak to him of Savette in loving terms, and do such tasks as would be the portion of an unmarried maid of the house. Further I would suggest that the abbey pay to Lovick the amount in wergild that Savette's lost wages would have brought him, for we, too, have been complicit in this wrong Cadilla maneuvered. As for Cadilla's relation to us, she shall continue to attend the offices and work in the infirmary for part of each day."

There was consternation. And silence. Then acceptance. The nuns, as one, were struck with the elegance of the solution. It seemed to fulfill a sense of justice within them. "Man's justice, not God's," they said portentously one to another as they walked, marveling that Emma should have parsed such wisdom. Dame Alburga alone had smiled wryly and said, "Methinks I see the hand of the old prioress in this solution."

Dame Mary had fretted, "But we, we sacrifice nothing."

Later that day, Emma crossed the outer court to Cadilla's cell, her firm step becoming less determined the closer she moved. In the murky depths of the entryway she paused. Even now in summer only a little light of the receding day was glancing off the pocked gray stone. *So easy it is now — too easy — for me to decide the fate of another, to pull out by her horns this snail from the*

387

curl of her dilemma. What right have I? First it was only counsel that moved me; now there is none that can.

Emma pushed open the door to Cadilla's cell as quietly as she could. Cadilla was, as she seemed always to be, in prayer, and started at the small, gritty pressure. Blinking aside prayer, her eyes remained cloudy and distanced. The abbess sat on the bench, and patted a place for Cadilla. "We have come to a decision about your punishment." Cadilla's eyes gained some focus as she sought those of the abbess. "Eyes that held," within expectancy, "some fear," Emma would tell Dame Aethwulfa. "A momentary terror only, though. Through it, she still glowed." As it started to become clear to Cadilla what the will of the community entailed, she gasped as if unable to breathe, and then lowered her eyes to her hands. "I felt as if my long strings of words were like ropes tightening around her newfound freedom within God. "God has forgiven you," Emma concluded, *fighting my way out of the tangle of my own words.* "You even seem to have forgiven yourself. But there is Lovick."

At the end of the abbess' words, Cadilla said into the dankness of the room and the bleakness of her heart, "It is just. I would that I be given the chance to make him some amend. Think you he can bear the sight of me ... anywhere near him."

"Nay." Emma's voice was slow and she shook her head with the futility. "Not at first. It will be ... an agony, harder than you know, to continue to love against his wall of hate and stubbornness. So you must give all of yourself to Jesus — it is only within Him that you can become bread and love to Lovick. He will know how to get there. In the end, you will fight to keep yourself from believing that you have done all this on your own; that battle will be the most persistent bondage."

"Cadilla," the abbess later reflected, "is no longer running from Him. I begrudge her that. We all run from Him. Why is that? Why do we all so resist giving ourselves to Him?

Aethwulfa's voice was starting to crack with the effort of breathing, "It is the 'I' part of our nature that resists."

"Perhaps the magnitude of her transgression hurried her toward that place of peace that we in our paltry sins seem unable to attain."

"Paltry sins? I am not so certain, my lady. Are they not, in our dismissing of them, far worse? Do not they hide behind their very banality?

Chapter Thirty-three

June 1148

Midmorning, or Nones

I

It was before midsummer some years later that the gate-keeper stepped out of his usual wide-legged stance, and, with a big grin, held out a grubby paw to a weary traveler. The man was suddenly familiar to others awaiting entrance to Shaftesbury and was soon encircled with friendly backslapping and other, shyer, but equally warm, greetings.

"I have been called again to Saint Edmund's at Bury," Master Hugo told the abbess over the crusts left from the sparse midday meal. The crusts, called trenchers, absorbed the juices of the soup, and what the two of them left would be given to the poor.

The abbess smiled an easy, raised-eyebrow smile wherein her dimple twinkled on the right side of her mouth. "You, Master Hugo, seem to have taken a circuitous route to get from Saint-Denis to Saint Edmund's. I thought not that Shaftesbury would be in your path?"

Hugo, too, smiled. "A new abbot has now been consecrated. You heard, I am sure, of the death of Anselm. Man's name is Ording, and he wants me to fashion a silver altar frontal for the main altar. It seems they have heard of that which is still unsilvered here," he raised a questioning eyebrow, "and have a need to be first in possession of a silvered frontal."

The abbess actually grinned. "The sanctity of a patron saint is now to be defined by the possession of a silver altar frontal?" Her expression changed to one of serious questioning. "We have had many good years since last you were here. Had you time to finish de Huseldure's monument, we could now afford the silver."

His gaze was equally level. "Indeed, I am here for just that purpose. There is much I would explain."

The day was unusually warm, even for June, with the hum of bees as they bustled around the clove gillyflowers in the cloister garth.

As the meal ended, the abbess rose. "Since this day is so mild, mayhap we might talk outside? It was miraculous," she continued in a whisper as they descended the stairs, "now that I think on it, that Master Levitas escaped without harm. Ultimately you — he — found refuge?"

"Aye. Abbot Suger, as we had hoped, was more than happy to have another accomplished goldsmith in his workrooms. None of the artisans were even threatened by his presence — that was the miracle."

"And Ralf?"

"You would hardly recognize him for the same lad. The lengthening that comes with manhood had been stunted — I suppose it was because of the bludgeoning of his village and the time he spent in the forest — but as soon as we reached Saint-Denis he seemed to sprout. The monks feed him, too, with wholesome fodder, though he will eat anything put in front of him."

"And you?"

"Lady, I have changed."

She studied him. "Tell me?"

"How to make it clear?" He sighed and looked toward Melbury. "You, and all who abide here in this place of peace, took

391

my tattered spirit and changed it somehow. It had been tarnished, more's the pity, during my years of wandering through Saxon lands and at Saint Edmund's. Mayhap 'twas the monks or mayhap 'twas a dearth within my own soul — who knows?

"What I then created did not etch itself on the trembling surface of the eye in order to lead those who saw it closer to God. The fact of the matter is, before coming here I felt worthwhile in the eyes of God and man only if my work was recognized as better than the efforts of others. I did not paint or carve to praise God, but for men to praise me. That has changed in me. I need such adulation no longer."

"Ah. Another miracle?"

"Another miracle."

"So."

"So, I have an itch, an eagerness, even, to silver — or gild — the wooden frontal I left you. He blushed under his beard. It matters not to me that few will see it."

"Ah."

2

THE FRONTAL WAS AS HUGO HAD LEFT IT. The reliquary had been put back on the chapel altar. Several pilgrims surrounded the altar in various stages of devotion. One of them moved closer, giving Hugo a clear view. *Ralf's horses.* Hugo shook his head. *Incredible. The lad captured a livingness that I have still never been able to reach. I'd forgotten. The truth of those images. Astounding.*

In the way of the convent, Dame Edith had heard of Hugo's arrival, and, as he stood, strangely affected by the frontal, knowing he had created it and yet seeing it as if for the first time, she made her way across the transept and stood waiting just inside the chapel so as not to disturb the pilgrims. Feeling her presence, he turned and moved to greet her.

"I heard," she whispered, beaming, "of your return. We are so grateful that you will finish it. How is Master Levitas?"

"Respected, Dame, and well pleased with his situation."

"Saint-Denis, is it?"

"Aye. Abbot Suger has great respect for such work as Master Levitas produces."

"Oh, I am glad. And Ralf?"

"He, too, is well."

"Does he continue as — as your apprentice?"

"Nay. He works on his own now. And is honored. Was it not incredible, Dame, that I should chance upon a child with such talent? He so easily could have died in the rape of his village, or another child with no talent could have been saved. But say it was he who survived, the odds are high that another man with no art in him would have been the one to chance by with need for an apprentice or — or slave. And Ralf's great talent would have been swallowed in wisps of smoke. Or it might have chanced — almost did — that I — I wouldn't allow Ralf to show what he could do. I probably wouldn't have allowed him anything more than sweeping and hauling, had not you picked up that carved bird. Much ashamed. And forever grateful to you. I never, on my own, would have noticed the talent that lives in those long-fingered hands."

She looked at him through the length of her lashes, "The fall of a sparrow."

"Aye. The fall of a sparrow."

She paused, allowing the concept to lie between them. "But the choice, even then, was yours," she said. "You had the privilege to see his talent and to use it, or to forbid the lad's growth. No. The miracle is not that you two should meet, but that having met, you should have put your own need below his and allowed his talent to bloom."

He shook his head. "It still seems incredible to me."

"Master Hugo," she said almost tartly for his 'Innocencia,' "if

393

you had it in you to understand the fullness of God, you would *be* God."

At first he didn't understand, then he shook his head again on a smile of incomprehension, "Aye, it is so. It must be."

"Innocencia" had smiled, bowed to him, and gone, gliding down the north aisle. *It's amazing,* Hugo thought, watching her go but idly focusing on the pilgrims, how swiftly the heart can be turned away from God. Hugo leaned against the wall on the far side of the chapel, and, letting his eyes flounder into the darkness, remembered the day he and Levitas had fled from Shaftesbury. They had been in the oratory, sequestered by order of the bailiff so that no "accident" should befall them.

Levitas had stood silent, looking at the completed frontal. Hugo shifted from one foot to the other, like a toddler, eager to share his accomplishment with someone important. Finally, Levitas turned and started to limp from the chapel, moving slowly, head down.

Hugo caught at the Jew's dirty mantle. "You have nothing to say? That's it? You are just going to leave?"

Levitas lifted up his face to his friend, his eyes sad. "Oh, my friend, my friend. I asked God for a friend, so he sends me one, and now you would have me sever this bond with words of no account? Truly, they would be only words, but they would hurt you more, I think, than I can know. I would not do that to a friend."

"It is worse for you to say nothing."

Levitas sighed deeply and searched Hugo's face. "Well, then, the composition is very good. You know that. The people jump out at the viewer. You have portrayed the story well, I think. The little I know of it ... "

"But?"

Levitas compressed his lips.

394

"You won't hurt me. God's truth, 'twill not, I promise."

"How can you promise that?" Levitas snapped.

"You are like a mother cat scaring off the tom," Hugo had snarled. "What is wrong with it? By the rood, what? I'd rather fix it if—indeed if—I find your words have value."

"Stubborn, conceited…" Levitas shook his head. "Bah. Forsooth, you shall have it your own way. Remember when first we met? You asked me of the 'Graven Images,' why we Jews think God forbade them?"

"Aye."

"Then look." Levitas turned Hugo around so he was facing the frontal. "Look at what you have done! Who is your God? Who there is being worshipped? You tell me."

Hugo looked, then shook his head and furrowed his brow. "Christ?"

"Use your eyes, man. No, not Christ at all! 'Tis the horse. You worship the horse. The horse is the god of the Normans. There are … let me count them … there are twelve horses in the central panel alone. Finished. Alive. Perfect. You Christians do not find beauty and truth in the man hanging on the cross. Your mind is not transfixed by him. No. It is on the horse that you focus. Graven image, indeed!

Hugo squinted intently at the panel and then brayed out a great guffaw, a laugh, a great gust of wind that sent tears streaming from his eyes. Then, much to the Jew's annoyance, he chuckled on and on. Finally, when he could control himself, Hugo sputtered, "Oh, Levitas. Levitas, you are right. And I saw it not. God help me, I saw it not."

Later, when they were already on the road, Levitas had revisited the thought, hoping for a more serious discussion. Hugo, however, was busy trying to untangle Bithric, who had chosen to go around the north side of a tree while Hugo had led to the south. "There is an old Hebrew legend," the goldsmith began when they had finally started off again, "that Abraham, the father of my people, had himself been an idol maker. There, in the city of Haran, he had made idols, and in that profession — our profession, if you will — had come to understand, as only an idol maker could, that idols are things made by hands and therefore no true gods. But the idolater — the one who worships — he understands this not at all. To his idol, the idolater gives all the powers of the god. The idol, to the idolater, becomes holy in itself, all-powerful, an answerer of prayer, and, even more harrowing to think about, the idol, unlike God, can be controlled by the idolater with sacrifices and gifts . . . ."

Hugo heard Levitas with only part of his mind as he tugged on the donkey's rope, for his mind was seeing again the chapel they had just left. When they had turned to leave, he turned back for one more look at the frontal and had been throttled by a visceral attraction that would probably never be overborne.

As they stood near the back of the chapel — the one hiccuping and wiping from his eyes the tears of mirth, the other exasperated — a blind man whom they had not noticed, another silent pilgrim caught up in his own journey, had started tentatively patting the frontal. Realizing it was not just a part of a wall, he had explored it methodically, slowly at first, caressing the forms, fingering the shapes, and then, finally, as if stung, had drawn his hands away from the agonized form of the Christ sagging in the center panel. Tears had sprung from the milk-clouded eyes and coursed down the man's furrowed cheeks. "I was blind," he muttered, "but now I see, oh, my poor Savior, what you sacrificed."

Jesu Christ, God's Son, whose hands were bound
for my love full sore, govern and teach mine
hands and all mine other limbs that all my
works may begin and graciously end to Thy most pleasing.

—A priest's prayer from the Bodleian, ms 3/14

396

Glossary

alb – worn by priests, a full-length white vestment with long, close sleeves

amice – for priests, an oblong of cloth worn around the neck

aumbry, ambry – a recess or closed cupboard made in a wall to hold vessels or books

bavin – a bundle of brushwood or kindling

berserker – a Norse warrior who was believed to possess super-human powers

burel – a kind of coarse sacking cloth

carrel – a stall in the cloister aisle, with a bench and a desk for writing

chalice – a footed goblet used for serving wine in church

chasing tool – a tool for ornamenting a metal surface; also a tool for setting gems

chasuble – resembling a poncho, the outer vestment of the celebrant at mass

Chi Rho – Used as a monogram, the Greek letters chi (X) and rho (P), the first two letters of the Greek word for "Christ"

choir – the smaller area of a church, in front of the nave; separated from the rest of the church by a screen, and within which each nun has a roofed wooden stall

cloister – the connected covered aisles around a court, for walking, reading, meditating

cresset – an iron vessel to hold burning oil, which can be mounted as a torch or suspended

curfew – a dome-shaped pottery vessel used to cover glowing coals and keep them live overnight

demesne – the lands of an estate not granted out to tenants

Domesday Book – the survey of the lands of England undertaken in 1086 by William the Conqueror

dortor – dormitory

effigy – an image of a person, placed atop a tomb

ewery – a place for keeping ewes and lambs, and for milking or making cheese

fulled – a kind of finishing of fabrics, using a substance called fuller's earth

frator – the dining room

garth – an enclosed yard or garden

glean – to gather what has been left in a field after the harvest

herbarium – an herb garden

hide – a measure of land equal to between 80–120 acres

hogmany – New Year's Day

lappet – a piece of cloth that is part of or attached to a head-dress

latchet – a thong or loop used to fasten a gate or a shoe

laver – for washing hands, a large basin or trough next to the refectory

leech, or laece – a healer, sorcerer, or maker of charms

moiety – half of an estate

monstrance – a receptacle in which sacred objects are exposed to view

nave – main or long room of a church

necessarium – toilet area

officina – workshop for drying and working with herbs

oratory – a place of worship, a church

organarium – a tool for producing tiny balls of silver or gold

palfrey – a small and gentle riding horse

panniers – large wicker baskets carried on a horse or donkey

plate – dishes and utensils of silver and gold

press – an upright type of closet

reeve – the elected spokesman for the serfs who is responsible to both serf and landlord

reliquary – a small box, casket, or shrine to hold objects associated with a saint

reredorter – a toilet area

reredos – an ornamental screen, drapery, or carving behind an altar

rick – a stack of hay protected from the weather by thatching

scorper – a jeweler's chisel used to engrave and pierce metal

sicker – stable; safe and free from danger

socage – tenure that includes the payment of a money rent, agricultural service, or military service

thane – an Anglo-Saxon or English lord, or member of the hereditary military caste who owned five or more hides of land and whose wergild was 1,200 shillings

transept – the arms of a cross-shaped church

trow – to believe, trust, or hope

verily – truly

vestment – any garment worn by a priest during a religious service

wadmal – a coarse, hairy woolen fabric

wergild – the fixed price to be paid by a man-slayer as compensation to avoid a feud

withy – a flexible willow twig or branch, often woven into a fence

wist, wot – know

NOTES

THE TIMES

DURING THE MID-TWELFTH CENTURY, England was embroiled in a brutal civil war. Henry I, a strong king and the youngest son of William the Conqueror, died in 1135. The people of London rejected Henry's daughter and heir, the Empress Matilda (Maud), and instead crowned her cousin, Stephen of Blois. Then, the Bishop of Winchester, (Stephen's brother) gave Stephen the keys to the royal treasury at Winchester. The war that ensued between Stephen and Matilda pitted baron against baron and brother against brother-in-law as the Norman followers of William the Conqueror took advantage of the crown's weakness to increase their holdings and power. The conquered English — those who had owned the land less than one hundred years earlier — were trapped and crushed in the ensuing anarchy.

THE ABBEY

SHAFTESBURY ABBEY CHURCH must have been awe-inspiring. The ruins indicate that the nave stretched an incredible 250 feet, making it second in length to Winchester Cathedral, the longest nave in Europe. The original Saxon church, built somewhat after the founding of the abbey by Alfred the Great (around 888), was substantially enlarged sometime between the late eleventh and the early twelfth centuries. During that period, the building of huge castles and cathedrals preoccupied the conquering Norman elite. Shaftesbury, like other abbeys built at the time, thrusting and powerful atop its hill, enclosed vast spaces dedicated to God, but also served as a reminder to the surrounding populace of the iron-fisted power of the conquering Normans.

Graven Images

DURING THE TWELFTH CENTURY, AS IN THE RENAISSANCE, all the arts (graven images) flourished. Sculpture, stained glass, painting, and manuscript illumination were all used to express the pervasive religious devotion. As would happen to a greater degree during the Italian Renaissance, however, the awe and admiration engendered by these works started to slide away from God and focus instead on the artists and institutions that had formed them. This was not a new problem. Controversy over icons and images had preoccupied the church over many centuries. Christianity, with its roots in Judaism, took the commandment against graven images very seriously, yet by the end of the tenth century, theologians had convinced themselves that sculptures in three-quarter round differed enough from sculptures in the round that such images were not to be considered idols. With the increased interest in relics (body parts of dead saints, or objects associated with saints or with Christ), the impetus toward acceptance of sculpture in the round was strengthened. Bejeweled reliquaries took the likeness of the venerated saint and were sculpted in the round, to allow pilgrims to worship from all angles. By the twelfth century, there were differing points of view regarding this proliferation of images. Deploring lavish decorations, Abbot Bernard of Clairvaux wrote, "costly polishings and curious carvings and paintings attract the worshiper's gaze and hinder his attention."

He advocated a return to complete austerity, while Abbot Suger of St.-Denis felt that no display could be too lavish to express his joy in God and His creation.

MASTER HUGO

MASTER HUGO WAS A REAL ARTIST who lived during the twelfth century. We know nothing of him, beyond what Jocelyn of Brakeland, a monk at the monastery of Bury St. Edmund in East Anglia, wrote: Abbot Anselm (1121–1148) commissioned a Master Hugo not only to illuminate what is known as the Bury Bible, but also to cast in bronze a set of huge doors or gates. Later, still at Bury, but under the succeeding Abbot Ording, Jocelyn says that Hugo carved an elegant cross in walrus ivory, and silvered an altar frontal for the high altar. To have been able to work in so many mediums, Hugo must have been an artist of extraordinary skill. Perhaps he was trained in the Rhine and Meuse valleys, in what had previously been the Ottonian Empire, where the Gospel Book of Otto III, an altar frontal of gold plate, and a pair of bronze doors (all of which still exist) bear a striking stylistic resemblance to Hugo's Bible and cross. According to Jocelyn, Hugo finished the Bury Bible in 1135 but did not complete the cross until 1152. I have taken the liberty of placing Master Hugo in Shaftesbury, and later in France, during the intervening years. There is no evidence to support this, as none of Shaftesbury's ornamentation survived Henry VIII, but artists of this period often traveled from place to place, and a rich community like Shaftesbury would have wanted and received the very best.

Abbess Emma

Because no history of Shaftesbury Abbey survived the disso-
lution of the monasteries, the dates of the tenures of the abbesses
of Shaftesbury are not always firm. What information we do have
comes from other sources such as deeds, wills, and charters. There
were no records offices at the time, so charters and deeds were kept
by the owners of the properties and brought forward along with
those who witnessed the original documents when ownership was
threatened or questioned. The witnesses tended to be well-known
figures and were key to the verification of property rights. Thus
Abbess Emma is recorded to have appeared before King Henry
and his barons at Ealing in 1130, and again before Stephen in 1135,
to prove the abbey's rights to various properties. It is from these
royal records that we know that Emma was abbess of Shaftesbury
from 1130–1135, but how long before or after those dates is not
known. There is no record of Emma going before Matilda in 1140,
but had Emma done so she would have been accompanied by her
vassals and others who had witnessed the deeds in question.

The Reredos

Master Hugo's reredos or altarpiece is a figment of my
imagination based on the altarpiece in the Chapel of Grace at
Grace Cathedral in San Francisco, California. This altarpiece,
reproduced on one of the bookmarks included with the book,
is not twelfth-century English, but sixteenth-century Flemish. I
examined the altarpiece, which seemed a perfect example of the
problem posed by using images in worship. Here the artist has
emphasized the horse over the image of Christ in a scene that
is supposedly focused on the crucifixion. Bernard of Clairvaux
specifically refers to knights on horses in his prohibition against
"graven images."

HORSES

THROUGH HIS TACTICAL USE OF CAVALRY, William the Bastard of Normandy was able to defeat the English at the battle of Hastings. For centuries, archers without stirrups had relied on the swiftness of their horses to outflank their opponents. The use of stirrups, however, allowed the horseman leverage, whereby he brought the increased weight of his armor, horse, and heavier equipment directly into the midst of the enemy lines.

The power of the horse not only changed the nature of warfare, but also changed the nature of the feudal contract. Successful knights required horses, and horses required large tracts of land devoted to feed. To arm a man in chain mail, helmet, and sword was expensive. Thus reliance on mounted knights for protection meant that the English thane—a man not so different from the others in his village, except that he had agreed to use his strength to protect them—was replaced by the Norman baron, who needed a huge tract of land to support his horses, and a castle to protect his people from other strong men who had knights on horses. Master Hugo's sculpture with Christ surrounded by all the horses of the Roman garrison reflected, without his even knowing it, the Norman, not the Roman, view of the horse and of battle.

MUSIC

IN HIS RULE, ST. BENEDICT ORDERED that the Psalms of David be chanted seven times each day. This praising of God, called the "Opus Dei" or "Work of God," was the most important part of the monastic day. Over the course of any given week, all 150 psalms would be chanted at least once. Because psalms rhyme thoughts, rather than sounds, monastic chant developed into antiphonal singing: one side of the choir chants the first part of the verse or the statement of the concept up to the asterisk; the other side reiterates the concept in the slightly different words that follow the asterisk. Preceding and following the chanting of a given psalm, a soloist or cantor chants an antiphon, a little embroidered song that changes according to the season of the church year.

In the twelfth century, tropes appeared. Those from Limoges, St. Gall, and Jumieges are documented; few others were written down. Most began as mere sounds added to parts of the Mass or the offices, a covey of notes extending a word such as "alleluia" into a jubilate of great length. Perhaps the new longer naves and higher transepts, which sent notes rippling into the darkness, were the impetus for the tropes. Later, words were added to the notes, often with little regard for the sense of the setting—nonsense words that happened to fit the glorious sound. Reforming bishops, disturbed by this practice of adding nonsense to the well-thought-out structure of the Mass, strove to stop the practice. Not until the Council of Trent in 1545 were the choir books purged of these "barbarities and superfluities."

LAW

ACCORDING TO HISTORIANS Dorothy Whitlock and Norman Cantor, English law in the twelfth century still relied on the principles of Germanic law as codified under Alfred the Great. The main idea was that law resided not in the emperor, as it did on the Continent under the Justinian Code, but in the community. Most cases were settled locally, where leading men of the community made up the juries, and testimony (one's word) could be verified and was therefore instrumental in deciding a case.

The Court Baron, the court in *Graven Images*, was just such a local court, held by the steward within the manor to redress "misdemeanors and nuisances" and settle disputes among the tenants. It was not a court of record. In it, a bare claim could be met by a flat denial. Both claim and denial had to be supported by "compurgators" or "oath-helpers" who, in claiming that "their man" was "oath worthy," accepted responsibility for him. In the case of a death, the slayer could pay compensation adequate to the rank of the slain. This "wergild" — oxen or money — was paid at the open grave. A man-slayer usually admitted guilt, as concealment made the crime "murder" or "slaying by secret means, poison or witchcraft," which could not be expiated by money payment. The ordeal or "judgment of God" in its various forms (fire, water, or the hot iron) was used only when no other judgment could be reached.

No woman could be outlawed, for she was never in the law. Nuns were considered dead to the world, thus not in the law, and thus could not inherit. Any man might lawfully kill an outlaw, even if the outlaw made no resistance.

Canon law (Church law) existed alongside codified secular law. This meant that those in religious orders were tried by a different set of laws than the general populace. Canon law tended to be more lenient; the church avoided the death penalty, preferring mutilation, so that the criminal could make amends in this world and thereby save his soul in the next.

DRAINS

WE THINK OF THE MIDDLE AGES as having rudimentary sanitary facilities, if any. Monks and nuns, however, went to great lengths to achieve cleanliness. The drains at Canterbury are at least three feet in diameter, and those displayed at the Weald and the Downland, an outdoor museum near Chichester, are considerably larger. I have no other evidence for the existence of drains at Shaftesbury except for their common use in other monasteries. As there are post-reformation references to manure carts going out of Shaftesbury in the spring, perhaps manure did have to be shoveled and carted away. There might, however, have been enough rainwater stored

407

in the chalky greensand to facilitate a downward-sloping drain. There is evidence for the existence of a well on the abbey grounds, and enough water seeped out at the bottom of the hill to feed a laundry, a tannery, and the abbey fishponds. "Reredortor" and "necessarium" are the terms used for the toilet facilities, which would have been placed upstairs near the dortor (dormitory) and downstairs near the warming room. Both areas are likely to have had separate cubicles. Washing of hands before meals occurred next to the frater, or refectory, where stood a laver or trough with running water, and cupboards above for individual towels. For washing hands and for drinking, the nuns at Shaftesbury probably used pitchers filled with water drawn from the well.

The Matildas

There are four queens named Matilda in post-conquest English history. The first was wooed and won by William the Conqueror over the objections of both her father and the pope. She must have been an extraordinary woman, because their son, Henry, insisted that his bride, the daughter of Malcolm and Margaret of Scotland, change her name from Edith to Matilda in honor of his mother. Henry and Matilda (Edith) named their daughter Matilda. For clarity's sake, this third Matilda is often referred to as Maud, but confusingly, not always. The fourth Matilda is the wife of Stephen of Blois, who stole the crown from the third Matilda (Maud). When Stephen was captured by Matilda (Maud) during the civil war, there is a span of time where Matilda (Maud), the daughter of Matilda (Edith) is warring with Matilda (the wife of Stephen). It is quite confusing.

THE JEWS

MASTER LEVITAS LIVED DURING A PARTICULARLY UGLY TIME in English history, when Christians persecuted English Jews. In 1141 in Norwich, a skinner's apprentice was found dead on Good Friday. Jews were accused and riots ensued. Scholars believe the boy had lost consciousness during a seizure and died naturally. There were riots against Jews in York where, as in my tale, the bailiff allowed the Jews to find refuge in the castle. In 1181 all the Jews were expelled from Bury St. Edmunds, ostensibly because of the death of "Robert," but probably because of the huge debts the abbey had incurred, which were canceled by the expulsion. Other riots are documented at Blois, Pontoise, and Saragossa, with the most famous at Hugh of Lincoln in 1255.

What precipitated the Christian violence against Jews during the twelfth and thirteenth centuries? According to Abrahams, in *Jewish Life in the Middle Ages,* when the Romans destroyed Jerusalem in AD 70, Jews dispersed to all the other parts of the empire. Were there solitary Jews living away from their brethren? The itinerary of Benjamin of Tudela from 1160 indicates that some Jews did indeed live alone, as Master Levitas chose to.

Over the centuries, Jews became dyers of silk and purple cloth, and glass manufacturers, as well as merchants and peddlers. They were renowned as gold- and silversmiths, especially at the refining of gold and the wire drawing of silver. In such conditions they may have been able to gather only on the Days of Awe, the High Holy Days — Rosh Hashanah and Yom Kippur — to expiate their sins. They might have had one Torah scroll among them and would meet in various houses.

With Charlemagne, and Europe's gradual emergence from the Dark Ages, Jewish communities began to encounter the hatred, hostility, and mob violence that we see Master Levitas endure. Settlements had grown. According to Joshua Trachtenberg in

The Devil and the Jews; the Medieval Conception of the Jew and Its Relation to Modern Anti-Semitism, much of the dislike of the Jews stemmed from economic friction. As land became scarce, laws were enacted forbidding Jews to own any. In an economy that relied on slavery, Jews refused to own slaves. Thus Jews tended to congregate in towns where they could assemble the necessary ten men needed for prayer. In a money economy, with its resultant need for a liquid cash flow, money lending was an occupation open to Jews, because they had amassed wealth over the centuries as merchants, and the church forbade Christians to lend, calling it usury. It was as moneylenders that William the Conqueror encouraged Jews to come to England after the conquest. He and his son, Henry I, offered Jews protection. In return the Jews agreed to pay the king a percentage of their profits. Norman England had an expansive economy; the king both taxed and borrowed to afford his wars and his extensive building programs. Abbeys, the nobility, and the clergy all built and all borrowed — far more than they could afford.

Emotional issues drove Christian hatred as well, envy being an obvious one. By Jewish law, at each of the three great festivals Jewish wives were given a new headdress, a new girdle, a new pair of shoes, and other clothing, to a value of fifty shillings. In an economy in which few women had more than one full outfit, such ostentation caused jealousy. Nor did Jewish men conform: their hats, commanded by the law for hygienic reasons, set them apart.

Purim festivals were often the tinder to the pile of stock grievances Christians felt. The festivals celebrated the Jews' deliverance from Haman by Esther and Mordecai during the time of Xerxes. Purim is a gay and noisy feast; mourning is forbidden, and the Talmud encourages participants to drink past drunkenness. As Purim fell during the Christian season of Lent, the conflict is obvious: a group of drunken revelers forbidden to mourn encountering Christians looking toward the crucifixion of their God.

There was conflict as well over graven images, which are forbidden to Jews. During the twelfth century, Christians erected many statues, particularly to Mary. It was rumored that Jews frowned at or made rude gestures toward such statues, which is possible. To a Jew, the statue of Mary was a graven image, an affront against God. But Christians felt that the Jewish disrespect was not toward the statue but the Virgin herself, and the common man, who relied on the statue for miracles, was angered. One sees this attitude reflected in "The Prioress' Tale" in Chaucer's *Canterbury Tales*, in which a Christian child, singing to the Virgin Mary as he walks through the Jewish quarter, is murdered by Jews.

It is tragically ironic that it was against the Jews, so often unjustly accused of cruel acts, that such brutalities were perpetrated. The Jews were expelled from England in 1290; at the expulsion, all debts owed to them were canceled.